Ninon and me at the

GRAND COMPTOIR

A NOVEL BY

KATHERINE WATT

Ninon and Me at the Grand Comptoir

A Novel by

KATHERINE WATT

Printed in the United States of America
First Printing, 2019

Luciole Publications
luciolepublications.wordpress.com
Print ISBN: 978-1-54398-730-0
eBook ISBN: 978-1-54398731-7
For inquiries regarding this book please email
luciolepublications@gmail.com

For Hervé, who gave me a home in which to write, entertained me with his musical antics and ready smile and, along with Ninon, made me just a little bit Parisienne.

Prologue

One of my big regrets for the past forty years was that I didn't live abroad in my twenties.

Little did I know that it would be so much better in my sixties. In my twenties I would have been so stressed out about what my career would be like, who would my husband be, and what would my future children be like. Now I know the career turned out quite well, the husband not so much but that did result in some great kids (and grandkids).

In my twenties I would have been poor and living in a smelly hovel with roommates I hated and complained about constantly; living on baguettes and whatever wine someone else would buy for me. Now, In my sixties, I have enough money to play with the idea of buying a Parisian *pied-à-terre* of my own, order the *dégustation* menu and opt for the wine pairings.

Perhaps more importantly, I see Paris through the eyes of someone who has traveled the world, kissed enough frogs to know which would turn into princes and which will stay frogs, be bold enough to insert myself into any scenario and to be comfortable just being me, on my own.

People exclaim that I am living my dream… I'm living their dream. I think it less my dream than my indulgence and the intentional design of the next chapter. In part, I am following ghosts. My small neighborhood on Montmartre's Butte found me by a happy accident. Some ten years ago when I rented my small but perfect apartment on rue Caulaincourt I had no idea that it would be my hopefully forever home a decade later. And while it was admittedly the bookshelf with a couple of hundred books that drew me back, some of those very books introduced me to a world that grabbed my curiosity and still refuses to let go.

Ghosts. Everywhere. A block away from my apartment is the building where Henri de Toulouse-Lautrec shared a studio with Suzanne Valadon. The sidewalks of rue Caulaincourt have been paved over many times over the years, but walk a short distance in any direction and you'll find yourself navigating the same cobbles that were tread by Degas, Picasso, van Gogh, and a host of others.

Every book I read, every google search, every wikipedia page, lead me to another and another and another. I wanted to understand my new home and with each layer I peeled of the onion I found myself looking for more. Starting with those expats before me; Gertrude Stein and Alice B. Toklas and their famous salons, Hemingway, Fitzgerald, and the rest of the "Lost Generation". It took me down the path of the artists that haunted my *quartier* in the early 1900s. It made me curious about those who came before them and I turned to Emile Zola. Still further back I dove and I spent six months devouring everything I could read about the French Revolution. And even still I am finding more. I just downloaded (but have not yet read) Stephen Clarke's "The French Revolution and What Went Wrong". I was excited to dig in as soon as I heard him talk about "fake news" at the time of the French Revolution.

I found Alexandre Dumas fils and his book "Lady of the Camellias". I was intrigued by the young courtesan and her popular salon. I walked the few short blocks to Cimetière de Montmartre to sit by their graves. I listened hard for their voices but didn't hear them. There was something else. Where was it?

Then I found Ninon and a partnership was born. She not only spoke to me, I felt as though she lived somewhere inside of me. I needed to tell her story. But I didn't know then that Ninon would bring me to my own story.

Ma Rue

Rue Caulaincourt. I would argue that it's the best street in Paris. But not just rue Caulaincourt, specifically the three or four block section where my apartment is. It took me awhile to understand that what makes my particular part of Montmartre so perfect is that I am situated on the curve of the street, allowing me to see down and up the street from any of my three big floor to ceiling French windows. Outside the windows, tiny balconies just cry out for pots of flowers. I put the last bits of my baguettes on the balconies for neighborhood birds, most often pigeons but sometimes robins that find their way to me.

The street is lined with trees, both home to the birds and harbingers of the changing seasons. When I first arrived at Christmas lights stretched across the street from each light post, creating a cheery welcome to all who entered the little village. After Christmas came the snow, not an every year thing for Paris. This year the snow came fairly regularly and piled up on the sidewalks and in the gutters. The sidewalks were very slippery in the mornings, before any bits of sun managed to warm the ice enough to turn to slush. The slush would freeze again in the late afternoon and make navigating the sidewalks a hazardous enterprise. In March and April the bare trees started to come alive again, first with tiny buds, then bursting into actual leaves; by May creating the familiar leafy bower that lines the *rue*.

Imagine my shock on a Sunday morning in September when I was awoken at 8 am by a horde of city tree trimmers. They closed off the uphill side of the street and teams of them were wielding their chainsaws and clippers from cherry picker lifts. Another was hoisted into the tree by a series of ropes. Neighbors I had never seen were standing in open windows and on their tiny balconies in bathrobes. Trucks followed their progress collecting the massive piles of clippings and hauling them off. By 9 am they had reached the trees outside my windows. The fellow on the ropes was engaged with a woman across the way, on the fourth story, arguing loudly and with expansive hand gestures, telling what to do and what not to do. Three of the workers congregated below, listening to her. They ignored her friendly advice. The next big tree the chainsaws attacked was not only pruned but completely taken down to a one foot high stump. The trunk was then cut into five foot lengths that were soon scooped up by a claw and deposited into a waiting truck.

By the time I left for a lunch engagement the parade of workers had the cutters at the top end of my perfect three block section of rue Caulaincourt, the branch scoopers in front of Le Cépage and the sweepers in front of my apartment. It was quite a nifty little process that amazingly left enough greenery to assuage my fears. What of the downhill side of the street? Would I wake up next Sunday to find more of the same?

Mine is a self contained little village. On that span of the street one will find three *boulangeries*, ensuring that one will be open on any given day. I regularly go to Maison Lardeux situated on the square less than half a block from my front door. It's where I buy my baguette, most of which goes either to the birds or in the trash. If there is one symbol of France I think it would have to be the baguette. Look out the window at any time, morning noon or night, and you'll see someone walking down the street holding a baguette. Moving to Paris I fell into the trap of feeling like I need to get my daily baguette to be a real Parisian. In fact, I nearly never eat them. They must be consumed within minutes of purchase or they become hard as rocks. True, there's nothing quite like the crusty end of a still warm baguette, munched on the way home. But after that I find little to enjoy about them. They are of course an excellent vehicle for amazing *beurre de Bretagne* and they do make decent *pain perdu* the next morning.

The *boulangerie* could provide a serviceable source of sustenance all on its own. In addition to several varieties of baguettes (tradi, aux graines, normal, batard), there are tempting and fattening *croissants*, *pain au chocolat*, *pain au raisin*, *choux*, sandwiches, pizzas and several types of quiche. Continuing down the counter you will find the pastries; eclairs of many flavors, tiny goodies of all varieties, *gateaux, tartes, macarons*; a feast for the eyes, the tourist camera, and a hazard for my waistline.

Two doors down from the *boulangerie* is the *boucherie*. Outside a rotisserie works most of the day, with chickens turning on the spit dripping their fatty juices onto baby potatoes in pans below. The butcher's cases contain a veritable cornucopia of seasonal offerings. My favorite time to visit is close to the Christmas holidays when the case overflows with whole pheasants, rabbits, black chickens, scores of loaves of *pâté en croûte*, shells full of tempting prepared Saint Jacques and *crevettes*, trays of *dauphinoise* potatoes with or without truffles. Fat sausages and other *saucissons* hang from hooks above the counter while loops of chains of tiny ones rest in baskets; the continuing feast for the eyes. The friendly butchers are always happy to help with recommendations as well as cooking instructions. After two or three visits, you become a regular, greeted enthusiastically, and allowed to take however long you like, regardless of the line forming behind you. After all, this is France.

Five doors down from my apartment is the *fromagerie*. There the cheesemonger will help you select a variety of cheeses for the perfect cheese board for either an apero or after dinner. His shelves are bursting with some fifty or sixty different types of cheeses; big rounds of comté, cheddar, swiss, emmental, cantal, runny rounds of brie, epoisse and camembert, giant chunks of roquefort and bleu, dozens of little chevres in all shapes and sizes and finally my favorite the Brillat-Savarin, a creamy white crusted cow's milk cheese with a layer of truffles in the center. Across the shop from the cheese case is a smaller case filled with butters from Brittany. They are like no butter I've ever tasted, some with flakes and crystals of sea salt imbedded, some *doux* or sweet.

Across the street from the cheesemonger Monsieur Vincent has his tiny *cave à vin*. His motto is

"I love two things; wine and rue Caulaincourt". There is barely room for one customer to stand in this space jammed with wines and champagnes. On the shelves lining the walls, stacked up in cartons and cases on the floor, wine everywhere. "*Monsieur*", I said, "*Je veux un bon vin rouge à offrir. Que recom-*

mandez-vous?" Monsieur succeeded in upselling me and I left with two bottles because he was emphatic that one would not be adequate for a meal. I gave one as a gift. The second sits in my wine rack for the perfect dinner. "*Monsieur, je veux un bon champagne pour une soirée ce soir.*" I left with three bottles "au *frais,*" already cooled in the shop's tiny refrigerator. "*Monsieur, je veux un bon porto à offrir,*" I asked when I was going to a dinner party and I wanted something a little different. I left with an impressive bottle, the best in the shop. Monsieur Vincent has funny hours so it's important to be watchful or you might end up resorting to wine from the G20, the small grocery store across the street. Not to worry. The G20 has an impressive array of wines and champagnes as well as other liquors.

It would be blasphemy not to mention the produce vendor directly across the street from me. Not only does this colorful shop provide all the currently in season fruits and vegetables one could possibly want, it's the perfectly picturesque view I see when I look out my windows. I contend that Monsieur is the hardest working man on rue Caulaincourt. He opens promptly at 8 AM and doesn't close until well after 9 PM; rolling his big stands of tomatoes, this season's fresh fruits and the orange juicing machine into the shop before rolling down the corrugated metal door. In the Spring I noticed cherry pits accumulating on my tiny balcony. A few days later I discovered where they were coming from. Small birds were stealing the cherries from the baskets on the stands in front of the store and flying to my balcony to enjoy them. Monsieur laughed when I told him about them. One December I asked Monsieur if he had asparagus for a recipe I wanted to prepare. "*Mais non! Ce n'est pas de saison!*" No, of course not. They are not in season.

Sprinkled among these most vital of shops are the florist, another gloriously beautiful storefront and indicator of the season, the rug man (God only knows what his business really is), the pharmacist, a hair salon, a Lebanese deli, a laundromat, a video rental store, a tiny toy shop, a vendor of vaping supplies and some five or six realtors. Add to these no less than ten cafés or restaurants. The street level of the Haussmann style buildings, shops and restaurants of rue Caulaincourt, punctuated by massive double doors that if you have the passcodes will give you access to the homes above them. All seven stories, no more, no less, what is found inside the double doors varies a little. Once past the front lobby filled with mailboxes, a second door invariably leads to a courtyard, sometimes modest, sometimes grand. All around Paris these little passages can provide amazing glimpses into the private lives of Parisians.

J'adore mon petit quartier, not only Montmartre, not only the Butte of Montmartre, not only rue Caulaincourt, but specifically rue Caulaincourt between number 41 and number 70; three charming blocks, with everything one might need to live happily in Paris.

Looking for Ghosts

It would be easy to simply say that I believe in past lives. It's really more a matter of something I've always known, since I was a very young child.

I was in Catholic school, in second grade. The priest came to visit our class and it was a free for all with all the "what if" questions.

"What if you are on the way to confession and you have a mortal sin on your soul and you get hit by a car and killed… Do you go to Heaven or Hell?" (What kind of mortal sin would a seven year old have committed?)

"When you die and you go to Heaven (we seven year olds seemed a bit obsessed with the idea of dying), how long are you there before you come back?" Father D: "You don't come back. You are in Heaven (or godforbid Hell!) for an eternity." Explain the concept of eternity to a seven year old.

I raised my hand: "You mean for a long, long, long time. And then you come back." Father D: (exasperated) "No, you don't come back ever. You stay in Heaven for an eternity. Forever."

At that point my seven year old self knew better than to argue. He didn't get it. We come back.

Through the years I started to find places where I knew I had been before; a window on the second floor of the California Gold Country. Another on the water front of a tiny Delta town. A particular alley in old Shanghai. A miniscule balcony above a narrow canal buried deep in the San Toma quarter of Venice. I had been to Paris many times before it happened to me here. I liked to say I slept around a lot in Paris. I stayed in all the usual tourist arrondissements over the years and even flirted with some of the further out neighborhoods. Once I found my home in the 18ème, I started to be surrounded by the ghosts of another time.

Every now and then I strayed; an apartment in the 8ème, a hip new hotel in So-Pi, but I always found my way back to my own special block in the 18ème; not just anywhere in the 18ème. On rue Caulaincourt, between 41 and 70, usually on a sunny terrass under the horse chestnuts at Cépage, now spoiled for me by Caroleen, but that comes later in my story.

I prowled around Cimetière de Montmartre, reading the inscriptions on tombs. For a brief time, I thought that maybe Marie Duplessis was whom I was looking for. *Mais non*, the tuberculin courtesan was a dead end.

It was after going down a string of rabbit holes, and digging deeper and deeper into the fascinating, grungy, smelly, ribald, fashionable, intellectual, seedy, drunken history of Paris that I discovered Ninon de L'Enclos. An educated woman in the 1600s! A self-proclaimed epicurean. A prolific writer. A courtesan of independent means!

Ninon

There is nothing more delightful in this world than a beautiful woman who has the same qualities of an educated man. In this way she has the best of both sexes. - Jean-Jacques Rousseau

Ninon sat anxiously in the salon of the small convent where she had lived for the past year, following the death of her father.

At twenty two, Ninon was hardly young. Most girls would be married with numerous kids (and probably more lost before or during birth) by now. She had lost her own mother ten years earlier and had been left much to her own devices over the intervening decade. Her mother and her father could not have been more different from each other. Ninon's mother raised her small pretty daughter with the presumption that the girl would eventually enter the convent. Her father, on the other hand, was an intellectual with a lofty position in society and entrée into the literary and artist salons of the times. He subscribed to an Epicurean philosophy and took care to press these opinions on his young daughter from her earliest infancy. It's hardly surprising that young Anne, as she was known as a child, preferred this approach to life, leaving behind the distasteful fruits proposed by her mother for the more sumptuous feast of ideas offered by her father.

She happily used her time reading everything she could get her hands on, eavesdropping on the conversations and meetings her father had with colleagues and writing in her journal. She had a talent for playing instruments, most notably the lute and her ticket to these early salons was that musical ability. She played, she stayed and she listened. At first she just soaked it all in, like a thirsty sponge.

But shortly she found herself debating some of the ideas of the old men, in her own mind, of course.

She was a careful and obedient girl, private with her developing views and opinions in those early years. However, in her private diary her mind was alive and challenging; challenging the ideas of the old men who expounded, at times ad nauseum, and documenting her challenges in her diary. One thing was certain. Ninon was committed to a life as prescribed by Epicurean philosophy. She pulled the small book from the side pocket of her small bag, a bag that held the meager belongings that she would take with her today.

She wrote: *"Aujourd'hui, un nouveau soleil se lève pour moi; tout vit, tout est animé, tout semble me parler de ma passion, tout m'invite à le chérir!"*

Today a new sun rises for me; everything lives, everything is animated, everything seems to speak to me of my passion, everything invites me to cherish it!

Tomorrow is truly a mystery. She had no idea what it, or the hundreds of tomorrows to come, would bring. They would be lived on her own terms. At that moment she resolved that she would forever remain unmarried and independent.

Fact vs Fiction: The Noctambule

L egend has it that a young Ninon was visited early on Sunday morning by a small man with white hair and black clothes known as *Le Noctambule,* the "sleepwalker". He told the young woman that he was there to offer her a choice of three things; the highest rank in the land, great riches and fame or eternal beauty. He had been wandering the earth for 6,000 years, he said, and he had only offered this choice to five women and she would be the last. The others were Semiramus, the ancient queen of Assyria, Helen of Troy, Cleopatra and Diane de Poitiers, French Noblewoman and mistress to both Henry I and II. Upon choosing eternal beauty *Le Noctambule* had Ninon sign a contract of sorts and promised her she would always be young, charming and healthy and would win any heart she desired. He told her he would return three days before her death, claiming her soul. Then he disappeared with a whiff of smoke and the scent of sulfur.

The Golden Age

The seventeenth century in Paris was special. In the largest European capital, French literature and the arts flourished; the era of Louis XIV, the Sun King. It was during this time that we find the enduring works of Molière, La Fontaine, Pierre Corneille, Jean Racine and a long list of others. French Science and Arts were given the opportunity to develop. The Paris Observatory, the French Academy of Sciences, the Botanical Garden, all were born during this time of openness and freedom, of literature, of art, of science and of love. Opera and ballet held their debut, the Comédie Française first opened its doors.

Versailles was being built. Le Palais du Louvre was home to the Court, but Le Palais Royal, built by and for Cardinal Richelieu, was a center of activity. This remarkable edifice, with its magnificent Queen's Palace across the square from the equally glorious King's Palace, was where private Salons hosted writers, artists, members of the Court and beautiful women. Ironically neither the King nor any Queen inhabited the palaces which today surround La Place des Vosges. *La fronde* was beginning to take root as taxes buried the little guy and the wealthy lived crazy austentatious lifestyles but revolution was yet to change the face of Paris and France forever.

Of course men predominated during the day. Women were born to be wives and mothers. Women who could not be wives or mothers could be nuns or whores. Prostitution was illegal in France. Courtesans were a whole other class of women; technically prostitutes but regarded differently because they generally saved their graces for one man at a time, their patron.

Religion dictated that sexual relations between a man and a woman were for the sole purpose of procreation. As such couples did not have sex for recreation. Men who could afford it kept a courtesan for pleasure. It was into this world that young Ninon de l'Enclos had her personal choices to make. And she not only made them in the fashion that suited her, but in a manner that would change Paris in the Golden Age.

Beauty Secrets

"**L**ouis XIV, believing that bathing removes a protective layer that keeps out disease, has washed only three times in his life. Instead, the scent of roses permeates the newly built palace of Versailles. Visitors are sprayed with rose water, with which the king also douses his shirts. In each room rose petals float in bowls of water, and courtesans anoint themselves with rose oil, each gram of which uses thirty kilos of flowers."

"A Year in Paris" John Baxter

Ninon may have had help from *Le Noctambule*, but she knew it didn't hurt to intervene on the behalf of beauty. Ninon's beauty secrets were not only unusual for her time, but the centuries have proven her to be spot on.

In the Golden Age, people seldom bathed. It was generally believed that water was dangerous and brought illness through the pores. So even the wealthiest and highly born of the time employed a *toilette seche*; powdered and perfumed but rarely washed their clothing and even more rarely bathed.

Ninon on the other hand, washed regularly and liberally with water. All of her. Her *bidet* rendered even her private places sweet and lovely. She also drank water liberally. She was religious about staying out of the sun and maintaining her alabaster complexion. She regularly employed a concoction of onion, rose water, oils and potions made from ambergris, a rare and costly substance coming from the sperm whale. Of course she used neither tobacco nor drugs of any kind so her skin glowed with health and wellness. She took care to get a good night's sleep.

Her diet was light and healthy which kept her slim. She didn't drink alcohol but instead drank tea with violet or very occasionally hot chocolate.

She was a woman who indulged in a lifetime of carnal love and yet only had two pregnancies, neither unwanted. As a contraceptive she would use a wool sponge soaked in wine, a type of early times diaphragm.

All of this contributed to a loveliness that was capped with black eyes that sparkled with passion and a beauty that was impossible to resist.

First Love

Armed with a pitiful inheritance but more importantly the network of political, artistic and social contacts her father had introduced to her, Ninon began on the path to a life as an independent woman.

She quickly captured the eye of the great Cardinal Richelieu who had all of France at his fingertips. Trying to impress and seduce the beauty, he hosted grand *fêtes* at the Palace at Rueil. Immediately comfortable in these grandiose and elaborate venues, Ninon was the toast of every event. She used her inheritance wisely to accumulate a wardrobe and some very carefully selected jewels to showcase her natural beauty; her clear white skin, her big black eyes, her open and generously bestowed smile with its row of pearly straight teeth. There was not one of Paris's noble men and not so noble men who did not notice and try to spend at least a moment in her presence. But they had to get behind the Cardinal in line. He was intent on taking her first "bloom".

"Ah, lovely Ninon!" the Cardinal exclaimed at the third of such *fêtes* at the palace. "Please, sit with me tonight."

How could anyone deny the man who was arguably the most powerful man in France? Of course she sat with him.

The man had deplorable manners. He ate with his fingers, grabbing half a pheasant from the platter at the center of the table and taking a greedy bite. He guzzled wine like there was no tomorrow. And the more he drank the more liberties he took. A hand snaked over and landed on Ninon's knee. She adjusted herself on the settee to move said knee out of arm's reach. By this time the Cardinal was perhaps a bit too tipsy to really notice. But his ardour was not diminished. He scooted over and placed his greasy fingers on Ninon's upper thigh. Ninon grimaced at the prints left by his foul digits on the expensive fabric of her dress.

"Mademoiselle, humor me." the Cardinal admonished.

"Monsieur, I have tremendous respect for you. You are a very powerful man. But I am not highly enough positioned to be worthy of your attention."

"Nonsense!"ejaculated the Cardinal. "You are bright, you are beautiful, and you are what I want right now!"

"But you, kind sir," Ninon hissed, "Are not what I want." And she gathered her sadly stained skirts and removed herself to the toilette.

That very bold move was truly unprecedented. Cardinal Richelieu was simply not a man to be refused. But rather than incense the Cardinal, Ninon's refusal increased his ardour. He requested her presence at another banquet a week later. For most of Paris society, an invitation like this was received with great joy. For Ninon it was more a command than a request. She knew she had to go and in retrospect it was a very good thing that she did.

It was a lovely evening and Ninon got to the Cardinal's grand palace at Reuil fashionably late, which by Parisian standards meant very late. She looked ravishing, as always. Cardinal Richelieu had been alert, watching for her arrival. He was well oiled with the palace's best wines by the time she made her entrance. It was nearly time for the guests to be seated for dinner, but the Cardinal delayed the call to the massive table and sent bottles of champagne around for all of the guests, indicating his willingness to spare no expense; the people's expense of course.

The delay gave Ninon a chance to circumnavigate the room, carefully keeping the Cardinal out of arm's (and finger's) reach. She graciously greeted the who's who of Paris, frankly a little weary of this scene. But wait! Who was that? Barely out of his teens and sporting just the earliest suggestion of a beard, Ninon spotted the young Gaspard de Coligny. It can clearly be said that Monsieur Gaspard fell immediately and desperately in love with Ninon. And to be frank, it was not long before Ninon shared his sentiments.

Ninon made her way towards Gaspard. As her target, Gaspard was a dead duck. The young man stuttered and turned a bright red. He had certainly experienced the pleasures of the female body, but Ninon was no everyday female. He was immediately under her spell. And Ninon decided that Gaspard was exactly what she was looking for.

We will give the young couple their privacy as they do their mating dance for the evening, all the while under the watchful and angry eye of the Cardinal. Suffice it to say that before long the two were lovers.

Cardinal Richelieu had never been particularly good at *not* getting what he wanted; it was just a fact of life. He had never had to be particularly good at strategizing how to get what he could not get other than by virtue of his lofty position. That night he retaliated by trying to make Ninon jealous. He flirted blatantly with Ninon's dear friend, Marion de Lormes. Marion, a pretty but slightly tired Parisian courtesan was delighted but not as delighted as Ninon who found her to be a wonderful escape. Let Marion endure the greasy gropings of the Cardinal!

Ninon and Gaspard enjoyed several blissful months of amour. As all new lovers they declared their neverending devotion and commitment to each other. It was a glorious time for Ninon. Her epicurean philosophy as well as an insatiable appetite for life made their time together very agreeable.

As time passed, the flame dimmed on Ninon's ardor if not her enjoyment of the physical moments of her time with Gaston. Certainly the physical and mechanical aspects of their coupling were spectacular. But that is what it became to Ninon; mechanics. She felt that it was time to move on; to embrace something bigger. She adored young Gaspard but he was so young. And so needy. And so she broke his heart. The first of many. But she did it ever so kindly, pledging that they should be friends for a lifetime. Ninon was to honor this commitment to each of her lovers; friendship for a lifetime. For poor Gaspard, a lifetime was not so very long. But it was long enough for him to marry two women, have four children and secure an important place in the annals of French history, being brought down during the St. Bartholomew's Day massacre, stabbed to the heart, thrown from a window and his head cut off.

For her part, following the relationship with Gaspard she declared: "I have noticed the most frivolous things are charged up to the account of women, and that men have reserved to themselves the right to all of the essential qualities; from this moment on I will be a man."

And So It Begins

L e Grand Comptoir d'Anvers was becoming very familiar. The staff always greeted me like a friend. I finally managed to get Philippe to call me by my name, instead of Madame W. We chatted about our week. In the evenings it can get rather busy; especially on jazz nights which was how I discovered the place. Today at 1:00 it's not too crowded. Could this be my writing place?

No ersatz Hemingways lurking. But there's a first for everything. Would they look kindly on me if I took a table for several hours?

My plan to use Cépage, my neighborhood café, was spoiled by Caroleen, who I eagerly befriended a couple of years ago. *Une amie française!* Someone to help me understand the psyche of a French woman. And maybe shed some light on French men as well. While not technically a French woman, Caroline moved to Paris where she became Caroleen (because it sounds so much more French) some thirty years ago and has been married to a French man for the last twenty five of them. As such, she was a self-described French woman. I had a hundred questions. Did all French men really cheat? Was the "*cinq à sept*" a real thing? And more recently, if you are invited to someone's home at 7 pm, should you really show up at 7:20 pm? Does the same rule apply if the invitation comes from an expat? (Caroleen's answer: Yes! The Americans always come traipsing up to the door at 7 pm on the dot! So inconvenient!)

After a couple of months, Caroleen was becoming a bore. Her stories had each been repeated dozens of times. Her cultural theories were beginning to be proven to be full of holes. Her politics were ghastly. I still need to test whether her views on Muslims reflect those of Parisians in general. It soon became very uncomfortable for me to listen to her rants about "All Arabs" in Paris, about every Arab woman in the city, wearing their "burkas" and spitting on her on the métro in their quest for forcing Sharia law on the women of France.

She sits with her laptop in the same seat at Cépage, next to the one available power outlet and after the first *café crème*, doesn't buy anything more until late in the afternoon. If I haven't come in by then to buy her a glass of something, she may spring for an *apéro* to earn the right to a bowl of munchies. Once she's gobbled those down, and usually mine as well, she grabs the arm of *la serveuse* and asks for more; shoving both bowls at her and making quick work of polishing them both off. I suggested that perhaps it was poor form to monopolize a table all day and not actually buy enough to justify the rent. "Nonsense"was her reply. "I'm family."

I noticed that my own welcome at Cépage got increasingly spotty. I had trouble flagging down the server. I could never seem to get another *verre*. And the previously friendly service had become downright rude.

I went out of my way to become especially friendly. Finally I started leaving bigger tips. Buying friends in Paris.

A quick survey of the room at Le Grand Comptoir showed several well placed power outlets. By 2:00 the restaurant has gotten more crowded. Gads, the French are on a later time schedule than I am used to!

Two glasses of wine down and nearly finished with my risotto. I realize I'm going to have to drink more slowly if I'm going to manage to spend the four hours I've committed to writing each day.

I suppose I could just ask Philippe, the owner. Can I write here two days each week? But first I need to determine, if in fact I can write here two days a week? Can I write? #imnohemingway.

At two in the morning I have so many ideas that seem brilliant in the dead of night. But by the light of day, maybe not so much. I had thought about asking Philippe to sit down and tell me the story of his life; all in French of course. But he is very busy greeting patrons and manning the bar. Enjoying a glass of champagne and singing, all the while singing little snippets of songs that play on the stereo. And some that don't.

Yes, I do think this will work. Now I just have to determine if I can write.

The Career Path

Any path to becoming a woman of independent means for Ninon may curl the toes of a young woman entering any western university today. In seventeenth century Paris a young girl had limited choices; find a husband, enter the convent, or sell your body. The latter option took a couple of routes; become an everyday run of the mill prostitute, or if one were beautiful enough, smart enough and clever enough, to secure an arrangement. In other words, to become a courtesan, a kept woman who makes her living by making love. At that time Paris counted some 30,000 common whores and another 10,000 luxury prostitutes.

Ninon's first arrangement was with Jean Coulou, councillor at the Paris Parliament and a neighbor in the Marais. He was a wealthy libertine with an equally unfaithful wife. She received 500 livres per month. By way of comparison, common whores got between 3 and 4 livres per meeting. This arrangement continued for nine years, until Monsieur Coulou's death. Ninon was not limited to this arrangement and soon added to it a second arrangement with Francois-Jacques comte d'Aubijoux who contributed to her coffers another 500 livres per month, leaving her comfortably well off.

By the age of twenty-five Ninon could no longer be bought and sold and she chose her lovers from those she liked. When the very rich Marc-Antoine Perrachon gifted her with a house worth 8,000 ecrus, she shortly returned the gift when he felt it entitled him to intrusions she did not welcome. She moved house a second time, and then finally a third time, putting her adjacent to Palais Royal, ground zero for the who's who of Parisian society. Her home at rue des Tournelles was by no means a sumptuous aristocratic townhouse, but more typical of the middle class bourgeoisie and the same maxim was at play in Ninon's day as exists today; location, location, location. Ninon was rubbing elbows with royalty. What is today Place des Vosges was the place to be.

Ninon's modest apartments required only four servants: a cook, kitchen helper, valet and chambermaid. The small but elegant salon limited the number of guests to an intimate but meaningful gathering. She entertained with decorum the cream of court and town. An invitation to become one of the Les Oiseaux des Tournelles was quickly becoming the hottest ticket to be had.

About Last Night

Today was supposed to be Ninon's day but then last night happened. I learned what it really takes to make a French friend(s)... Three bottles of champagne, and a little foie gras doesn't hurt.

Here I am, back at GCA my new writing café, and it's packed. Poor Philippe is running around like a *poulet sans tête*. My usual writing table is occupied, but clever girl that I am, I have grabbed another that has not yet been cleaned off.

Montmartre is nuts today. It's three days after Christmas and the streets are mobbed; literally, the streets. The sidewalks are empty, as my Uber driver pointed out. Yet the tourists are strolling in the streets with no regard for cars. I guess I am considered a local now and my driver snarled "*touristes!*" and continued to speak to me in French.

About last night...Stephanie suggested that Magalie, she and I meet for champagne at Le Terass at six pm. It was a dark and stormy night. I probed that we find a place indoors but they weren't having it. It's only a three block walk for me but by the time I arrived I was frozen. As luck would have it, there was a table in the inside bar. As even better luck would have it, by the time Magalie arrived, Stephanie and I had snagged an even better table inside and were comfortably ensconced with all of beautifully lit Paris laid out before us. By the time Lady Eiffel did her on the hour twinkly bit, we were well into our first bottle of bubbly.

Stephanie has been a careful friend for several years. Maybe more. I say careful because she is my landlord. Every time I am in Paris, whether staying in my usual apartment or not, we get together for at least a drink, usually a meal. I am always sensitive to her budget because I suspect she doesn't make a lot of money.

I pay every time I can get away with it. We've talked about many things; careers, men, fashion, food, men, Paris, friends, restaurants, men. A couple of times I've tried to talk about politics to test Caroleen's extreme pronouncements. But Stephanie usually shrugs, purses her lips and indicates she has nothing to say.

The subject of men is our favorite. Let me go on record as saying I have immense respect for Stephanie. She is an independent woman who is adventurous, thoughtful, brave and won't settle for less than she deserves. She loves dogs and has taken more than a few into her foster care until a good family could be found for them.

The closest we have come to having real girlfriend talks has been on the subject of men. Stephanie takes an annual week long trip to Club Med in Turkey with a group of friends. The last two years she has met men she liked. She even returned to Paris with a small hope the relationship may endure when she came home.

I'm curious why Stephanie has not met anyone she likes in Paris. She's beautiful. She's smart. She's successful. Maybe it's the line of work she is in. She works long hours and her contacts are usually clients (mostly foreigners), her cleaning staff, and her handyman. The handyman is a 70-year-old widow who gives her a good deal. She said the Telecom tech who came to fix her connection also gave her a good deal and offered her more services at her pleasure. She did not reciprocate the feelings.

I on the other hand, who am dumpy and old and don't zoom around Paris in high heels on a cute little yellow scooter seem to fall in love every other week since I hit this city.

I have always sensed a distance in Stephanie's relationship with me, despite our man gossip. Last night it was confirmed. She slipped and said that I was a client.

"Mais non! Nous sommes amies!"

And then last night happened.

I first met Magalie on Christmas Eve, when I had been invited to join Stephanie and her parents for a traditional family Christmas Eve dinner. At the last minute Magalie was also included.

Stephanie knows Magalie tangentially through work. She manages a cleaning business that supports a large number of short term rental agencies. Magalie, like Stephanie, is the typical *Parisienne* beauty. Think: chicly dressed, hair carelessly pulled into a haphazard ponytail.

The evening progressed completely in French. Stephanie's parents speak no English and at this point I didn't realize how very fluent in English Magalie was. The only English during the evening were Magalie's frequent outbursts of "Fuck!" and "stop" which was the word used for the current foster pup, a badly behaved, wiry little thing given to climbing all over everyone. Evidently the dog is being trained to be bilingual; stop and *descendre*!

After four or five hours of struggling to spend an evening all in French I realized one key truth about my future life in Paris. I was a completely different person in another language. I was not going to be clever or witty or interesting or amusing. It took every bit of energy I had to understand, translate in my head and respond. By the end of the evening, when I put on my coat and headed out into the cold night to climb all those Montmartre stairs to home, I was exhausted!

So when Magalie breezed in to La Terrass and oohed and ahhed at that spectacular view and the three of us had toasted to our collective health, I discovered that she was completely fluent in English. I was delighted that the evening was able to flow in a joyous combination of French and English. I told the two that I was counting on their frank opinions about all things Parisian, men, women, life… And when Stephanie cautioned that I was her client, I put that notion to bed. No more. We are friends. We are past the client relationship! By the end of the second bottle of champagne, the question was completely drowned.

Magalie told me about her year in Australia where she had an American boyfriend and learned to speak English. She told me about her time there working in restaurants (Double Bay – Double Pay!) and her time on a farm in the outback where she ate four avocados a day, and her time in Cairns where she met the American boyfriend.

"If you want to learn a language," she told me, " You must learn it in bed."

"But Stephanie told me I should take some classes!" I replied.

"*Alors*! *Bien*, but then you must learn in bed!"

Now I am very curious about what French I will learn in bed that I will not learn in class.

Magalie also spent a year in Mexico and learned Spanish in bed. She has just broken up with her French boyfriend of half a dozen years with whom she lives. She wants to move out, but she can't really afford to just now. She lives outside the *Périphérique* which requires three *métro* changes getting to and from work. She is waiting for the bank to tell her how much they would be willing to loan her so she can buy an apartment in the second arrondissement. Right now she's guessing about three square meters worth.

Her boyfriend, Jean-Claude, has an 11-year-old son by a woman with whom he lived for two years but never married. The boy spends every other week with JC and Magalie and treats Magalie very badly. Otherwise she would like to stay with JC but the boy is "*le paille qui a cassé le dos du chameau*" (the straw that broke the camel's back). They just bought a bigger bed so in her opinion it's really not a problem to continue to live and sleep together for the time being. The bed is so big they don't ever touch each other.

Over bottle number three we talked about whether Magalie's relationship with JC is really over or is it redeemable? Afterall, a seven year investment was not a small thing. If he could successfully convince the kid to treat Magalie more respectfully, or maybe the kid could just go live full time with maman, the fancy black lady with the "googles" (sunglasses) and the attitude.

By 11:00 pm the maître-d' from the adjacent restaurant started bringing us food; savory *choux*, mixed nuts and then, *foie gras*. When the third bottle was upended in the ice bucket we were all besties and Magalie and I were Facebook friends. To toast our fast friendship, the Maitre-d' brought us all a complimentary flute of more of the same.

Parisians are known for long drawn out adieus. Not me. When I'm ready to go, I go. I popped up, put on my coat, hugs and bises all around. Then I cleverly made for the restaurant elevator while Stephanie and Magalie sauntered to the bar elevator.

I walked up the hill in the cold Montmartre night, feeling warm in the confidence that I had broken the French girlfriend glass ceiling. All it took was three bottles of Moet and some good old HR skills.

As for Philippe, today I got a friendly hello and handshake and initiated *la bise*, the very French kiss on both cheeks, or in the air near both cheeks, which he eagerly came in for. We had a rather long chat about our New Year's plan, where was my family and then my retirement. When I left, I gave him a handshake and left him pining for *la bise*.

Cold Feet

Last night I had an attack of cold feet and such an overwhelming feeling of malaise. What the fuck am I doing?! I have given up an amazing job and a career that has been forty years in the making. Yes, it was part of the plan. And yes, I have spent the last three years preparing for this.

What if I can't write? What if I'm total crap at it? (Now playing, alongside the earlier tunes of What if my money doesn't last? What If I'm just lonely all the time? What if I can never function in French? What the fuck am I doing?)

The hangover from my attack of ennui kept me sulking around my apartment all morning and well into the afternoon. I couldn't decide where I wanted to go or what I wanted to do. Shall I go write? Shall I go eat? Shall I go back to bed? In my self-critical self I think, good grief K, you are a fucking stalker. Besides, we've already discovered in the wee hours of the Paris night that you can't write.

Voila! My guardian angel, in the form of Izzypop on an internet message board: "Put your warm socks on, K. You're in for a great adventure!

So I jumped in the shower, letting the stream of hot water rinse away the negative thoughts as long as I dare, without risking no heat in the apartment for the evening. (I am not sure how they are connected, but they seem to be.)

I texted Caroleen, "Are you working". This was beyond taking backwards steps.

"*Oui*" she texted back, "*je suis dans le Quartier Latin - tu es aux Cépage? jq quelle heure?*" (she never uses capital letters, and I have no idea what jq means but I get the rest)

I respond: "*Je suis chez moi. Je pensais y aller. Quel temps est bon pour vous? Ou un autre lieu?*" At least if I'm going to backslide, let me do it in French! I put on my metaphoric warm socks and headed out into the rain in an Uber.

I don't know if I can write, but By God, I will write! 1,000 words a day. Crappy words. French words. Maybe even a few surprisingly brilliant *bons mots*. Let my story unfold. Let Ninon's story unfold. It's only one year.

Two hundred and fifteen days I don't have to commute. Six hundred and forty five hours not spent in my car. $2,400 worth of gasoline! One month's rent! That makes me feel better. Maybe I won't run out of money. Two hundred and fifteen terrible cafeteria lunches that will be replaced by French onion soup, *moules frites*, *foie gras*, lovely cheeses, truffles, and wine at lunch! (to lubricate the written word, of course!)

And all the things I won't have to do; listen to the whinging of CC and PK and countless others. I will never again have to deal with the spreadsheet from hell. Or to put up with JY's temper tantrums. And never again have to endure the stink eye from my boss. No more flights from Hong Kong, Shanghai, Sydney or Berlin in coach. No more flying off (again in coach) to tell a dozen poor souls they are losing their jobs. No more jet lag.

The Uber driver asks me in French if I'm on vacation. "*Non!*" I respond, "*J'habite ici!*" "But the restaurant where you are going is very touristy". Really?

Tuesday was congenial and seemed to be all locals. Thursday was packed and seem to be a mash of big groups of locals (office parties?) and various groups of tourists. It's not a long walk from Sacré Coeur, up on the hill. It was busy all afternoon. Today was very quiet. Only a few tables, all speaking French. And no Philippe! So much for his pining away for my *bise*! New waiter; the other manager who is often there at night. Definitely not a tourist place. And it still feels like a good place to write.

This is where I'll put down *les bons mots et les mauvais*. After all, the enemy is not the badly written page; it's the empty page.

My old pal Hemingway said, "Never quit unless you know where your story is going next. It's time to tell Ninon's story.

Go Out

Go out... every day. Even if I have to force myself. Life happens outside of my apartment. Paris is out there. The Paris I adore. Not necessarily Paris of the Louvre, the Eiffel Tower, the Seine. It's the small neighborhoods, the regular Parisians who live and work and eat and shop and ride the bus. It's the Uber drivers and the waiters and the ladies in the *boulangerie* who are gradually and perhaps grudgingly recognizing that I'm part of the neighborhood; the Pakistani girls at the G20, themselves immigrants to Paris who greet me and wish me *une bonne journée*, the interesting assortment of mecs who work at the *boucherie* who always treat me exactly as they do the old lady in front of me, buying small bits of everything, and the young mother behind me, keeping an eye on the baby in the stroller outside that won't fit into the tiny shop.

People coming to Paris want to know how they can live like a local. My neighborhood; my block, on rue Caulaincourt, between 41 and 70, is certainly the place to do that. And while the little Montmartre tourist train goes by my apartment several times a day it doesn't stop. The number 80 bus stops. The locals get on and get off, always greeted with a *bonjour* from the driver.

What other warm socks can I add to my quiver? Better language skills; whether they be from a class or from a bed. Or both.

Caroleen

T here is a crazy contradiction in the way Caroleen describes herself and the way she behaves.

"A French woman never goes out without being completely put together!" In the dozens of times I've seen her she always looks the same; summer and winter. I suppose the scarf is a nod to being French, summer or winter. In the winter she is hidden beneath a black wool poncho, a little pilly. Her streaky hair looks finger combed and pulled into some sort of top knot. She wears a bit of makeup, mostly eye liner. Her resting bitch face sports more of a sneer than a smile.

The thing that boggles the mind about Caroleen is how she absolutely devours any food that appears on the table, whether it's for her or not.

We were supposed to meet at Cépage for une verre at 5:30. She showed up twenty minutes late, having just met with clients (like that?!) To be fair, she had her nails done. I was finishing a glass of wine and she plopped down and snatched my little bowl of pretzels wolfing them down in an instant. Be my guest. I wasn't going to eat those. Crazy, my plan was to treat her for a New Year's *apéro*. I ordered two glasses of champagne, half a dozen oysters and some frites.

When the champagne arrived we toasted to our health and a prosperous and profitable New Year. Then the oysters arrived. She nearly swooned.

"For us?"

"One for me and five for you!" I don't really like oysters but I feel that I must eat one. For "*chance*". For the "*Nouvelle Année*".

"But they taste like the sea!"

So I've heard and I'd really rather go into the sea and swallow a mouth full of water.

By the time I had managed to swallow my oyster she had literally inhaled the other five. At one point I feared she was going to climax! Then she made fast work of "our" *frites*, stabbing four or five at a time into her mouth.

"Another champagne?"

"Sure! We should have gotten a bottle!"

Thierry

I first saw Thierry maybe five years ago. At the time I didn't know he was Thierry. I only know from the moment of first eye contact there had been another life and that we had shared it.

All that from a single moment of eye contact, you might say? Stop the presses. Is this going to be that kind of book? Not to be dramatic, but sometimes this past lives thing just works that way.

And for five years it has teased me. In this life he is too young, too married, and too much of a father. Well maybe the too young part isn't such a problem. He does fall into the sweet spot for me age-wise. And after all, France is the country with a President some twenty six years younger than his wife. But the wife and the kids are a bit of a problem.

So that's where I played with the idea of *cinq à sept*, or the fantasy of just one week, secluded somewhere together, to get it all out of our (my) systems. And to remind him not to take so damn long the next time around!

But even I don't want to get in the way of a family. And every time I come to his restaurant, the thing that stands out more than anything; more than the sexy beard, that smile, those eyes, is that wedding ring!

For a couple of years, I thought that my part of this story was about Thierry and who he was before he was him and I was me and this life was this life.

He says I am his favorite client. It's not that the connection, however inappropriate, isn't there. It certainly is. But this story… my story… is about something else this time around. And I just haven't figured out what yet.

Of course, that doesn't mean that it's not still fun to connect and flirt and maybe become better friends. Who knows what twists and turns this life will take. After all, I live in Paris!

Daniele C

A nother wrong path, but it's becoming very clear that these wrong paths take me interesting places and towards the place I think I'm supposed to be going.

First there was Daniele J, my celebrity chef crush who actually ran with the bulls. (And look how that turned into an actual let's hold hands moment.) It was by virtue of stalking him that I discovered Hotel L and by liking it on Facebook that I was lured by the tiramisu martini. I promised to do a research trip for my BFF C's annual holiday party. Sitting at the bar, videoing the making of said cocktail it just happened to be the then every other week appearance of Daniele's jazz group at Bar L. I've no idea why he caught my eye. Too skinny. Too hairy. A bit greasy. A drummer. But he did.

Fast forward to stalking him and falling in love with him and following him to every jazz club in Paris. Then that fateful day, following *rentrée*, when every Parisian returns e*n masse* from the August vacation he came back with a wedding ring!

I was devastated. Daughter number one said "like you thought you had a chance to be with him?!"

The every other Wednesday at Bar L turned into every Wednesday at GCA. It took me a stupid long time to actually go. I Google street viewed it. I watched GCAs videos of the sessions. I made reservations. I cancelled reservations. And then I took the plunge. It was great.

Each time I was greeted by Philippe. Soon he remembered my name. He played a bit part in my weekly jazz interludes. All my focus was on Daniele, who occasionally even seemed to notice me.

Until one night while I watched Daniele and Philippe told me a story in French that I didn't quite understand but seemed to be how I went from Bar L to GCA. For the first time I noticed Philippe with new eyes.

So fast forward to a place to write and a man with a continual soundtrack playing in his head and the *bise*.

And let's just see where this path leads.

New Year's Eve

The man across from me in tiny Truffes Folies pulled off his sweater, revealing a t-shirt that said in huge blurry letters "The Future".

Among the things that came to mind; I would never wear a t-shirt to Truffes Folies (where by the way it smells like what Heaven must smell like), Have I already had too much to drink on this New Year's Eve Day, although it's only lunch time (For anyone counting, champagne and two glasses of Côtes du Rhône helped wash down the *foie gras* and artichoke tortellini with black truffles), and finally If that "The Future" is representing my future it would have bright shooting stars and neon letters. The only mysteries about my future are good ones. How will it play out? How will my book turn out? How will my story turn out? How many more times am I going to fall in love? (When will Ninon's story start to be written?)

The sun came out but the wind howled as I staggered to the bus stop. I'm trying to be mindful of burning through my life savings. Uber is usually quicker and more comfortable but the number 80 bus takes a very scenic route, crossing the Seine at Pont d'Alma. Look to the left; there's the Eiffel Tower. Look to the right and there are the Grand and Petit Palais. Avenue Montaigne, my favorite glamour street in Paris always dazzles at the holidays with Plaza Athénée and the Dior Atelier setting the standard for the bejeweled decorations and window dressings. It may be freezing, but that doesn't stop those wanting not only to see, but mostly to be seen from grabbing patio tables at L'Avenue, wrapped in scarves, furs and hats. I notice that the same refugee family has been living on a mattress just adjacent to the chi chi restaurant, the passersby with their Louis Vuitton, Gucci and Jimmy Choo bags blind to them.

A couple of blocks further and the bus passes the Artcurial building, one of the most beautiful buildings in Paris right before it circumnavigates the Franklin D. Roosevelt roundabout. Look quick to your left, the Champs Elysées leads majestically to the Arc de Triomphe and the Grande Arche de Défense beyond that. To the right, the Place de la Concorde with the Egyptian monolith and the Grande Roue at the holidays. The controversial great ferris wheel is certainly a landmark from all vantage points of the city. The elderly King of the Romanian Gypsies who owns and operates it won the right to run it this holiday season - a small concession by the city's Mayor for refusing to allow his Christmas Marché along the Champs Elysées.

The bus continues past the ritzy streets getting increasingly ethnic and increasingly more like the real Paris as it nears Gare St. Lazare. Here's where Claude Monet painted his famous series of steam trains arriving at the station in the late 1870s. (and where today you can catch a train to Vernon to visit Monet's impressionist home in Giverny).

The next couple of stops are packed and people shove onto the bus loaded down with rolling shopping carts, luggage and baby strollers. This is where I often snicker at the cliché of the well coiffed, well dressed Parisian. There are no rules. Parisians come in every size, shape, color and smell. All of the restaurants and shops for the next couple of stops are Chinese, Thai, Italian, Chinese and African. Turning right at Place de Clichy the neighborhood takes on a whole other feeling; grunge tourist, with a host of tacky souvenir shops, cheap restaurants, local markets, news kiosks. Boulevard de Clichy veers right and enters the sex zone. The Moulin Rouge pulls in the huge tour buses unloading scores of Chinese at nine and eleven. Irish pub. Cockney Bar. Shop after shop advertises sexy; girls, toys, lap dancers. It may be the only street in the world where you can buy an Eiffel Tower vibrator.

Bus number 80 doesn't turn onto Boulevard de Clichy. Instead it heads up hill, crossing over Cimetière de Montmartre where it enters an entirely different world; my world. Two more bus stops and I'm home. To the one perfect block in Paris.

Welcome 2018

I'm tempted to say that 2018 isn't starting out well, but I'm definitely looking at things from a glass half empty perspective. I did a lot of nothing until three o'clock when I finally figured out I had to go outside. I planned to take a bus to the river and bid adieu to Paris for six weeks. Waiting for the bus was rainy and cold and dreary. I decided instead to Uber to GCA. It took ten minutes for the Uber driver to show up and by the time he arrived I was cold and wet. Then I had accidentally put in Le Clou so when we got to Avenue Trudaine, the road was closed for pedestrians and cyclists (who obviously weren't going to be out in this weather). I explained to him that I wanted to go to Place d'Anvers and you would have thought I said I wanted to go to the moon. *Quel inconvénient!* Sheesh! So I let him drop me at the corner of Boulevard de Clichy and Place d'Anvers and swam the rest of the way.

The place was packed; with families it seems. In fact there was only one table left and the people at the next table grudgingly moved their coats over enough for me to sit. No Philippe. But seated at a warm table with a carafe of wine and some vegetable soup I feel like I'm in my right place. Definitely better than Cépage, (which I think I have successfully bought my way into by now)!

On top of that, I am waitlisted for a business class upgrade for my flight back to San Francisco tomorrow; number two on the list and it's sold out. All I can hope for is that two people will either cancel or not show up. Dare to hope.

I always feel so sad to be leaving and this time even more so. I've been telling everyone *"j'habite ici"* and although it's just a tiny bit premature, I really feel like this is my life now. And the six weeks "in the way" are a vacation; to get my Visa, clean out my office, and say my goodbyes. And parties! One in Encino, with the beautiful people. The second at Beverly's home with my 50 closest friends.

So my glass is more than half full. It's overflowing.

On Writing

Je suis ici! Pour une année. I have arrived at my new apartment a little after eleven and met Tara, Stephanie's BFF. She's a sweet little thing from Ireland. We agreed to have lunch together soon.

I've stayed in this apartment twice before and it's fine, but I don't feel as warmly about it as I do my usual one. I will stay in this apartment for three months and then move in June for nine months. Maybe I can do some things to make it feel more like mine. It's certainly convenient to Le Cépage! It's in the same building.

My plan is to write two days at Cepage, two days at GCA and one at Le Cafe Que Parle. Sprinkle in with the Bibliothèque Mazarine and the Terrass.

Everyone at home says that I am so brave to do this. I don't feel particularly brave. Maybe indulgent. Flying to Paris, taking a taxi to my apartment, going about my daily activities either alone or with someone, feels very normal. After all, I came eight times last year alone. What feels brave to me is leaving my job; walking away from both the prestige and the money. I've heard that the average book earns its writer $10,000. I earned that in two weeks in Silicon Valley. I think writing a book is more a labor of love than a job or a career. It's about creating something and putting it out into the world.

I listened to John August's podcast "Launch". He talks about the desire to write a book, a novel. He has been a successful screenwriter but a book is something he will create in total. To begin he feels like he has a very personal, very private thing he wants to create. It actually sparkles with flashes of light. It's completely his own thing until he decides to share it. He sends his first eight chapters to a publisher. It's no longer his personal baby anymore. He describes the anxiety of waiting for feedback from the publisher. Now, Mr. August has a big advantage. He's a known creator. He's sent his chapters to a top notch publisher. I'm pretty certain that the run of the mill first time writer does not enjoy the pleasure of attracting an eye so easily. After a few short days he gets the feedback he's been waiting for. They love it. And then his baby is truly not his any longer. They give him an advance, my two weeks pay in Silicon Valley, and ask for 80,000 words in six months. Now Mr. August has an actual job with an actual deliverable.

80,000 words at 1,000 per day, five days a week is four months of writing. The sparkles are gone. He overruns the six months by two. I wonder how he pays his bills on that $10,000.

Then come the edits! Hundreds of edits from things as minor as challenging regional phrasing and Oxford commas to editing out entire story lines and changing a major character's personality.

How will I feel about someone attempting to rewrite my words? Once I contributed an essay to an anthology about being a working mom in Silicon Valley. I loved my essay. The editor cut it to shreds. She cut out sections that I felt were critical to what I was trying to communicate. And it was her book.

The Rug Man

For six years I have been watching the Rug Man. He has a small shop across the street from my apartment, ostensibly selling imported Persian style rugs. His hours are incredibly irregular although the sign on the window proclaims them to be *mercredi*, *jeudi*, *vendredi* et *samedi* from 11 to 7. The thing is, I have never seen him sell a rug. He typically stands on the sidewalk in front of the shop, watching people walk by, in cold weather, hot weather and everything in between.

Year after year Monsieur has stood outside his shop, never selling a rug. Occasionally he pops over to Cépage to have a coffee or a beer. Caroleen tells me he's a cad; that he made unwanted advances. She told him "*Non!*" that she's married. According to her he replied "a little spice on the side makes life more interesting". I can only surmise that there must be more going on at Tapis Berthoud than rugs, since to my knowledge he's never sold one. Until…

One January he had a big *SOLDES* sign and I decided to go see about buying a rug to bring home and put under my dining room table. Monsieur Bertoude speaks no English and at the time my French was pretty pitiful. We pointed and gestured and Monsieur pulled out a number of rugs, nearly flipping them like the Turkish rug sellers in old town Istanbul. I finally settled on a rug with a pretty tree of life pattern for 700 euro. Un petit problem. I wanted to pay with a credit card but Monsieur said his machine was not working. "Cash please". No doubt he was trying to avoid paying taxes. Silly me. I didn't happen to have 700 euro in my wallet! We ended up looping in the produce vendor next door. I think I actually ended up buying 700 euro of mushrooms and somehow the two of them worked it out, probably cutting out the French Tax authorities.

Today while I am writing and eating lunch at Cépage, Monsieur walks in with a son! *Le garçon*, about 15 years old looks exactly like his father. They sit across from each other, heads at 90 degree angles, both looking intently at their phones. Excellent father-son time. I look up from my writing to see them both watching me! Monsieur has completely turned in his chair. I smile at them and look away. Did they hear me writing about them? Will I be offered some spice on the side?

Les Chiens ne Font pas des Chats

(The apple doesn't fall far from the tree)

J'ai besoin d'une nouvelle amie. Ou j'ai besoin de me divorcer de Caroleen! I need to find a new friend! Or I need a divorce from Caroleen! What a miserable person she is turning out to be. We met for *un verre* last night, me buying of course. She sat down, unhappy with the table I had chosen and being forced to sit on the chair across from the bench seat. I was working on a glass of Côte du Rhône, which came with a small bowl of peanuts. Bises out of the way, she scooped up a handful of the peanuts. Our short conversation about the derivative of the French word for peanuts, *cacahouètes*, was the only non offensive part of the next two and a half hours. She surmised that it comes from the word "caca" or "pooh". Maybe so. Little drops?

The rest of the evening was a one-way dialogue about the evils of Muslims. "And I'm a democrat!" she kept saying. According to Caroleen they are taking over Paris. And it is not a good thing.

The lid to her tagine had fallen off her stove top and broken so she needed to buy a replacement. She and a friend took the *métro* to Belleville, a neighborhood in the 19th arrondissement, where there are a lot of Arab markets. (She also noted that bundles of herbs are one-third the price there than they are at the Chinese market in the 14th arrondissement. Evidently, the Arabs are good for something!) She bought the tagine she was looking for and her friend pointed out a suitable café where they might get *un verre*. But no, upon looking in they saw only men. They walked on a bit more and the friend pointed out another café, again full of men. They decided to take a chance.

They sat down and the server came over and admonished them; "Look about! Don't you see that there are only men in here?"

Caroleen launched into an anti-Muslim tirade. "This is Paris! We are not ruled by Sharia Law. You cannot prevent us from having coffee here!"

"Weren't you afraid he would spit (or worse) in your coffee?" I asked.

"It doesn't matter! I wish I had videotaped him. In fact, I think I will go back and this time I will video tape him with my phone!"

She went on to opine about Madame la Maire, ranting about how she had passed a law requiring any apartment sold to first be offered to the Mairie for the lowest price bid. The Mairie would then purchase the apartment and give it to refugees (Arabs), who will in turn bring in fifteen other refugees (all Arabs) to live in the tiny studios.

"Look about you!" she ranted. "Notice all the hijabs slinking into the buildings around you!"

I personally have not seen any slinking going on around me. And in this cold weather most people are wearing some kind of hat, scarf or fur lined hood. She specified two nearby buildings where she saw a slinking Arabess. Sharia law is taking over Montmartre!

Caroleen asks for an aperol spritz and shoves both little bowls at the reluctant waiter, "Plus snacks!" He smirks and brings her another bowl and her drink, along with another glass of wine for me. Both on one check which of course will be left for me to pay.

At this point the subject changed from Arab takeovers to scams in general after I mentioned a conversation I overheard at the nearby bus stop. A British woman was speaking to companion about someone in the building across the street making ridiculously low offers on all of the apartments before the city takes over the building, a beautiful old building on one of the best blocks in Montmartre, for a major renovation. It turned out to be a scam.

Which launched into the telling of a scam that happened to her and her two young guests at Le Cépage. They had three coffees on the *terrasse*, and the bill was eleven euro. She placed on the tray one ten euro note and one one euro coin. She repeatedly, like ten times, pointed out that as she stepped into the restaurant with the tray she held her thumb firmly on the ten euro note. She handed it to the "new Arab" waiter and then she and her two young guests headed up the street. A minute later the watier was chasing them up rue Caulaincourt.

"*Madame*! You only left one euro! You owe me ten euro more!"

That sent Caroleen into a rage. She marched him back to the restaurant where she pointed to the several cameras in the ceiling corners.

"Let's look at the cameras! I gave you eleven euro. You will not get away with this!"

Eventually the waiter acquiesced with some feeble comment about maybe the ten euro note blew away (at which point she repeated for the eleventh time the claim of holding it firmly on the tray with her thumb)

She reported the scam to the newish manager who remarked, "No! I trust him! I brought him in myself." The next day she reported the scam to the owner, Marcel, who demurred "Oh I hope not."

A few days later she heard from another patron that the scam had been repeated and both the "Arab" waiter and the new manager were fired.

It's kind of funny. I have been to Le Cépage many times over the last seven years and I don't recall any new Arab waiters or short term managers. All of this must have happened in one of those eight to twelve week gaps between my visits.

Which brings us to the current manager, who Caroleen calls "an evil little faggot". Caroleen reported that this past week he actually turned off the internet in an attempt to make her leave. When she accused him of doing so, saying that Marcel had proclaimed "*C'est chez vous*", which she very generously translated as "you are family" he denied having turned it off at all. It was soon magically working again.

"But of course the mean little faggot was lying! And now he always ignores me and will not wait on me at all. Or on F, by association! And probably now YOU by association as well!"

He actually had waited on me before she came in. I just spent ten euro buying my way back into the good graces of the pretty waitress who had shunned me by association on my last visit. I don't think I can afford to be associated with Caroleen any longer! Now that I am living in the same building as the restaurant, I must figure out how to detach myself, or divorce the bitch!

"What about working at Le Refuge?" It is after all the restaurant attached to her own building on rue Lamarck!

"It's the next best. But the coffee is not great. '' The one cup of *café crème* she buys to give her access to the table, the power outlet and the free wi-fi all day.

Maybe I should offer to meet her for *un verre* there a couple of times to distract her.

"How about Chez Ginette?" just up the stairs from her building.

"No, it's really a restaurant." Wait! Le Cépage is a restaurant!

"What about Bibliothèque Mazarine? Have you been there?"

"Can anyone just go in?" asks the tour guide extraordinaire.

"Oui, you just have to show your passport. It's so beautiful. I plan to write there once or twice a week. Terribly historical. But with wi-fi, power outlets and air conditioning on hot summer days."

"Tell me next time you go! I'll go with you! I can use my press pass."

"But I have to do serious writing when I go…" Maybe that was a bad suggestion. And press pass? Huh? Does she not have any simple ID?

By now it's 7:30 and a plate with a lobster goes by. Caroleen stares greedily and looks at me expectantly. I can't afford to be friends with this woman on so many levels!

"I've got to be going," I say.

She checks her app for the time of the next bus; nine minutes. My walk home is one minute. I pay the bill and my change from the twenty euro note is six euro fifty. I take the five leaving the one euro fifty for the waiter. We sat at the table for nearly three hours.

Why do I think she pocketed the change after I left?

Locked out!

What a fright. Home from an afternoon of writing at GCA and my door key won't let me into my apartment. I got through the first four doors without a problem, using the fob on one through three and the passcode for number four. But the actual key won't work in the door lock! I panicked! Did the Mairie catch up with my property manager and deem me an illegal leasor? Or was I just clumsy and didn't use the key right?

Lorna laughed at my text. "Were you drunk?"

"No!"

But here I sit at Cépage with another glass of wine a bit worried. Lorna said the said they had the same problem when they arrived at their apartment on the Ile Saint-Louis, years ago. They tried for hours and nobody would help. I think this door is my kryptonite! It's the same door that Lorna closed last year, leaving the keys on the counter and her luggage behind the locked door when we left at 6 am for a flight to Spain.

The brand new waiter at Cépage has agreed to help me when he gets off at 9 pm. It's now 7 pm. Today is his first day and we've already exchanged our details; me living in this building since this week, him starting today. Maxim. Loves the SF 49ers, especially Joe Montana. His offer feels a bit intimidating.

Who is the Patron Saint of Locks and keys?

Maybe I'll just try again. "Push up on the door while you turn the key" suggested Lorna.

Eleven Days in Paris

I am completely overwhelmed with all of the emotions and experiences I have had in the last several days. I told Elliott that I am sure there is some chart somewhere that explains the ups and downs of expat lives in transition. Elliott responded that the chart would probably turn into a multi-tome anthology of all the writers who came to live here. Big swaths of Pushkin and Hemingway, bits of Turgenev and Gertrude Stein, spiced with James Baldwin and sloppily flambéed with late Wilde.

In some crazy way living in Paris sends me back into my twenty year old head, but without money problems, future career worries or a ticking biological clock (in the 70's we thought all childbearing should be done before the age of thirty).

Last night I went to Wednesday night jazz with Magalie. After our champagne orgy she did indeed get back with her boyfriend and was optimistic that things would go well. He was drawing appropriate boundaries with his son and realized how close he had come to losing her. She texted me, "Would you like to go for a drink on Wednesday". I responded, "I'm having dinner at GCA with live jazz. Would she like to join me as my guest?" So I booked for two, which I rather suspect gave Philippe pause.

He greeted me with *bises* when I arrived. "*Pour deux?*" he asked, with a look.

"*Oui, j'attends un ami*", a noun that when spoken designates neither masculine nor feminine.

He takes me to my usual table and asks "Or would you prefer…" indicating a table further into the room.

"*C'est bon.*"

I settle back into my *banquette* and listen to the jazz. Daniele, playing the drums still makes me sigh, with his three day beard and his dark Italian eyes. But now the real heart palpitations are because of Philippe. Oh what a fickle girl I have become!

"An *apéro*?" Philippe asks. "How about if I bring you a *coupe de champagne*?"

"*Oui, merci!*"

Magalie arrives only a few minutes late "*le métro*". Warm greetings and introductions to Philippe and our waiter (whose name I asked but didn't write down. These French mens' names are impossible to understand and harder to repeat or remember).

Magalie tells me about her boyfriend's come to Jesus moment. We talk about Paris apartments after the new short term rental laws. She expresses concern about Stephanie's business future. I tell her about my worries that Stephanie will be surprised by one of the apartment owners telling her that they have gotten an offer they can't refuse. I've heard too many of these stories, alternating with stories about leaking pipes in neighboring apartments and warnings to get a lawyer. Magalie tells me that if the owner wants to sell they are obligated to offer it to the renter first, but I'm not sure I believe her. How can I let the owner know that if they decide to sell their apartment, which I am probably renting illegally, please speak to me first! Full cash payment. Let's make a deal!

I remind Magalie about our conversation about the best way to learn French. We laugh about it again and I motion to Philippe, "I want to learn with him."

She looks him over and raises her eyebrows, "Is he married?"

"I think not."

"He's nice looking. Is he the manager?"

"No, he's the owner."

"Even better! Does he sometimes sit with you?"

"Yes" (I exaggerate) "We talk about my novel. He wants to be the hero."

Magalie laughs. The evening goes on. Lovely jazz, good food; *parmentier de canard* for her, *tartare de boeuf* for me, two bottles of Bordeaux.

Towards the end of the evening Magalie leans in for a confidence. "I don't think he likes you that way."

My face freezes into a mask of frank interest in what she wants to say as she goes on with "He doesn't look into your eyes or focus attention on…" My face appears accepting I hope but my head cannot absorb the words. "You never know when the right person…" I can't think.

I wasn't looking for anyone! I like my solo lifestyle. I certainly wasn't looking for rejection!

My phone buzzes, indicating a new message. Aimee.

Aimee was my translator at my cooking class a year and a half ago. We had lunch the week after but then both kind of dropped the ball to follow up. Yesterday she "liked" a picture I posted on Instagram of the Paris rooftops from my living room window. I shot her a message, "I'm living in Paris now! Would you like to have a drink sometime?"

"Hello *Parisienne*, I know that you came back. Philippe, (the Grand Comptoir owner) told me. I would be happy to have an apero with you…"

What a weird, small, incestuous city this is! How on earth do two people from two completely separate parts of my Paris life come to be talking about me?

I choose to see it as a sign. I think my 37 year old well intentioned Parisian friend is wrong.

Eager to get out of the apartment where my upstairs neighbor seems to be doing what can only be jogging in place (in wooden clogs) right over my head, I pop into Cépage to see if Caroleen might offer a bit of distraction.

"Are you working?" I ask as I take the table next to her.

"Yes, and it's very important and I can't chat."

"No problem, I'll just have lunch and read."

For the next half hour she lectures me about the facts of living in Paris as an American that I absolutely must be aware of… this is what she gets paid good money for! Older French dislike and distrust Americans but the young ones love us. Don't ever talk to the French about money. The census? There is not a census going on! (This in spite of posters in the lobby of my building and on bulletin boards of shops and restaurants.

"You should NEVER tell anyone anything about yourself! Just lie. Tell them you don't speak French! Tell them you're visiting a friend! We would never tell them anything. What if he is trying to find out if you are renting legally and he reports you to the Mairie? Did he show you his identification?"

"When I lived in the Marais… and I had a dinner party for my husband's stupid relatives… and I know how to entertain; candles, music, art… and his wife whacked him under the table…"

"I thought you wanted to work!"

"I told you I can't work when someone is next to me. Pass me your bread basket. I want to take a photo of this beautiful gluten. Look, where do they get their bread when the *boulangerie* is closed? You know, this bread is much better!" She eats two pieces.

"You know, when they bought the *boulangerie* they had to keep all of the employees. You can never let anyone go in France." She began to choke a little on the bread she inhaled. "Can I have some of your water?"

I pass my glass to her.

"Do you have a cold?" she asks.

"No"

"Well I do so now you shouldn't drink from that. I guess I'm going to have to go home to work."

She paid her 3.80 for the coffee she had ordered several hours earlier and sipped the rest of my water. Marcel, the owner walked by and glanced at her.

"He always flirts with me! I wonder if I'm his type."

WTF?! He might have *almost* smiled at her.

Les Salons

Les Oiseaux des Tournelles: An invitation to Ninon's salon was the most sought after ticket in the City. Her guests included the absolute who's who in Paris in the mid seventeenth century; Charles de Marguetel de Saint-Denis, seigneur de Saint-Évremond, soldier, hedonist, essayist and literary critic, Écrivains Jean de la Fontaine, Molière and Paul Scarron, Bernini, the acclaimed Italian artist in town briefly to do a sculpture of the King and propose a new façade for the Louvre. Madame de Maintenon, the secret wife of Henry was often in attendance. Even Cardinal Richelieu and Cardinal Mazarin, who was suspected to be the *vrai Papa* of the Sun King. All were eager to enjoy the pleasures of Ninon's hospitality.

Fast forward to the early twentieth century, between the Great Wars. Gertrude Stein and her life long partner Alice B. Toklas watched a gaggle of artistic creatures track through their Saturday evening salons on a regular basis. Most famously among them were Ernest Hemingway, Scott and Zelda Fitzgerald, Pablo Picasso, Toulouse-Lautrec, Sherwood Anderson, Henri Matisse, Ezra Pound, accompanied by a host of talents and thinkers as they forged a new reality, modernizing literature and art.

I came to Paris determined to host a modern day Salon; à la Ninon, à la Stein. Clearly my apartment was too small to invite but a few people at once. I have neither the art or accoutrements to set the stage, not the well enough stocked bar nor the appropriate barware to host such an event but I could easily visualize the guest list. My imaginary Salon was getting to be a bit crowded with *habitués* if they all accepted!

Where to host these show-stopping events? (And how much will they cost me? Caroleen suggests that they not be hosted and that the guests pay for their own drinks. Why did I ever tell her about this?)

I considered venues representative of Ninon's grand salon on rue des Tournelles, or decadently decorated with Matisses and Picassos on the rue de Fleurus. First to come to mind was the beautiful restaurant Le Mandragore at Hotel Particulier, hidden deep on a private cobblestone alley in a secret garden in Montmartre, former home of the Hermes family. If it doesn't have a Michelin star it should.

I have been to a private book event in the lovely dining room. The plush velvet chairs and *canapés* (only the French word for "sofa" adequately captures the essence of these lush versions of sofas). Gorgeous damask curtains hang from the windows and candelabras and chandeliers provide the exact right lighting. The room was perfect for a lively discussion on living in French.

The practical side of me saw Euro signs. Such a privatized event would not be cheap. Twelve to fifteen people, a dozen bottles of champagne or wine, platters of canapés (the small food items, not sofas) and coffee to send my guests out into the night, would quickly total 1,000 euro! One salon a month would put a big dent into my own dining out budget.

Another location that seems intriguing is Maison Souquet. Its two red lights at the door, welcoming guests is a nod to the buildings past life as a "House of Pleasure" and make it feel like the perfect place to relax and discuss... whatever. Caroleen offered to go check it out with me. At 20 euro per cocktail, I'm pretty sure I'll be picking up the tab. Maybe I will check it out alone. Or maybe I'll continue the search for a more affordable venue.

Le Clou and the GCA both have upstairs rooms for privatization and both owners love me, but while they may be serviceable, both seem more suitable for football events and the patrons of the downstairs restaurants would be traipsing through to use the toilettes. Not quite the atmosphere I am looking for. The back room of Le Cépage? Certainly close to home and more affordable but a far cry from the Hermes family living room or a 1920's brothel. You get what you pay for.

USA Today says there are 40,000 restaurants in the twenty arrondissements that make up the City of Paris. I will just have to keep looking. Without Caroleen.

An Accidental Salon

I t started with a text.

"Elliott, where is the best place for grilled squid in Paris?"

Elliott is the go to man if you want to know anything about food or wine in Paris. Never a man of few words he quickly responds, "Very interesting question. And I have an answer that very few would probably think of. .. A bit odd but there is a Croatian *resto* by Ternes. Au Petit Paris in the rue Rennequin. Great flame grilled squid. Not to mention meat and vegetables. And fantastic Croatian wines. If you want to go, let us know. Haven't been in a few months."

That's how a text turned into my second dinner as part of Elliott's ragtag group of expats. Ragtag is probably not a good descriptor of this group. Elliott clearly curates his groups with the same talent and care that he curates his wine pairings. Tonight's group, at six smaller than the Chinese New Year event at Maison Dong, included Elliott and his wife Joan. I am still trying to figure out how that coupling happened. One day I'll figure out how to ask. She's a head taller than him, lean as a whip and rarely utters a word. He's as gregarious as the day is long, holding court at every opportunity. I suppose that his *monsieur je-sais-tout* savoir will get old to me after awhile, but for now, I have a lot to learn and appreciate his verbosity. I suspect that still waters run deep and that there is a lot Joan could teach me as well. It just may take a while to get there.

Siobhan is a quiet Irish girl who has been in Paris for three years. She doesn't contribute much to the conversation but this is the second dinner we have sat side by side and she feels companionable. I think *un verre* one on one might reap an interesting friendship. I will follow up on that.

Joao is a Brazilian entrepreneur and business owner of indeterminate age living in Paris. I like him a lot. He has an amiable manner and a great smile. Further investigation finds he is wicked smart but in a not pretentious way. At Maison Dong he passed me his iPhone and said "Let's be friends", shorthand for let's connect on Facebook. In one short week my Facebook account has somehow spammed his. He's nonplussed.

"What shall I do?" I ask

"Change your password."

"I don't know my password" I admit sheepishly.

"Click forgot my password"

"But it's connected to an email account I no longer used and I don't know that password"

Joao shakes his head and rolls his eyes. He figures out he may continue to get spam from me.

Joao has told me about a language school that he attended for four months. He thinks it has helped him a lot. Besides, it was fun and he met interesting people. He thinks that two hours each day was just the right amount of time. I say I think I may check it out (since I don't seem to be jumping into bed with Philippe in a big hurry).

Joao has agreed to join Magalie and I for a jazz dinner to talk about Brazil. Magalie thinks she'd like to go live there for a year. Joao thinks she's nuts and is eager to talk her out of it. I'm doing my part to facilitate the spread of Paris friendships.

Rounding out the group at Au Petit Paris, and over forty five minutes late (Joan made her a plate and poured her wine before the fish course arrived) is Mariia, a pretty and obviously incredibly smart Russian girl. Mariia is a delicate Ruski doll with blond hair pulled back in a knot and the palest skin I have ever seen. She uses her hands a lot when she talks, her slender fingers emphasizing her words.

Before Mariia arrived Elliott expounded on Yugoslavian restaurants in Europe in the last twenty five years and the evolution of the culture outside of the former Yugoslavian countries after the war. It seems that Munich and Montmartre were two big centers of Yugoslavian people with wonderful restaurants and markets. No more.

Elliott stands to introduce the first wine, a delicate Prosip from Dalmatia. I only remember because I took a picture of the bottle. Joao does the same, for his education. Elliott seems pleased. We feast on roasted peppers and a charcuterie platter that makes my arteries moan. A creamy, garlicky pepper, tomato spread is perfect on the basket of fresh baguette, a nod to Paris I suppose.

Out comes a tray of the grilled calamari that gave birth to the idea of the evening. I eat all the legs. And two bodies. Elliott stands to introduce the second wine; a blah blah blah, whose grapes were grown on the blah blah blah, with just the right exposure to the morning blah... I stop listening. I'm eating legs. Joao notices and gives me his last legs. I give him a body.

At some point Elliott and Mariia start talking about Russian and Romanian writers and how poetry was impossible to translate because it could never say the same thing at all. They speak of Nabokov beyond Lolita and how Edgar Allen Poe only truly became great when translated by Baudelaire. Pushkin, Dostoevsky, Turgenev all fall into place.

The meat platters arrive and Elliott jumps up to talk about the Alatan Plavac barrique (from Hvar). The two platters groan with abundance; lamb, beef, pork, chicken, bacon, cevapcici (a minced pork and beef mixture formed into scrumptious little sausages, Elliott's self proclaimed "guilty pleasure"). All are interspersed with sliced onions, grilled eggplant and more meat. Elliott stands to tell us about the next wine and the conversation moves from literary to culinary.

Elliott: "I cook often at home. Always three courses with two different wines."

Me: "Sometimes I make pancakes for dinner. And if it's Friday, I may pair it with a Sidecar... or even two!"

Elliott: " I make excellent pancakes! In fact, I was often asked to cook for my father and his important friends. Pancakes was the one time he actually complimented my cooking…" (Aha! A key to Elliott's need to know everything!)

Me: "Sometimes I just have popcorn."

We ask for another bottle of wine, this one the Grand Cru of the previous wine.

"But I always thought it was best to drink the good wines first and then to revert to the lesser wines" (I think I may have even mentioned two-buck Chuck).

"Nonsense! First of all, you don't drink wine to get drunk. I refuse to include those people who insist on drinking so many *apéros* before dinner that they come to the meal drunk! Wine is to be savored! To enjoy! Few even comprehend the notion of terroir…"

D'accord.

The meal concludes. The bill is divided. *Bises* are exchanged.

Elliott says they have a car outside and would be happy to have the driver run me home after he drops them. Nice.

We pile into the car, Elliott in the front, Joan and I in the back. Elliott talks the driver's ear off about the benefits of Chauffeur Priv vs Uber.

They get out at their apartment and the driver zips me home. "*Il parle beaucoup!*", I say.

"*Oui*"

Later when I am in my bed thinking about the night I realize I have been to a modern day salon!

Today I texted Elliott: "I am proud to be one of Les Oiseaux d'Elliott I am in the middle of writing a Ninon chapter and I realized that what you do is really a version of a modern day salon. I suggest this name. I would love to discuss Salon culture, both past and present soon."

Elliott responds: "Thanks for the kind words! But sadly we are a poor reflection of the salon of the past. But if we can hold on to a little piece of it, that might be a nice thing to have done."

Watch me!

Madam Monique

My plan was to choose an elderly woman who speaks no English and invite her to have coffee with me once or twice a week. The idea was hatched at a bus stop on Av Montaigne. It was raining and a well outfitted elderly woman began to talk to me about the newly designed bus stop structures. "they simply are not functional!" she said (in French). I knew I was not lingually equipped for this conversation so I pulled out my old tried and true "*Je suis désolée. Je ne parle pas français.*"

"Oh!" she said, "are you English? It's raining cats and dogs! Cats and Dogs! What exactly does that mean? I always thought the English liked cats and dogs."

"Well, I'm American. But that's a good question!" I since have looked it up and it seems it comes from olde-English when the animals may have been on top of the thatched roof and it rained so hard that the animals would fall through the thatches and into the houses.

"I haven't spoken English since I was in school!" Her mastery of the language was excellent given that her last experience was clearly a long while ago.

The bus came and we both got on, sitting in different places. I was leaving in a couple of days, but I wished I could have invited her to tea, and arranged to practice my French with her on a regular basis. The seed was planted.

Since that day, the idea has been refined. I have half a dozen friends who I could have coffee, or drinks with, some who even say "let's speak French today!" But our conversations quickly revert to English, primarily because of my inability to have any sort of meaningful conversation in French. I can order a meal. I can (sort of) of have a conversation in an Uber car between my home and any reasonable Paris destination. "*J'habite à Paris maintenant. Je suis de la Californie. Depuis six mois.* (OK I like lie? a little bit, it's easier to say than to try to explain that I came a lot and now I'm here to stay). *Je suis écrivain. J'écris un roman. Oui, j'aime la neige.*" A real, meaningful conversation always means switching to English.

So, the primary requirement for my enseignant was that she spoke no English. There would be no back-tracking.

I popped into Cépage for a bowl of soup, careful to sit in a seat where Caroleen would not want to sit. (She is very particular about sitting only in the seat at the end of the second row of banquettes, just before the serious diners, next to the only outlet, but where you could arguably justify occupying the table as long as your *café crème* paid the rent).

Madame Monique sat at the table next to mine. Of course at that time I did not know yet that she was Madame Monique.

As I've mentioned before, a whole host of elderly patronize Cépage on a daily basis. They are known as the *Montmartois*, the elderly who eat their hot meal of the day, chat with their friends, keep abreast of the neighborhood gossip. Some sit together. Some alone.

Madame Monique is a mumbler. She carries on an ongoing dialog with nobody. After awhile the conversation started to include me, and occasionally the good looking gentleman on the other side of her. (Where did HE come from?!)

I think at first she was talking about her fish dish and wondering why they had not given her any sauce on the side.

"*Madame,*" I asked, "*parlez vous anglais?*"

"*Non*" she responded regretfully.

"*Bon!*" I said enthusiastically. "*J'ai besoin de quelqu'un pour pratiquer mon français!*"

I went on to ask her, in what I thought was a reasonable rendition of French if she would like to meet with me a couple of times each week to help me with my French.

She seemed to love the idea. She would meet me at 1:00, actual days unclear and we would work for one hour and she would be *mon enseignante*.

From there I was able to determine that Madame was born in Paris in 1936. During the war, her family moved to Poland. Her husband had passed and she had never had children. She did have a niece *(une medecine.* Each time she said niece it was followed by *la medicine)*, who lives in the second arrondissement and is of course very busy.

During the course of determining our agreement to meet, Madame tore a page from her little notebook and wrote her first and last name, her address, her digi code, and her telephone number. She said she lived just *"deux minutes à pied"*.

Madame finished her meal, paid her bill and we agreed to meet *demain* at 1:00 for one hour.

Just five minutes after she left she flew back into Cépage and plopped down next to me, much closer than she was previously sitting. She unleashed a rapid-fire dialogue. From the best I could tell, it was all French, she could not come tomorrow. She had forgotten that she had to be at home because there was a leak in the plumbing in the apartment above her which was dripping into the apartment below. IF she was not there, it's likely that the people in the apartment below her would try to fix the blame on her. They were extremely *méchants* (evil) and she is an old woman and he is trying to force her to sell her apartment because she has a bigger balcony than he does. There was much gesticulating at the Century 21 office across the street, leaving me a bit concerned that in fact her apartment might indeed already be on the market!

If repetition is helpful in learning a lesson, Madame Monique is perfect. *Ménchant. Balcon. Vielle dame. Ma nièce le médecin.* All got a lot of repetition.

No, she could not meet me tomorrow but she seemed to agree to my suggestion that we meet on Monday at 1:00. Several times Monday at 1:00 for one hour was reinforced. Again, the little slip of paper with her name, her phone number, her address, her digicode, the *deuxième étage, à gauche. D'accord!* There was more about the *ménchant* person who wants to sell her apartment and the leak and the *nièce le médécin.* She is sitting so close to me we are pressing against each other. If she were a man, I'd be crying out "Me too!'

Finally Madame scurries off. I take a big breath and relax. *Le beau monsieur* smiles at me knowingly.

I have my *enseignante.* If today's lesson is any example I believe that meeting with Madame Monique will in fact help me improve my conversational French. Today we talked about the difference between *seule* and *seulement,* including the genders. While this is something I already knew, I had in fact misused it while speaking with her. Her pedantic correction showed an attention to detail and clarity.

I am so grateful that there are three days between that exhausting discussion and Monday!

Monday rolls around. It's arctic cold, -1 degree, -10 with the wind chill factor. I pop over to Cépage, fortunately about thirty steps outdoors between my door and the restaurant. I go early for lunch, a salad. I'm working on getting in my five fruits and vegetables. Does wine count?

One o'clock comes and goes. Every time the door opens and closes I look up. No Madame. At 1:45 I assume she isn't coming. I have to admit that I have mixed emotions, part disappointment that I'm not moving forward with this stage of my life in Paris. Part relief. Did I choose someone who will need too much from me? Am I prepared to be someone for a lonely old woman to lean on?

I wrap myself up in scarf and puffy coat and head back to my apartment; fifteen steps to the front door, then another fifteen across the wind tunnel that is my courtyard, into my toasty apartment.

Tuesday, as I sit in GCA, three glasses of wine in, watching it snow outside and Philippe doing his lovely Philippe thing, it occurs to me: did Madame expect me at her apartment at 1:00 on Monday? Is that why she was so insistent that I understood her address, her digi-code, her *deuxième étage, à gauche?*

Did I stand Madame Monique up?

She Turned Them Gay

C aroleen asked me if she's in my book. I shook my head. "Because I will read it you know."

I guess I don't need to worry. I suspect the last book she actually read was… well, maybe never. But F is likely to read it. He's gotten me to download Emile Zola's "L'Argent" in both French and English. For that matter, when I couldn't remember the name of the Zola book about the unfaithful wife in the notions shop near the Seine she did offer up "Theresa Requin" with a dramatic shudder. I truly cannot imagine her reading it.

"Remember the photo I posted of me in the eighties?" She asked, referring to a photo she had posted on Instagram that week; big hair, big makeup, baby doll dress with oversized coat and shoulder pads the size of Mayfair. The hashtags were #EatonPlace #Belgravia #daysofwine #roses #parties #antiquing #friends #Kingsroad #drinks #soirees #Mayfair #writers #artists #poets #magic #love # beauty #fashion…

She slides her laptop toward me. "Should I add this paragraph?" It's a massive list of names, most of which mean nothing to me but clearly meant to allude to nights spent partying with the likes of Twiggy, McCartney, Sting, Boy George and George Michaels, the last two who were actually in her paragraph.

"I don't know. Sure. Why not?" I don't know what she's trying to accomplish, other than showing me how fab she used to be.

She still has big hair but it's kind of in that wild, combed with your fingers and pinned back with some bobby pins and sunglasses plopped on top way. Her hair, by the way, smells like it could use a good wash and her black poncho is getting pillier by the day. However, "A French woman never goes out, even to the *poubelle*, if she's not completely put together!"

"Ah, London!" I say. "Do you still go often?" After a month in Paris I'm dreaming of a trip on the Eurostar.

"No!" she spits out. "I am boycotting London. It's been completely taken over by Arabs. They hunch in the doorways, sneering at you from under their headscarves. Spitting at you! But in the day…"

"Maybe you should write a book" I offer up, eager to get the subject off Arabs, her catch all for any one of Muslim faith.

"Oh I should… Sam North wrote a book about those days. You know, the old woman who owns those big mansions and would let out the rooms to young boys. Sam North wrote a book about the house on Chapel Street turned into a boarding house. He changed the names of course. Mrs….. still knew it was her and sued that author!"

"How did it turn out?"

"Oh, she died. The real Mrs Gorse took young boys and turned them gay."

"You can't turn someone gay!"

"Of course you can!"

Again I change the subject to avoid another long lecture about something ridiculous. It's not my habit to let people get away with such outrageous statements. I have learned with her there is absolutely no way I will convince her of the foolishness of her beliefs. Our hours of arguing about her outrage for all Muslims has left me frustrated and exhausted of any hope to make her a nicer person.

La Séduction

E laine Sciolino wrote a book about it. "La Séduction". Page one begins with a quote from Voltaire:

It is not enough to conquer, one must also know how to seduce.

I raise my hand high and say "I suck at it".

Ms Sciolino says a *grand seducteur* might refer to "someone who never fails to persuade others to his point of view."

Well, I'm great at that!

A colleague in my past corporate life once told me I was manipulative. When I asked what he meant by that he said "you get people to do things and make them think it was their idea all along." I told him I preferred to think of it as influence. Maybe, thinking like a French woman, it's a matter of seduction.

Sciolino goes further to say that seduction is bound tightly with the notion of *plaisir*, "the art of creating and relishing pleasure of all kinds... they give themselves permission to fulfill a need for pleasure and leisure..."

Consider Philippe. What is it about him that has appealed to me? For a full year I barely noticed him. He was the guy who welcomed me, albeit warmly, each time I showed up for a Wednesday night jazz dinner. I noticed that he buzzed about, humming and singing to the music. It seemed to me that he would rather be performing himself.

For the first year or two all of my interest was on that sexy drummer. I'm not even sure when the needle on my infatuation compass swung to Philippe.

Once, during my long stay in Paris before moving here, he said something to me, all in French, about knowing that I had been watching Daniele at the Hotel du Jardin. (My pea brain substituting "stalking" for "watching") I was startled and confused.

"You were there?"

"No."

By then I had my own dedicated table, we were *tutoying* and on a first name basis.

He continues to buzz around, always with a song not far from his lips and lots of friendly words. Maybe Magalie is right. Maybe I'm just part of his revenue stream, albeit a friendly revenue stream. But I need to know. And if I can influence Philippe to see me that way, to seduce him into a bit of *plaisir*, I want to. I need to up my game.

What would Ninon do?

First stop, La Pharmacie. I picked up a hairbrush (no more finger combing for this girl), some mascara and a bit of eyeliner.

"Comment dit-on eyeliner?"

"Eyeliner"

Now down to Le Café Qui Parle to reread La Séduction and have some lunch. Oh la la it's cold! -3 degrees and ice on the sidewalks, although the sun is shining. While I wait at the crosswalk, a guy on a motorbike looks directly at me and holds the stare. I look right back, do an exaggerated little shiver and smile broadly. The light changes and he moves on. *Une petite séduction.* Fake it til you make it.

A bowl of celery soup with a floating island of *foie gras* and a glass of wine in the shadow of the studio Toulouse-Lautrec shared with Suzanne Valadon. Take a deep dive into *le plaisir.*

Who are these people?

People come to Paris for a hundred different reasons. Like New York, London, San Francisco, it seems like nobody was born in Paris. People leave Paris for a hundred different reasons. Some come to study, my own daughter and niece among them. Perhaps the dream doesn't live up to the expectations. They are poor. Living accommodations are dreary. The language barrier is more difficult than they expected. The French are rude. The city is dirty. The crusty baguettes have worn holes in the roofs of their mouths. When their year is over they return home where the stories of living in Paris are far sexier than the reality was.

Some come to pursue their art. With its rich history of art, literature and music, the City beckons would be artesans of all kinds. But can the City deliver on its siren call? When asked where do today's Hemingways hang out and put pen to paper, John Baxter, expat cum writer cum tour guide pooh poohs the notion entirely. The City, he claims, is entirely too expensive for the starving artist today.

I would argue that today's writers are the bloggers who habituate the coffee shops primarily in the ninth, tenth and eleventh arrondissements, taking advantage of the free wifi, a warm dry place to sit, and maybe a bit of *camaraderie*, all for the price of a coffee. They clog up the tables for hours; the scourge of café owners. A trend for enterprising landlords is to charge a day rate, or even, like the Peloton Café, to ban laptops altogether. (I wonder what they would do about me with my notebook and pen?)

For the better backed among us, those with working spouses, or retirement nest eggs sufficient to support the Paris lifestyle, life may be a bit easier. We can pick and choose our working venue, careful not to overstay our welcome by eating or drinking on the cheap.

Some come to work. Yesterday at a special Elliott curated Sunday Bacchanalian Roast, I surveyed the five other women at my end of the table; a Brit, an Irish lass, a Spaniard and two Americans. They have been in Paris between three and twelve years. All came to work. All had done a good job of adapting to their new city. While each seemed more than content to stay, none were opposed to the idea of following their job to a new location.

"What about love?" I asked. "Have you met anyone here that would make you stay forever?"

No. While each had dated a French man, none lasted very long and each of those relationships had cross cultural issues that got in the way. In fact, each of these attractive, successful and intelligent women in their thirties was currently single. And looking.

Quatre vingt dix
neuf per cent

Ninety nine percent! That was the consensus of the ladies at Floyd's Bar Sunday afternoon. At first they unanimously said 100%, but then they qualified the virtual totality with a possible one percent margin of "no". What do these 99% of French men do? Cheat on their wives!

I have to look around any room I'm in and wonder; Do you cheat on your wife? Do you? How about you? Or are you perhaps that amazing one in one hundred who doesn't? And if you don't, if this is such a totally accepted thing; why don't you?

"Keep in mind", one of the women said, "their wives cheat as well."

Bien sûr, mathematically it stands to reason, if all these men have something on the side either the women must all have something going on the side, single women must be dating a lot of married men, or some smaller percentage of married women are really really busy with multiple lovers!

For my part I sit there trying to wrap my head around this possibility.

"You have to understand," the Spanish girl says "It's different here. A lover on the side doesn't take anything away from the marriage. It doesn't minimize how much they love their spouse. It's just sex."

"Hmmmm" I really have no words.

Maybe that's why, if Caroleen is right, French women are so distrustful; why they listen to and delete their boyfriend's messages.

How would I feel, knowing that my guy had a lover on the side? That once or twice a week, he crept away for a *cinq à sept*? If I didn't know for sure, would I be forever wondering? Watching? Worrying? Why even get married to begin with?

Sitting on the terrace of Le Clou and enjoying a very French cheeseburger and *frites*, some sun and wine, I watch the beau Thierry working. Is he the one in one hundred?

Le Cours de Cuisine

I started following the Hotel du Jardin on social media after I enjoyed an amazing dinner that was hosted by their two Michelin star chef, Julien Rocheteau, and guest chef Stephane Jego, from L'Ami Jean. That was how I learned about Saturday's *Cours de Cuisine*. "Spend the day in a Michelin Star kitchen!" was the advertisement. Limited to six people.

So I signed up and showed up at 9 am on Saturday morning. Soon the Chef came out to greet me. It seems that the other students had cancelled at the last minute.

"Well, surely you want to cancel the class." I said, part sad, part relieved.

"*Non! C'est bon.*" The class would continue. Me, Chef Julien and the translator, Aimee, who they had thoughtfully provided for me. Aimee was actually thrilled because she would participate with Chef Julien and me.

We sat in the bar area and enjoyed coffee while Chef invited me to ask him any questions. I put on my interviewer hat, trying my best to ask my questions en francais.

"You are only 34 years old and you have already earned two Michelin stars: what is next for you?"

His shrug and quick tilt of his head to the right said "a third star, stupid!"

The Oxford English dictionary has some 233,132 words. *Le Grand Robert de la langue française* has only 100,000 words (with 350,000 definitions). A great percentage of the French language is with shrugs, pouts, snarls, puffs of air from the side of their mouths, murmurs, eye rolls, growls, punctuated with *oh la las* and *bah ouais* and *merdes* and *putains*.

"*On y va*" and into the kitchen we went. Chef gave me a white apron and showed me where to wash my hands. First up, we would be making his signature starter, a langoustine concoction with not less than fifteen ingredients and thirty seven steps. First step, peel the raw langoustines. Chef gave that task to the stupid American, after showing me how to do them first. It seemed simple enough.

On my very first *langoustine* I punctured my finger and spurted blood. The class would have to be cancelled! It's not possible to have human blood in the kitchen, especially not a Michelin star kitchen. Pas de probleme. Chef produced rubber gloves and proceeded to put one on my offending hand. My wet hands made the task all the harder, an errant finger jutting out to the side, the spurting finger rapidly filling with blood. "It's going to be a long day," Chef murmured in French. that I understood.

I finally got six of the little devils (at twelve euro each, Chef told me) properly peeled and into water to be gently parboiled. Then Chef showed me how to roll them individually into a sheet of seaweed, making little langoustine cigars. The cigars were sliced into thick nickel size rounds which I arranged carefully into three ring molds. Into the ring mold went a jellied liquid that I watched Chef prepare. These were put aside to set while we made squid ink lace which eventually was broken into little triangles to poke into the unringed rounds. Out of a drawer came a tin of caviar and sheets of edible silver. Dabs of *crème fraiche*, little mounds of caviar, the triangles of squid ink lace and our entree was ready to serve.

Aimee, Chef and I took our pretty little *entrées* into the private dining room and he popped a bottle of champagne. While my mind calculated the cost of these little starters I sipped champagne and prodded the Chef with more questions. I learned about his family, his wife and his hobbies. Aimee happily translated and enjoyed the champagne and *langoustines*. It was all very *sympathique*.

Back into the kitchen to start on the main course; homemade ravioli stuffed with a rich cheesy mixture served on top of an elegant sauce and accompanied by three perfect scallops. This all atop a plate dusted with squid ink dust, made from the rest of the crushed lace. We spread flour and eggs on a marble table top and proceeded to make the pasta while simultaneously mixing the cheesy stuffing mixture. Rolled, rerolled and rolled again, the pasta was cut into strips and the stuffing placed in dabs at exactly the right spots, sliced and folded to be molded just so. Chef and Aimee's raviolis were perfect. Mine much less so and were tactfully named Ravioli Katrine.

Chef took a shortcut and seared the scallops while we watched, quickly plating the main courses and pulling a white truffle out of the magic drawer and shaving it over the plates.. We grabbed our plates and headed back into the dining room where Chef opened a bottle of crisp white wine for us to enjoy with our meal and added a basket of fresh mini baguettes. The meal of course was delicious. I suspect that by this time Chef was getting a little tired of his new best friends and was eager for the day to be finished. Aimee took a smoking break.

The dessert course; *soufflés*! We beat eggs, we folded in flour, we prepared the little individual *soufflé* pans. Around us scurried other kitchen staff who washed our dishes, wipe up our spills and cleaned up our messes. We waited for our perfect little risen souffles to come out of the oven.

Back into the dining room where he sunk a dab of chantilly into our picture perfect masterpieces and poured in a bit of grand marnier. Too salty! Well, I guess that even a Michelin starred chef makes a mistake now and then. Or maybe it was the distraction and fatigue of putting up with this annoying American. I have to say that Chef remained charming and gracious throughout the entire day. He autographed my apron and set me off with la bise, I'm sure, glad to see the back of me!

I will never prepare any of the things we made that day. Well, maybe I will attempt a *soufflé*. But I absolutely gained an appreciation for why a Michelin starred meal costs what it does. The magic drawer with expensive ingredients; the crazy number of steps each course required; not only does Chef need to engineer, create and serve innovative dishes, he needs to work with vendors to procure the freshest and best product, buy artistic dishes for presenting his masterpieces in the exact right light, hire a staff both inside and outside of the kitchen, pair with the right wines, procure the right wines… Five days a week from morning to night. He stands on his feet all day. He deals with unappreciative clients, difficult vendors, unruly staff. And then after the day is over, he comes back the next day to do it all again.

Shortly after I took my class the Michelin people came out with the next years stars. Chef Julien was downgraded to one star. I felt somehow responsible. He left the Table du Jardin and started a new restaurant, La Scène Thélème. He quickly earned his first star. What's next? I imagine that Chef would shrug and give a quick tilt to his head.

Le Divorce

Finally! You can only hang around with bat shit crazy so long before you realize that makes you the crazy one!

I actually walked out on Caroleen last night. Well, I told her I was leaving and she said "Yes, I think I should leave. We should both leave." But she didn't. I suspect she stayed behind to pick up my change.

I don't even know how to tell the crazy story. You could not make this stuff up.

"Am I in your book?"

"Yes Caroleen! You are too fucking crazy to not be in my book!"

It started with an invite for an *apéro*. What is wrong with me? I hadn't seen her in several days. My memory is evidently short.

Her favorite table was occupied and I got there first so I got to choose. I took the comfy bench seat. She was stuck with the chair against the aisle.

Maybe that's why she started out on the defensive. Maybe it was because I'd had several fun busy days without her. She hates that I have so many friends already.

The attitude manifested itself immediately. It was happy hour. I ordered a margarita; she ordered an aperol spritz. An older lady came over from a couple of tables away. "Are you Americans?"

"Yes!" Caroleen responded, then she quickly qualified that she had lived in Paris for a long time and had a French husband.

Madame was German but moved to Paris with her French artist husband and lives in the 18ème in an artist atelier on rue Ordener. Quickly Caroleen piped up about her German mother and her roots *allemande*. (Caroleen detests her mother and disowned her some years ago.)

Madame said something about loving New York. Caroleen lived in New York! She knows it well!

Madame suggested that we should speak to each other in French. Caroleen looked at me and shuddered. Madam left.

"You're looking rather pretty" Caroleen said. I had put on lipstick. "I always go out with a bit of something; lip gloss (chapstick?), eyeliner (yes, about that eyeliner – you really have to be careful about that after fifty… Meow)

"That reminds me, something I'm putting in my book" (You have a book now? Is it like the website you've been almost finished with for two years? Meow MEOW)

"I go to a store, for example Mac, and say, "I'm not familiar with your line. How would I use your products if for example you had an evening soiree? And *voilà*, you are made up for the evening!"

Great! So you are advising visitors to Paris to pull a fast one to get a free makeup job. Do you advise them to pop into Galeries Lafayette for a ball grown and carefully tuck the tags in so they can return it after a ballet at Palais Garnier?

I shared with her my thoughts about nobody being born in Paris. That everyone seems to come from somewhere else.

"Nonsense! There are hospitals here! People are born every day!"

"Yes, of course" I respond. "But children of people who came here from somewhere else. For example, where was F from?"

"F is Parisian!"

"He was born in Paris?"

"Well no, he was born in Provence but…"

"Exactly, what I'm wondering is why do people come to Paris? Why did F's family come to Paris?"

"For work opportunities. There were no jobs in the provinces."

"And you, where were you before you came to Paris? And why Paris?"

"I was in London, and I think I came here to be close in spirit to my Father. I was a Daddy's girl."

"Was your Father born in Paris?"

"No, my Father was born in the South."

"How did he meet your German mother?"

"During the war." She sipped her Aperol Spritz. "My father was doing classified work for the British and the Americans during the war. And he met my mother."

"That must have been controversial!"

"Yes, they couldn't even get married for many years. They married in New York after my first brother was born. Why are you asking all the questions? You know I hate talking about myself."

I told her that I had just watched a documentary about women during WWII in France; women in the Résistance.

"I can't imagine what Paris was like during the war. And I don't understand how an entire nation of people were so easily convinced to follow Hitler."

"Because he was the solution to the Jewish problem! My mother is still a Nazi, and while I don't agree with her, the Jews really did control everything! The banks! The media! It was a solution to the Jewish problem."

I sat there with my mouth hanging open.

"It's a problem today in the US. There have been times when I have had articles declined simply because I'm not Jewish. The media, the banks, the movie industry... all controlled by Jews!"

"Have you followed the Harvey Weinstein situation? Have you seen the list of all the offenders? All Jews! And have you seen the women making the complaints? No Jews! They just don't fuck their own!"

At this point I was determined to change the subject. "French women, you said before that French women are very jealous. How about Macron and his wife who's so much older?" I was reaching.

"He's gay! She's his cover." She spurted out.

"No he's not! I read a piece disproving that rumor!"

"No, he's gay. Everyone knows. He wears two rings because he has a gay husband. Look how he holds his head and looks down his nose. I have gay friends and they have a thing called gaydar and they all know! Why are you asking me all these questions?"

Good god! Jews. Arabs. Gays. Is anyone safe?

"Have you been following the Italian election today?" she asked.

"I haven't had time to read about it yet."

"They are going all Right! Everyone is going Right. It's the immigrants. Nobody is controlling the Arab problem. It's a real problem!"

"We need to change the subject" I said firmly.

"No! We can't change the subject! This is important. France needs to get out of the EU!"

"Caroleen, we need to change the subject. I can't talk to you about this. You know you and I have very different opinions about this."

"We have to talk about it! It's important! It involves all of us. You live here now! It involves you! This Arab problem is out of control!"

"We have to change the subject or I will leave."

"Fine! Let's talk about jealous French women and other petty things that don't matter. F and I are going to have to leave Paris and leave France and you just get to be an American. Think about trivial things and ignore the important things."

"That is BS!" I raised my voice. "You are not leaving Paris. You and I have very different opinions about this and neither of us will change the other's mind. I've said this before and you continue to go on and on. After you text me that you're sorry you kept on but it's important to you. You do it again and again. How dare you accuse me of being trivial!"

I paid the tab for both of us (again) , "I'm leaving".

"Well, I guess we both should leave." But she stayed seated while I put on my coat.

"*Au revoir*", she said airily.

I walked the seventy eight steps home, my blood boiling, feeling completely impotent. My phone buzzed, indicating a text.

"Thanks again for the drink – just joined F at Francoeur – great group of French guys talking Italian vote all at the same time. Great fun – no one agrees on anything. *C'est la France*"

I deleted the text.

I deleted her Instagram account.

I blocked her from mine.

Stupid I know. But I felt divorced at last. It's a pity that she'll probably get Cépage in the division of assets. I'm sure they'd rather have kept me, too. I tip better.

French Girls Think Differently

French girls think differently than we American girls. And they really don't want to talk about it.

I'm not talking about fake French girls like Caroleen. She is, however, the perfect example of why even twenty five years in Paris can't make an American girl think like a French girl.

I would never say a bad word about Stephanie. I love her with all my heart. I call her *la soeur de ma coeur*, the sister of my heart. The first time I met her, some five years ago, when she greeted me at my apartment as the new owner of the rental agency that manages my two favorite rental apartments we clicked as kindred spirits. She is strong, independent, intelligent and brave. And she's pretty and very French. She was even born in Paris. Every day she jumps on her scooter, rain, snow or sun and runs her business. She vacations alone in Bali and once a year with a big group of old friends at Club Med in Turkey.

In the time that I've known her she has had men friends but no single boyfriend. There are a couple of men who are disappointed about that, nearly as disappointed as her mother who wants grandbabies. She refuses to settle. She owns her own impressive apartment in Montmartre where she entertains generously and fosters rescue dogs until proper homes can be found for them. I've been fortunate to be on the receiving end of her hospitality and every time I've been to Paris we meet for lunch or dinner.

Now that I'm an actual pretend "*Parisienne*", I'm grateful to have Stephanie as my first French girlfriend. She introduced me to Magalie, making two French girlfriends.

Stephanie has been back from Bali for ten days but she has been slammed with work so last night was the first time we've been able to get together… for Wednesday night jazz dinner at Grand Comptoir d'Anvers.

When I finished up my Tuesday writing session, Philippe asked "Demain soir? Pour la jazz! C'est vrai?"

"*Bien sûr*" I assured him. "*Pour deux, s'il te plaît*".

"*Deux*" his eyebrow shot up. "*Ah, oui! Avec Aimee!*"

"*Non! Aimee es Vendredi*" I had agreed to meet Aimee for an apero at GCA on Friday evening. "How do you know this stuff?"

Lost on him. Sadly it seems like Philippe's English is getting worse and my French is going backwards. Even Duolingo has downgraded me from 70% to 68%! He's taken to pulling Guilloume over to translate for us. I've seen Guilloume feed him other English responses for clients too. Maybe it was just not so good ever.

I walked into the restaurant and Philippe dashes over to me, la bise in front of the band, Daniele tonight!

"*Mon table!*" I exclaimed, seeing it occupied.

"*Un peu de confusion.*" Philippe said sheepishly. "How about this one?"

"*Pas de problème*" Actually this one was much better. Right across from the lovely Daniele, impossible not to be noticed. I make a mental note to ask Philippe to please make this my regular table.

The dour new manager heads over to ask me if I would like something and Philippe shoos him off. "I will take care of Madam." Philippe whips out a white table cloth and sets my table. Guillaume comes over and shakes my hand.

Stephanie comes in looking fab; faux fur coat, knee high boots, cute little dress. We exchange *la bise* and she settles into her seat and takes in the ambiance of the restaurant. Philippe comes over and I introduce Stephanie. I tell him we would like a bottle of Pinot Noir.

Stephanie said she's checked out the menu online and is very excited to try the *boeuf bourguignon*. After Guillaume opens the wine, I do the tasting ceremony and he pours for both of us. We tell him we are ready to order; the *boeuf bourguignon* for her, *poisson* for me.

I tell her about the divorce. She congratulates me and we toast to that. She tells me about her Bali vacation and the newest foster pup and that business is booming. We are well into the second jazz set and the second bottle of wine before I tell her about my disappointing conversation about Philippe with Magalie. She listens without comment. I tell her about my previous obsession with Daniele.

"He's very cute!" she says, "I've noticed he's been looking at me." Between sets he bumped her chair going from the restroom back to his drums. He put his hand on her shoulder and apologized.

During the third set we've nearly finished the second bottle. Philippe has spent a lot of time at our table. For that matter, Guillaume has too. Only the dour manager has managed to stay away.

Philippe takes our photo and we send it to Magalie. Then we take a selfie including Philippe. We are laughing and talking and Daniele calls out, *"Alors!"* We were so busy talking that we hadn't noticed the last number had ended and nobody was applauding. Philippe jumps up clapping loudly. Stephanie and I join in.

Now Stephanie's chair is turned about 80 degrees giving her a more direct view of Daniele.

Aha! An opportunity for me to observe first hand *le regard!* Nineteenth Century French writer Stendhal says you can say everything with the look, and you can deny it because it can't be quoted word for word. I guess when two girls are sitting at a table and twenty feet away sits a drummer, it's kind of impossible to say who the drummer is actually looking at. I do think however that Daniele played his heart out last night. And married or not, Stephanie was under his trance. I can certainly understand that. I've been under his trance for nearly three years.

Wine is gone. Cognac comes out, followed by a final *coupe de champagne* for each. When the final song of the final set ends and Daniele stands up to introduced his group I am buzzed and clapping loudly, happy with the attention we've gotten from Philippe and the fact that Daniele was playing for our table. OK, for Stephanie most likely.

I pay the tab and we are ready to leave. Stephanie pops up and heads to the end of the bar where Daniele is standing. OK. American girls… watch this! A French girl in action. "I'm going to talk to him."

How many years have I watched him end his set and stand at the end of the bar while I slink out, maybe with a nod or a thumbs up, content to wait until next time. I follow about ten feet behind, to give Guilloume a 10 euro note and to say *au revoir* to Philippe. By the time I'm finished she turns away from Daniele and he's looking at me.

"*Merci beaucoup.*" I say and follow her out.

"What did you say? And what did he say?!" I ask while we wait for our Uber.

"I told him how much I enjoyed the music. He just said *merci*." She wistfully added "He's not interested."

The Uber driver dropped her off, then me one hill further on. I staggered into my apartment, peeling off my clothes as I made my way into the bedroom.

This morning I woke up thinking about French girls and American girls. French girls believe they are what they want others to believe they are. American girls who learn about this secret can try to believe it. They might even convince others they believe it. I don't know if I will ever believe it.

I reached over and grabbed my phone off the nightstand. There was the picture of Philippe, Stephanie and me. When I looked at it last night I felt like I was the intruder in a snapshot of the two of them. This morning the photo was clearly of Philippe and I with Stephanie in the corner. My phone buzzed, a new Facebook notification.

Daniele had sent me a friend request. I almost fell out of bed.

Days of Confusion

Sitting in GCA and I'm just stuck. La Séduction has me confused and maybe even a little sad. Some of the things I read make me feel rather French after all, and then huge swaths of it leave me sure I will never be French.

Still a bit high from the Daniele friend request and struggling with the differences between the way my French girlfriends think and the way I do, I didn't tell Stephanie about the friend request. I'm discovering a great deal of competition, even when you think someone's your friend.

Thursday night I had dinner with Charlotte at Bulot Bulot, a new hipster oyster bar in Montmartre, on rue des Martyrs. It seems like everything in Montmartre and the 9eme are going hipster. The restaurant is a teeny tiny place with very uncomfortable seating for the 15 or so patrons they can actually accommodate but time spent with Charlotte is always good. I hadn't seen her since before Christmas so took a little bit to establish our connection again. She has an amazingly busy, interesting life and she knows everyone. Her blog, app and podcast have such cache that she seems like a true celebrity. Celebrity aside, she is completely down to earth and we just click. We see things the same. We talked about Elliott and Joan. Joan remains a mystery to her as well and in 15 years of friendship, she's never done anything with Joan alone, Elliott alone, yes. But never Joan. I told her I was determined to crack that. She responded "Good luck with that!".

I asked what Elliott's job was and she said he does some sort of consulting. "He's very smart; one of the most well read people I've ever known. And incredibly generous. He frequently shows up with small gifts, perfectly thought of just for the giftee. To each of his curated dinners, often including a couple of dozen participants, he brings wine from his own cave, not expecting anything in return other than good conversation and fun. Very generous. We've just never talked about money and how he gets it. Maybe family money?"

"Elliot has alienated a few people. He will be the first person to admit that. But he has always been a good friend to me. I think you will learn to appreciate all that he brings to a friendship."

For my part, I'm admittedly a little more catty, commenting that I think that maybe Joan wears the pants in the family. "Black leather" I add, "And a whip"

She bursts into laughter, her cool cocktail spraying an oyster.

Charlotte is generous with her connections and has invited me to two follow-on things; dinner with the girls, her closest gal pals, and dinner at her own house in a couple of weeks. That dinner will include Elliott and Joan and Elizabeth and her husband. Elizabeth is a neighbor and very good friend, another American who's been in France for nearly two decades. She is a blogger, a tour guide and an expert in all things French cheese. For the dinner at Charlotte's house, I was assigned to bring a "soft cheese". Charlotte cleverley has her guests bring different cheeses as a way to involve them in *partager* and sharing the meal. How can I possibly choose a soft cheese that will pass the test of the cheese expert?

I shared my panic with Charlotte at Bulot Bulot. This is how lovely Charlotte is, "Oh no! Don't worry! I just do this because it seems like a fun way to involve my guests! But wait until you meet Elizabeth! She's great! She's very easy going." And so she is. But that comes later.

I could ask Elliott of course. He's been tasked with a hard cheese. If I ask him it would just be Elliott's cheese plate with me just bringing what he recommends. This must be perfect. My local fromagerie has a soft white cheese, I don't know what, with a layer of truffles. It was fantastic... to my unsophisticated cheese pallet. I thought it was exceptional, but what if it is pedestrian?

Aha! Ask Thierry! After all I took his wine and cheese pairing class last summer. I shot him a text and he quickly responded "A Saint Nectaire can be nice, or

Epoisse, but it's strong, or Pont L'Evêque." I googled them all to prepare myself with a bit of knowledge on their source, terroir, age, and the names of the cows that gave up the milk. I think I'm set.

Then Friday evening happened. I was scheduled to have an *apéro* with Aimee at GCA at 7:30. 7:30 seems a little late for an *apéro* for me but when in France…

I got there early but thought I could write a bit. Philippe was just leaving, jacket on, motorbike helmet in hand. Bises.

"*J'attend qui?*" I ask him. He seems a bit confused. "Who am I meeting?" I ask, "You seem to know my social calendar." Aimee, I confess, and he decides to wait as well. Maybe we'll get the truth behind all this gossip.

Aimee comes in a bit ruffled. She seems maybe a little nervous. It's been over a year since we've seen each other. There is something waifish and fragile about her. No makeup, hair pulled into a ponytail, her only nod to French femininity is a pretty glittery sweater. She collects a quick bise from Philippe and then we order from Guilloume; a beer for her, a margarita for me.

We spend the next hour catching up. We relive our fun *cours de cuisine* at La Table du Jardin with two Michelin star chef, Julien Rouchteau. She fills me in on Chef's loss of a star. We both laugh that it was probably because we were in his kitchen. She knows that Julien has gone to a new restaurant (with one star) but she has not been there. She, like me, has noticed that the *entrée* on the new menu is the one we made at our class!

"How do you know Philippe and how does he know you know me?" I get right to the point. The mystery, however, was never completely solved. Veronique, Aimee's sister is the Directoresse of the Hotel du Jardin and she lives across the street from GCA. Evidently she is at GCA at least three nights a week, sometimes with Aimee, sometimes with Aimee and their mother… She parks her car in the lot under Square Anvers, adjacent to the restaurant. OK, I get it. Veronique is a local and a regular but it doesn't explain how my name comes into it.

Aimee tells me about her difficult six months of unemployment since we last saw each other, about some web development training and her discouraging job search. She has been told she is too old (she's 40!) and too inexperienced. She finally got a job with a famous Parisian bread chain, creating a point of sale website. She beats herself up everyday worrying that she's not good enough. Her employer constantly reassures her that she's too hard on herself and that she's doing great. But she's not sure.

We talk for over an hour and our glasses are empty. "Would you like another drink?" she asks. "I have to take a quick break and go out for a cigarette. Only number five for the day!" She's trying to quit.

Ten minutes later she's back, with her mother and her sister! I "almost" met Veronique a couple of years ago when I used to go to Hotel du Jardin for their Wednesday night jazz. I jump up and there are bises all around before they join us.

Veronique has aged ten years! Or at least it seems that way to me. I remember her being a very pretty petite blond, very charming and very French. She seemed to have gotten puffy, messy and sarcastic; friendly enough, but somehow cynical about my being here. She introduces me to her mother in French. They say that her mother's English is like my French. I get the implication that my French is nonexistent.

Veronique asks Aimee if she had seen Philippe. "Yes, he gave me a *bise*". Then she asked me about the job I retired from. She seems to know a lot about my new life.

"So, when you and Philippe talk, what language do you speak?" she asks with a bit of a sneer. Can you do a friendly sneer? Evidently Parisiennes can.

"A bit of French. A bit of English. We kind of help each other."

Hmmmm, could it be that Veronique likes Philippe? There's something more than a little off about this potential friendship. I'm disappointed. I think I could learn a lot from Veronique. Maybe as competitors for the same man, there's even more I could learn from this woman!

The evening proceeds and we decide to have dinner. Philippe is long gone. Guillaume is our willing server. We mostly talk about Veronique's job, the changes she's making at the Hotel du Jardin, the monthly regional theme menus, promoting Julien's sous chef to head chef, trying to win back that first star. Her focus for the du Jardin has gone from the Royals of the 1600s to Hollywood royalty, focusing on celebrities who have been guests in the past; Marlene Dietrich, Orson Welles, Elizabeth Taylor. When I ask about the woman's portrait in the bar, I had imagined one evening that it was perhaps Ninon herself, she said "I hate that painting! I want to replace it with Marlene! And on the other side, Elizabeth Taylor!" Her French accent is so strong it takes me several times before I understand who she's talking about.

To be honest, I'm not crazy about the direction she's taking the lovely hotel. She seems to be infatuated with America, specifically Hollywood America. She recently went to California for a conference and she loved loved loved Santa Monica (again it took several tries before I understood) and her "convertible Mustang!"

She has never been to San Francisco but she said she'd like to go. But she adores Los Angeles! And maybe New York city. I told her we should trade lives. But in reality, I don't want her job. Too much pressure, not enough reward. And I certainly don't want her thirty square meter apartment! Actually, I think I like my life just fine.

Saturday I loafed around. My activity for the day was dinner with Charlotte and her friends in the evening. My only venture out in the daytime was to the *boulangerie* to get a croissant. I made a mushroom and cheese omelet in my little French kitchen. I'm saving euros now that Le Cépage is off limits to me! Caught up with a bit of cleaning, reading and studying French. I even took a little nap to build up my stamina for a night out on the town.

In the early evening I was Facetiming with Izzy and a little message flashes across my phone screen. "Philippe waved at you"

WTF! The gods are playing with me. First Daniele. Now Philippe. I choose to take these as signs. Maybe I'm not invisible.

After I finish with Izzy I send back a little kiss blowing emoticon. Later he responds, "Thank you. I hope to fine"

Don't try to read between the lines.

Today I woke up to an "Invitation from Daniele to Jazz at Pop Up du Label" Me and his 2,000 other Facebook friends. This social networking stuff is going to make me crazy!

Dinner with the Girls
(and Gareth)

I continue to struggle with the concept of on time here. When is it expected that you show up *en retard*; when should you be on time; what if God forbid, you arrive early?

Dinner with the girls was set for 7:30 at Le Yacht Club in the 9ème. So far the rule, as far as I can tell, is if you are expected at a French home, be fifteen minutes late. Never on time, Never more than twenty minutes late. What I don't understand is why you don't ask me to come at the time you really want me to be there.

At a non-French home you are most likely expected at the time stated, although it's possible that you will show up and the hosts are still in the shower, or one has gone to the market, or people are at various stages of dress or undress.

For dinner with the girls, all non-French, at one of the newest neighborhood hotspots, I would assume you show up on time.

So I arrived at Le Yacht Club at 7:30. It was completely empty. I walked down the street a bit and took some photos of Eglise Notre Dame de Lorette, then a few of the pretty flower shops nearby, walked back to Le Yacht Club ten minutes later; still empty. I hitched up my big girl panties and walked in.

"*Bon soir! Je suis avec Silvie.*" Silvie made the reservations.

"*Bien sûr!*" the server said and pointed at two tables in the center of the large dining room, indicating that I should take my pick. I pointed at another, along the wall with a questioning look. Frankly quite a lot can be communicated without ever saying a word. "*non...* an incomprehensible French sentence or two.." clearly all the other tables are spoken for.

It's only a few minutes before Silvie sails in. We have never met before but several people have told me I need to meet her. Canadian by origin, she's been in Paris for over twenty years. She married and divorced in Paris, has a teenage daughter, runs her own apartment rental business and lives not far from me in the 18eme.

She seems to be friends with everyone; Elliott and Joan, Charlotte and T, Stephanie, Siobhan. Yes, clearly I need to meet her. She's a voluptuous, outspoken woman, obviously comfortable in her own skin. She is just getting over a bout of bronchitis and a business trip to Las Vegas followed by a conference in Paris. Obviously this is a busy lady. "I'm so happy to meet you at last! I've heard so much about you and everyone tells me I must meet Silvie."

Clearly she's never heard of me. Or perhaps she's simply not interested.

Charlotte and Elizabeth come in, at this point only thirty minutes *en retard;* muttering something about the *métro*. So, on time seems to be a fluid concept; thirty minutes give or take, mostly take, and murmurs about the metro (unless, like me you have an aversion to the metro).

Bisous all around. Another cultural lesson: inclusion into a group earns you *bisous* immediately. Coming on to a scene on your own means having to earn the *bise*. It took a year to move from a hearty handshake to *la bise* with Philippe. I got my first *bise* from Thierry only last week, after nearly two years of eating at Le Clou. The next visit his hands were full and I got a friendly "*ça va?*"

The girls are all travel writers, tour guides and bloggers so loads of photos were required; photos of the still empty restaurant, photos of the bar, photos of the menu, followed by photos of each of the exotic cocktails. We all tasted each other's. I was happy I had chosen mine, *la Barbe Noire* (Black Beard, going along with the nautical pirate theme), Jameson, bitters and *cassonade flambé et rallange au tonic* with a dried orange slice.

Charlotte is right. Elizabeth is lovely and very down to earth. She tells me about her coming to France, originally to a small village in the south where she and her husband bought a house. Yes, she agreed, living in a small village outside of Paris is the best way to learn French. Eventually she and her husband relocated to Paris where she is leading small cheese tours and writing about cheese. I like her instantly and am looking forward to getting to know her better at Charlotte's dinner party.

Silvie takes the lead in ordering the first round of tapas and Elizabeth chooses a bottle of white wine. The wine is poured and another ordered immediately. Silvie tells us that Gareth will be joining us. I can't help but wonder how Gareth got included in the girls night out.

"Gareth is in town and I told him he needs to get his stuff out of my cellar since I'll be moving soon." Silvie has been living in her ex-husband's old apartment and since he's moving to the South soon, she will have to move as well. "I helped him load it into a taxi and he's unloading it into someone else's cellar. Then he will join us."

Everyone seems fine with it so who am I to bicker. Another bottle of wine is ordered, along with a second course of tapas. The razor clams are deemed too sandy to be eaten and are sent back. The waitress is unapologetic but takes them. The aubergine is delicious. If I could return, I would make a meal of the aubergine, the squid and a couple of *Barbes Noires*. In fact, I think I will! Another bottle of wine is ordered.

Gareth blows in. He is very tall, Finnish and flamboyantly gay. He immediately declares that he and I will be very good friends. He tells me about going back and forth between Paris and Finland, and about the new guy he's fallen for. He tells me I'm beautiful and that he knows I've got an amazing sense of humor. He guesses my age, subtracting sixteen years. Why is it always the gay guys who get me? Then he tells me I absolutely have to get some Louboutins. Maybe he doesn't get me. No way I'm spending hundreds of Euros on shoes with red soles and five inch heels.

At 9:30 the restaurant is absolutely packed. It seems impossible for the servers to navigate between tables. The guy behind me is smashed up against my chair. People ebb into and out of the restaurant to take smoke breaks. The sidewalk in front is jammed with smokers. Nobody (other than our table) seems to be over 40. Another bottle of wine is ordered.

Gareth tells me about his accident last year when he fell down a flight of stairs and was in a coma for eleven days. (Aha! Maybe that's why he took sixteen years off my age!) It is so noisy it's hard to hear exactly what everyone is saying. Are their voices slurring, or are my ears just slurring? Another bottle of wine is ordered. Silvie explains; "They are turning people away. I offered to consolidate our table so they could take another couple of customers but they assured me we're fine." I cover my glass when the wine is poured. Anymore and I will be in trouble. I'm thinking it might be time to call this lovely night over. Another bottle of wine is ordered.

Suddenly the check is requested. Nobody seems sober enough to do the math. "Let's divide it by four and let Gareth pay the tip. He didn't eat." someone suggests. Seems reasonable enough. 95 euros each. I think Gareth gave the prettiest waitress 20 euro. I wonder briefly if she shares it with all the others who have waited on us tonight.

Sloppy *bises* all around and I'm at the door to call an Uber. I don't really remember the trip home. I see that I texted Charlotte at some point to see if she got home safely. She didn't text me until the next day. With a headache.

La Chope

I can now see that getting together with people from the travelers' websites is going to get old. The fact that Noelle wanted to meet in Paris should have been no surprise. That's what she does. She travels, finds out who else will be "in town" while she's there, and sets up meetings. She says she felt like we knew each other from the travel board. I don't think I was particularly aware of her. I was no stranger to meeting others that way, so I agreed. When she emailed me I suggested either La Chope for some Sunday Jazz Manouche or Wednesday for the jazz dinner. She chose both.

La Chope is a fun little café in Saint Ouen, in the heart of Les Puces, the famous Paris flea markets. I took a bus and got there early to be sure to get a table. The only one available was a high table wedged into the corner between the end of the bar and a few feet from the entertainers. I actually thought it was quite nice because it wasn't smashed against the other tables. It would be great for talking and getting to know each other.

Noelle came in and spotted me right away. "Oh no!" she groaned. "This isn't going to work at all. If I knew this was what the seating would be like I wouldn't have come."

Oh no… what to do.

"Well, let me see what I can manage". She struggled to hoist her not insignificant heft onto the chair. I offered my arm, a hand, what could I do to help? "Don't fuss!" she snapped, "Let me do it!" I tried to adjust the table to give her more space and knocked my wine glass over; on the table and on her. Well, this is going really well.

Finally she's perched awkwardly on her chair looking very uncomfortable, and I've mopped up the spilled wine and handed her some towels.

"Red or white" I ask.

"I don't drink."

Le sigh

I check out all of the tables occupied by people eating. There are only 4 chairs in the café that are not high chairs. A mother and daughter in two of the low chairs look like they might be ready to go. Chairs where you can put your "feet on the floor" was a requirement I didn't know about. Within ten minutes and some very quick moves on my part we managed to get those seats, dirty plates and all.

It took another fifteen or twenty minutes for the plates to get cleared, the small staff running ragged. Clearing the plates didn't include wiping the table and there was an annoying blob of something in front of me. At least I wasn't still smelling the leftover food.

I guessed Noelle to be about my mother's age, early eighties, but my mother looks younger. She's a retired lawyer living outside of Boston with a variety of interests; symphony music (she plays the flute), French Literature, theater and opera. She calls herself a long time Francophile and speaks pretty passable French, certainly better than I do, and she corrected me repeatedly. She has significant mobility issues so you have to hand it to her for traveling to Paris solo. Her husband chose to stay at home.

There were two young guitar players. Noelle seemed to enjoy them and we ordered lunch, grilled tuna steaks and foie gras. She said they are two of her favorite things. Things were finally looking up!

While we were eating, an obviously more professional group of performers burst into the room; two guitarists, a violist and a base player. The room was charged! They played faster and faster and louder and louder and sang together, individually and together again. A bevy of thirty and forty something women came seemingly from nowhere. They loved the group, whooping and hollering and singing along. I looked at Noelle and she was loving it! I was so glad. After our poor start the day seemed to be a success!

Noelle leaned across the table to me, "I'm really enjoying this! Thank you!"

The A-Team finished and the young guys returned. We sat for awhile, talking more, gossiping a bit about other people on the travel board, about her life in Massachusetts and my decision to move to Paris. She was astonished at the progress and connections I have made. I kept reminding her that I've been working on this for years.

I paid the bill (I especially can't keep paying the tab for all these visitors to Paris!) and we agreed to try to share an Uber. Her controlling and impatient side came back.

"Let's just put your address in and then ask him to drop me off enroute."

She wasn't having it. "There's a way to do this" she snapped. Ultimately she put in my address and then asked the driver if she could add another. "Pas de problème" he assured her.

I always get a little cranky when someone doesn't pay attention to the scenery we pass, especially in Paris! We arrived at *chez moi*, dumped me off with her hardly noticing. She was busy figuring out the Uber app. But we would see each other in three days, at GCA for jazz.

Again I arrived early and got my regular table. By now Noelle and I are old friends. She talked a lot about her life, college, law school, a summer in Colorado, meeting her husband, Woodstock." She loves Paris because "people like you and me, we are both the same age and size and we are invisible."

What?! This woman is my mother's age and half again my size!

"Not so in Paris." She baffled me. One of us doesn't have an accurate view of ourselves. I caught my reflection in the mirrored glass across the room. It wasn't me. I was sure of it. She definitely has moxie and not a shred of self-effacement. Maybe it's an East Coast thing.

I'm getting weary of this getting together with online people. But unfortunately there are two more coming up.

The Dinner Party

I've looked forward to the dinner party for months. Charlotte said she wanted to give a dinner party for me when I moved to Paris so I could get properly introduced to the right people. Charlotte is a busy girl. Travel plans, work, social commitments and a February detox, all got in the way, so by the time the dinner party actually happened I had met all of the participants except Elizabeth's husband. Not to worry, I'm still really looking forward to it. I feel like it admits me to the inner circle; Charlotte, Elizabeth (and husband) and Elliott and Joan; the special friends.

Charlotte has brilliantly implemented the aforementioned Cheese Board Policy. Thierry's recommendations "A Saint Nectaire can be nice, or Epoisse, but it's strong, or Pont L'Evêque?" sent me to Google. Who knew they'd each have their own Wikipedia page? So I studied up. Epoisse is a nice cow cheese from the Côte-d'Or, first consumed by Louis XIV, Brillat-Savarin consecrated it the King of Cheeses in the 1800s. Saint Nectaire is another cow cheese, from the Cantal region. Looks a little blah. Pont L'Evêque cow cheese, from Normandy this time. The only thing that looks different between it and the other two is that it's square. Next stop: Fromagerie down the street.

Just as I head out it starts to snow. I pop into the shop. "*Bonjour! Je voudrais un bon fromage doux pour une soirée ce soir!*" I say. The nice man leads me over to a long case full of cheeses. He starts to point to things babbling *en français*.... And I spy something I've had before! A Brillat-Savarin *aux truffes*! Perfect!

I read about Monsieur Brillat-Savarin in David Downie's excellent book, "A Taste of Paris". Monsieur was a man after my own heart; an self-described epicurean, a cook, a writer and France's first food critic! So I wasted not another minute and asked for two selections of the truffle infused goodness; a big one for the party and a small one for myself. I paid the man and rushed across the street to the *cave à vin* for *un bon porto*, something nice in a bottle to bring with me. Once home, I got back online and studied up a bit on Monsieur B-S, I wanted to be prepared to spout a few clever words of wisdom myself when the cheese board came to the table.

Charlotte lives across town in the 15ème. According to Google maps, it would be a 36 minute drive. I was told apéro would be served at 7:00 pm. Checking my mental rule book; show up 15 minutes late for French dinner parties, on time for restaurants (although that had proven to be false information) and pretty much be on time for American hosts. I assumed a 5-10 minute wait for Uber so put in my request at 6:15.

I knocked on her door at 7:02, the first to arrive. "Annoyingly prompt guest!" I said, handing her the cheese and port, when she answered the door.

"This is perfect!" she responded. We made our way into the salon of the very small apartment, the coffee table set with snacks and cocktail napkins that read "I have Mixed Drinks About Feelings". "I was going to do cocktails" she said, "but Elliott said he's bringing two really unique bottles of champagne." She showed me around the salon and dining area, which took about thirty seconds. We sat for a couple of minutes and she jumped up and said, "if Elliott's not going to be here NOW, we're having cocktails!" and we headed into the equally tiny kitchen to shake up a couple of Sidecars.

We didn't get far before a knock on the door announced Elliott, fresh from the five story climb and Phil emerging from the miniscule elevator. Phil, a big teddy bear of a guy on crutches, was recovering from a recent hip replacement. Thank God for the miniscule elevator. Elliott's backpack full of champagne and wines was on the floor in the elevator.

"I never take elevators," Elliott remarked, "after getting stuck in one even smaller than this one for three hours." Oh good. Something new for me to worry about.

A few minutes later both Elizabeth and Joan come up the stairs and we are treated to *la bise* all around. Phil picks a comfortable spot on the sofa and I take a chair next to him and we talk about his hip replacement while the others fuss in the little kitchen. Elliott bursts in to tell us about the very rare champagne that he has brought, a single type of grape, completely metal casked, that .... Okay Elliott, I'm not really listening to your wine blathering anymore. Glasses poured all around, Phil sets his gin and tonic on his stomach while he tries the champagne; a couple of sips and he reverts to the gin and tonic.

For the next hour we talk about the kinds of things that people talk about at dinner parties: Charlotte's partner is skiing and the family is group texting incessantly, leaving her wondering why she wanted to be in that text group after all, Elliott opens a second bottle of champagne and explains the differences in the grapes and the terroir and why we never would have been able to drink them the other way around, the little spreads in the bowls on the coffee table which Charlotte really isn't sure what they are because they came in little jars from her partner's brother but they are not labeled, Phil's latest horse racing results, Elizabeth's recent food tour customers. It was all pleasant, the kind of stuff you'd expect at a dinner party.

Charlotte beckons us to the dining room. The table has been beautifully set with china and the perfect glassware for each of the wines that she brought up from the cave for this "special occasion". Elliott however, has some wine ideas of his own and inserts two unusual whites and reverses the order of the reds that Charlotte had intended serving. He replaces Charlotte's soothing background music with his own, Irish music, in honor of Saint Patrick's day.

First course is a beautiful radish carpaccio with three kinds of radishes atop a mound of *crème fraiche*. Elliott pours his first white and gives us the two minute lecture about the wine. The carpaccio is delicious. We talk about the market where Charlotte found the black radishes and Elliott brings the focus back to this unusual little wine.

Entrée plates are removed and out comes a steaming heavy tagine of *cassoulet*. It smells divine and tastes even better. We all help ourselves to plates full of chicken legs, pork sausage, beans, onions, carrots and whatever else is in the lovely stew. Elliott opens the first of Charlotte's two special wines and pours without any discussion. The wine is perfect and I tell Charlotte how much I appreciate her raiding her cave for the occasion. The *cassoulet* is delicious and we all take second helpings and make fast work of the second bottle of red wine. Nobody is feeling any pain.

In due course the dishes from the main course are swept away by Elizabeth, Joan and Charlotte, I'm in a corner where it's pretty much impossible to get out and besides, I'm not really sure where they are all going into that teeny tiny kitchen, not to mention where all the dishes and glasses are being piled up. Out comes the most remarkable cheese board; what Elliott quickly dubs the Four Country Cheese Board! There are seven cheeses and I can't begin to say what they all were; something pecorino with peppercorns, a couple of hard cheeses that Elliott sliced very thinly, almost like shavings, something from Greece, my Brillat-Savarin (which to my relief, Charlotte drools over) and a couple of other soft rounds of lactose goodness.

Elliott opens and expounds on a Greek white wine that he just happened to run across that very day. I toss out a Brillat Savarin aphorism: "A meal without cheese is like a woman without an eye" to which Elliott responds with three more of B-S's famous expressions in French. The Irish music gets louder, and our exhausted hostess falls asleep at the table.

Nobody seems to think anything of it and we continue to work on the cheese board. Finally I suggest to Elizabeth that we might want to put Charlotte to bed. She asks our snoozing hostess if we can just close the door behind us, will that be ok? Charlotte seems to mumble assent as she is led into her bedroom.

After another half hour of talking, Elizabeth, Joan and I do a reasonable job of clearing the table and putting the leftover cheese away. We load as many of the dishes as possible into the tiny dishwasher. Then everyone prepares to go. Elliott asks if I would like to share an Uber. Sure, I would love to. Phil and Elliott's now empty backpacks are loaded into the teeny tiny elevator and the rest of us head down the five long flights of stairs.

We step out into the snowy night in a part of Paris that I am completely unfamiliar with, Phil and Elizabeth to walk the half block home, Elliott, Joan and I to wait for our Uber. The app says it's there. but Elliott couldn't find it. Suddenly things take a surreal turn. Elliott and Joan are hurling F-bombs at each other, blaming each other for something to do with the misplaced Uber and I'm not sure what. He's calling the number of the driver shouting at him, shouting at Joan, completely blowing a gasket. Finally we figure out it's there, about 2 doors down with it's lights blinking and Elliott is hurling insults at the driver! Wait a stinking minute here, we're supposed to get into this car and be driven through a snowy night across the city. Be civil Elliott! The driver was pissed and we drove for half an hour in complete silence. When they reached their apartment in the 17ème he asked the driver to take me on to the 18ème. I was pretty sure I was going to have to walk at that point! But he bised me goodnight, told me not to give the driver another penny and off they went. As soon as the door closed I apologized (in French!) for Elliott's behavior and tipped him five euro for the 2 minute (uphill in the snow) drive.

What a night! I guess I am part of the inner circle now.

The Lost Generation

Gertrude Stein called those expats who prowled the cafés and bars in Montparnasse between the wars The Lost Generation. I believe, they still exist, and they are still lost.

At the dinner party Elliott asked me if I was interested in having dinner with he and Joao the next day. Joao was at loose ends, about to leave for Brazil for a month, and Elliott was going to take him out to dinner and see him off. Sure I responded. After his very poor behaviour on the sidewalk outside of Charlotte's I wasn't sure that he'd really be very comfortable seeing me the next day and frankly I wasn't sure I wanted to hang out with him again. Perhaps the former because I didn't hear anything the next day.

But Elliott made a long and seemingly extremely profound post on his Facebook page about "his people" who seemed to include geniuses, lunatics, addicts, drunks and perverts, plus a few other choice descriptions. There was brilliance in the post, and arrogance and vicissitudes that frankly left me baffled. It was "liked" and "loved" by 42 people, some, the very people I'd met at the Elliott curated dinners. Comments followed calling Elliott fucking brilliant, accolades, tears and love poured over the leader of what Elliott refers to as his "tribe".

Not my tribe. I like a good party. I can drink but these people can DRINK! I'm not part of the Lost Generation.

Taking Inventory

Another jazz dinner, this time a rollicking night with Magalie and Stephanie. Although it was "musical version" (every other week, Daniele organizes a vocal version and he doesn't show up), this week Daniele is not there because he has a gig at Sunside with Luigi. Uttering that sentence feels very strange for me; "gig", "Sunside with Luigi", as if I'm an insider, or a wanna be insider in this world of musicians. Strangely I've been getting FB requests from Daniele's friends all week. Marketing no, doubt.

Now I sit in a very busy Cépage on Friday morning trying to make heads and tails out of the last couple of days. I braved Cépage at 9 am this Friday morning, not sure what I would do if Caroleen was here. I've only been once since the divorce; an evening meeting with Siobhan. Caroleen was not there. It was amazing that one of the waiters who would not even make eye contact with Caroleen was absolutely flirtatious with us, wanting to engage in French chit chat.

I've discovered a new emotion I haven't experienced in decades; jealousy. Oh sure, I've had twinges of envy; towards someone in Business class when I didn't get an upgrade, when another VP who I felt had a less impactful year than I did got a bigger bonus, that Jojo Moyes or Meg Clayton or Michele Gable seem to effortlessly spit out good book after good book. But in general, I'm very satisfied with my life; more than satisfied. I've managed to design it pretty much exactly as I like it. If things need adjusting, I adjust them.

People tell me I'm lucky. I doubt that they know the hard work that went into getting where I am. Paris was a plan several years in the making. A plan that not everyone would even think of creating. I didn't want a big house full of expensive furniture, yard, pool, husband. I wanted a career, a relationship with my daughters, friends who mattered to me, and adventures. And I worked hard to develop and maintain them.

To a person, everyone remarked how wonderful my plan to move to Paris was. Everyone was "jealous". I would argue that they are envious; like I am about someone else's upgrade, the bigger bonus or literary success. For the most part, it's not a path that others aspire to.

So now I am sitting here and the days are hurtling by. In six weeks I have collected an interesting assortment of friends. I struggle with the use of the word friends. To me it implies a strength of relationship one cannot develop in days or weeks, even six of them. However, there does seem to be something that happens in this expat life that puts relationships on fast forward. It is a bit like going to summer camp as a kid. We are thrown together in a uniquely strange and exciting environment and set of circumstances and we quickly scramble to assert our own role in this new world; the leaders, the followers and the hangers-on.

Here's where the camp analogy ends and a certain amount of real world enters. Paris is a city. A big important world-class city. A city with an allure that makes people want to experience her magic. So while the expats come and go, some for decades, others for a much briefer tenure, there are real Parisians in our midst; people to whom Paris is the only home they have ever known. They struggle with jobs, aspire to vacations in the South, or maybe even to Spain or to Morocco or even to New York City. They ride the Metro, navigate through city traffic on motorbikes, walk (and walk and walk and walk! This is why Parisians are not fat.) They spend hours on café terraces drinking, smoking and gossiping with friends.

They do buy baguettes. The do like to complain; about the weather, traffic, noise, politics. They do say *bonjour*, to everyone who enters their personal space. They do la bise to their friends coming and going, even if there are ten people sitting in one place, all ten will get the bise, coming and going. They do say *"enchanté"* when they meet someone new. And it does sound lovely.

I felt from the beginning it would be important to make friends not only with expats, but with actual Parisians. Herein lies the rub. The Parisians you will meet when you move to Paris are nearly all in some kind of client relationship. Stephanie is my landlord. While we clicked from the very beginning, until the night of endless champagne, and there have been many lunches and dinners in the five years between our first meeting and that night, there was always a tiny formality, a caution on her part. I was a client.

I have been lucky enough to be treated very well by so many Parisians; the handsome Thierry who continues to insist I'm his favorite client, the charming owner of le Café Qui Parle and his equally charming beau-frere, the owner of Le Café de la Butte, Philippe who always rushes to welcome me with la bise, even the celebrities Mario and Stéphane Jego, who now personally welcome me with *la bise* when I go to L'Ami Jean. But to all of them, I am a client. Maybe they toss in a cognac or a glass of champagne, but the truth is these are friends I pay to be my friends. Not only do I pay them, but I'm an American who pays them. How do I get past that?

I think that Magalie was the catalyst that changed the relationship with Stephanie; bold outspoken, hold nothing back Magalie. I still cannot get Stephanie to comment about politics beyond pursed lips, downturned eyes and a tsk tsk that says "it's terrible". I can't get an opinion out of her. Yet she will share the most intimate details of a love affair that went sour. Maybe she doesn't follow politics and the lip pursing is the easiest way not to disclose that she doesn't know. (Stephanie completely disagrees that 99% of married French men cheat but she won't offer a more accurate number.)

And Philippe, well that's going nowhere. I'm stuck at *la bise*, *ça va*? (lots of ça vas). This could be a function of limited language skills, his and mine. I have watched him sit with other regular patrons, generally at the bar, chatting intimately. But he doesn't do the same with me. He knows I'm writing. Does he not want to interrupt? Or perhaps does he, like me, realize that it's impossible to be clever, interesting, witty or even understood in a language that one is not comfortable with? While I thought that Philippe's English was about on par with my French, I'm discovering that his English is actually very limited. Which brings me back to the topic of jealousy.

Wednesday night jazz dinner. Like I said, no Daniele this week. There was a substitute drummer. When I arrived, wholesomely greeted with bises and seated at "my table" by Philippe, the night's performers were already into their first set. The drummer was horrible! This could be a long night! Fortunately the number ended and the drummer stood and bowed to the enthusiastic bravos of his drinking buddies, quickly replaced by the group's actual drummer.

Guillaume rushed over to welcome me with a handshake (I guess *la bise* is reserved for a more informal relationship, we haven't graduated to it yet) and I order a bottle of Côte du Rhône. I'm well into my first glass when Stephanie and Magalie arrive together (friendly greeting from Philippe but no *bise*).

Magalie says hello with kisses and a big hug, deposits her coat and rushes upstairs to use *les toilettes*. Stephanie takes off her coat, hat and scarf and settles in while I pour her a glass of wine. Magalie breezes back down the stairs and takes a seat next to me. She's effortlessly beautiful, slim in her tight jeans and long sleeved scooped neck t-shirt, an ornate belt with dragon buckle turned to the side of her tiny waist. Both girls have their hair pulled into a messy knot, one that if I tried to get away with I would just look... messy.

In walks a forty something blonde with a boy, about ten. Both go straight to bar stools where they get Philippe bises. Friends or something more? She's ruben-esque, squeezed into designer jeans of a size I wouldn't have thought you could get in Paris, and trendy sneakers. Philippe pours her a glass of champagne and one for himself, a coke for the boy. He continues to do his restaurant owner welcoming people, applauding and bravoing the band, making sure we have what we need, overseeing the happy patrons thing, always returning to stand by her, wedged into a small space between her and another mec, someone Philippe introduces her to. They chat and sip champagne.

The restaurant is jam packed. Stephanie and Magalie decided that we should try to speak only French. That is quickly derailed by the noise and we agree to take a break tonight but going forward I need to speak French. Magalie encourages me to attend classes at the Alliance Française. She tells me about a client who did and with three months was fluent.

Philippe brings me my *soupe à l'oignon*. The blond glares at me. I take a tiny pleasure in that glare. Philippe goes behind the bar now, takes a sip of his champagne and then a bite of something from her salad with his fingers! *Quelle intimité!* Am I truly turning as green as I feel?

Philippe makes his rounds of the restaurant, checking on everyone. At our table he spreads his arms, flutters his eyelids and sighs, as if to say "quelles beautes". Now I am jealous of my friends! Guillaume brings Magalie and Stephanie's meals, tuna steak for Magalie, *boeuf bourguignon* for Stephanie. Just at that moment Philippe passes and I gesture "where's mine?" He rushes to the kitchen to see about it. I was kidding! Guillaume is doing an amazing job handling the throbbing restaurant. My salmon tartar quickly appears. We finish off our second bottle of wine. Magalie chirps on about l'Alliance Française. Yes, I promise I will go see them.

Digestifs are ordered, cognac for me and something green and minty for Magalie and Stephanie. I spy an impossibly handsome man at the bar. He is looking at me (it seems as if everyone at the bar is looking at our table… is it my imagination?) I try to send him "*le regard*". A beautiful dark haired woman sits next to him. Soon they are touching each other in insanely intimate ways; he strokes her arm, lightly touches her neck, traces her fingers. They both wear wedding rings but I doubt that they are married to each other. When the band breaks between sets, they go out to the terrace to smoke. She perches on his lap and they share a cigarette. I play with the idea of taking up smoking.

A second round of *digestifs* appears. I notice that both Stephanie and Magalie have green teeth! I am very glad I'm drinking cognac. Magalie invites Stephanie and I to dinner *chez elle* in two weeks time. "Not on Wednesday," I say, "it's jazz night." "OK, Thursday! I will cook you dinner. And we will only speak French because my partner does not speak English!" How much French can I learn in two weeks?

A third round of *digestifs* comes and I think this one is on Philippe. He must be feeling particularly gleeful tonight. The bar and restaurant are jammed, the music has been great, lovely women everywhere flirting with him. I am the only one without green teeth, but my skin must be glowing chartreuse by now.

The music ends. The check is requested and split. The very inebriated three of us pile on scarves, hats, coats. I can't be sure but I think I am the only one who got bises. And I got very bold, planting actual smooches firmly on both of Philippe's lovely cheeks.

Gareth

I definitely sold Gareth short at the girls' night out. Maybe I didn't think he had any business being there. Gay or not, he wasn't a girl. After the dinner we texted each other that we should get together for lunch or dinner. The ball was in my court and I kind of let it drop.

At the Wednesday jazz dinner Gareth somehow came up and Stephanie and Magalie both said "Yes, we know Gareth well!"

"Let's see if he would like to join us tonight." I suggested. They both agreed.

I shot Gareth a text to which he eventually responded "Tonight I'm not free, but let me know in advance and I will be."

"Two weeks from tonight?"

"If I'm still here in two weeks. I normally will leave next week on Wednesday unless I have some really good news from my past job interviews."

"How about lunch tomorrow? Le Clou, Avenue Trudaine, at 1:00?" I ask.

"That's good with me!"

Ms. Toujours en avance arrives at Le Clou at ten to one. Sweet Thierry seats me at my usual inside table and I tell him I will wait for my friend to arrive before ordering something to drink.

Then all hell breaks loose outside. An unruly mob of dozens of students just let out from the high school around the corner, all in various stages of cheering on and trying to prevent a fight. The melee looks like it will unfold right in front of the restaurant. Lovely Thierry rushes out to break it up. Fifty something unruly teens vs one handsome Thierry. I think it says a lot about my Thierry's character. I hope it does not say he is foolish.

Soon the familiar police klaxon sounds. Then another. Then a mass of police and *pompiers* descend on the area. The teens are invisible as quickly as they appeared.

Again the timing thing. 1:15 came and went and no sign of Gareth. I buried my nose in my book and pretended not to be concerned. How long should I wait until I decided he wasn't coming and admit to Thierry I had been stood up. AT 1:20 I texted Gareth: "Are you still coming?"

"Yes, I'll be there now." He texted back. And there he was.

Handsome and stylishly dressed, all six foot four of him. He apologized for being late; he had come from the 12ème. *Le métro… bien sûr.*

I asked him if he would prefer red or white (wine) and he politely deferred to me. I recommended a bottle of the Walden. It's what I've been drinking at Le Clou since it opened.

Thierry opened the wine and poured us both a taste. "Nice!" said Gareth, admitting he really prefers red and we both briefly grimaced over the seven bottles of white we took part in consuming at the girls' night out.

We made small talk and then perused the menu. "*Tartare de boeuf au couteau!*" he got very excited. "When it's *au couteau*, I never pass it up!"

I had recently been involved in the *au couteau* debate and hadn't realized that I was having the good stuff all this time at Le Clou. "*Moi aussi*" I told our waiter, pushing my craving for a hamburger out of sight.

"Tell me about your interview."

For the next two hours we ate and drank and talked about Gareth's frustrations with his job search. He had been working in fashion merchandising for Collette for five years before they closed their doors in December. Before that he worked for Chanel for five years. Job searches in Paris are evidently slow and painful.

The story was very much like that of Aimee. In Gareth's case he did not lack confidence and indeed contacts. It just seems to be a very slow process. He had a very good headhunter working enthusiastically with him and had generated interest from Louis Vuitton, Adidas and Hermes. He had set a target date for himself that he would have to return to Finland if he hadn't gotten something and that date was Wednesday!

"Don't go!" I said, "You are very close. You need to be in Paris. This is where your future is! I'm sure of it!" I told Gareth about my recruitment background which seemed to give him confidence, hopefully not misplaced, that I knew what I was talking about.

We talked until we were the only ones left in the restaurant. Thierry had gone home for the afternoon. The poor waiter had cleaned all the tables, the glassware, and set up for the dinner service. We asked him if he wanted us to leave. He assured us we were fine. We kept talking while the cook left. We talked about our lives and loves and hopes and dreams. At one point I even confided to him that I was pretty sure that Thierry and I were involved in a past life, some 400 years earlier, in Paris. He believed me.

Finally we put the beleaguered waiter out of his misery. I insisted on paying (I have to stop doing that!) He protested but I assured him that when he landed that perfect job he would take me for a grand lunch, with champagne. We toasted to that with his coffee and my water glass.

When I got home I got a text.

"Thank you K for a great lunch! I'm so happy to have met you (see you again in this life) This is just the beginning of our friendship. *Bisous et à très bientôt.*"

I think I have made a new real friend. Not French. Not really an expat. Identities in Paris are fluid.

So today I've been here six weeks. It's really flown by. I think it's a good time to take a brief inventory of where I've been and what I'd like to say I've accomplished at the end of the next six, when I "go home" for a short while.

For the positive, I've written some 28,000 words, a good chunk of a 100,000 word novel. I've learned that if I sit down and start writing it will come. I've learned that if I'm patient and live my life, things happen that I can write about. I've made friends. Making friends in Paris is on fast forward. Friends that I expected would be important to me turned out to be less so. People who I didn't expect seem to play a more significant role. I'm certainly connected with a huge number of people. If I invite someone for a drink or coffee that network keeps expanding.

I've learned not to waste time with people not worth my time. Caroleen. I've been clever about balancing expats and locals. Expats can suck you in and they offer loads of entertainment and you can learn from their experiences. But they can also trap you into an "other space", not really Parisian and not helping my language skills, although oddly they all seem to speak excellent French. French people take much longer to get to know, certainly longer than the high-speed expat relationships. I have discovered that French people who have lived abroad, particularly in non-EU countries are a bit more open to *vraiment* friendships. French people who have only lived in France can be very reserved. I've learned that because someone has some sort of business relationship with you, whether they are a restaurant owner, a waiter, the Boulanger or the fromagerie owner, no matter how friendly and welcoming they are to you, they are not your friend. That is not to say that they might not someday become a friend. But the likelihood seems quite remote. You are a financial opportunity, perhaps a pleasant one, maybe even their favorite client. But they will never take you as a permanent fixture on their landscape.

Paris is a melting pot. The French are slow to integrate outsiders into their world. Muslims are a large portion of the population, but are sadly and generally distrusted by many. Concerns might be understandable given the recent attacks in Paris and Nice. French are not appreciative of this American's inquisitiveness and questions. I am yet to crack the code of having someone honestly and frankly tell me how they feel. But then, it's only been six weeks.

French men flirt. All the time. With everyone. That doesn't mean they see you as a potential bonafide domestic partner. Americans are simply not used to that.

I would imagine that the experience for American men with French women is completely different. French women don't flirt. They expect to be pursued all of the time. They ignore. I think an American man would simply give up. And what about gay men or women. I have no idea.

Where am I going? At the hearty encouragement of Magalie, I have signed up for French classes with l'Alliance Française. It's very expensive so I'm allocating an expenditure of no more than 1,000 euros; 8 weeks, 3 days a week, 3 hours a day. Let's see how much I have improved by the time I leave on May 12. In the meantime, I'm going to try to speak only French. That means getting out more with fewer English speakers. When I'm out with friends, I will try to speak only French. That should work with Magalie and Stephanie, who encourage me to speak French. With Philippe, of course. In every café and restaurant, no problem. But how about with the expat dinners with Siobhan, Charlotte and Elizabeth. Can I convince them to speak only French? They all speak it perfectly.

All F'ed Up

My mind is abuzz and I can't even really get my arms around how I feel. So I decided to work and do the five employee evaluations that were requested from me. The hotel in the corner of my building is undergoing renovation and for the past two days the incessant drilling is sending me around the bend. Although it is technically only Spring, Parisians are declaring Summer is here and it's too nice to sit inside anyway. I took myself and my laptop to Cépage to do the evaluations. Dumb idea! The drilling just got closer. So as much as I said I wouldn't, I packed things up and headed to GCA.

About last night… Stephanie wanted to come with me to jazz night. Great! I got there first, as usual, and took the seat facing out, where I could see up close and personal the musicians.

"One of these days I'm going to get here before you and I can sit there!" she said when she came in.

"Would you like to sit here?"

"Yes!"

So we switched. The windows were open and the terrace seats full. I could see the people on the terrace. Period. I couldn't see the musicians at all. (It never occurred to me that was the case for her!) I could see Philippe every time he buzzed out to the terrace to see how things were going.

Like that the night progressed quickly. During the third set a trumpet appeared from somewhere and I twisted my seat to watch. It was a bit awkward since Daniele and I have clearly acknowledged each other in the last couple of weeks.

The blonde girl was at the bar, without her kid this time. Philippe talked to her a bit but it didn't seem as intimate as before. Stephanie commented that he had an admirer. But where it got weird was Stephanie's clear interest in Daniele. And her assumption that he was her game now, not mine. I love Stephanie and her friendship means a lot to me but this was just weird. And I didn't like competing. But two and a half years it too long for me to give up the chase, when I'm finally making progress!

He looked over at our table a lot and Stephanie was certain he was looking at her.

Fast forward to the end of the music. Daniele came over to our table. I can't even really remember what I said but I was a bit drunk and I did melt a bit into fits of giggles.

"Why are you laughing?" he asked. (Stupid American stereotype… laughing about nothing)

"I'm not laughing" dumb… I was laughing. But I stopped.

None of the rest of the conversation makes any sense and I can't even re-enact it to get some kind of order. I just remember in no particular order; "*Je suis Katherine*" (I know) "*Je suis une grande fan*" (I know, I see you here a lot) Stephanie: "She comes every week." "This is Stephanie" (OK) "I really enjoyed Larry Browne last week. He and I are from San Francisco" (He's a good friend of mine) " You speak English, right?" (Yes) "Parle Italiano?" (Yes, do you ? Are you Italian?) "No but I speak a little" (My mother is Italian).

At some point he corrected my French telling me it was very important that I get it right. "I need a tutor. Would you like to be my tutor?" (Yes, but you have to be willing for me to be very tough) Oh heck yes! (How many languages do you speak?) "Just English well" (English is not a language) "Of course it is!" (Not really) And there must have been some more but I can't remember it. All I remember is that I felt like a total idiot! It was not a good feeling.

And Stephanie's teeth were green again. She said, "Magalie is wrong. Philippe obviously is interested. He looks at you a lot and comes to say things throughout the night."

Is this the consolation prize? Is she throwing me a bone? You can have Philippe but I get Daniele (who by the way directed his entire conversation to me).

Time to go, Uber arrives fast for once. Philippe comes outside to say goodbye. Instead of *la bise* I give him another big old kiss smack on his cheek.

And now I'm working in the restaurant. He commented that my book must be progressing well. If he only knew.

Honor Among Thieves (and French Girlfriends)

Wednesday rolled around again and I happily found myself with plans to go to Wednesday night jazz night alone. The last few weeks I've been buried in friends; friends from outside of Paris, and Magalie, Stephanie and Siobhan. So I haven't done an evening alone in over a month. I've missed it. The nights with others have been lively (Philippe said "you have a lot of friends!") But they've changed the nature of my interactions with Philippe and Daniele. It seems so odd to me to think that eating alone ever felt awkward. I am missing it.

Early Wednesday morning I found an email from Stephanie who has been on a *petit vacance* in the South.

"I might see you tonight. I go with my girlfriends to Comptoir d'Anvers tonight so we might see you I guess?" Bisous. PS: Did you book your stay at the Terrass Hotel?

OK, I'm not exactly sure what this means. Maybe I'll see you from across the room? Feel free to wave? Let's all sit together? Shall I up my reservation?

One thing was very clear. She was coming for Daniele. I don't know about thieves but there is no honor in French girlfriends!

I showed up at 7:30 and took my usual table. A smile from Daniele who was well into his first set. Guillaume set my table with a white tablecloth and a bottle of red. He knows what I like. I was texting with my daughter in California and didn't notice Stephanie and friends, along with Bob (Bub) the newly adopted dog) at the bar right in front of me. They had evidently been there for awhile because they were sipping their drinks when Stephanie came over to say hello.

I heard her friends say "Oh! Katherine's here!" although I only had met Tara. After introductions, a bit of fuss over Bub and some discussion with Philippe it was agreed that I would join them at a table Philippe was getting set up in the other part of the restaurant, out of the line of sight of Daniele.

The table was declared ready and we all moved. Guillaume brought my wine, which was quickly decided would be the group's wine (which was followed by four more bottles through the night).

I have to admit, the friends were lovely and I enjoyed getting to know them, two Irish girls and one from the UK. What's with all of these Irish girls? So far my expat circle seems to be weighted heavily with Irish girls, at least half a dozen. Mary Murphy (seriously!) is loud and gregarious. She declares herself to be Stephanie's wingman tonight and will grease the skids and make this thing with Daniele happen. WTF?! Clearly Stephanie has brought the group up to speed on all things Daniele, except for the fact that I like him and have for years!

Mary Murphy, God love her, is no slouch when it comes to being a wingman. As soon as the band took a break she was out of her seat and across the room having a conversation with him. Her own boyfriend/life partner/father of her three year old child is evidently a guitarist and she knows a thing or two about these musicians. A short time later she is back with a report on the conversation. It's not positive. She thinks he seems defensive.

Over the course of the rest of the evening she gently and kindly discourages Stephanie from continuing to pursue this.

"Look at him" she says as he sits with his group during their break. "He has his arms folded across his chest. He's not an open person!"

"And he's married!" I chime in.

She does that thing French people do with their mouth, emitting a sarcastic little puff of air. "So?!"

I do that little thing I do every time I hear that, rolling my eyes and briefly shaking my head.

I'm not a huge fan of stereotypes but there is, after all, a reason they become stereotypes. Here are a few things I've learned. French girls are very frank. They don't mince words. It can feel very unkind when they tell you "You are a bit fat." "You look tired, are you getting enough sleep?" "He's just not interested in you!" But it is more than just frank. It really is an ingrained gift to play with your self-esteem and confidence in order to come out on top. I have watched French girls say that they are going to concede a point in the interest of keeping a relationship, but still asserting that they are, in fact, right.

Learning this about your French girlfriend is a gradual thing. At first they seem very sweet and eager to become your BFF. Last night we were waited on by Amal, Philippe's newest waitress. The girls loved her and she was efficient and friendly and quick to bring us what we wanted. Of course she's whippet thin and pretty and she reported to the group that she knew immediately when she was waiting on me last week that I was special and that she liked me. Very charming and impressive. Not at all the stereotype of the rude French server. But then this is Rive Droite, where those stereotypes quickly fall by the wayside, in favor of hipster beards, tattoos, mohawks and multiple facial and body piercings.

Don't be fooled! Amal is lovely now. But she will ultimately be true to form. Who knows, she may be doing unmentionable things to Philippe in a secret closet as I write this!

Irish girls are also frank and outspoken in a way that takes a bit of getting used to. Siobhan knows I am interested in Philippe, but when he was in a snit because I paid too much attention to the trumpet player she called him controlling and inflexible and it was no wonder he had trouble finding a manager to stay. This after an hour of watching him work at the end of a very busy jazz night. Even though I have spent hours going back and forth with her over whether "A" is interested in her.

"Just say you're not interested if you're not interested," she lamented. (But A is Brazilian and a man. Do Brazilian men say those kinds of things?) "So.. do you think he's interested"?

My guess is no, but I'm not going out on that limb. I'm an American girl. I'm tactful and kind of evasive.

"Mary, can you be my wingman?!" I ask.

"Absolutely! Philippe! Restaurant man! Another cognac for my friend please! In fact, come have a cognac with us!"

Philippe wasn't having it.

So the evening was a bit of a strike out for everyone. Stephanie got nothing from Daniele. (At least I got a smile and a nod) I told Philippe I would soon be leaving for three weeks and "tu me manques!"

"Tu vas me manquer" corrected Mary

He met me on the sidewalk while I was waiting for my Uber to dispense not particularly intimate bisous.

"So you will be away for three weeks?" He asked.

"Not yet" I responded "Soon"

Stephanie, Bub and the UK girl shared my Uber home.

"I'll see you on your birthday at Le Terrass!" Stephanie said when she and Bub headed for home.

"And GCA on Wednesday?" I asked.

"I don't know," she demurred. "I'll let you know". That's a no.

I went to bed feeling glum. I messaged Daniele. "The music was lovely tonight. Merci beaucoup."

Minutes later he replied "*Merci à vous!*"

I woke up feeling even more glum.

A Duel

Place Royale was born some fifteen years before Ninon so by 1627, when Francois de Montmorency-Bouteville tragically lost his life in a duel in that same square, the public space was fairly well established. Closed in on all four sides by royal edifices, the King's on one end and the Queen's on the other, it was a grand, sandy, open field for cavalcades, tournaments, games and most recently the endless duels that seemed to become more and more of a problem in the square.

When Cardinal Richelieu returned to Paris he was confronted with these duels right outside his own windows, seemingly on a daily basis. In an attempt to curtail these ghastly events, a fence was erected and the square became a private space where only the well healed locals were allowed to enter. Sadly it still did not diminish the occasions of these gruesome battles.

These barbaric events did not come without a great deal of forethought and formality. There were rules and conventions behind a duel; beginning with the perceived offense. Upon feeling insulted one party would signal the offender that recourse was required, specifically a duel! A thrown glove or often a letter describing the offense and the expected recourse. You have been served notice good sir. The battle is on!

Declining a duel is a whole other matter. One may decline if there is too great a disparity between the parties based on age, societal status, health... any number of disqualifiers. But regardless of reason, one can scarcely get out of such a combat without seriously losing face or appearing a coward.

At this point "seconds" are chosen. Each party designates a person who is responsible for all further communication. The principals at this point stop talking to each other and it is the job of these trusted parties to try to resolve matters without bloodshed. If an apology can be negotiated all the better. The matter will be considered closed.

When no such negotiated conclusion can be reached the circumstances of the duel must be determined. It's clear that negotiations were not typically very fruitful since literally tens of thousands of duels occurred in France resulting in over 400 deaths in the thirty years bridging the 17th and 18th centuries, a period where dueling was outlawed.

The next matters to be decided - if a duel could not be averted - were the field of honor, where the action would take place, the conditions and what would be considered a successful outcome. Typically the location chosen would be very isolated , such as the Bois du Boulogne, a enormous forested area to the west of central Paris. But the Palais Royale was boldly chosen by many, thumbing the participants noses at the Cardinal, the Royals and showing the world one was not intimidated.

The conditions might be a duel to first blood, until one man was sufficiently wounded so that he could no longer continue the fight, or to the death. More often than not matters were concluded before resulting in death, giving the aggrieved party or the defender sufficient satisfaction and "face". Too often however the matter was not resolved without a body on the dueling field.

Ninon was walking in the early morning, just as the sun rose, through the square enjoying the beginnings of an Autumn day. The first light showed paths were littered with dry brown leaves. A place where royalty and the hoi polloi came to chat and discuss a lot of nothing, Ninon felt certain that she would not run into anyone she knew this day. Indian summer was hot this year and the household got little sleep on these fetid, humid nights . She really wanted to get some fresh air and let the phantoms of her days clear from her mind.

Alas, that was not going to happen. Entering the square from the west were two gentlemen formally dressed with elaborate hair pieces and epees. Ninon looked to the south entrance and saw two more - equally formal - approaching. Alas, it seemed she would be treated to a duel at dawn. Ninon veered toward the northeast quadrant of the square in an attempt to avoid the matter. The parties met in the center. Without much ado the principals squared off with the seconds standing at the wait. Ninon slipped behind a tree to avoid being noticed but somehow could not help but watch from her hiding place.

It was over shockingly quickly. The parties were not well matched. Within minutes one man: the offender? the offended? who knew? Was lying on the ground dead. The victorious party and his second turned on their heels and marched back to the southern entrance from which they came. The second of the dead man hoisted the body over his shoulder and slowly made his way back toward the western entrance to the square.

Ninon stepped from behind the tree and walked slowly to the battle ground. She stood over a patch of bloody gravel. A life ended. For what purpose? She would never know.

Une Pause et un Nouveau Départ

For the past week I've been sad. On Monday I will leave this apartment and check into the Terrass Hotel, down the street, for 5 nights. I have been miserable about leaving this apartment, which I've grown to love and this life that I feel so ingrained into. Even though there are pleasures on the other side; friends, family and the most amazing little two year old granddaughter, as well as the excitement of bringing them to Paris in June. I feel like a newly germinated plant that has just taken root and now I'm being plucked; from an apartment that feels like such a sweet home, from friends, from my wonderful neighborhood, from the cafés and restaurants where I have earned my "favorite client" status. From Philippe and Daniele and Thierry.

Family Incoming

S o much family. Daughter, two granddaughters, ages two and eighteen. Ex husband. Ex-husband's fourth wife. And somehow I'm footing the bills for all of it. In some cases, completely unexpected.

For example; Ex and numero 4. The daughter and granddaughters were completely planned and anticipated with great enthusiasm. Izzy's second trip (and hopefully an annual event), Olivia, a high school graduation gift. Ex and wife claimed that it was a completely unexpected delight. They just concluded a Swiss tour and had five days to blow in Paris. That coincides just perfectly with the days that I paid to bring everyone to Paris. A lunch or dinner was suggested.

"How about Jazz Manouche at La Chope on Sunday?" I suggest.

"Sounds great!" they agree.

So I book.

While the Les Puces de Saint Ouen are hardly off the Paris tourist track, the back restaurant at La Chope very much is. Some tourists might find their way to the bar if they are lucky. I found it when I was invited to meet a group of Charlotte's friends. It took me half a dozen visits to discover the restaurant in the back room. It's pure magic, like stepping into Alice's Wonderland. Ground Zero for the Paris Romanian gypsy culture, Sunday afternoons are my favorite time to visit. There is always live music on the stage, graced by a massive portrait of Django Reinhardt himself.

The huge room is full of oddities: carousel animals, a photo booth, framed guitars formerly owned by famed jazz guitarists, miniature replicas of ferris wheels in recognition of the Grande Roue, owned by the controversial Marcel Campion - seventy something year old godfather of Paris's Romanian gypsies (who just happens to own La Chope), photos, and paintings, both good and terrible. No space is left empty. The room is full of formal tables set for diners and in one space there is a kind of conversation pit with long canapés and throw blankets.

Most Sundays Campion himself is holding court at his reserved table, surrounded by family and his henchmen. It's a rare Sunday when he doesn't pick up his own guitar and join the performers in the front bar for a long set. This Sunday was no exception.

We all show up. The music is great. The "A" team is on tap. It's hot. We have wine, an extraordinary cheese and *charcuterie* board, lunch mains, more wine. After two hours everyone decides to go check out the brocantes. They all leave me *en masse*. Except me and the 250 euro check to be paid.

So where did I go wrong? Did I somehow make it appear to be an invitation? Or did I just forget? That Ex is a sponge, a taker, an entitled leach? That's why he is Ex. That's why I have sworn over and over again for the last thirty five years… never again!

Well, again happened.

Back to Work

And then I got sick. A terrible terrible cold in the middle of a terrible terrible heat wave. My apartment was an oven. Outside was an oven. I languished in front of the two fans, one situated on the bedroom dresser pointed directly at the bed, the other in the living room, pointing at the couch. I wanted to do nothing but lay in front of one of the two fans but every time I laid down I broke into a wracking cough. I longed to go "home". I googled airfares, not even thinking clearly enough to realize the flight would have been hell. The fares were outrageous. I was stuck. In Paris. In hot hot hot Paris.

It would have been nice to read but my face hurt too much to put my glasses on. It would have been nice to sleep through the duration but my wheezing breathing was too disturbing. It would have been nice to die.

And then I felt a tiny bit better. I could put my glasses on. I lost myself in the Perigeaux with Bruno the Chief of Police. And as I felt a little bit better I got the very good news from my property manager that a man would come on Friday at 9 am to install a new air conditioner! I turned the air conditioning so low that I actually wanted to wear a sweater. I could sleep under my comforter. I devoured a second Bruno book.

My cupboards and refrigerator were bare. I finally forced myself out to try to buy something to eat. I got as far as the *boulangerie*, about a half a block short of the intended marche, grabbed a couple of small quiches and dragged myself back home, to the comfort of my 17 degree bedroom. The two small quiches would last me two days if I was careful. I was careful.

I missed two jazz concerts and most regretfully a weekend in Burgundy with Stephanie and Magalie!

"Have you gone to the Doctor?" Magalie asked. "Go to the Doctor! Don't just stay that way!"

It is a cold. We don't go to the Doctor for a cold. I almost felt like I needed a Doctor's excuse to pass on the planned weekend away. Maybe the French go to the Doctor for colds. Who knows? I'll have to check this one out later. When I can find someone who speaks English. I found my "sickness French" was woefully inadequate. I had to google the word for cold…. rhume. Hmmm. Sounds appropriate. Maybe I have rheumatic fever. Maybe I have tuberculosis! I googled rheumatic fever. Not good news. I downloaded a third Bruno book.

Sunday morning I woke to find I had slept nine straight hours! I lay very still and took inventory. I think I was going to survive this. I checked my phone and found texted pictures of Magalie and Stephanie enjoying champagne in a beautiful vineyard setting. I even felt a little regret that I was not there. They were having a wonderful time, they reported, but missed me very much. Nice.

I got up, brushed my teeth, took a shower and washed my hair. I opened my kitchen windows to the world. Oh my goodness. Paris is so beautiful!

I think I will live.

Just in time for a very busy week. My calendar tells me I have dinner with Charlotte on Tuesday night, the last jazz evening before the vacances on Wednesday, dinner with the Elliott tribe on Thursday and Friday… *le Bal des Pompiers*!

But first, I must get back to work. It has been weeks since I have written a real word, much less 1,000 of them a day. Between the family visit and then my malady I have gotten very off track.

Jolie Laide

The French, who are more attuned to the magnificent mysteries of womanhood than most, may be the only people in the world to treasure the concept of jolie laide, the plain or even ugly woman who is so well at ease in herself and so cheerful in her soul that she becomes lovely.

Bruno, Chief of Police
Martin Walker

I'm not suggesting that I'm plain or ugly, but it's been a rare day that I've thought of myself as particularly jolie. Sure, there have been a handful of times in my life that I've felt really pretty. But to be so at ease in myself and cheerful in my soul… allowing myself to become lovely. That is magic.

La Fête (and then some)

July arrived with a burst of activity. The National Holiday, on July 14, what most Americans mistakenly call Bastille day (who exactly was St. Bastille, one American friend asked) was nearly dwarfed by the fact that France worked its way to the lofty position of the finals in the World Cup. Not since 1998 had France been that successful. The Country was going nuts. Every cafe was crowded with football fans. And after each victory, every French citizen seemed to personally celebrate as if they had kicked the winning goal. Horns blaring down every rue and boulevard in the City late into the night! While the Champs Elysee was ground zero for the celebrations, with massive crowds bringing out the gendarmes in riot gear and tear gas, my usually tranquil neighborhood celebrated for hours after every victory.

My personal *fête* started on Wednesday night when I ventured out for the first time after my battle with *le rhume*. Intending on catching the last jazz *soirée* of the "season", I actually caught the football match between England and Croatia and was sucked up into Football fever.

My ex-colleagues in England and Croatia and the US were also wrapped up in the excitement and texts were flying. When Croatia pulled it off in the last minutes of the game my Croatian friend texted: "My friend has two tickets for the world cup finals, Croatia: France on July 15th in Moscow. Unfortunately the game is starting at the same time as his pre planned wedding. If anyone else wants to replace him, his wedding is at the Croatian Catholic Church on Lincoln Avenue, San Jose and his girlfriend's name is Ivana, she has long blonde hair." This is serious stuff!

Thursday night I continued my post rhume re-entry into Paris life with apero and dinner of tapas with Elliott, Joan and our Brazilian friend, Joao. We met for *apéro* at a newly opened hotel with a lovely inside courtyard terrace in the 9th. Elliott and I got there about half an hour before everyone else and had lots of time to chat. I forgot how great Elliott is at chatting. Although he definitely has his biases (the Champs Elysées and Avenue Montaigne are both truly a waste of space but these little neighborhoods in the 9th are fantastic), I do learn a tremendous amount from him. His references to authors and books alone are worth the effort of sorting through the vast volumes of Elliott's opinions. I am tremendously grateful for this friendship.

Besides, where else would I have learned about Le Petit Barcelone? Elliott calls it the one good Spanish restaurant in Paris (but then he says only one in ten Spanish restaurants in Spain are good). Definitely dive-restaurantish, the hole in the wall place on a tiny side street of the very diverse 9ème was a place you'd have to know to visit. The four of us ordered a vast assortment of tapas for partager. Or rather, Elliott ordered a vast assortment of tapas, with Joan reminding him what he did and didn't like. But that is always the right way to go. Say what you will, but Elliott knows his food. My only request was the squid. I'm surely glad that Elliott had the foresight to order the padron peppers. I may go back myself just for the squid and the padron peppers! And maybe those little sausages on a stick. Of course, the wine flowed generously. And the conversation! We talked about bullfights and bullfighters (something that put a spark in Joan's previously unsparked eyes) which led to Hemingway and then F. Scott Fitzgerald and reading Gatsby out loud (the only way)... twice. I think we even halfway agreed to take a trip to Arles next April to watch the bullfights in the ancient Roman amphitheater. We talked about potential vacation spots, where to buy the best house outside of Paris so you can get away for weekends, but not be completely overwhelmed by the nightmare of the weekly commute. (Hmm, maybe I should buy a house outside of Paris...) And we gossiped. I love gossiping. I love having smart, interesting friends in Paris. I love long evenings and café life in Paris.

I dragged my almost not rheumy, definitely inebriated self to the spot where Elliott had arranged to meet the Chauffeur Prive driver (another one of his weird biases.. why not just ask him to come where we are? We quick-stepped three blocks to where he was impatiently waiting... well everyone else quick-stepped, I wobbled a bit drunkenly and definitely mindful of the cobbles in this ancient sentiere.) We again negotiated with the driver about a second drop off location. Elliott again had a confrontational conversation in rapid fire French about dropping Madame off at a second location. I again tipped the annoyed driver 5 euro. A successful and fun night.

Next up - *Le Bal des Pompiers*! Why do Firemen have bigger balls than Police-men? They sell more tickets of course! Traditionally, on July 13th and 14th, in conjunction with the National Holiday, the fire stations of Paris open their doors to the public and host the Bal des Pompiers. My French friends Stephanie and Magalie texted me: come on Friday for *apéro* at 7 pm and then we will go to the Bal des Pompiers in the 18ème. Bring a bottle of bubbles and something to eat. It is a "good atmosphere".

Still rheumy I drag my sniffy self to my local *cave* to get a bottle of the cham-pagne Monsieur Vincent was telling me about on the last visit. I picked up two and popped them in the fridge to cool. To satisfy the request for "something to eat" I stopped at the fromagerie and picked up my favorite Brillat-Savarin. I've yet to find anyone who didn't swoon over the truffle-infused brie. So so good.

Elliott had warned me about the tradition of *les Bal de Pompiers*. Originally, he said, introduced to recognize the contribution of the firefighters in France, and a coming together of community, old and young, it had recently and sadly transitioned into a rowdy party for the younger crowd. "Go early" he advised, to see the neighborhood locals and to buy your tickets for the drawings. Further-more, "the pompiers are all extremely handsome and it is a tradition for them to get some action in the shadows of the fire station during the night." Of course, this means some level of willing participation on the part of the women of the sentiere, anxious to participate in that action.

Wait a minute, are there no female *pompières*? Of course, that sends me to my friend Mr. Google who tells me that since including women in their numbers, less than 5% of today's firefighters in Paris are female! I hope they are getting a piece of the action!

Of course we are well lubricated by the time we walked the block and a half from Stephanie's apartment to the firehouse (thank GOD she is well protected!) and there is already a rowdy and jovial crowd. Elliott's right; the music is definitely geared toward the younger crowd. It feels a bit like the parties I went to in college. And Elliott's also right; there's nowhere to sit. My sick and slightly drunk self is desperate for a place to light. Before long I run into Caroleen and F. Then into a couple other of my expat friends. I'm amazed that in such a short time I've become a part of the Paris scene. Or at least the scene of Montmartre.

I've tasted the infamous Firemen's Ball and I'm ready to go home. I make my excuses to Magalie and Stephanie and head towards chez moi; just three blocks and the 105 stair steps between rue Lamarck and rue Caulaincourt... or another couple of blocks and stair 43 steps plus 400 meters. Not a big deal, unless you're crippled with a summer cold.

July 14th dawns clear and sunny - unfortunately my head not so much. I really need to think about drinking less. I spend about half a minute worrying about what mon foie may be looking like these days. The cleaners are coming today so I have to go somewhere by noon. I drag myself into the kitchen and make fresh coffee in my French press. While it's "brewing" I wash the three or four dishes that are still in the sink from yesterday. There is absolutely no activity on rue Caulaincourt. The buses seem to be running toward the marie but nothing is arriving in the other direction, towards the Seine. All of this morning's activity centers around the Champs Elysées, a massive military parade and the spectacular aerial flyover the Arc de Triomphe with the red white and blue smoke trail. A tiny part of me wishes that I were not averse to crowds and could catch a view of it all just once in person. Naaah, I will watch it on TV.

Clearly a good decision. I watch President Macron driven from the Elysée Palace up the famous boulevard and back down to his viewing station at Place de la Concorde. I see close up while he greets each of the many different branches of the military's leaders. I note the intimacy with which he shakes their hands, makes almost intimate eye contact, then grips their arm or hand with his second hand. I make a mental note how genuine and effective it seems.

The endless stream of military and police cadres who parade in front of the President is impressive. I can only imagine that last year, when the (#notmypresident) leader of the US sat beside Macron for the parade, he had to be wetting his pants for something so extravagant.

I'm torn. Do I want to watch this extravaganza in person or am I better off viewing it all on TV? I head to Le Cépage for *un cafe crème* before taking an Uber to GCA to do a bit of work. It's so *tranquille*. Even though the terrace is crowded with *Montmartrois* it is nothing like what I imagine the crowds on the Champs Elysées to be. I got to see everything on TV. I would have seen a small slice of the action in person. And yet, when a friend posts a video of the dramatic red, blue and white fly over, I feel like maybe I made the wrong decision.

I worked at GCA for several hours, enjoyed maybe the best meal I've had to date for lunch; *dorade* and grilled *courgette* with a bottle of rosé. I rave effusively about the *courgette* and *dorade* which seems to make Philippe extremely happy. Is he insecure about my impressions about GCA? I rave on social media about other working lunches (and the *beau patrons*). Am I not effusive enough about him? Am I so invested in working when I'm at GCA that I don't appear to be interested? Does he have any idea how much of my time spent at GCA is about him? He puffs up his chest and grunts something to the effect that he was involved in the decision to put this combination together. I'm very happy to have made him feel this good. Note to self: more compliments. A nearby table wants to know about *caviar d'aubergine*. He asks me to translate. Eggplant, I say. "Eggplant?!" He's learned a new English word today.

The remaining challenge of the National Holiday… *les feux d'artifice*. The fireworks. Last year Christine and I watched from L'Oiseau Blanc. They are advertising the dinner for a mere 575 euro per person, excluding alcohol. It was a once in a lifetime experience. Last year was the once. As tempted as I am to inquire whether they still have a table for one, 575 euro (*sans alcool*) is a lot of money! It is spectacular. Fireworks shoot from the structure of the Eiffel Tower. But I think my once in a lifetime was last year. I can see the very top of the tower from the bench on rue Caulaincourt just half a block up from the Terrass Hotel (where they offer dinner for 275 euro *sans alcool*) . It's only about six inches of

Eiffel Tower. For some reason six inches come to mind, although it's probably some 75 meters of Eiffel Tower) but maybe some of the *feux d'artifice* will show. And then it will be an easy 400 meter walk back to *chez moi*. Or I could watch on TV. And see the whole thing. Free.

Girls in Short Shorts

In the winter the French are so wrapped in clothing that there is barely an inch of skin that shows. They wrap massive scarves, nay - blanket themselves - in wool and fabric. But come summer, skin is the word of the day. I am working in GCA, watching the girls come and go. As does Guilaume, and I dare say Philippe. Shorts. She bends over to retrieve her purse and her butt cheeks show at the bottom of her very short shorts. Both of them look.

We Are the Champions of the World

France has won the World Cup. Cue Queen and put the tune on replay (and replay and replay and replay). The City has gone mad.

I am sad that I care about this so much. But I'm happy that they won because I know that it makes Philippe so happy. *"Demain est la fête"* he said when I wished him *bonne fête* on the National Holiday. *"Tu espères"* was my response.

But Paris, and probably all of France, cares about it in an insane way. Every café and every restaurant on every street in Paris is jam packed with celebrants. What if they lose, I wonder? How will the French react?

I chose to watch alone, from home, although options abound. I somehow felt that the stress of the event and the potential disappointment in the case of loss, was something I preferred to face alone. I did however open my windows to the cheers and honking of the celebrants on rue Caulaincourt.

And they were plentiful! Oddly there was absolutely no vehicle traffic on the street. No buses came and went, no trucks double parked to discharge their goods to the local shops. Other than the big crowds that gathered in front of Nepo's, Les Loups and Le Cépage, the street was eerily quiet.

I've learned a lot about soccer in the last week, having watched my first and only three games. First of all, I've learned it's both stressful and boring. Unlike American football and baseball, where your team actually gets it's "ups" or controls the direction of the game, the ball just gets kicked, headbutted and bopped about endlessly with nobody really seeming to be in control. The first two games that I watched each had one goal apiece. So in 90 minutes, plus some unexplainable extra minutes tacked on to the end, athletes ran around a massive field and tried to move the ball into the other team's goal. Boring but oddly stressful.

France's first goal came on a penalty against the other team. Evidently the Croatian teammate pushed, kicked or touched the French guy in some inappropriate manner. The French fans (and my neighborhood) went wild. The referee took a break on the sidelines while he reviewed the action on a laptop for several minutes. Yes, it seemed he had been fouled. The French player had an opportunity to kick the ball into the goal, guarded only by the Croatian goalie. Score!

The neighborhood went nuts. Suddenly there was moto traffic on the street, blaring their horns, waving their flags (hey, where are their helmets and why are there three people on that moto?) The fans at all three cafés went wild. They jumped and shouted and sang in the street.

Just minutes later Croatia scored an actual goal. Silence! I have to admit, I felt a bit good for Croatia. Afterall, I have Croatian friends, and they are clearly the underdog here. And my friend's friend skipped his own wedding for this event! But at the same time, I was sweating and anxious and fearful that Croatia might actually win!

Another goal by France left a margin of comfort at halftime (I presume that's what happened at 45 minutes into the game when both teams took a break and the advertisements took over). I checked social media and indeed it was full of posts that France was leading at halftime.

I poured a glass of wine.

In the next 45 minutes (plus 5 mysterious minutes) France scored two more goals, each to the absolute delight of my neighborhood. And with some time to spare, Croatia countered with another goal. Very respectable effort on the part of the Croats! And possibly worth missing one's wedding for. The extra five minutes passed in an excruciating 300 seconds and it was over. In Moscow, where the game was played, Macron leaped in the air, a moment that was caught on film for the enjoyment of millions of French and all the citizens of the world.

The French team leapt onto the field in a massive dogpile and rue Caulaincourt erupted. Red, white and blue smoke filled the street. Horns blared (for the next twelve hours). Blue, white and red conga lines snaked up and down the rue for hours. Flags flew everywhere. People say that you can tell the French by the black clothing they wear. Not on this day. Everyone is dressed in red or blue. Everyone has the French flag painted on their body. Everyone waves a French flag, or wears a French flag, or sings *La Marseillaise*!

I wonder if the street is blocked. There are no cars for hours (but there are motos; honking incessantly) Rue Caulaincourt is a river of people coming from up the hill; singing, dancing, shouting, waving flags. Where are they all coming from? That's when I realize that every cafe and bar and restaurant in Paris is filled with people celebrating France's victory at this moment. Rue Caulaincourt is just a small representation of what's happening at Place du Tertre, Rue des Abbesses, Avenue Trudaine… and that's only my small part of Paris! The Champs Elysées is one massive swarming mass of humankind. On the Champs de Mars people have been picnicking all day, their spots claimed for watching the game on the massive screen. The same thing with the Esplanade des Invalides, La Bastille and Place de la République, every little rue and boulevard in the 10th and 11th lined by trendy bars and bistros; they were all teeming with people insanely happy and celebrating France's 20 year return of the World Cup trophy. People were leaping into Canal St. Martin. People were climbing the lamp posts and news kiosks. People just jumped up and down. For hours. And hours. And hours.

I went to bed at midnight. At 3 am I woke to honking. What is even open at 3 am? Evidently nothing has to be open to honk one's horn.

I sensed that I was awake. I didn't really want to open my eyes but I sneaked a peek to see how much sunlight there was, a sure clue to the time. Hmm, I guessed, 7:50? Sure enough it was very close to 8 am, my usual time to wake up these days that I didn't have to be sitting in my Silicon Valley office by 7 am. It was eerily quiet. I look out the window onto rue Caulaincourt. One woman walks a dog. One jogger runs by. Not a car. Not a sound. The produce man hasn't pulled open his sheet metal door yet. It's Monday. Most of the shops on rue Caulaincourt are closed on Monday but today is eerily quiet. I rather suspect most Parisians are calling in sick today!

I go into the kitchen to make coffee. While I wait for the kettle to boil so I can add the water to my French press I check my phone. Social Media tells me the French team is coming home today. The parade on the Champs Elysées will begin at 5:30 PM. The following metro stations will be closed while hundreds of thousands line the world's most famous boulevard…

I am meeting Charlotte for dinner at 8. Will I be able to get there? Once again #youcantgettherefromhere.

Maybe tomorrow things will again be normal.

You'll Get What You Get

When you get it, you'll like it. Or you'll go somewhere else. And I say this with love. The French really don't want my feedback (or anyone else's from what I can tell.)

For the last few years I've really been wearing rose colored glasses with respect to the stereotype of the rude French. I've argued that nearly everyone I've met has been lovely. The exceptions might be places that are primarily populated by tourists; the Jules Verne, very expensive Michelin starred restaurant that Alain Ducasse just got booted out of, any restaurant facing the river and especially those with a view of the Eiffel Tower, any restaurant on rue Hachette. But even as I list these I can think of more exceptions than rude culprits. Thierry's tiny restaurant on Quai de la Tournelle faced the river and had a lovely view of the flying buttresses of Notre Dame. He and his staff were absolutely lovely to me. Service at some of the especially great places I've been; L'Oiseau Blanc atop the Paris Peninsula Hotel with it's glorious view of the Eiffel Tower, Sacré-Coeur and the rooftops of Paris, Les Ombres, L'Ami Jean, La Scène Thélème… all top notch eateries, some with Michelin stars, all with plenty of people traveling specifically to experience their fare, and all extremely kind and gracious.

As I get to the small bistros and restaurants in my local area it is even more the case of friendly service and helpful staff. The longer I am here, and the more I am accepted as a part of the neighborhood, it's as if I'm a part of the family. Even the manager that Caroleen tagged "the evil faggot" greeted me warmly and asked how I was, moving a second table close to mine to accommodate my laptop, wine, salade nicoise, and water. This is the guy who turned off the wifi when he'd had enough of Caroleen. Clearly the key is it pays to treat people how you want to be treated.

But dig a little deeper and there is an attitude in Paris that says "the customer is not king". In fact, *le commerçant est roi* and the customer is a customer.

Last night I met Charlotte for dinner in the Marais. I was curious about a restaurant I'd been reading about, Vins des Pyrénées, and asked her if she'd been. She said it was on her list, let's go. Our rendez-vous was set for the unfortunate time that The World Champion Soccer team was arriving back in Paris and was to parade down the Champs Elysee on top of an open air bus. Hundreds of thousands of people lined up all day for the route. Would things ever get back to normal in Paris? The two buses I would have to take to make my journey 1,50 euro were disrupted, even the metro had closures. So I was left with no choice but a 30 euro Uber ride.

Normally I've learned to maximize the value of my Uber rides by turning the driver into a language tutor. At least I feel less guilty about the cost. Last night, I was not in the mood, and preferred to watch Paris go by. Even away from the Champs Elysées, where *tout le monde* was gathered, the streets, cafés and sidewalks were jammed with people, drinking, smoking, walking, moto-ing. Suddenly jets flew in front of us, leaving a trail of blue, white and red jet stream! The driver and I gasped in unison! Only in Paris!

Thirty minutes later the driver dropped me in front of a charming little bistro, on a narrow street just two blocks from Place des Vosges. I was fifteen minutes early for our reservation, but *pas de problème*. I was seated at a table next to the open window. At 7:45 the restaurant was nearly empty. Only one other table was occupied by four American women.

The waiter asked if I would like something to drink. "*Un cocktail?*" "*Oui*" he brought me a menu. A long list of trendy named but interesting looking cocktails; Zelda, People are strange, L'homme pressé, Medicis, Vol de nuit, Elliot Ness, Le résistant, Come fly with me. I debated between the Zelda and the Come fly with me and in the end opted for the Zelda.

Fifteen minutes later Charlotte arrived, right on time. Five minutes later Zelda arrived, a wannabe Manhattan with a foamy egg white topping and dried rose petals. Were they edible, I wondered?

Charlotte asked for the cocktail menu. The waiter suggested that she might not want to order a cocktail because they were taking a long time. Huh? There was a bar not 15 feet away from our table. Evidently the cocktails were made at the bar upstairs, Le 1905.

"Aha" said Charlotte, "that's why this was on my list. It's the bar I had heard of."

The waiter launched into the history of the restaurant, Les Vins des Pyrénées. In 1905, the original owner built the house and this is where he bottled wine from the grapes that were shipped in from the Pyrénées, to "Port St. Emilion"

"Is there a Port St. Emilion in Paris?" I asked Charlotte.

"Not that I know of. I would like a cocktail she said. I'll have the Elliot Ness."

We asked for the food menu and ordered. We asked for the cart du vin and ordered. Why did we have to ask?

The wine arrived before Elliot Ness. By the way, my Zelda was fine, not earth shaking but tasty. I didn't eat the rose petals.

We shared a starter of lamb croquettes. They were piping hot and very good but a bit awkward to eat since we weren't given any small plates. We each stabbed one with a fork and munched on it, dipping it in the very nice yogurt sauce. Our *plats* arrived; *poulpe et piments* for me and a *croque aux truffes* for Charlotte. I think both were fine but unremarkable. Maybe the best part of the meal was the Pouilly Fuisse, and certainly the conversation.

It was an excellent gossip fest.

"I feel guilty," I admitted. "Everytime I see you I gossip so much!"

"I guess you feel safe with me!"

I like that. I felt decidedly less guilty.

We finish our meal and ask for the bill, heading upstairs to check out Le 1905. It is lovely! A space full of nooks and crannies and lovely little seating areas. We choose a space on an outside terrace. Behind the building apartments with windows wide open to the space between buildings. Golden hues suggest interesting things going on in the apartments. Our small terrace has space for half a dozen. A couple sits at the next table having dinner. We should have eaten up here! Maybe Zelda and Elliot would have made it to the table more quickly.

The young waiter turned on electric fairy lights and the small patio was magical. I think there was some kind of unobtrusive but pleasant music playing. The same young waiter brought us the same cocktail menu we gotten downstairs. We decided to go off menu.

"I'd like a very dry martini." Charlotte said. That evolved into a discussion about the exact recipe for a dry martini. I still say good martinis are very hard to come by in Paris! I asked for a Sidecar. Crickets. "Can you ask the bartender if he can make one?" I suggested. They can make a Le Résistant, a Come fly with me and an Elliot Ness but a classic Sidecar?

Maybe 10 minutes later the waiter came back to tell me that Sidecar was a go. He would have been back sooner but he had a lot of cloth napkins to fold. Finally the martini and Sidecar arrived and both were good.

Bottom line, here was a restaurant and bar that have so much potential. They could be great. But they are ok. With potential. And neither of us is probably going to make the effort to trek across town to come back. Later it occurred to me that there could be an excellent business in consulting with places like this. A few simple modifications; getting the cocktails to the table quickly, better trained servers, more customer service, could turn a really lovely location into a place worth traveling to.

But this is Paris. Parisians don't take kindly to advice and suggestions. Maybe there are enough people already in the 4eme to keep the place busy enough. And who asked for your opinion anyway?

Philippe, who supposedly likes me and beamed when I said the grilled cour-gettes and dorade were the best thing I'd ever eaten at GCA, won't make me a Sidecar, even though he's got all the ingredients behind the bar.

You'll get what you get..

"Ce n'est pas assez d'être sage. Il faut plaire."
It is not enough to be wise. You have to please.

A woman who has loved only one man will never know love.
"What would Ninon do?" - Louis XIV (aka Sun King)

Epicureanism:

When we say… that pleasure is the end and aim, we do not mean the pleasures of the prodigal or the pleasures of sensuality, as we are understood by some through ignorance, prejudice or wilful misrepresentation. By pleasure we mean the absence of pain in the body and of trouble in the soul. It is not by an unbroken succession of drinking bouts and of revelry, not by sexual lust, nor the enjoyment of fish and other delicacies of a luxurious table, which produce a pleasant life; it is sober reasoning, searching out the grounds of every choice and avoidance, and banishing those beliefs through which the greatest tumults take possession of the soul.

- Epicurus, "Letter to Menoeceus"

Of all things which wisdom has contrived which contribute to a blessed life, none is more important, more fruitful than friendship.

-Cicero

An Insurance Policy

Upon leaving the convent, Ninon knew she had two choices; take a husband or get a job. Having committed to never doing the former, she planned for the latter. What she needed was an insurance policy, something that would guarantee her future and remove any hint that she may be tainted material. Marquis Henri de Sévigné was just the ticket.

Henri was not unattractive. He was just a vain and impetuous young man. He was easy pickings for the clever but young Ninon. More importantly, he was from a family of means and could be precisely what she needed to guarantee her future as an independent woman.

While Henri was just not unattractive, Ninon had been fortunate to be born quite lovely. Her year in the convent merely added to the discipline and habits required to maintain her natural gifts. She lived a life protected from the sun so her beautiful white skin was unblemished by the savagery of the everyday elements. Ninon was resolute in protecting her attractions. She ate well, didn't drink, in fact drank an extraordinary amount of water, which flew in the face of contemporary convention, and slathered her entire body with bull semen. As a result, in addition to her god given (although Ninon doubted the existence of a god) gifts she was slim and had alabaster skin that was wonderfully soft to the touch.

At twenty two, she was not only lovely to look at she was delightful to listen to. She cleverly asked all the right questions and reacted to the responses with exactly the right balance of interest and boredom. Young Henri was no match for our Ninon. In due haste he set her up in a modest but lovely apartment on rue des Tournelles, truly an address to be coveted and just a block from the Place des Vosges.

Although Ninon did not love Henri (in fact she really didn't even like him) she recognized that he was vitally important to her future as a Parisian courtesan. She learned from him. And he was a naive and willing teacher. She quickly learned when to withhold and when to give; when to listen and when to talk; and after six months Ninon learned when to cut and run.

By then Ninon had feathered her little nest on rue des Tournelles quite well. She had the beginning of a lovely salon, with stylish but comfortable furnishings and a few pieces that would become the beginning of an extraordinary art collection. She quickly became adept at the art of love and was not learning anything more; at least from Henri. He had become engaged to his cousin Marie and Ninon decided it was time to move on to a new arrangement.

Henri was of course, destitute. In spite of his engagement he was quite used to getting what he wanted and he wanted to continue to be spoiled by the attentions of the lovely Ninon. He wanted to have his proverbial cake and eat it!

It was at this very early and pivotal stage of Ninon's career as a courtesan that she determined she had allowed this to go on too long. Three months was her new limit. She also wisely decided that she would have just one lover at a time. But no one lover would overstay his welcome in her bed.

Avril 1667 rue des Tournelles

"**H**ave you seen that Italian's bust of the King?"

"I have heard that he was brought here to redesign the entire Palace!"

"Noooo, not the entire Palace." "X" tutted, emitting a tiny puff of air from his snarling lips. " He's just been invited to submit a proposal for the east facade. A proposal you silly twits!" "X" had strolled over to the periphery of the cluster of gossipy women. Why are they here? he wondered. How on earth did Ninon allow these vapid soulless nitwits into her salon? What on earth did she think they would contribute? Even their powders and paints and tresses and abundance of decolletage add nothing to the scene. If I were looking for frippery I could go spend an evening with one of my own mistresses. They are always eager to supply me with the latest gossip along with more salubrious satisfactions. This time his puff of dissatisfaction included an audible grunt.

The women merely took a few steps further into the luxurious room, away from Monsieur X and continued their chatter.

"Did you hear what he did to his mistress? The woman was the wife of his workshop assistant."

"No… don't tell me. I saw him on the square the other day. He was staring into space. Just gazing at the horse chestnuts as if he expected them to do something. He's actually rather handsome, in that dark, oily, Italian kind of way. It was truly odd how he stared for a very long passage of time."

"Well, this was years ago," Madame A was not to be deterred from her story. "Before he was married and had all of those little Italian brats. He had a long time affair with the wife of his workshop assistant. What did the thankless trollop do? She started sleeping with his brother!"

"Oh my…"

"True! Of course the sculpture was enraged!"

"What did he do?" Madame X asked, on pins and needles, exactly the reaction Madame A was looking for.

Madame A took a long sip of her sherry and looked around the room surreptitiously, as if daring nearby ears to listen in. Everyone was engrossed in their own discussions, or gathered around Ninon, hanging on her every word. Clearly Madame A had an audience of one. She sighed heavily, disappointed that she had wasted this juicy tidbit of gossip on the vain and silly Madame X. She looked around the room again, desperately hoping to find more eager ears for her story. It wasn't going to happen.

She took a dramatic breath, one more sip of her sherry and launched into the denouement of her tale.

"Well, he engaged with one of her servants." She glanced again longingly at the group surrounding Ninon.

"Go on, please…" plead Madame X.

"And he had the servant slash up her face with a straight razor!" She waved her hand in the air for effect while Madame X gasped and spilled a bit of her own sherry on her abundant decolletage.

"No!" Madame X finally was able to utter as she used her lace hanky to delicately mop up the spill on her generously exposed bosom

"Mais oui." reinforced Madame A. "Of course the woman is terribly scarred and absolutely hideous."

"And the sculptor? What happened to him?"

"Absolutely nothing."

Madame X wrinkled her nose, looking for more.

"Well, you know how those papists are. The Pope hastily arranged a marriage to a woman half his age whom he rendered a breed mare. She bore him a passel of children."

Madame X was deep in thought, trying to fathom some part of the story, not clear exactly what.

"And his servant and the woman…" Madame A whispered conspiratorially, "were both imprisoned! For infidelity and assault."

"No!"

"Mais oui." Madame A shrugged.

In the heart of the salon, Ninon herself was deep in discussion with several Messrs about Gian Lorenzo Bernini themselves. Not the gossip, but the merits of his being brought from Italy to make an important proposal for a significant new Palace facade.

Although she had been a frequent presence in Paris's most notable salons, she had only recently inaugurated her own at l'hotel Sagonne on rue des Tournelles, very well situated adjacent to Place Royale. The salon at l'hotel Sagonne fast became "the" place to be. Ninon's habituées were quickly dubbed the L'oiseaux de Tournelles".

Ninon looked lovely as usual. Her long hair, grown out again after a period of sporting her infamous "bob ` la Ninon" (the result of her cutting off all her locks to console the desolate Marquis de Villarceaux upon ending their "arrangement") fell in luxuriant curls around her shoulders and across her own famous poitrine.

An Embarrassment
of Riches

W riting every day is becoming part of what I do. It's certainly a change from my corporate life. I wake up by 8, get up by 9. I used to be sitting at my desk at 7 am, unless of course I was traveling somewhere; China, Malaysia, Australia, India… Now I get up when I can't wait any longer to answer the call of nature. I've made myself a rule, not to leave my room until my bed is made up; at least I will have one small bit of discipline in my life. So I make my bed and then head to the kitchen to make coffee.

While the french press is steeping, I turn on my laptop and the lights and fans. I check on my tiny balcony garden, basil, thyme and chervil along with the pansies and petunias, giving them a drink of water. Then I plunge the coffee and spend the next hour or two checking and sending emails, checking my social media accounts, doing my Duolingo. I'm on day seven hundred and something of Duolingo.

Then I decide where I am going to write today. I've started to feel completely immersed in Ninon's life; the mystery of how it all evolved is gradually unfolding. Where did she go when she left the convent? What did she feel like? Was she afraid?

I'm drawn to 36 rue des Tournelles. It looks nothing like it must have looked when Ninon walked these streets over three hundred years ago. Now it's completely gentrified and part of the trendy and tourist saturated fourth arrondissement - the Marais. I once had dinner at the small café on the corner.

"I'm writing a novel about a woman who lived on this street in the 1600s. Do you ever wonder what it was like here then?" I asked the waiter.

"I've only been working here for a couple of months." he responded.

Today I wrote at GCA. Philippe helped me find the right table on this very hot Paris afternoon. Not this table. Too noisy, they are doing construction across the street. This side is better, facing the park or facing inside?

"Facing inside of course. *J'écris mieux ici. Je ne sais pas pourquoi. Je pense peut-être tu es mon muse.*"

I'm not sure he understood my American accent. But he seemed pleased. I'm GCA's Hemingway. And Le Clou's Hemingway (yesterday the lovely Thierry was wearing the SF Giants cap I brought him and proudly pointed it out to me), I'm also Le Cépage's Hemingway where Laurent thoughtfully sets up a second table to accommodate my beverages while I write and admonishes me to stop writing for a bit while I enjoy my *dorade*. "*Quand tu travailles, travaillés et quand tu manges, manges!*" When you work, work and when you eat, eat!" He's right of course. Monsieur durade gave up his life for my enjoyment. It is my obligation to enjoy it. And I'm Les Loups' Hemingway, handsome Rafaele eager to make sure I have what I need at my regular table. Such an embarrassment of riches. So many handsome waiters and restaurant owners and the glorious opportunity to write at my leisure! All patrons of the arts.

A Holiday

I t's time for a break. I have been in Paris for over six months and other than the trip to the US I have not stepped foot out of the city.

But where to go?

The parameters; I must be able to take the train. I don't want to rent a car. I will be going alone. I don't want to be lonely. I do want it to be peaceful. And different from Paris. Not a city. I would prefer that the journey does not involve more than 3 hours on the train.

How about Bretagne? I seem to recall reading about St. Malo on the northern coast of France and it seemed lovely. I'd recently read "The Little French Café Bistro?" which transported me to Bretagne. It sounded charming and different and peaceful. I pulled the book up on my Kindle and found it wasn't indeed Bretagne, but Kerdruc, more than 200 kilometers from St. Malo, more than 500 kilometers from Paris and not accessible by train. Google images showed it was indeed exactly what I was looking for but it wasn't going to work.

Could I make St. Malo work? There is the old Grand Hôtel des Thermes on the beach that looks old and stately and very very restful. Should I go there? I'm desperately wishing I had my copy of "Hungry for France" which I left in San Francisco, too big and heavy to fit in my suitcase. It was full of ideas for restaurants and small inns and places to stay. Maybe I should go buy a new copy here in Paris. I'm envisioning a quiet place to think and write and look at the seaside, a cozy restaurant nearby with only the freshest seafood and delicious local wines.

Hmmm, would Philippe fit into this picture? Maybe this is a trip better saved for a month or two from now, after we figure out exactly what comes next.

So how about Lyon? I have always loved Lyon. And while it doesn't fit the "not a city" requirement, it's certainly smaller than Paris. That charming hotel we stayed at in Vieux Lyon, Coeur des Loges, was small and cozy, tucked deeply into the ancient part of the city, amongst the traboules and shops and cafés. Lyon is known by its local gastronomy. A first class train ticket is only 65 euro and the trip is just under two hours. How about two nights in Lyon and then on to Geneva for a couple of nights? I remember having dinner on the terrace of a beautiful hotel on the lake. I google the hotel and find I can get a room for three nights for a reasonable rate. I see myself taking a boat ride on the lake, maybe to Evian. Or a train to Lausanne or Vevey or Montreux for the day.

It breaks all the rules. It's not even in France. But it sounds lovely. And not lonely. Maybe a trip is born.

And another trip conceived. For later. And not alone.

Hunan Food, Bartleby, Guy de Maupassant and Tattoos

riday night was another Elliott curated evening; first *apéro* at the Hotel Parister, where I had met Elliott, Joan and Joao the week before enroute to the "only good" tapas restaurant in Paris. Then to L'Orient d'Or, a Hunan restaurant right around the corner from the only good tapas restaurant in Paris. Elliott seems to have a thing about Chinese. Personally, as many times as I've been to China in my other life, I could happily leave it behind. But I go for the conversation, not the food. Good thing too, at 50 euro for a Chinese dinner, plus taxi fare to and fro, the Chinese food would have to include foie gras, which it didn't!

But the conversation and the sense of community is always well worth it. I sat next to Pierre -Yves (my first Pierre in Paris!) who introduced himself by saying that I knew his wife, Deborah. Hmmm, I don't think so. But Pierre-Yves turned out to be a very interesting dinner partner and well worth the 50 euro price tag for so so Chinese food and drinkable rosé.

Pierre-Yves is a collector of rare first and second edition novels. He told me with great excitement about his latest find, a second edition copy of somebody I'd unfortunately (and making me feel ignorant) never heard of, for a veritable steal. Bravo Pierre-Yves! I mentioned Ninon to him and for once discovered I had met someone who actually knew about her.

But the seventeenth century literature and courtesans was not really Pierre-Yves's thing. He preferred to talk about Emilie-Louise Delabigne , or the Vallee de

La Bigne, a nineteenth century courtesan, who started her career as a Lorette before transitioning into a very famous bedmate to the who's who of the art world. Pierre's English was far far better than my French, but still he struggled at times and while I understood there to be some issue with Napoleon III that put her career in danger, I wasn't clear at all what exactly it was.

Pierre-Yves is currently reading Herman Melville in French. "Moby Dick?" I ask.

"No! A much shorter book!"

"Bartleby" I grasp from my college literature classes.

"*Oui!* Do you say '*je ne préfère pas.*"?

"*Oui!* That is the essence of Bartleby!"

We talk some more about the challenges of translating authors from English to French and how hard it must be to capture the feeling the author intended to convey with his carefully chosen words. And then the conversation transitions to Guy de Maupassant and his rampant syphilis ("Everybody in Paris in those days had syphilis," said Charlotte) and his mistress, Blanche Roosevelt, an opera singer and novelist in her own right, and a night in a restaurant with Henry James in London.

Where would I ever have a conversation like this in San Francisco? With a stranger. Or at least with a new friend! I must remember to ask Elliott for Pierre-Yves' contact information. I wonder if he would be interested in a monthly book group. He can even choose the book and the other participants! I just want to be in a world where these are the kinds of things we talk about.

Then we pony up our 50 euros and move on to a bar nearby; nearby being, as Elliott puts it, "two blocks away." Warning: when a Parisian (having lived in Paris for 20 years, Elliott qualifies) tells you two blocks, it's probably five. Eight of us hightail it to a bar five blocks away where we manage to find tables reasonably close to each other. This time I find myself sitting with Magella, a fifty something Irish woman, cum Australian, cum Parisian who's newly married to a twenty something very handsome Tunisian and Jeremy, a twenty something American software engineer who is currently working in Berlin. The conversation of the next hour or so is tattoos, what and where ours are, who did them, and who are the most awesome tattoo artists in Europe.

When did tattoos become the lingua franca of the day? I remember when we had a good idea and we got a T-Shirt with the message. "Seize the day" "This too shall pass" (Jeremy's message along with a pocket watch on the inside of his left arm). A bale of wheat representing the meals that he and his best friend had in University on his right calf. A massive tree with roots on his chest and stomach representing something that completely went over my head. I wonder what that one will look like in years to come when wheat is replaced by barley and Jeremy is a fat middle aged man. Well, maybe he won't get fat.

(For the record, I currently have none, but am considering a very small one on the inside of my wrist of a grasshopper, wearing a beret and playing a fiddle.

"How is your pain tolerance" Jeremy asks me? "Inside the wrist is a very painful place." He shows me his "Go button" tattoo on the inside of his left wrist. "But wait, you have kids… did you give birth?"

"Yes…"

"Well then you should be fine."

Whew! I'm so relieved. But wonder about maybe getting a temporary tattoo.

After another twenty minutes of so of looking at tattoos done by the best tattoo artists in Europe on Jeremy's phone I start to monitor precisely how often taxis go by this bar with green lights, an indication that they are available. Maybe every few minutes. I think perhaps it's time for me to take my leave. I give Magella my share of the tab, and start the lengthy process of *la bise*. As luck would have it, a green taxi nears just as I step onto the sidewalk. I walk into the street and flag him down (to think I used to be afraid to do this!) and in half an hour and 10 euros I'm back in the tranquility of my own little neighborhood.

Life on the outside is endlessly fascinating. But it's good to have one's own sanctuary to come home to!

Life Happens Outside

Saturday night rolls around and I have no plans. A week of living with Ninon left me exhausted. Although force of habit pushed me to go to GCA and write, something told me I needed a break, so I spent a lazy afternoon lounging around home doing chores, tending my garden (that took about ten minutes) and laying on the couch in front of the fan with Bruno. This was evidently to be my summer with Bruno. I was now on book number four of the Chief of Police series. I sleep with Bruno. I wake up with Bruno. Today I spend a lazy Saturday afternoon lounging around with Bruno.

By evening I was trying to decide whether to have popcorn or scrambled eggs for dinner, about the only two things I had in the larder. Neither particularly tickled my fancy and I decided to pull myself, and Bruno, together and go to Le Clou.

I didn't bother with a reservation, thinking if I got there by eight, Thierry's crew would surely accommodate me. Accommodate me they did! Every table had a little yellow sticky, indicating a reservation, but the guys managed to secure my regular table on the terrace.

I propped Bruno up against my *carafe d'eau* and enjoyed the ambiance of So-Pi (sans Thierry tonight). My entrecote *"saignant" avec frites* was perfect but the ambiance was better. I found myself pulling out my notebook to jot down a few notes about the groups sitting around me.

An elderly trio adjacent to me; two *madams* and one *monsieur*. One of the women has clearly exceeded her plastic surgery quota and her very open eyes ogled me throughout their meal. For some reason she clearly wasn't happy with my being there. Because I was alone? Because I was drinking an entire bottle of

Côte du Rhône? Because I had the very good fortune to be dining with Bruno? Maybe her eyes just didn't close any further.

A British family sat at the table next to mine; Mom, Dad, boy teen and girl preteen. All wore glasses. Clearly they were genetically related. They spoke enough French to transact their requests. The teenage boy quickly got on my nerves. By the end of their meal, I wanted to murder him. I put it into my iphone translator and told my server *"s'il était mon fils, je devrais le tuer!"* They ordered fish and chips.

The two servers tag teamed each other in making sure I had everything I needed. The older of the two had both arms full of tattoos. I considered asking him for a reference for my grasshopper. His jeans are rolled up about 6 inches above his bare ankles. For some reason what works in Paris would never work in California. He's already got a significant belly and I only briefly wonder what tattoos are under that shirt. Back to Bruno. No gut, no tattoos, no bad habits.

The restaurant is very busy. I can stop worrying about Thierry and whether or not he'll be able to pay his bills! The boys turn away several people without reservations. They are running all night. Le Pirate (My two year old granddaughter Izzy tagged the bar manager a pirate when she was visiting and it's stuck) comes out to check on how I'm doing and if I need anything. Nobody seems in a hurry for me to move on so they can turn my table. Bruno and I are doing fine.

No dessert thank you, but I'd like a glass of cognac. The pirate brings it to me. Later Monsieur Rolled Up Jeans brings out the bottle and refills my glass. And then again. I think I will be swimming home.

The sun had long set and So-Pi has a special glow. If I were not so toasted from the Côte du Rhône and the cognac I would consider walking to LuLu White's for an absinthe nightcap. But I know that I'm at my alcohol limit for the day.

Nothing much happened Saturday night but it was perfect. Me. Bruno. The boys at Le Clou. Much better than popcorn for dinner.

Housekeeping

I've got to get out of my head. Out of Ninon's head. I find myself making stuff up; having conversations with people. I've had long one way conversations with Philippe, Daniele and even Caroleen. I think that I'm so used to my life filled with people all the time that conversations beyond the brief give and take of a restaurant or shop is weird after too long.

It may be good for figuring things out. Or maybe I'm making up what I'm figuring out! So by the end of the day yesterday, I figured out that Caroleen is probably actually crazy. She's certainly paranoid. And Daniele is an egotistical one note pony. And I really don't know anything about Philippe.

Yesterday evening I lost my internet connection. I was completely cut off from the outside world! After a day inside, in front of fans all day, I played Candy Crush (there I said it) for hours on end, moving from the rocking chair by the window to the couch. Never moving from in front of some blowing device. I had planned a quiet dinner of popcorn and an evening with Bruno. It was too hot outside to go anywhere. I deserve a break now and then, I rationalized. Then the wifi went out. Even though wifi didn't play into any of my extravagantly exciting plans for the night, I felt panicky!

I brushed my teeth, washed my face, packed my computer bag, put on real clothes and went to Cépage. Whew, a connection! I texted Stephanie with the problem and told her no amount of unplugging and plugging seemed to help. Her response: "Have an aperol spritz and if it isn't working in the morning give me a call." Well… pretty much. And no, it wasn't working in the morning. Personally, I think it's the cable box. I can see when I plug it back in it tries to connect and the lights flicker for a moment, but then no, it doesn't work. I'm no technician but….

So I get ready and pack up and head back to Cépage. Stephanie's response; "Hi K, Stéphane will pass by this morning as I myself have to leave Paris this morning (some personal problems, I hope to be back for our apero on Thursday."

This probably isn't the best time to remind her that our apero is on Friday so I let that slide. "Does Stéphane have a key? I won't be home." Back to the "you'll get it when you get it and you'll be happy with what you get" Parisian thing. And this is supposed to be from a friend. What if I was one of her other clients, here in Paris for one week? No wifi is not an option. No telephone or television isn't an option. And yes , I still love Stephanie (and hope everything is ok) but she seems to have a lot of personal problems or health problems or vacation!

But I guess I will get it when I get it and will be happy with whatever it is.

So it's not happening at Cépage. I catch an Uber to GCA. I'll write. Maybe I'll figure out what's going on with Philippe. On the way I feel like I'm going towards an end. So be it. I can move on. I can dive into Ninon. I think she has an important lesson or two for this loser.

I've never been to GCA in the morning. When I arrive it's just the new waiter, no Philippe. I take my working table and ask for a cafe creme. Darn. I forgot my kindle. I was going to bury myself in Ninon's own words this morning. *Pas de problème.* I will just look at the book I need on my Amazon Prime account. Nope. I don't have the password on my Mac. Darn. Everything is heading downwards. I'm scowling and frustrated when Philippe comes from the kitchen and comes over with kisses. "Ça va?" I scowl at him. (But still I notice something new as he kisses me; cologne." Can I be charming? Can I say good morning? No. I simply grunt "*j'ai un problème*". Nice. I'd want to be around me! Not.

OK, I've calmed down. Got my Amazon password so I can read Ninon's words online. I've had two cups of coffee so I'm adequately caffeinated. I've caught up with my emails and messages. And now I'm sitting comfortably and watching Philippe work. His morning is interesting. There are deliveries. Some he sends into the kitchen. A beverage delivery man arrives and a trap door opens under

Table 30. All the times I sat there for dinner and jazz and I never realized I was sitting on a trap door. He pushes a button and a lift comes up. The delivery man loads boxes of beverages on it and leaves. After a bit Philippe lowers the lift again and closes the trap door. Who knew the secrets of Table 30?

There are the regulars. They come in, grab a quick coffee, catch up on the latest gossip, read the front page of *Le Parisienne*, and then blow out. Some get hand-shakes. A few get la bise. I still can't get over the whole la bise thing. Women. Men. It makes no difference. And the transition from handshake to la bise. When does that happen? I tried to remember the first time Philippe gave me la bise. Was there something that changed that caused it to happen? Was it when I took the liberty of *tutoyering* him? Thierry has given me la bise a couple of times. Most of the time it's just a wave across the room and then later a small conversation. I remember the first time, being very surprised by the roughness of his beard. La bise has surprised me by letting me experience the scent of a man. When Stéphane Jego came in for la bise (why did I earn it from him?) I was surprised by his clean soapy smell at the end of a long lunch shift. Today I was surprised by Philippe's cologne. There's an intimacy provided by *la bise*. And then there's not. They seem to be rather freely given.

There's a much livelier selection of music on the stereo than in the afternoon. And Philippe always has a song on his lips. He sings along. He whistles along. I think of it as his personal soundtrack. This is definitely my preferred writing place. For whatever reason, I feel connected to something.

Wherever this goes or doesn't go. It's going to be hard to stop ... stop whatever it is I feel for this man.

Worlds Collide

Sitting in GCA. It's incredibly hot. I've just eaten lunch and I'm writing and finishing a bottle of rosé. Philippe is doing all of the tricks that keep me on the line; walking by making comments, making sure I have what I need, singing snippets of songs as he passes, and keeping an eye on my business. I looked up, and at the bar, enjoying a beer is Thierry!

"Thierry?" I call out!

"Ah!" he comes over... *la bise.*

"Would you like to sit?"

"No" he defers and points to my laptop. (Philippe watching all the time) I ask him about my St. Malo vacation idea. I fumble with terrible French and he assures me that it's a great idea and that it will be much cooler than Paris. He says five days is perfect and I will find great restaurants and will not be lonely being alone."

He heads back to the bar to finish his beer and read his paper. Before long Philippe is chatting him up.

When Philippe sits to enjoy his lunch I ask him to sit closer, so I can ask him questions. About a vacation. It's a disaster. I think he said St. Malo is good. Five days is not too much. Good food. Good wine. But he wouldn't sit closer. I don't want to intrude on his lunch. And he doesn't want to intrude on my work. I ask him if he knows Thierry.

"Non, how do you know him?"

"In a past life." I blow it off. That seems a little upsetting to him. Perhaps my Cardinal Richelieu tactic was as big a disaster as it was for him, securing Ninon. But he got Marion. And me?

Question: Why is Thierry drinking a beer at 2:12 at GCA on Wednesday and not at Le Clou? Part of a mystery. Why GCA? This is the second time I've seen him pass by GCA, but he lives in the 13ème. And he works two blocks away. Why isn't he at work?

Question 2: Old man sits at Philippe's table while he's eating lunch. Who is he? He was here earlier. Why did Philippe decline sitting at the table close to me. He's facing me. Just 10 feet away. So obviously… what obviously? He goes from happy and flirty to annoyed and seeming a bit jealous. We can't have a decent conversation in French… or English. My four hours here has been a roller coaster ride. I know no more than I did when I came. Maybe less.

Question 3: Shall I have a boule of ice cream? And where do I go for dinner tonight. It's too damn hot. I believe my internet is working, per Stephanie. But who knows?

An Alcohol Fueled Day

I had an interesting day yesterday but maybe most interesting is the way it affected me. I had made a lunch date with Evelyn, a woman I met through an old childhood friend. Evelyn, like me, had recently retired and decided to move to Paris. While it may seem like we have a lot in common, that may be where the commonality ends.

We both had held executive positions and had faced the challenges a woman finds in climbing the career ladder in Corporate America. We both were single, me long time divorced, she widowed, I don't know how long, she didn't really seem to want to talk about that. We both had grown children and grandchildren. But most significantly, we had both somehow chosen Paris.

Everyone comes to Paris for different reasons. Everyone stays in Paris for other different reasons. It can be very hard to articulate the reasons.

We agreed to meet at the brasserie at Hotel de Crillon, one of Paris's select five, six, whatever the lofty number of stars is. Evelyn's requirement was that we choose an air conditioned restaurant. Air conditioning in Paris is a rare commodity and is often considered an indulgent luxury, typically required by tourists and foreigners. For example, I am sitting in GCA right now writing. It's 95 degrees and blistering hot in Paris. But there is no "*clim*". The windows are all open, people sit on the terrace and Philippe has, as a concession, opened the awnings all the way to create maximum shade. I will admit, it was awfully nice to walk in the front doors of the luxurious hotel and feel the blast of cool air.

The Crillon is indeed beautiful. Flowers abound. Comfortable sitting areas are artfully and cleverly arranged and I made my way back to the restaurant. Most of the guests were dining on the courtyard terrace in the center of the hotel. Although the tables were all covered by huge umbrellas, it was still 95 degrees. I asked to be seated inside, where it was air conditioned! After all, that was the criteria in choosing the venue. I was about fifteen minutes early and asked for *une carafe d'eau* and a glass of wine, something like a Côte du Rhône. What was presented and poured was called something different, but at 20 euro a glass, it was obviously decent. (I'm paying 20 euro right now for the bottle of rosé I'm enjoying at GCA). I tried to connect to the wifi and while the server was very helpful, it wasn't happening. No problem. I'll just take a taxi home.

Evelyn showed up right on time at 2:00 pm. We did *la bise* and exchanged pleasantries. Then she launched into the "What brought you to Paris?!"

I laughed, "Right to the point. And the million dollar question that is difficult to answer! I was going to ask you the same thing."

The waiter arrived and asked if we knew what we wanted. "Whatever that is she's drinking," she said.

And to eat?

"I'm sorry to be such an American. I want the steak and fries."

"Not a problem" the waiter responds. "*Steak frites* are very French!"

"With *béarnaise* sauce please"

I order the poulpe with chorizo and a salad. And ask if we can just get a bottle of the wine.

"*Bien sûr!*"

Then she shared with me that on our previous meeting I had ambushed her with questions. I was completely taken aback. I'm sure that a wall of some kind went up but I found myself putting on my professional face and looking like I would like further elaboration. In reality I was thinking, "WTF? We had just met, we had similar circumstances and I was trying to get to know you!" But clearly that wasn't something she was used to or comfortable with.

She asked me what I thought about Judith, the other part of the-living-in-Paris group at the dinner.

"Well, I don't think I will have an ongoing friendship with her."

"But what did you think!"

"I thought she was nice enough but like many Americans who have been in Paris for a number of years she believes she knows everything about living here and I found that some of the things she said are just wrong."

"So what did you think of her?" She wasn't going to let me get away without a frank and preferably harsh critique.

I shrugged.

"She was completely self absorbed! She's one of those pretty girls who gets away with being pretty and getting what they want for years. Then the day comes when they aren't necessarily pretty anymore and then what? What will she do then? She went from husband - who evidently she's still using to promote her business but who cheated on her - to boyfriend. She lost her job and told us far far too much personal information, and by the way, the French do NOT talk about their personal lives. Then she moved in with this Luis character who evidently is happy to support her. Again, getting along on her looks. And for most of what she said being wrong, it was ALL wrong."

OK, I guess she had a stronger opinion than I did.

"We went for drinks after dinner on rue de Bac, I don't know… somewhere where Mitch wanted to go. You had gone home. After awhile I had to leave and go meet my family. I couldn't show up coming from the metro. My son-in-law is very well placed and it would not do for them to see me arrive in any manner other than their view of me. So I had ordered an Uber Black. And I was concerned that the street was too small for the driver to find me. It seemed to be a walking only street."

"Were you perhaps on rue Cler?" I asked.

"Yes! Exactly! So the driver was speaking to me in French and I asked her to please talk to him. She told me, 'you have to walk over to this spot so you can find the car', but the driver was standing right next to me! Right at my shoulder! So she obviously didn't know what she was talking about!"

Unforgivable? I guess.

"So, what brought YOU to Paris?" I asked. Haha, I cleverly sidestepped HER questions. And she fell for it. I guess I wasn't ambushing her anymore.

"Well, I retired and I had to decide where I was going to live. I have a home in Atlanta, I have a beautiful condo in Marina del Rey. But if I live in Marina del Rey I will always be that Corporate Director of XYZ Corporation. I wanted to open a fresh door. Somewhere where nobody knew who I was. Where I could do whatever whenever.

I have a son and four grandchildren in Georgia. I have a daughter and grandson in Ibiza but it's just too hard to get out of there; a taxi, a bus, a boat, a plane. I thought of Madrid. I thought of Barcelona. I thought of London, of course. But it was always Paris."

OK, that doesn't really tell me why, other than there are direct flights.

Our food arrives.

Evelyn has an absolutely fabulous apartment in the Marais, adjacent to the Port de l'Arsenal, a pretty bit of waterway that runs from the Canal St. Martin to the Seine. Her apartment is huge, 140 meters (mine is 54), three bedrooms, a massive salon and dining room, big windows, modern kitchen, two full American style bathrooms. When I put in the digicode to enter the lobby I knew it was going to be something grand. Marble. Everywhere. A lovely old fashioned cage elevator with a bench in it. And a concierge! I would love to have a concierge; someone to accept my Amazon deliveries! Someone to arrange a handyman when I needed something done. Someone to ….

The same group of us who had met for lunch in the 7ème were invited to her home for lunch. We were instructed to leave everything on the tables. The cleaner would take care of it all. Then she rushed JoJo off to a pre arranged appointment to get her hair cut, colored and a much needed facial.

Goodness, was she paying for this extravagance? Did JoJo know what she had in store for her? Clearly Evelyn didn't do anything on the cheap. She left Mitch and Judith and I in the apartment telling us, just lock up when you leave.

Mitch, JoJo's easy going agreeable husband, had worked for Evelyn in a past life. He clearly held her in great esteem. After a short time I asked Judith, "So what do you think this place costs?" Evelyn told her that she had hired an agent to find her an apartment. He wanted desperately to put her in the 8th or the 16th, both chi chi residential areas, resplendent with embassies and five star hotels. But she felt too removed. When she found this apartment in the Marais she knew she had found her home. She took a three year lease and had her belongings shipped. She arranged with the concierge to hang her art and replace the lighting fixtures she didn't care for.

But back to the question at hand, "What do you think this place costs?"

Judith responded, "Probably 2500 euro!"

"What? No way!" I blurted. "I pay 2500 euro. This has to be 5,000 at least!"

"No! How big is your apartment?" I give her the details and assure her that I feel it's appropriately priced and she is aghast. "No, way, you're being ripped off! You should pay no more than 1500 euro!"

"But it's furnished and all the utilities are paid for; phone! water! electricity! Wifi! And I get a weekly cleaning (I lied, trying not to appear too ripped off, it's only bi-weekly). In my defense, I have looked at the area comps and most one bedroom furnished apartments in my quartiere are in the same ballpark, maybe slightly higher. But most importantly, I love my apartment. I love my location. I love my view. Simply no other apartment will do. The comps in the neighborhood are slightly more expensive and they are NOT in my perfect location!

But more importantly, there is no way this massive and elegant apartment in the Marais is 2500 euro. So I had to find out.

As Evelyn continued to trash the absent Judith, I mentioned a couple of things that she was wrong about. I didn't want to out right ask her what her apartment cost but…

"She thinks I'm am being ripped off on my rent." I dropped.

"Well, what are you paying?"

"2500 euro, but it includes…"

"For how many square meters?"

"54"

"Sounds reasonable."

The waiter comes by to see how we are doing. "Can I have some more of this béarnaise sauce?" she asks.

"*Bien sûr* Madame!"

"Would you mind me asking what you pay?"

She squirmed but responded "4500 euro. Plus I pay power of course. And 45 euro a week for the cleaner." (Honey, you are ripping that poor woman off!) So bottom line, she's probably coming in around 5,000 euro. I pretty much nailed it.

Evelyn has a three year lease. She asks me, "So tell me about this visa business. How did you get a long term visa?"

"You don't have a visa?" I asked, surprised.

"No, I didn't think it was a big deal. I just have to leave France every 90 days."

"And stay gone for 90 days!"

The restaurant staff was hovering. We were the only ones left in the restaurant. Maybe we should take this to the bar. She took her wine. I wanted a Sidecar.

Seated in the bar our conversation turned to men. She told me she would love to find a nice relationship. But she's a sixty something year old grandmother.

"Are you kidding?! I ask. "How old do you think you look?" Evelyn clearly has the visage of a woman who has been pampered; facials, best hair care.

"I don't know" she answers.

"Seriously, you could pass for 45."

"NO! Do you know how old I am?"

"I assume you're around my age."

"And that is?"

"67"

"OK. But no."

"Yes! So tell me about this restaurant manager you mentioned. The one who is always glad to see you and who brings you your glass of red wine in the late evenings."

"Oh, he's in his 40s, pudgy, but he's a restaurant manager!"

"But you just told me you want to be somewhere where all the windows are open, nobody knows who you are, you can do whatever you like. Maybe you like to flirt with a 40 something year old restaurant manager!"

She tells me about a professional organization she's just been invited to participate in. She's had several lunches with the former ambassador to someplace and they were somehow summarizing their relationship.

"I think you are very protected." he said, correctly. "We have had several lunches now and you don't let down your guard."

"We have had six lunches, monsieur, and I can tell you where they all were.

"You can tell me where we ate lunch?" he asked.

"Yes, we ate at L'Oiseau Blanc at the Peninsula Hotel, at the Ritz, at Le George V, at Le Meurice, at the Plaza Athénée…"

"You can tell me all of these restaurants, but you can't tell me about you. About who you really are and what you want."

She sidestepped the question and avoided completely where Monsieur intended to take this conversation…to the bedroom.

"Why?" I asked. "Why don't you allow yourself a little pleasure? Why not be a new person?"

"Do you know that you are very quick to jump in with reponses?" she asked.

Well I have no idea how to respond to this. Is it a criticism? Constructive advice? I think I said nothing. What could I say?

"Maybe if you gave people longer to complete their thoughts…"

"I'd get more information?" OMG, I just did it Finished her sentence. But nobody anywhere had ever called me on this before.

Then she started telling me about an important man from Saudi Arabia who was, what.. courting her? He had three wives but he could still have one more! He was handsome and incredibly charming and she seemed to be drawn to him.

I kept completely quiet. What could I add? And I was still bruised from her admonition that I was too quick to finish her sentences.

I ordered another Sidecar.

Over the course of the Sidecar she continued to talk about the Arab. That I was "pretty enough, cute blonde hair, obviously needed to lose…" but she wasn't telling me anything I didn't already know. What was the most difficult conversation I had during my career? She once wrote a short story and actually won a contest for it.

I just drank my Sidecar. It was good, but at 27 euro per they should have been good!

"Oh look!" I said, glancing at my phone! "I have to run. I have a rendezvous with *mes amies* at Le Terrass at 6:30." (Had we really been there for four hours?)

Evelyn was headed back to the US for a month. She had to get this visa thing straightened out.

"I guess our next lunch will be in September! I'll be gone from the 2nd to the 10th but then…"

We kissed goodbye. She headed to the *métro*. I grabbed a taxi to Le Terrass to meet friendly fire.

I woke with a fuzzy head. A shared bottle of wine at Le Crillon, two sidecars, two bottles of champagne at Le Terrass followed by a bottle of much less expensive Pinot Noir and a short swim home. I peeked an eye open to get an idea of the time. It was quite light; maybe 8 or 9 am.

I closed my eyes and ran through the happenings of the previous day. Evelyn who put me in a very strange place. My lovely friends at the Terrass who adore me. My phone beeped. An invitation to dinner with Elliott and friends. But the conversations with Evelyn wouldn't stop running through my head. Why was I allowing it to dominate my feelings about myself and my life in Paris?

You need to lose some weight. You jump too quickly to finish sentences. You're missing so much.

Canicule

I learned a new French word this week. Heatwave. And what a bizarre one it has been. For that matter, what a bizarre summer it has been.

Before I forget, here's another new French phrase; *Avoir le cul bordé de nouilles*. It means essentially "to be a lucky son of a bitch". Literally? To have an ass full of noodles.

Parisians eschew la *climatisation* (or more familiarly *la clim*), claiming that it's really only hot one or two days a year. So far it has been hot one hundred and two days this summer! OK, maybe that's a petite exaggeration. But it has been hot hot hot way too long.

So yesterday when I headed out to work at GCA my phone told me it was 97 degrees, about 37 degrees c. *La clim* in my bedroom is set for 17 degrees c. I could have worked in my room. But no, in my imagination the words come ever so much more freely when the lovely Philippe is in my line of view.

I collected my *bisous* and took my usual table, where miraculously a (hot) breeze seemed to circulate around me. The windows were all thrown open wide, the awnings on the terrace extended to their maximum to protect people on the terrace from the direct sun. The marche at Place d'Anvers was going full storm. I considered a brief shop there but was too lazy to walk across the street.

Philippe set me up with a bottle of water, a bottle of rosé on ice, another bucket of ice for my glass and my water, and eventually the tarte a lieu that it was just too hot to eat very much of. But I wrote. I wrote for four hours! I wrote through a sudden monsoon which left the air humid and hot.

At 5:30 ish I hopped into an Uber and headed to Saint Ouen to meet Elliott and friends at a hip new hotel near the brocantes. "It's too hot to stay home so I snapped up their offer for an air conditioned room plus extras for 99 euro." The extras included a pizza, a bottle of rosé, breakfast and a 2 pm late checkout the next day. Sounds awfully good! But I have *la clim* so I'll just come for drinks and dinner thanks.

I taught the bartender to make a perfect Sidecar and joined Elliott out on the terrace. Soon Siobhan came. Elliott told us about two twenty something American girls who would be joining us; one a promising singer trying to make a career for herself in Paris. The other he said was a model. Then we heard about the various models and ballerinas who Elliott had dated in his young life and the impact they had upon his choices and habits later in life. Personally my expectations for the two were very low.

The girls, J'aime (!!) and Jenny turned out to be lovely. J'aime, the model told us she was an actress in LA and was hoping to expand her career in Europe. She had big beautiful brown eyes and a friendly open and interested attitude.

More bottles of wine arrived. Then prosecco. I was done. I said my adieus and grabbed an Uber home. I had the absolute best conversation with my Uber driver. He raved about my having accomplished the French language so completely and quickly and couldn't believe how brave I was to move to Paris all by myself. I had to use the English word for "*pas courageux;* indulgent" Ha! Google tells me it's *indulgent*! It's interesting that people who I pay all rave about my mastery of French. My friends, not so much. Magalie nitpicks my genders and plurals, "*les vacances*", she admonishes. "Vacances sont toujours plural" That's good. I need someone who doesn't let me get away with mistakes. As Daniele Chandelier said "will she be TOUGH!" Magalie is tough but loving. And she did say that I am so much better than before.

I pour myself out of my Uber with a *"cinq étoile! Et une sixième étoile pour la clim!"* Five stars! And a sixth star for the air conditioning!

He laughs. *"Cinq étoile pour vous aussi!"*

I take extra care crossing the street because I know I have had a lot to drink. I step up to my door and dig in my laptop bag. OH FUCK! Can I really have forgotten to put my keys in my bag? SHIT SHIT SHIT!

No keys.

I walk up to Cépage and sit at a table on the terrace and empty out everything in my bag; laptop, notebooks, kindle, wallet, iphone, headphones, assorted euros and used kleenexes. No keys.

I texted Stephanie. No response. The manager comes out and asks what I would like. I told him my problem.

"I could call the pompiers?" he suggests. Maybe they could break into my apartment for me.

I don't think that's a very good idea.

I check Le Terrass hotel on my phone. They have rooms.

I make my tipsy way down rue Caulaincourt to the hotel. Even though it's 11 pm it's blistering hot outside and the rain and hail has made mushy work of the fallen tiny flowers and pollen that have been snowing on Montmartre all week. By the time I arrive at Le Terrass I'm a sweaty mess.

"J'espère que vous avez une chambre ce soir! J'ai laissé mes clés dans mon appartement et j'habite seule!" I hope that you have a room tonight. I left my keys in my apartment and I live alone.

I'm in luck. They have two rooms. I can get one for a meager 200 euro. "You will sleep very well tonight, Madame, with *la climitasion!*"

I should have stayed at the MOB Hotel! I could have gotten a pizza and a bottle of rosé for half the price!

"J'ai la clim chez moi" I have air conditioning at home!

"C'est vrai? That's very unusual!" He adds "the good news is, you are a *Parisienne!* You don't have to pay the city tax!"

OK, I guess there's a rainbow in every storm.

My room is fine. But I'm not in the mood to enjoy it. I peel off my clothes and lay naked on the bed. The air conditioner doesn't seem to want to turn on but the room is cool enough. What's up with that? My phone is nearly dead and I have no charger. A text comes from Stephanie. "I'm not in Montmartre but Stéphane can come let you in now if you want. He can be there in 10 or 15 minutes. Let me know if you're not there so he can go back to sleep."

Poor Stéphane seems to pick up a lot of Stephanie's loose ends. And mine too now it seems.

I reply, "I'm at the Terrass for the night. Brian comes tomorrow at noon. Can you please let him know he'll need to let me in?"

I turn on CNN. There's an upside! It's dismal and I turn it off and pull Bruno into bed with me. "You get to sleep with me naked tonight, Bruno!" I have no toothbrush, no hairbrush, no pajamas… I'm a mess.

I spent a restless night, resorting to Bruno at 2 am, 3:30 am, 4 am… Every time I noticed myself adding things to the story I tried to sleep again.

At 8 am I get another text from Stephanie, just before my phone is about to die. "Brian will be there at 12:30 or I can come earlier if you like." I hate to be an inconvenience but… yes please! We agree to meet at my apartment at 11.

I hike up the hill to Cépage at 10. I arrive a sweaty mess again. Laurent brings me coffee, juice and a croissant. At 11 I go sit at the bus stop in front of my apartment.

Stephanie arrives fresh and adorable in a little mini skirt and tank top. "Did you walk up the thousand steps?" I ask.

"Yes! and usually I get to the top panting but today I feel great!" She looks great.

She lets us into the lobby, into the second door, beyond which I could not get. I take the elevator. She takes the stairs. I'm in my apartment!

Off she goes for a weekend away to Reims. She and Stéphane are staying at a nice hotel with a pool and having dinner at Domaine Les Crayères. I hope Stéphane is getting something nice for all of this covering Stephanie's ass. She says he's like a brother. I hope it's an incestious brother relationship!

I brush my teeth and wash my face and brush my hair and change my clothes. Not enough time for a shower. I pull myself together enough to go out before Brian arrives for this week's cleaning.

I repacked my computer bag with my fully charged laptop, iphone and KEYS, which will forever henceforth live in the pocket of this bag. I take out my trash and head down to Les Loups for lunch and writing.

Sitting on the terrace, right next to the door is Caroleen. I seem to run into her or F everywhere these days! I ignore her and walk into the restaurant. After a bit she comes in and chats with the barman. I don't give her the time of day. Such is life in a small village.

La Fiesta

I take back every snarky thing I ever said about Elliott. *Oui*, he talks a lot. And, *oui*, he could give others just the smallest opportunity to speak. But this weekend he went miles and miles above and beyond.

Friday night (THE Friday night before the big lock out) during the hail storm while drinking on the terrace, I mentioned the thing I miss the most in Paris is good Mexican food. That afternoon at GCA Philippe was discussing some new menu items with the chef and I overheard them talking about a Mexican salad.

"Mexican!" I blurted out. "That is what I miss the most in Paris!"

Of course, Philippe was not interested in my advice. He never wants my advice!

But Elliott took my remark and ran with it.

"Anytime you want, just say the word and I'll make you a great Mexican meal. The only problem is my kitchen is too small and our apartment is too filled with books (evidently he has 5,000 books and is in the process of beginning to give them away) to host anyone right now. But I'd be happy to do so at anyone else's house."

"*Chez moi!*" I said. By this time I had had a bottle of wine with lunch and was on my second Sidecar at the MOB Hotel.

"How many people can you seat around your table?"

My table is a coffee table that leverages up to be a makeshift dining table. I've never seated anyone AT it before but I do a mental configuring. "Six?"

Charlotte warned me about the feasts that Elliott cooks in other people's kitchens! But the die is cast and all I have to do is provide the space, the kitchen, tableware and the music. Siobhan will bring the ice. Elliott will bring everything to prepare the feast and to make pitchers of margaritas. The girls will bring their loveliness. Sounds good. The only downside is that I was hoping to catch a little bit of the Tour de France arriving in Paris, but I probably never would have gone anyway. It's one of those you can't get there from here things and hopefully the last big event that creates havoc on the streets of Paris for awhile.

Thus my first dinner party was born.

Saturday I finally got home from leaving my apartment that I had finally just gotten back to after the lock out debacle and wanted nothing more than a short nap. Bing. A text. From Siobhan; "I found ice. Can I bring it to you now?" Maybe I'll ignore the text for a bit. Bing. A PM on another app. Bing. A voice message. Clearly I need to respond.

"Sorry," I type into my phone. "I was napping. Yes, of course, come anytime."

"On my way"

Two minutes later, "The door doesn't seem to be working." I had given her the wrong digicode.

"I'll be right down." I carefully grab the keys and head down to let her in.

She's standing outside with a huge bag of ice talking to a friend. I guess I'm going to have more company than I thought! But the friend was just coincidentally passing by. She introduces us, we do *la bise* and she heads off to wherever she was going when she ran into Siobhan in front of *chez moi*.

Siobhan unloads several bags of ice into my fortunately empty freezer.

"Would you like a glass of wine? Or prosecco if you prefer?"

"Which would you prefer? Which would you rather have an open bottle of in your fridge?" She opens the fridge. "Wow, a nice big fridge! Can I make a suggestion? Put everything into this drawer here and leave Elliott lots of open space."

"I guess the wine." I say.

I take out a bottle and open it, pouring each of us a glass. I put the bottle on the table. She pulls her feet up under her on the sofa and makes herself at home. I wistfully say goodbye to my nap.

The afternoon morphs into a long discussion of Siobhan's misguided love life. After a couple of hours she tells me she's going to dinner with Elliott and Joan, would I like to come? And she has to go home and take a shower and put some makeup on.

"No thank you," I say. Elliott on Friday and Elliott on Sunday is already over my allotment of Elliott. "I've got a reservation at Le Clou."

We had agreed to start the Fiesta at 3:30 so I had a leisurely morning to do the very few things I needed to do. I took inventory of my table and glassware. I could manage six easily but the guest list has swelled to seven. We would have to use some mismatched dishes and glassware. I could take the odd place settings for myself. Not a problem.

I put away my personal things, made sure that there was nothing embarrassing in my bedroom or bathroom. Everything was stuck in drawers and closets. The apartment looked good. Elliott texted me with questions and comments throughout the morning and early afternoon.

"Do you have gas or electric stove top?"

"Gas"

"Do you have spoons and bowls for 9? Ariella and beau are coming."

Uh oh.

"We may have to do buffet style. My table looks like it expands though!" I send him a picture of hinges on the edge of the coffee table top. "I've never done it though. Siobhan can help me figure it out."

A few minutes later, "Ariella and beau aren't coming. Seven will be perfect. Do you have gas or electric stove top?"

"Still gas."

"Oh sorry! I was cooking and missed that. Yay! Perfect."

"I'm headed to the market. Is there anything you need?"

"Nope! All is good."

I make a quick trip to the market for napkins, toilet paper and some plastic cups.

J'aime texts to say, "I'm so excited about the fiesta! I should be there between 4 and 4:30."

A few minutes later from Jenny, "I am working. I should be there around 4:30. Very excited! Oh, by the way, my boyfriend is coming."

At this point I am finished worrying. "Great! See you soon!"

Siobhan arrives and is a whirlwind of activity. "OK girl wonder", I intreat "Help me figure out how to raise and extend this table.

Siobhan is nothing if not capable. The table is raised and opened. It's huge! We can easily seat 8, as long as two people sit on the sofa. We're only short one chair. Somebody gets a stool, which is really one of my little night tables which has doubled in the past as a Christmas tree stand. Looks great! Just a little crowded with that big table in the small room but it works.

"I'm not sure that the intercom phone works or what button to push to let people in." I confess.

Siobhan lifts the phone at the precise moment Elliott has buzzed. She pushes a button and he's on his way in. I step out into the hallway to greet him at the elevator when he comes up the stairs.

"You didn't take the elevator?"

"No! But the stuff is in there." I had forgotten that Elliot doesn't do elevators after getting stuck incident.

He opens the just arrived elevator and pulls out a large carrier bag and a trolley. "Joan will be along shortly. She went to help a friend move a heavy table." He peruses my kitchen. "This is very nice!" he exclaims. He opens the fridge, "I love you, Katherine! You have provided me with an empty fridge!"

"You can thank Siobhan for that!" I said. "She suggested I make space for you."

He unloads his groceries and soon the counter is covered with groceries, bottles and other things I haven't even identified yet. But it looks very promising!

He tests the burners and pokes through the drawers for pots, pans and cooking utensils that he needs. He puts on an apron and sets to work. He's got big freezer bags full of sauces, marinating meat, carnitas, and other goodies waiting to be integrated into the fiesta. He's got thermoses and bottles of wine and bottles of tequila.

Soon Joan arrives with another carrier bag. Out comes a massive cocktail shaker. For the margaritas.

While he's cooking Elliott takes pauses long enough to tell us what to expect from the meal. "As with wine, I always lead with the lightest foods and move towards the richer, more complex courses. So while most Mexican meals start with chips and salsas, you won't find them on my table until the third course. I don't want you filling up on them and not being able to really appreciate the two earlier courses."

We nod in understanding but I'm frankly eyeing the bag of freshly fried tortilla chips.

It's 3:30 and we are still missing some of our guests. "I know Joao will be a little late, he's always late!" laments Elliott, "But where are those girls!"

"Oh, they texted me, they will be here around 4 or 4:30"

Oops. Elliott's face flashes from irritation to rage. "There is NO excuse! We said 3:30 and I slaved to make sure that things are ready at a prescribed time!"

"My fault" I sheepishly confess. "They told me that yesterday. I should have told you."

"That's still inexcusable! We talked about this on Friday. This is simply not ok!"

Joao arrives stylishly late and when 4:30 comes Elliott decides that we will begin with the margaritas without them. The shaker is shaken and the glasses we have been using for champagne (thank you Siobhan) are used for the fresh margaritas that Elliott has mixed. We toast and appreciate them while Elliott tells us about the one hundred and thirty year old tequila that he got on his last trip to Mexico. It's evidently only available from a specific part of Mexico just outside of ... (or at Bevmo for $69 a bottle I find later. Note to self: get a bottle on my next trip to San Francisco as a thank you gift.)

Next up; small glasses serve as bowls and appear on our plates with soup. "This is a deconstructed tamale" Elliott tells us. "See what you think."

It's actually delicious! And yes, it tastes like a very good tamale.

"Wow!" I exclaim! "Elliott, Paris needs this restaurant!"

He grins.

"Seriously! I know that opening a restaurant is not something you ever want to do, but Paris really does need this restaurant. This is Michelin quality stuff! I especially like the way the spicy heat doesn't hit until you've already been eating it for awhile."

Elliott beams! "This is the result of repeated iterations of attempting to get this exactly right. I'm glad you enjoy it."

Elliott starts to open a bottle of white wine but changes his mind and puts it back in the fridge, selecting another instead. "I think that this is the white we should start with." He fills our glasses and then serves up the next course; shrimp mango tacos. He's even prepared a separate smaller bowl of it for the vegetarian girl, who still hasn't arrived. The tacos are small and delicious.

Again, I say "the perfect next course in this restaurant that Paris needs!" These things are Michelin size and quality. The wine of course is perfectly matched.

The next course is where the Michelin comparison ends and things just get good and real. And really good. Out come the freshly fried chips, a huge bowl of fresh guacamole, bowls of red, green and white salsas, sour cream, grated cheeses, beans with meat, beans without meat (for the vegetarian girl). And the second white wine, a stellar white Burgundy. OMG! This is what I've been missing. The chips are perfect. The salsas and guacamole are fresh and amazing, even better than anything I have found at home. I didn't even try the beans. My satisfaction quota reached its limit.

And the girls and the boyfriend arrived. Boyfriend was introduced and *la bise* performed by all. We scooted around to make room and Elliott happily ran into the kitchen to bring the little margaritas, then the deconstructed tamales followed by the mango tacos, with and without shrimp. Where was the flash of rage? It was gone and Elliott was again the perfect chef/host. The girls and boyfriend were oblivious to the trouble and irritation their tardiness had caused. I was fine. I was eating those perfect chips with their perfect accompaniments.

Elliott said the next course would require about fifteen minutes of cooking. We all enjoyed the rest of the white Burgundy and talked with only two quick pauses to fan the air when the smoke alarms blared. A magnum of old vine Morey-Saint-Denis was opened and Elliott tasted it. He went back to finish whatever it was he was doing to prepare this course while the wine breathed. J'aime poured herself a glass.

"NO!" admonished Siobhan. "It's breathing! You have to wait for Elliott to pour!" J'aime quickly gulped it down so she wouldn't be caught by Elliott. Siobhan looked disgusted.

Elliott brought out a foil wrapped pile of hot corn tortillas and a platter of sliced roasted steak. "The ones on the left are rare, the ones in the middle medium and the ones on the right are well done."

I took two corn tortillas and a couple of pieces of the rare. I added some of the green tomatillo salsa and sipped my glass of red. Tres contente.

Poke a fork in me, I'm done. But no. Elliott brings out course number five, a big bowl filled with foil wrapped burritos! The big flour tortillas have been pre-wrapped and are full of spanish rice, beans, beef, jalapenos, who knows what else and are about nine inches long and as big around as a baseball bat. There are two labeled "earth goddess" that are for the vegetarian girl. I peeled off the foil from one end of mine and cut off a small bit. "I'm going to save the rest for later!" I said.

"Not a problem" says Elliott "I've got more here for you to keep and for everyone to take home." He holds up a plastic bag with several more of the beasts.

At some point I stand up and start to clear away some of the dishes. "No! Sit down" blurt Joan, Siobhan and Joao in unison. They jump up and clear and start to wash and dry glasses and dishes. The pretty girls sit at the table continuing to look pretty. In the meantime, Elliott is making a very big deal about opening a very special and old bottle of tequila - different from the one that was a million years old and very hard to find - for us to sip while we digest. The dishwashers are back in their seats and someone produces a cell phone with a game app. Elliott goes first. He swipes up and then holds the phone to his forehead, facing us, while a series of words or phrases appear. We give him clues so he can guess the words. When he gets one right (or gives up) he tilts the phone quickly downward and a new word appears. We all shout clues madly at him and he gets maybe three right. Next up is Joao, then Siobhan, then me…. and we go around the table two or three times, refilling our tequila glasses all the while. It is interesting how harder or easier the game seems to be depending on one's country of origin, age or for that matter attractiveness! The French boy was a disaster. Joao, growing up in Brazil but spending many years in London and Paris and being very well educated did much better, but still struggled with some cultural references. Elliott, Joan and I did well. And the pretty girls were a disaster.

Joao disappeared for a few minutes and returned from the night market downstairs with a bottle of whisky and we all started to work on that. The pretty girls decided they had to head off to another party. And eventually Elliott and Joan headed home.

Joao and I put away all the leftovers and finished the last of the washing up while Siobhan turned the massive table back to a coffee table. We had finished off the whisky so we opened the only bottle of alcohol left in the house, a bottle of inexpensive prosecco in the fridge and talked. Siobhan ranted about the pretty girls and the boyfriend.

"Who comes to a dinner party, first of all an hour and a half late, and EMPTY HANDED?! It's simply not done. I can't believe that Elliott let them get away with that. And for him to jump up and wait on them like that, preparing all of the courses that they had missed while we waited. And the boyfriend... he may look good but he was so rude! I went into the bathroom after him and the seat was up and there was piss all over the place!" She tutted and huffed some more and then promptly fell asleep on the couch.

Joao and I talked.

Finally Siobhan awoke from her brief beauty sleep and she and Joao headed out into the night. It was just past midnight. I looked around my apartment. It was cleaner than when the guests arrived!

I would call that a successful dinner party! I didn't have to shop, cook or clean up.

Petites Vacances

The entire country of France is suffering from *la canicule*. Warnings were being issued by people who issue such warnings to stay out of the heat, stay hydrated, stay cool. People with jobs outside were cautioned not to go to work.

I looked at the weather forecasts and there was one small area of the country where the forecasts were more moderate; Bretagne! So St. Malo it was! I booked a small vacation taking me out of the City. I had waited too long to stay for the five nights I had originally intended so decided I would leave on Wednesday and return on Friday night. That way, if I regretted my decision, I wouldn't be stuck there too long.

Tuesday Philippe asked, "So you go to St. Malo tomorrow?"

"*Oui*"

"*Pour une semaine?*"

"*Non! Seulement trois jours.*"

"*C'est parfait! Trois jours.*"

I'm not sure why he endorsed the three day option but it made me feel like I was doing the right thing.

The train ride was great. After getting out of the Paris the countryside got greener and prettier the farther away we got. The last thirty minutes of the ride was stunning with every possible shade of green. The trees were lush and the ground covered with thick masses of berry brambles. The train followed the path of a small river and the forested areas broke every mile or so for huge pastures with cows. Tiny farms looked exactly like what I would expect French country farms to look like, an old tractor, some geese wandering freely, chickens cooped, goats and sheep. I was revelling in the magic of my mini break.

We arrived at St Malo station. It didn't look like much, but train stations rarely do. I was in *voiture 1*. I grabbed my rolling suitcase and deboarded. It was a long train. *Voiture 1* was the closest at Gare Montparnasse, but the farthest in St. Malo; about 40 *voitures* far! On the barren (and long) voie running alongside the train it was hot. But the station was small and the taxi queue was right out front, sans taxis. I was number three in line.

The longer we waited, the hotter it got. Customer number two had a cat in a pet carrier who grumbled and howled and meowed unhappily. Finally a taxi came and customer number one was off. After a hot and howling ten minutes Monsieur *le chat* finally was off on his way. My turn came after another seven or so minutes.

"*Le Grand Hotel des Thermes*" I told the driver.

The taxi skirted the old walled city and headed east. We quickly arrived at the stately old hotel. What a Grand Old Dame she was indeed. Sitting on the oceanfront, the massive building was perhaps the most impressive in St. Malo, short of the old fort, which shamefully I never visited because I didn't leave the premisses for the next forty eight hours.

A bellman insisted on taking my one little rolling bag and heading toward my room. I protested. "Just tell me the number and I will find it."

"No, Madame, I will take you."

And I never would have found it. Up one elevator, across the Bar La Passarelle, where I got my first impressive glimpse of the sea, down a long corridor, turning into another, then into another, then up (or was it down?) another elevator to a small corridor that housed my room. I hadn't paid the extra hundred euro a night that was required for a seafront room and in retrospect I was grateful. I had a nice balcony facing a garden of the also impressive home next door. It was lovely and quiet and although I could hear the waves in the background, the more imposing sound was birds; pigeons cooing and seagulls crying. And it was blessedly cool.

I sat on my balcony for awhile and gathered my thoughts. Then I went in search of sustenance and the Bar with that amazing view. I snagged a window seat in the room near the grand piano and a chubby young barman came over to welcome me and ask what I would like.

"Puis-je avoir une Sidecar?"

"Desole, Madame, non," he said as he shoved the menu closer to me.

"D'accord, je veux un Manhattan."

Bad idea. At least the Manhattan came with a bowl of peanuts and another of olives. The piano man arrived and started to play lounge music. I gazed out the window at the sea. The tide was a long long way out. The bellman had told me "the sea is very low. It will rise at twenty two hundred hours." Below the bar I could see Le Terrass restaurant. It looked promising. The other two options were the Le Cap Horn, *"restaurant gastronomique vue mer,"* and La Verrière, the big formal dining room I could see through plate glass windows en route to my room. The former looked like something I would like for the next evening, the latter like a cruise ship dining room, something I would like maybe never.

"Non, désolée," I responded when I walked onto the deck of Le Terrass for dinner and was asked if I had a reservation.

"Pas de problème." The server walked me to the prime table with a corner view. Lucky me. He handed me a menu and left me to enjoy the view. The view was incredible! To the left was the old city of St. Malo. To the right a jutting bar of land that created a perfect little bay where the perhaps three kilometer beach stretched. As the bellman had said, the tide was low and the beach was huge. At 8 pm, it was light and every type of beachgoer was enjoying the perfect weather. There were surfers, sailors, swimmers, waders, frisbee throwers, sand diggers, metal detector surveyors, runners, walkers, sunbathers, land sail racers... anything you could do on a beach was being done.

I ordered a bottle of wine and a starter of foie gras followed by a fish main dish. It was glorious. I felt guilty that I hadn't bothered to book any of the restaurants that Elliott had recommended. But the food was perfect. The view was perfect. And I was happy. Why should I feel guilty! I sat and ate and drank and read my current Bruno the Chief of Police novel until the sunset at just before 10 pm.

Then I signed the bill to my room and staggered my way back to the room, making perhaps only three wrong turns on that first trip. The bellman was right. I wondered if I could call on him again for further trips back to my room.

I woke up late after spending my first night of vacation with Bruno into the wee hours. I lounged in bed. I felt guilty about not getting up and going; going to the old wall city, going to explore this neighborhood that was so very different than Paris, with its stone roofs and quiet streets. I made a cup of hotel room coffee and sat on my balcony enjoying the birdsong and the garden next door. A huge hammock hung from two trees in the yard. I fantasized owning that house, lying in the hammock all afternoon with Bruno, doing nothing I didn't want to do.

Finally my stomach grumbled enough to force me to go out somewhere so I took a shower, washed my hair, dressed and headed out. I finally found the Bar with the amazing view and peeked out at the beach. Filled with people reveling in the perfect weather! Down below I saw Le Terrass beckoning. So I strolled down and asked for a table.

"Do you have a reservation?"

"*Non, désolée*" I said, eyeing that corner table.

"Hmmmm…" all of the tables had little reserved signs. Uh oh. They seated me at a table very close to the front desk. OK, I still could see the ocean. It was still shady. There was a lovely breeze. They handed me a menu.

What came over the next three hours was one of the most lovely of gastronomic and sensual experiences of my life. *Moules frites*. Beautiful, fat, juicy and so plentiful I couldn't eat them all. Crispy fries. Fresh local rolls with the most amazing local butter I've ever eaten in my life. I didn't need the rolls, I had the *frites*, but I needed some kind of vehicle for that incredible butter. I knifed big slabs of butter onto tiny bits of roll and popped them into my mouth. For an hour I plucked the little *moules* out of their shells and popped them into my mouth. "*Un autre verre?*" I asked. Another glass of wine.

"*Dessert?*"

"*Bien sûr!*" Even though I couldn't finish my *moules* I had seen the *kouign amaan* on the menu. It's a Breton specialty, a crusty pastry with butter and sugar folded in again and again and again until the result is a delicacy so rich and sweet and buttery that it defies description. It came in a big puddle of caramel cream and topped with a globe of rich vanilla ice cream. It would have been perfect for sharing. And I somehow managed to eat the whole thing by myself!

I signed my bill to my room and looked down to the old walled city at the end of the boardwalk. I definitely needed to do some walking to work off this lunch. So I walked one hundred or so steps to the lounge chairs on the deck and chose one in the shade overlooking the beach. I flipped off my sandals and settled in for a nice read.

That's about how my St. Malo vacation went; eat, drink, relax, read. I google street-viewed the streets of the old town. It was lovely! I google street-viewed the restaurant that was recommended by my friend. It was lovely! I sat on my little shady private balcony overlooking the lovely garden of the house next door and read my novel. Feeling guilty, I promised myself that I would get up early tomorrow and walk down to the old town. I didn't have to check out until noon. And my train wasn't until 4:30. I could even check out earlier and leave my bag at the desk, walk down to the old town and have lunch at the lovely little restaurant in the old town.

But the next morning found me lounging on my little private balcony, sipping the coffee I made in my room, reading, spying on the neighbors in their charming little garden, and feeling a little sheepish. I definitely sold St. Malo short! I simply did not give it enough time. I would come back again and spend an entire week. I would stay in the charming hotel in the middle of the walled city, the one across the street from the charming restaurant that I never went to. Not this cruise ship of a hotel with old people wandering around in their hotel bathrobes and hotel slippers!

I checked out at noon, left my bag with the front desk and made my way back out to the Terrass restaurant. I ate the most wonderful meal of cod, risotto and *cèpes* with a *beurre blanc* on the side that was so good I took the tiniest bites I could to savor every single morsel. I lathered the amazing bretagne butter onto tiny bits of roll, making each bit an excuse for a glob of the delicious butter. I sipped a nice cold bottle of rose; a whole bottle all by myself. And for dessert, a trio of crepes with apricot preserves and chantilly. I didn't read. I didn't write. I just ate and drank and tasted every single bite and every single sip. It was decadent.

I dragged the lunch out until the last possible moment and then collected my bag and took a taxi to the train station.

I could live in St. Malo, I decided at that moment. Not in the cruise ship hotel of course. But on one of these little streets in the neighborhood. It was so lovely, so cool, so fresh, and so quiet. This is something definitely to investigate on my next visit… soon!

I arrived at Gare Montparnasse to a blistering hot Paris and trudged through the station, looking for the way out. Stepping out into the Paris evening, 9:30 was still light and people were lounging about on every planter box and stairway. I made my way to the bus stop where the 95 bus starts and ends its journey, climbing into an empty bus just as the doors closed and it headed toward Montmartre. This might not have been the very best of ideas as the bus was like a sauna. Crossing Paris from corner to corner we passed every amazing thing that is Paris. As the sun set and the lights started to come on the cafés along Boulevard Saint-Germain were stuffed with rosé drinkers; Café de Flore, Les Deux Magots, Café Bonaparte… not a Hemingway or Fitzgerald in sight but still pulling in tourists and locals alike. We breached the Seine and crossed Pont du Carrousel into the street passing into the grounds of the Louvre; to the left the entrance to the grand Tuileries, to the right, the Pyramid of the Louvre - now lit brightly as night descended. Continuing on through the Carrousel courtyard diners enjoyed their meals in elegance at Café Marly. We continued on past Palais-Royal and the popular Café Nemours and headed up Avenue de l'Opera. The steps of the Opera Garnier, what I contend to be the most beautiful building on earth, were crowded with people. At the top, couples were dancing the tango. Such a glorious Paris night!

Continuing on past Gare Saint Lazare and into the Clichy neighborhood, Paris taking a turn into a grittier ambiance. I was dripping with perspiration, not so clever as the woman across the aisle from me who had thought to carry a folding fan. I wondered where I could find one. Past the Lebanese diners, the falafel take outs, the KFC, across Boulevard de Clichy, the Moulin Rouge just a block down the street, I got off at Caulaincourt Clichy. Here the little tourist shop and café were closed and nobody sat at the bus stop. The sign was not lit but I had noticed at the previous stop the 80 bus was just about 5 minutes behind. This far up the hill there was a slight breeze and it was glorious to be off the bus. I sat on the bench and enjoyed not being hot; being back in Paris. The bus came, taking me the next two stops uphill. I stepped off at Square Caulaincourt. This far up the hill the breeze was stronger and the street was quiet. A few people lounged on the terrace of Le Cépage. I walked the half block to my door. The guy in the mini market downstairs was outside, sitting on the ice cream cooler, enjoying a smoke and I said "*Bon soir*" as I always do when I arrive home at night.

"How is the American girl" he asked.

"*Bien*" I responded.

I am home.

La Canicule Continues

I always heard that Paris was empty in August but I didn't know how true that was until I experienced it myself. Some say it's the best time to visit, you'll have Paris all to yourself (and the hundreds of thousands of other tourists; not exactly my favorite thing when visiting a foreign location).

I haven't been down by the river other than that bus ride after dark, so I can't say if it's as deserted as everyone says it is. I do know that rue Caulaincourt is deserted. *Tout est ferme*! The butcher has gone on vacation until the end of August. The wine seller until the middle of September! The *fromagerie* closed. The Vietnamese restaurant, closed. The Florist closed. The real estate offices, all five of them, closed! The *boulangerie* is closed for good! A sign is posted on the window that there will be a new enterprise coming. I certainly hope it's a *boulangerie*! Only two things remain open; Le Cépage and the Produce vendor. Thank goodness I won't starve.

And the heat goes on…

Saturday I had booked at Le Clou. It was becoming a Saturday night habit. A good one I would say. In the late afternoon I got a text from Elliott. "It's too hot to cook. We are looking for somewhere heavily air conditioned for dinner. What are you doing?" Assuming that he and Joan were not talking about my bedroom, I responded that I had reservations at Le Clou, where my favorite waiter had promised that if it was hot enough he would wear his speedo to work. It was certainly hot enough. I told Elliott that I was not sure that Le Clou was up to his standard, that I ate on the terrace, and the food was good but nothing special. If they wanted they were certainly welcome to join me.

A short time later he came back with, "We'd love to! Shall we call them and use your name to tell them it will be three?"

I told him I'd tell Thierry. (And oh by the way, he asked, could we make it a little earlier?)

So Thierry said, of course, and we were booked for 7:30.

And this is where I take back everything I take back taking back every snarky thing I ever said about Elliott!

I knew this was a mistake! I told Elliott, "Set your expectations very low! This is not an Elliott caliber restaurant!" To which he responded, "On days like this, food is primarily fuel."

I got there a bit early to make sure to get a reasonable table on the small terrace. We were pretty much sardineed into a corner but the space for four would certainly work for three. It was pretty empty. I ordered an Aperol Spritz and had a hard time getting it. The waiter with the promised speedo was not working. The three who were there were the waiter who had been onboard for about three weeks, the one who started last week and the Pirate. No Thierry.

A short time later Elliott arrived with his omnipresent rolling market tote at hand. He took in the surroundings, obviously not impressed, planted *la bise* on me and sat down. We exchanged pleasantries and he waved madly to get the attention of any of the waiters. The new fellow was waiting on a table adjacent to us, speaking German to the patrons. Elliott's ears perked up and he joined in the conversation, in German. It seems the young Cuban (I knew this by the huge tattoos covering his right forearm) had left Cuba to go to Germany, via Munich.

Elliott asked what whiskies they had. "Low expectations, Elliott. Don't expect much from their bar!" They settled on something and a short time later the Pirate brought out a glass of whisky and a large glass of ice water.

Elliott told me about a picnic he was planning for the next day. Would I be interested in going? Maybe. He will add me to the Facebook invitation.

"Our picnics are not what you might expect." he explained. "No blankets on the grass. I have acquired a folding table and folding chairs to accommodate these events. Tomorrow's will be at Park Martin Luther King."

"Did you just say that with a French accent?" I asked.

Ignoring my comment he went on. "It's originally intended for just eight people, but I think this might get a bit larger."

"Please don't feel you have to include me." I demurred.

"Nonsense! You are always welcome!"

Joan showed up a bit later but I could not get out of my seat, tucked away into the corner as I was, enough to greet her with a proper *bise*. She bent to me. Finally, way too late for Elliott's taste, we were able to order a bottle of wine. "White of course.. we simply cannot tolerate a red in this heat!" He asks the waiter who has been there for two weeks what the year of one of the five white wines on the menu is.

"2017" he responds after checking. I internally groan. "No, that's good," says Elliott. Restaurants like this often try to pass off old whites." Two minutes later the waiter returns to apologize. They are out of that wine. I groan again.

"No problem" says Elliott. That is not uncommon. He orders a Chablis that is evidently of a suitable year.

The wine comes along with a big bottle of cool water.

We talk about the picnic and who is likely to be there.

"How do we get to order?!" demands Elliott, frustrated at trying to get the busy staff's attention.

Thierry walks in with his wife! I've never seen his wife in person. She looks a bit dour and Thierry doesn't look particularly happy. She disappears into the restaurant and he tends to a few things. He sees me and brightens up with a big wave! "Ça va?!" I tell him I have been to St. Malo and liked it very much. Elliott asks who he is and I tell him that Thierry is the owner, who I have become friends with over the past two years.

The German couple's meals are delivered. He's got a steak and both Joan and Elliott wrench their necks to get a good look.

"No! It is not grilled." Elliott expounds on restaurants that say "*grille*" on the menu but then served meat that has been cooked on a flat surface, not allowing the meats' natural juices to run off and…." blah blah blah

"And you can tell by looking at the guy's steak?"

"Yes, of course. Joan looked and it's definitely not grilled! It makes me so mad when restaurants say on the menu 'grillé" and they have no grill! At one restaurant we went to they brought me out a steak that was clearly not grilled. I told the waiter, 'take this away! I cannot eat it!' The waiter was confounded and didn't know what to do. He insisted it was grilled. I told him that was preposterous and stood up with my plate to head into the kitchen! It scared him so badly he didn't know what to do!"

By now Elliott has taken on the look of rage I have seen only three times before; when the taxi wasn't where he thought it should be at Charlotte's dinner party, again with an Uber driver when Elliott ordered it with a starting destination three blocks from the restaurant we were dining (so it would be "easier to find us") and for a brief moment at the Mexican Fiesta when he realized the pretty girls would be late. It passed quickly but I found myself thinking, "OMG, please don't storm into Thierry's kitchen!"

We finally manage to order after Elliott has flailed his arms and complained loudly that we would like to place our order. Joan orders a fried shrimp starter with a special fruit salad entrée, Elliott orders a hamburger, *bien cuit*, with the sauces on the side and some grilled onions and the feta starter. I order the feta starter and the *dorade* with *frites*. I love the *dorade* with *frites*. It's the first thing I ever ordered at Le Clou and has never disappointed.

"I would never order fish in Paris." admonished Elliott. I didn't ask why.

"So!" I say, taking the focus off the ineptitudes of the restaurant staff and the shortcomings of the food and wine list. "I want to ask you about the Somerset Maugham book." (Elliott had told me, as a writer I really must read *The Razor's Edge*.)

"In the very first chapter" I began, "the narrator says a writer should never attempt to write about someone from other than his own country. Do you agree?"

"Well, you have to realize that Maugham is an unreliable narrator!"

Huh? Elliott, can you just answer the question?

At that point Elliott lectured me about the nature of the "unreliable narrator" and all of the instances when the literary device has been used to further the progress of the tale. He went on to outline the countless times that Maugham violated his own principle by writing characters that were not French. And I knew that the "conversation" would be precisely what Elliott wanted to be and the merit of Maugham's principle would never be discussed. I also knew that the book discussion sessions that I had proposed to Elliott would not be pleasant at all. I can't fathom how Charlotte got through the entire works of Shakespeare over a year or two of Monday nights in their small 17th arrondissement apartment!

The starters arrived. Elliott took a bite and declared, "it's actually not bad." Then he proceeded to polish off all but one of Joan's fried shrimps, so they must not have been too terrible.

We talked about tomorrow's picnic. Elliott told me how his picnics were far and above the normal picnic and that he intended to organize *Le Diner en Noir* soon. That started a rant about *Le Diner en Blanc*.

"I was involved in the first of them. When there were only fifty or so people on the Ile-Saint-Louis. And then it turned into that insane thing with thousands of people. It's ridiculous!"

We have finished our starters and our water carafe is empty. Elliott is gesticulating wildly at any staff who will pay attention, "How do we get these plates removed?!"

I calmly asked for another *carafe d'eau* and another bottle of wine.

Our mains arrive, Elliott's burger indeed has the sauces on the side but no onions. He plucks a *frite* from the bowl and declares that they would be ok if they were actually crispy. Mine seem crispy enough. He cuts his burger in half and grumbles about the bun. "Hamburgers in Paris never have the right bun, always a brioche, which makes it impossible to pick up."

"I always eat mine with a knife and fork."

"Yes, as do all Parisians". He picks up half of his burger and takes a bite. It must not be terrible because he doesn't complain.

Somehow the topic of reservations came up. I mentioned that it was evidently a big problem for Paris restaurants and that many people make reservations but failed to keep them. "Even L'Ami Jean said that after they reconfirm reservations by phone people don't show up. And that's a very hard reservation to get."

"Oh yeah, it's that restaurant in the seventh that all the Americans like." I'm pretty sure that he knows it's one of my favorites.

We talked about popular restaurants in Paris; expensive restaurants. I stumbled trying to recall the name of a place; "It was started by an American couple who originally had people come to their home."

"Verjus," he said. "Braden and Laura are friends of mine. When they acquired their serving ware they got some stuff they didn't end up using. It's in my cave for when I start my own restaurant. I've never eaten there though. I don't like their wine list."

I should add that Joan's contribution to the conversation is a few mumbled words, impossible to understand. After the Mexican feast, when she had done such an amazing job of cleaning up, I was prepared to forgive her for all of her failure to contribute to any of our conversations. But my forgiveness was unraveled.

It was hot. Elliott complained that the heat was exacerbated by the glass barriers that divided the close in terrace from the sidewalk terrace. He complained about the inadequacies of the servers. He complained about the food. He complained.

"You should be embarrassed!" he declared. "As a regular customer, bringing friends, they should be far more attentive!"

I just mumbled something about it being an off night.

Finally Elliott started to gesticulate wildly for the check. The two week old server acknowledged us and then continued to bring menus to new diners and plates to others. Finally after fifteen minutes he came and Elliott asked for the machine while Joan got out her calculator and figured out the per person charge. When the machine came out Elliott proffered his American Express. Sorry.

"Strike three!" ejaculated Elliott.

He used another card. I used mine. He said "Our taxi is coming, dear. You really must talk to the owner. This is simply unacceptable."

I was quietly seething. I waited for them to get into their Chauffeur Privé (and probably abuse another driver) and I went out to order my own Uber.

When I got home my blood continued to boil. Would I have been disappointed had I been by myself tonight? Maybe. It certainly was an off night at Le Clou. But after two years of wonderful nights, I was prepared to forgive one off night in August when it was so very hot. What I was not prepared to forgive was Elliott's horrendous treatment of the staff. And his rudeness about reacting to what he knew was one of my favorite local spots.

Did he need to prove something?

In the end I decided that people are allowed to like what they like. They don't need to apologize for their preferences. What they aren't allowed to do is abuse the restaurant staff. Doing that only makes one look petty and insecure.

In the morning I texted Elliott.

"I'm sorry, I forgot that I have a rendezvous for an *apéro* at five today. I'm going to have to miss the picnic. Have fun!"

I decided that it's time for me to take a break from Elliott.

Beverly and Dave Visit

What does it feel like to be completely adored?

Let me begin by saying that I completely adore Beverly as well. I first met her when she was my Contract Recruiter, responsible for hiring dozens and dozens of highly technical and usually bizarre Engineers, as well as anyone else the company needed to bring on board. We instantly bonded. Our backgrounds were very similar; divorced single moms with grown kids in assorted stages of making it on their own. We both had difficult exes and a long history of interesting relationships.

That may be where the what we had in common ended. Beverly was tall and beautiful, model thin with a wardrobe that didn't end. She got her hair professionally done every three weeks and weekly manicures and pedicures. She loved a good massage and facial and went to twice weekly Zumba classes. She had a beau, Dave. Dave was recently divorced with a difficult ex and two boys just graduating from University. He had a great career as a high level something or other with one of the Big Four accounting firms and traveled the world extensively. He was gone most of the week and returned on Friday, staying at Beverly's apartment.

Dave adores Beverly. Heck I adore Beverly. Our CEO adores Beverly. The job candidates adored Beverly. She was the perfect person to have on my team. Beverly deserves to be adored. She's just plain nice. When I was working, she was my favorite travel partner, so I made her the Director of Global Staffing so I could create excuses for her to travel with me.

And travel we did. We went to Singapore, Australia, Malaysia, India, China, Texas and Anaheim! Everywhere we went Beverly was upbeat and happy and in love with the people and the place. And they loved her back.

I mostly got to take advantage of my perks from years of frequent flyer status and when I couldn't share them with her I promised her she was on her way to accumulating the same. She gamely went to the back of the plane and made friends with the flight attendants, enjoyed the free wine they would slip to her and slept in a middle coach seat. More than once a flight attendant would come up to me and say "So you are moving to Paris!"

"How do you know?"

"Your friend was telling me all about it."

We'd reconnect at the gate of our destination and I would take her with me through the lanes that had no lines that were afforded to the very frequent global travelers. Then we collected our bags and headed to our hotels where I was special only in that I was the Executive and she was special because she was Beverly.

Here is a perfect example of the love that Beverly garnered. We were in Hyderabad, India; from my perspective, a nightmare of a place. The new highway that was just opened and clean and empty on my last visit was now crowded with trucks, incessantly honking, littered with refuge on the roadsides, clusters of signs advertised shopping centers, cellular services and housing projects. We stopped at one point to wait as a water buffalo crossed the highway.

"It's so beautiful!" effused Beverly.

I looked sideways at her surprised. "What rose colored glasses are you looking though?"

She just kept smiling and watching out the window.

We arrived at the Lemon Tree Hotel, in the middle of the high tech district. It smelled thankfully very lemony. And it was clean and spacious. We were assigned to rooms on the "Lady's only" floor. Interesting.

"Let's dump our bags and meet in the bar!" Bev suggested when she saw the poster advertising this week's special cocktail. Beverly loves a good bar and a tipple, which makes it even easier to enjoy her presence and to like traveling with her!

So we did just that, dumped our bags and met in the "Slounge". Slounge became our ever after catch phrase for hotel bar. Indian cocktails are made with ice made with Indian water. Not touching that! Indian wine is dreadful; the red absolutely undrinkable, the white maybe barely bearable. Indian beer might be drinkable but I don't drink beer so that left me with the white. Or nothing. To be honest, I kind of preferred nothing.

But every night of our three nights there we met in the Slounge. We laughed. We talked about the day; about the interactions with the stubborn and argumentative Indian HR Manager, with the rest of the eager but slightly inept staff, about the luncheon they hosted, about the shopping trip foisted on us, about the tour of Golconda Fort in 117 degrees.

Every morning we met in the breakfast room. One of the bus boys attached himself to Beverly. He wore a t-shirt that said "new kid on the block" indicating that he was a trainee. She asked for coffee and coffee appeared in front of us in no time flat. He brought her pancakes, a fried egg, more coffee. All without her even asking. He asked her about her impressions of India. ("It's beautiful! I love it!") He asked her where she had been. He brought her more eggs.

On our last morning in India the infatuated boy piled our table with coffee, eggs, pancakes, eager to talk to his beloved and hear more about her love for his home country. She was in a rush. She wanted to hit the gift shop and see about that pearl necklace in the shop window. And then she had to pack. Off she went. I flagged the lad down and asked for a cup of coffee.

"Later" he said, "I have to clean these tables."

So my point is, everyone adores Beverly and it's impossible to begrudge her any of the love that is showered on her. Dave really really adores Bev. He shouts it from the highest social networking platform. He tells anyone who will listen how he was so lucky to have been the man she agreed to marry.

They got engaged in Paris, at Chez Francis over a dinner of Sancerre and oysters while the lights of the Eiffel Tower twinkled. They had a Parisian themed wedding with mini Eiffel Towers awash in twinkly fairy lights on every table. The tables were named after Parisian landmarks; Champs de Mars, Grand Palais, Pont d'Alma.

The wedding was beautiful. When the doors to the venue for the ceremony opened and Ed Sheeran belted out "Take me into your loving arms", Beverly literally ran down the aisle to her waiting husband-to-be. She of course was gorgeous. Dave was radiant. He had won the golden ticket. There was not a dry eye in the house. Everyone adores Beverly.

They honeymooned in France; two weeks in Paris and the Côte d'Azur. Beverly in a bikini at fifty something. At the office she planned her packing out loud. She was taking twenty four different dresses for two weeks. The question was, how many pairs of shoes?

Twenty four dresses! I don't own twenty four dresses! I don't own five dresses!

What would it be like to be so adored? For most of my life I have felt appreciated, valued, cared for, but never out and out adored. I wonder if I'm maybe a bit like Groucho Marx, I would never really want to be a member of a club that would have me. I think it would be very hard to be around someone all of the time. If someone adores you all of the time do they become less… less… less what? Less worthwhile? Less desirable? Just less?

I sit and write. Philippe sits on a stool across from me. He hums. He whistles. He watches me write.

What do I want?

Beverly and Dave are arriving in Paris tonight. We are having dinner on Friday. I wonder if I can get some one-on-one time with her. I could talk to her. But I'm afraid that maybe she is too busy being adored by Dave to get that one-on-one time. Maybe that is the downside of being adored.

Le Dépositaire

Ninon looked into the mirror on her dressing table. She was ready, she felt, to receive her old lover M. d. Gourville. Yes, she was sad when he left. At the time she cared about him deeply. But his affiliation with the Prince of Conde and that whole mess of *la Fronde*... when his effigy was hanged and burned in the square it was obvious that he needed to leave Paris quickly.

He had a great deal of money that he was unable to take with him. Hedging his bets he divided it between two caskets. The first he left with the *Le Grand Penitencier,* the Cardinal, of Notre Dame. The second he entrusted to Ninon. And off he went just in the nick of time saving himself from sure death.

Ninon had missed him. He was a good partner and an excellent lover. But of course he was easy to replace. In no time at all her bed was warmed by another and she had forgotten poor Gourville. And also forgotten the casket of cash under her bed.

Until the messenger arrived yesterday. He had a lovely note from Gourville. "Cher Ninon, Enough time has passed and the political climate has changed adequately for me to finally return to Paris. Of course my first thoughts are with you!" (And, he did not add, the immense fortune of cash that I have left in your care.) "I beseech you to allow me to visit you at your earliest convenience."

"Oh dear" sighed Ninon.

"I have missed you desperately and the moments we have shared." He did not mention the extreme anxiety he experienced on discovering that the Cardinal had used the money that was left in his care, claiming that any such deposit was destined for charity under the rules of the Penitentiary. In other words, too bad, so sad, your money is gone!

"Until I cast my eyes upon your lovely visage, I am forever yours. G"

Of course Ninon had no way of knowing that Gourville had also left a large sum of money with the Cardinal. Furthermore, she did not know that money had been squandered on the Cardinal's purposes and that the desperate Gourville was aware of the breach. She simply was not looking forward to informing the dear man that her heart, and all of the delicious private time that came with it, was no longer his.

But Ninon was nothing if not familiar with this conversation. She looked again in the mirror, took a deep breath and prepared for the confrontation.

Gourville was standing in front of the fireplace in the Grand Salon when Ninon entered.

"Ah my dear! You are a sight for sore eyes! You have no idea how I've missed you."

Ninon allowed Gourville to take her hand and grace it with the gentlest of kisses. "Monsieur Gourville, I am delighted that circumstances have allowed you to return to Paris! I look forward to your rejoining our Salon. Will you be with us Friday evening?"

Gourville blanched at Ninon's use of the formal "vous" instead of the more intimate "tu" that he had enjoyed during their partnership. But he was encouraged by the invitation to return to Ninon's coveted Salon.

"Please have a seat. Can I offer you tea? Coffee? Un verre de vin?"

Taking a seat on the overpadded settee did little to increase Gourville's comfort level. How would he bring up the casket? At this point, he was assuming that Ninon had spent the money in the same way the Cardinal had. He was destitute! He was broke!

Ninon had poured Gourville a glass of wine from the decanter on the lacquered sideboard. She took nothing for herself, other than a deep breath.

"Ah Gourville," she began, "A great misfortune has happened to me in the consequence of your absence."

Here it comes, Gourville thought. I am a pauper! He could not meet Ninon's eye, such was his distress.

Ninon, for her part, was certain that he was distraught at the loss of her love. She quickly went on, pulling the bandaid off the wound, "I'm sorry if you still love me, for I have lost my love for you, and though I have found another with whom I am happy, I have not forgotten you. Here," she turned to her escritoire, "Here are the twenty thousand crowns you entrusted to me when you departed. Take them, my friend, but do not ask anything from a heart which is no longer disposed in your favor. There is nothing left but the most sincere friendship."

Gourville was, of course overjoyed. Certainly the icing on the cake would have been resuming his love affair with the beautiful Ninon, however, given the duration of his absence he did not expect that to be the case. After the distressing news from the Cardinal he was astonished by her loyalty.

He quickly masked his glee and put on a morose mask. "My dear Ninon. Of course I am distraught at the loss of your love. I trust he who now enjoys your passions is worthy. My love for you is such that I wish you only the most perfect happiness." He turned away from Ninon to take a deep breath.

Upon confessing the betrayal of the Cardinal, and his expectation that he would find the same from Ninon she was highly offended.

"You do not surprise me." she said, with a sly smile. "But I am surprised that you suspected me on that account. The prodigious difference in our reputations should have assured you of that." She added with a twinkling eye, "Am I not the guardian of the caskette?"

The Boys, Writing around Craziness, and Postulating about Intimacy in France (Paris?)

Philippe is so happy when he's with the boys. There are three of them today. One a pudgy grey haired fellow, perhaps fifty who is often sitting at the bar, drinking a glass of wine. The second, a slightly less pudgy, a bit younger dark haired guy, also drinking chablis. And the third a very handsome guy probably no more than forty, slim, wearing some interesting wrist jewelry. He drinks chablis as well. Philippe drinks champagne. He seems to like champagne as it's his tipple of choice at the Wednesday night jazz nights. The four of them stand and sit at the bar just feet in front of me. They talk quickly and I pick up about ten percent of what they say.

Philippe pops away every so often to greet a new customer, bring them l'ardoise, say merci and avoir to someone who leaves. The conversation with the boys goes on.

He's not any less happy to see me and he dances to the music in front of my table, making sure that I see him. Since I gave him a bottle of wine for his birthday he's brightened considerably. He seems genuinely happy when I show up. He seems nearly gleeful the entire time I'm here. A different Philippe from the guy who was getting to be just tired. Maybe it's because he loves summer?

Today's weather is perfect. The *canicule* has broken. Yesterday it rained and thundered and washed Paris clean. Today there is a bit of a breeze and the temperature is a perfect 70 degrees. Yesterday was perfect as well even though it was a bit rainy and overcast.

Yesterday I opted to write at Cépage. Sometimes I think that Philippe can use a break from me. Or at least maybe it's good for him to miss me; to not take for granted that I will write here every day.

Crazy Caroleen was there; sitting not in her usual spot by the power outlet but at the end of the banquet I usually sit on. It was too drippy to sit outside. I paused for half a step and then braced myself, walked in and sat at the far end of the same banquet. I was not going to let her chase me away.

A new waiter greeted me warmly. Crazy Caroleen and I purposely did not look at each other. She was evidently nursing her cafe creme and had her smartphone earpieces in and was speaking to someone; probably letting her equally crazy husband know that I was there.

The waiter brought me *la carte* and I made a quick easy decision; *magret de canard* and *un verre* of chablis. I was having dinner with Elliott et all so didn't think a carafe was a good idea today. My poor foie is taking the brunt of my good life in Paris.

I opened my laptop and started to write. Shortly my duck arrived. The new waiter admonished me, "*Quand vous travaillez, travaillez. Quand vous mangez, mangez!*" What's with these guys? Are they cut from the same cloth? I closed my laptop and enjoyed my duck, purposefully not looking at Caroleen who was purposefully not looking at me.

Soon her regular seat near the power outlet became available and she moved. On her way she purposefully greeted and dispensed les bisous as if to show me, "See, I have friends here! I belong more than you do!"

I finished my lunch, opened my laptop again and became serious about writing. Ninon was certainly more fascinating than the crazy one and I was transported again into seventeenth century Paris. When I looked up again two hours had passed and I had finished my writing for the day. Caroleen was gone and I hadn't even see her leave.

I paid my bill, packed up and headed home to prepare for my evening out.

The boys have moved to Philippe's regular round table to eat lunch. They are on their fourth glass of white wine each (Philippe is on his fourth glass of champagne, it seems an odd choice for lunch). They continue to rattle on and I still can't understand much of what they say. And I thought I was getting so fluent.

The afternoon manager just arrived. He walks in and immediately stops at my table to say hello and give me a handshake.

A handshake. He goes to the boys table and shakes the hand of each of them. He stops at the day waiter and shakes his hand. Soon Guillaume will arrive. Whose hand will he shake. Surely mine. He always does.

In French there is no simple word for "hug". That doesn't mean that French people don't hug. You could say étreindre, but that doesn't really capture the simplicity of a hug. *Embrasser* sounds like what you want to say, but that actually means to kiss, bigger than *la bise,* a real kiss, a romantic kiss. The French don't hug casually. That coming together of bodies, the physicality of embracing someone is saved for far more intimate relationships.

Yesterday I collected eighteen *bisous*. Every coming together and parting of a group takes literally forever while each person deposits the requisite two *bisous* on each person's cheeks. Often I am expected to deposit *la bise* on the cheeks of someone I am just meeting. It seems that *la bise* is warranted or not by virtue of the connection with another. If I am meeting someone who is the friend of someone I regularly would greet with *la bise, la bise* is in order.

Guillaume arrived for work, forty five minutes early. All four of the boys got la bise; Philippe got a handshake. I got a friendly handshake and a "ça va". The girl behind the bar got very playful *bisous*. A short time later the afternoon bartender arrived, the three boys got *bisous*, Philippe got a handshake. Is it a respect thing?

The boys have just opened a bottle of red. I ordered a *tarte au citron.*

Back in the "Nunnery"!

J ealousy is a wicked thing. Many of the women of breeding and beauty were *habitués* of the Palace. Ninon was a rare creature indeed; raised by a liberal and forward thinking father, long absent her conservative and pious mother, she was free to socialize and read and think and discuss and create. Her admirers were many and at times her enemies were even more numerous - generally the women of Paris.

Some women were blessed with a naturally svelte figure, some with lovely complexions, some had beautiful shining hair, some had intriguing smiles, some even with good teeth. Seldom did a woman possess all of these in a perfect combination along with a brilliant wit and intelligence and the ability to charm and win the confidence and admiration of every… man.

Anne the Regent Queen did not have an easy start to her time in the Court. Spanish by birth and beautiful by Spanish standards she didn't look, sound or act like a French lady. Betrothed to Louis XIII at only eleven to insure a military alliance between France and Spain, and married by proxy a short time later, she had been forced to consummate her marriage to Louis at the very early age of fourteen. The two did not like each other much and their forced couplings were met with resentment and unhappiness. Anne detested her mother-in-law, Marie de Medici. It was only a short time before that situation was remedied. At sixteen Louis formed alliances with the Duke de Luynes to make progress in removing his mother, resulting in a *coup d'etat*.

With Marie out of the picture, he then turned to Frenchify Anne, sending away her Spanish staff and replacing them with French ladies. The Duke encouraged

Louis to become a real husband to Anne, resulting in a series of miscarriages and stillbirths. These of course took their toll on Anne and she grew hard and embittered. Any genuine affection that had developed between the King and Queen died when Anne fell down a flight of stairs, causing her final miscarriage and the end of any pretense of love between the King and Queen. The King spent most of his time after that away from the Palace and Anne spent most of hers gossiping and making trouble with her ladies in waiting.

As part of Spanish Royalty, Anne's job was to visit churches and convents across France. This offered her another great opportunity to make trouble and she developed close and controversial relationships with several convents. These controversies aside, it was easy enough, when Anne got good and fed up with the complaints and whining of her ladies in waiting about Ninon to banish her from Paris to a convent.

Anne's first choice for Ninon was *le couvent de filles repenties*, the Convent of Repentant Girls. At this point M. Baudon, one of the highly respected Oiseaux who enjoyed the ear of the Queen, cagily approached Anne and hinted that maybe this was not the best choice. After all, Ninon was neither a girl nor a repentant. "This could be very embarrassing for you, your highness." He craftily suggested.

Anne was nothing if not malleable to the suggestions of a handsome man. The order was revised allowing Ninon the choice of her future prison. Ninon was not too concerned. She knew that her legions of admirers would not abandon or fail her and she would be out shortly. She cleverly made her selection.

"I am deeply sensible of the goodness of the court in providing for my welfare and in permitting me to select my place of retreat, and without hesitation I decide in favor of the Les Grands Cordeliers."

The joke was on Anne. Les Grands Cordeliers was a select monastery very specifically only for men. Women were expressly prohibited. As the Captain of the Queen's Guard, who brought Ninon's message to Anne was one of the Oiseaux, the preference was honored and Ninon became the first woman resident of house. But of course, it had been years since Ninon declared that she would "be a man".

Ninon's retreat was short lived as her admirers and fans entreated the Queen with a thousand reasons to commend Anne, noting her brilliant qualities of mind and heart, rather than a need for her punishment. When the Duc d'Enghien, not known for lightly praising the values of women joined the hue and cry, the Queen had no choice but to save face and let Ninon go home.

As a result of the escapade, Ninon's popularity soared. Her cheekiness at choosing Les Grands Cordeliers, the magnitude of the protestations and appeals for her release, the humiliation of the Queen, all gave Ninon a cache even greater than she had before. All of Paris resounded with her wit, her spirit and her philosophy. Everyone wanted to get close to her. Entree to her salon was THE ticket of the day. Even the cleverest of Paris's women saw the wisdom of gaining access to her charming circle.

Ninon had become, through this travesty, the acknowledged guide and leader and everyone in Paris submitted to her influence without envy or jealousy. Ninon was at the top of her game and nobody but nobody questioned her authority.

Francais

A s I work on learning French I become increasingly baffled and increasingly interested in how the language evolved and continues to develop as new words are introduced. L'**Académie française** is the French council that determines all things related to language. First established by Cardinal Richelieu in the sixteen hundreds, (that man had his fingers in a lot of pies), it exists with many of the same conventions and habits from over four hundred years ago.

The council is protective and has rigid laws pertaining to and preventing anglicisms sneaking into the French language. The forty member council, known as Les Immortals will spend days arguing over an appropriate French word for "hashtag". They came up with *mot diese.* Translated in English, that would be "harsh word"

I guess these guys are also the culprits for determining whether a noun is masculine or feminine. This is totally mind boggling to me! There seems to be little rhyme or reason as to which gender is assigned to a specific word. And yet, of course, the other parts of the sentence all reflect the gender of the noun, so if you get it wrong… I am always being corrected by someone. "*Un Oeuf!*" Really? And egg is masculine? *Une carafe*! "That's how I knew your French was not so good!"

Le visage (the face) masculine

La bouche (the mouth) feminine

Un oeil (an eye) masculine

Le nez (the nose) masculine

Le menton (the chin) masculine

La joue (the cheek) feminine

Le front (the forehead) masculine

Why are the mouth and the cheek feminine but the rest of the face masculine?

La langue (the tongue) feminine

Is there some kind of trend or methodology here?

The chest (*la poitrine*) is feminine, but breast (*le sein*) is masculine!

A storm is feminine. Thunder is masculine. Lightning is feminine. A heatwave is feminine.

The Transmigration of Souls

A belief held by two thirds of the human race.

"Has it occurred to you that transmigration is at once an explanation and a justification of the evil of the world? If the evils we suffer are the result of sins committed in our past lives we can bear them with resignation and hope that if in this one we strive toward virtue our future lives will be less afflicted. But it's easy enough to bear our own evils, all we need for that is a little manliness; what's intolerable is the evil, often so unmerited in appearance, that befalls others. If you can persuade yourself that it is the inevitable result of the past you may pity, you may do what you can to alleviate, and you should, but you have no cause to be indignant."

Somerset Maugham, The Razor's Edge

School Yard Fights

When I was thirteen years old I had my one and only schoolyard fight. It actually was not in a school yard but on a dirt road that served as a fire access road that we used as a shortcut to walk home from school. My family just moved into town, from the poor track where we had lived for the last ten years. It was a major move for us. Upward mobility! Now we got to walk home from school, the town's Catholic School.

The house around the corner from the shortcut was a massive Victorian, kind of falling apart. It sat on a big corner lot and had a wrap around porch. At one time it must have been rather grand. Those days it was pretty trashy. As was the family who lived in it. There were, as in most families in town in those days, a bunch of kids, mostly nondescript. It was hard to tell one kid from another. And that was particularly true of the two girls my age; twins, Arlene and Marlene.

For some reason they decided that these new Catholic kids would not be allowed to pass their ratty house nor get to the shortcut. The ultimate result was a big neighborhood brawl with my brother and sisters and all our neighborhood friends coming to the support of me, and the big family of ne'er do wells, far more experienced in the ways of hand to hand combat, coming to fisticuffs in the short cut.

Long story short, our neighborhood shockingly won. There was something about dirty fighting and Arlene getting punched in her boob which was probably going to halt its growth forever. But we had established dominance of the shortcut and while I was still a bit terrified when I rounded the corner and saw that big house, all future trouble from the twins came in the form of verbal taunts. I shortly found a different route and skipped the shortcut and their block altogether.

There followed decades of only peaceful behavior on my part (although I can't say the same about my siblings). Until now. I had my second school yard brawl. This time the Social Network was the battle ground. I kicked the hornet's nest and the hornet came out ready to sting.

Nearly every day I posted on my Facebook page an update of my writing progress, often with a picture of my lunch and my laptop. It helps me feel connected to friends and family across the ocean, and judging from their feedback, they enjoy it as well. Crazy Caroleen doesn't have a Facebook account. She doesn't believe in Facebook. She thinks people are stalking her; her insane mother, her evil sister, her greedy thieving nephew, and don't even get started on her husband's relatives. She does however post a nearly daily photo depicting her fabulous Paris life on Instagram, complete with fifty ridiculous hashtags (mots dieses); #bistrochairs #parisbistro #pariscafe #montmartrelife #igersparis #aperitif #apero #peoplewatching#streetstyle #frenchwomennevergetfat #imsofabulous #livingoffotherpeoplesmoney #youdbestupidtobelieveanythingisay #dontyouwishyouwereme #blahblahblahblah…

After the divorce Caroleen blocked me from her Instagram page so I frankly have no idea what she posts anymore. But I had a sneaking suspicion that she still takes a peek at mine, and that she probably looks at my Facebook page as well. So after the lunch at Cépage last week I went low. Yes, I went low. It was beneath my dignity. And the hornet stung me.

On my daily lunch post I said something about "working at Cépage and Crazy Caroleen was there, nursing her one *café crème* for hours on end as she used their wifi and power". I also posted the waiters admonition that when I'm eating, I should be eating; when I'm working, work. And a picture of my *magret de canard*.

It took less than eight hours for the post to show up on my own Instagram account from a newly created account. "You sure eat a lot. One of your Facebook friends did a screenshot of your post and sent it to Caroleen! Do you know that it's illegal to try to destroy the reputation of a good person? We are looking into legal action. You are a Grotesque Fat Fuck!"

Ouch. The sting got to me. Those three words played again and again in my head. While I would like to say it had no impact on me at all, it sadly did. Not the threat of legal action. That's silly. And to be honest, the grotesque fat fuck comment faded and felt more like a sad attempt to sting that wasn't very creative. But it totally ruined my ability to use Cépage for a writing venue. There is no way I can go there and take the chance of running into either her or her horrible husband. Cépage! One hundred easy steps from my front door! For that matter, I'm not even sure I want to run the risk of running into her at Les Loups. Or Le Café de La Butte. My entire neighborhood (where she doesn't even live) is ruined! I've given up the shortcut! After all of these decades. I should never have posted what I did. I went low and I lost.

I deleted the post and posted my own. "Nice try. I knew you were looking." Trying to grab back a little control. But after my excitement about getting back Cépage, whether she was there or not, I lost it again.

What would Ninon do?

Progress

I came to GCA to write today. What can I do? I can't go to Cépage. It's some kind of holiday and Philippe is standing on the corner out front. Waiting for me? He greets me with la bise when I get out of the cab and complains that the restaurant is empty. All of Paris is *en vacances*. It's true! Nobody around but tourists. (How quickly I have come to eschew tourists.)

He sets me up with two tables; one for my beverages, the other for my work stuff. Did he see that on Facebook? The guys at Cépage do that for me. Or at least they used to, when I could still go there. He's never done it. Maybe it's just because there is nobody else in the restaurant.

He talks about inspiration and some other things I don't understand at all. I tell him that he is my inspiration; his singing and his dancing. He sings and dances for me. I showed him the progress of my book so far; 130 pages. He's surprised! What does he think I've been doing all of this time?

"So, 250 pages total?" he asks.

"Nooooo, probably at least 400." I say. He pantomimes a fat book. I laugh. I don't think Philippe is much of a reader. I'm quite certain he doesn't read English. There's little concern he'll read my book.

"A best seller!" he declares.

He has a lot of confidence in me. And he's proud of his contribution to the arts.

A very pretty girl in very short shorts comes in looking for the toilettes. He points the direction. She heads off up the steps. He doesn't even look. Saturday the new waiter told me "I like you." A while later he confided, "I would like to go out with you." "I only have eyes for Philippe." I told him. His eyes got big as saucers. As the afternoon wore on Philippe was clearly not happy with him. He probably asked out all of the female clients. Philippe scowled at me. I said "Another one bites the dust." He did that thing French men do with their mouths and indicated that I was right.

He's an odd duck. So why am I so interested in this odd duck?

Marquis de la Chatre
- called away by duty

"Have no scruples about the quantity of your pleasures, but only of their quality." Ninon's father's last words.

It was hot in Paris. Hot like it can only be hot in Paris; sticky, stinky, cloying hot. Ninon was in her apartments, tempted to throw open all of the windows to allow in some fresh air, but the air outside was anything but fresh. The waves of the glass panes in the windows barely concealed the waves of steam rising from the cobbles, a combination of heat, horse leavings, the evaporating rivulets of effluence tossed from the windows of the neighboring apartments, and other piles of detritus. It was days like this one could only wish to be elsewhere; anywhere other than Paris.

Ninon gazed in her dressing table mirror. She mopped the perspiration from her forehead and powdered her face. She briefly wished she were going with Chatre. She had allowed him to occupy her boudoir longer than most. She had developed a great affection for him. He was clever and handsome and funny and the art of love making seemed to come instinctively to him. She was actually very sad to see him leaving. However he was being called to his family estate in Provence to deal with a matter of utmost urgency.

Provence. Oh that sounded almost heavenly. Yes, it was hot there as well. But certainly the air was fresher, if for no reason than there was more of it. More trees. More rivers. More fields of glorious sunflowers and lavender and wide open greenery. Cicadas rather than street traffic and neighborhood squalling provided the background music. One could go days without seeing people other than those in your own employ. And while the horses still shit and people still tossed out their personal refuse, there was more space for it to be absorbed. More air to breathe.

But it was not to be. Ninon had matters of her own that demanded her attention; her salon had become so popular that it was now a nightly event, the biggest event in the City these days. De la Chatre may be gone for months and she could simply not be absent for such a duration. Months! She exhaled deeply and went back to her toilet. He would be here soon and she wanted to be at her best.

"Madame", her maid interrupted her deep thoughts. "Monsieur la Chatre is in the salon."

"*Merci*" Ninon responded. "Please offer him *un verre* and tell him I will be with him shortly."

Ninon knew that although she was not ready to end it with la Chatre, naturally, it would be necessary to bring this to a close. She was not want to go without a lover for weeks, certainly not the months la Chatre was expecting to be gone. She took a deep breath, applied a dab of scent just above her bodice and rose to meet her lover.

La Chatre jumped up from his seat when Ninon entered the salon. "My beloved!" He moved toward her to take her into his arms. Ninon moved instead toward the window, considering for one moment opening it to relieve the oppressiveness of the heat of the still stuffy room. Looking on the cobbles below made her realize the folly of that idea. She allowed la Chatre to grab her hand and bring it to his lips.

"I am most devastated that I find it impossible not to leave you now. How can I go?"

Ninon pulled away. Her lover was certainly better than most, fastidious about his wardrobe and personal cleanliness, but it was impossible to come from the streets of Paris without some of the fetid atmosphere clinging to one's garments.

Having been outside all day, La Chatre had become desensitized to his own state and completely misinterpreted Ninon's distancing herself. He felt that she had begun the process of separation before he had even left! His entire aspect deflated as if the air had been let out of his body.

"Alas my darling, the love you inspire in others is very different from the love you feel. You will always be in my heart, and absence will be a new fire to consume me."

Ninon clutched a scented lace handkerchief and took a long sniff of it. Lowering it to her side she moved closer to la Chatre and allowed him to pull her close.

He continued, "To you, absence is the end of affection. Every object I imagine I see around you will be odious to me, but to you they will be fascinating."

Ninon could not deny this logic. Her history certainly proved that this was likely to be true. But she still loved La Chatre and wanted to put him at ease.

"*Mon cher,*" she protested, "why must you assume that your absence will lessen my love for you? Can you think so little of me? To believe that my ardor will be diminished by your absence? Please have some faith in me; in our love for each other." Ninon took two steps, distancing herself just a little and raising the handkerchief to her face again.

"My love for you will certainly endure this brief separation. You can be sure of my fidelity and know that I will think only of your return."

This conversation went on for an hour; La Chatre expressing his fear that his beloved would forget him; Ninon protesting and pledging her constancy to her lover. Finally La Chatre had a bizarre idea but became fixated on it. He asked Ninon to commit a pledge of fidelity in writing!

"If you will do a thing, you will stand to it." he exclaimed! "What will tend to quiet my mind and remove my fears ought to be your duty to accept because my happiness is involved and that is more to you than love. It is your own philosophy. I want you to put in writing that you will remain faithful to me and maintain the most inviolable fidelity."

Ninon became completely exasperated. "Such a thing is just too bizarre!"

But her lover became increasingly obstinate and refused to leave. "Let me dictate the document!"

Ninon was becoming exhausted by this debate. There was no other way to draw this to a conclusion. "*D'accord,*" she sighed. "Tell me what you would have me write."

And with that la Chatre dictated a most strongly worded vow, using the most sacred of terms, almost like a wedding vow. And Ninon, knowing that there was no way to get her lover to leave, and feeling decidedly less in love with him by the moment, signed the crazy document.

With that, the Marquis took Ninon into his arms for one last passionate kiss and confidently headed off to the South, to do his business.

Of course there was a line of suitors waiting their opportunity to become the next of Ninon's lovers. Within two days she was won over by the pretty words of one who was certain that he was the next worthy candidate.

For two days the rain had fallen, relieving the City of its crippling heat and washing, if only temporarily, the streets of the grime and grit and stink and mess. Ninon had been able to throw open all of her windows and expunge the fetid, stuffy air of her rooms. Paris seemed fresh and clean.

Two days later, she gave in to a new lover. "*Ah Ah le bon billet qu'a la Chatre!*" (Oh the fine bond that la Chatre has) repeated breathlessly three times.

Monsieur Chapelle
- A love denied

Voltaire's Comedy of the Prude (act I scene III)

Il ne font pas qu'on s'étonne

Si souvent elle raisonne

De la sublime vertu

Dont Planton fit reveti

Car compter son age

Elle peut avoir vecu

Avec ce grand personnage

Let no one be surprised

If she should be advised

Of the virtue most renowned

In Plato to be found

For, counting up her age

She lived 'tis reason sound

With that great personage.

Ninon on "Amour"

L ove is merely a taste founded upon the senses, a blind sentiment, which admits no merit in the object which gives it birth, and which promises no recompense; a caprice, the duration of which does not depend upon our volition, and which is subject to remorse and repentance.

I Suck at Being in Love

Before I said I suck at Seduction. I may suck even more at being in love.

Somehow I ended up in a bit of a funk. I'm not really sure why. My writing session at GCA at the beginning of the week went well. Well, it went well from a personal perspective. Maybe a little less well from a writing perspective. But I felt very much like something different clicked with Philippe.

It was another hot, quiet August day. Not much was opened in the neighborhood, or any neighborhood. The restaurant was mostly empty with just a middle aged couple sitting at the bar and an occasional tourist taking a seat on the terrace. Things were a little out of whack. Philippe wasn't there when I arrived but the unfriendly, part-time manager was working. And Guillaume was working, even though it was too early for him. The couple at the bar kept looking at me. I got the distinct feeling that they knew something about me but I had never seen them. Kind of like Aimee and her sisters, everyone seems to know something about the American girl who writes at GCA. It all felt upside down and weird.

I may be reading way too much into this but this part-time manager gives me a very strange vibe. He seems to look at me in a way that says "I know what you're up to and I don't like it. If there is anything at all I can do about it I will stop it." As if he's protecting Philippe against me. Protecting him for someone else. Maybe the blonde? He seems to have the same, maybe even stronger relationship with her that Philippe has.

After a short bit Philippe came into the dining room. Where did he come from? From outside? Or just from his office upstairs? I didn't notice. He came to me right away and gave me kisses on both cheeks. How was I? Did I need his inspiration? I was distracted, lost in Paris of the 1600s. It took me a bit to realize he was standing in front of me and asking me questions. And there was a new twinkle in his eye. He was looking at me like I was someone special. And I was lost in Ninon's world. The couple at the bar glared at me. The part-time manager gave me side eye.

When I left I felt different. I can't really say why. I just felt like he knew. He knew that he felt the same way.

I went home and pulled my shell around me. I spent two entire days watching Netflix. I watched every movie that Netflix recommended when I searched "Hugh Grant". I watched a ridiculous number of love stories. Of course they all had happy endings. I mourned my own personal absence of a happy ending. I descended into a gloomy bad feeling about my own lot in life.

I'm struggling with Ninon. I don't feel like I really know her. There are so many contradictions. Her epicureanism. Maybe I don't really understand epicureanism. Today when you say the word people think "ah, you want to eat good food and drink good wine."

Let's revisit Epicurus's own words:

"When we say... that pleasure is the end and aim, we do not mean the pleasures of the prodigal or the pleasures of sensuality, as we are understood by some through ignorance, prejudice or wilful misrepresentation. By pleasure we mean the absence of pain in the body and of trouble in the soul. It is not by an unbroken succession of drinking bouts and of revelry, not by sexual lust, nor the enjoyment of fish and other delicacies of a luxurious table, which produce a pleasant life; it is sober reasoning, searching out the grounds of every choice and avoidance, and banishing those beliefs through which the greatest tumults take possession of the soul."

Absence of pain in the body and trouble in the soul. Sober reasoning. Searching out the grounds of every choice and avoidance and banishing those beliefs through which the greatest tumults take possession of the soul.

It feels very elusive. What does that mean in my own life? How do I insure against absence of pain and trouble in my soul? How do I exorcise those tumults that tend to take possession of my own soul?

But Ninon was also given to distractions of the heart. She fell in love quickly and often. And it seems like she also fell out of love as quickly and as often. This coupled with her intelligence, her cleverness, her ability to share her philosophy both in writing and in person, were her legacy. She was clearly special, standing above all other women, not because she was more beautiful than other women, although she was, and not because she was more educated, although she was, but because she had something no one else had, neither women nor men.

And then there was the whole friendship thing. Friendship was said to mean more to Ninon than all else. There was nothing she wouldn't do for a friend. I have read story after story of times when Ninon came through for a friend.

So what is bothering me? I just don't feel like I know her. For all the stories I have read, both about her and in her own words, I just don't feel like I know who Ninon was. When I took my deep dive into all things Hemingway, I felt like I really knew the man. I didn't particularly like him. But I felt like I could see him; the stubble on his cheeks, the boozy but searching look in his eyes, his belly not quite covered by the ratty shirt not quite tucked into the belt of his pants, that don't quite fit right. I could see the dirt under his fingernails, the cigar ash in his beard, smell his boozy breath and not so fresh body odor. I could see him looking through me, deciding that I wasn't worth his notice.

Ninon would not have looked through me. I think she would have looked at me, into me, wanting to know what I needed. How can she help me? I think that Ninon can help me. I think she was put in front of me at this time, in this place, to help me get through this challenge. To learn to love. All I have to do is open myself to her. To hear her lesson. It's not too late. And if I don't listen, I will not love in this life.

The old me would seduce the part-time manager who doesn't like me and hate myself in the process. The old me would give Philippe away to one of my friends What will the new me do?

Caroleen Strikes Again

Stephanie texted me: "Going to be in the neighborhood to greet some new clients. Would you like to meet at Cépage for a coffee at 10:30?" I haven't seen Stephanie in a few weeks. It would be good to catch up.

It was a perfect morning. Although two weeks remained to August, and September's Indian summer loomed a long time off, the weather had cooled down by a lot and some trees were beginning to turn gold. It was warm enough to wear short sleeves and enjoy the terrace. Signs of life had started to pop up; cleaners and painters freshening up the restaurants that had been closed for the past three weeks. The butcher was open and chickens turned on the rotisserie, dripping their juices on the baby potatoes below. The realtors office was open and I saw a *"Vendu"* sign on an apartment above. I didn't even know it was *"A Vendre"*! It fits the profile of what I was looking for a year ago; *"on rue Caulaincourt, entre numero 55 et 65, face à la rue, sur la deuxième étage ou plus"* While I have decided that I dodged a bullet by not being able to buy an apartment, I would have liked to take a look at it.

I arrived at Cépage and carefully snuck a peek to see if Caroleen was around. Not inside; not outside. I took a seat outside. Laurent greeted me with a hearty handshake and looked at his watch. *"Un peu tôt!"*

"Oui, j'attends une amie." I told him. I'm waiting for a friend. I ordered a *café* and a croissant.

Stephanie arrived and I introduced her to Laurent. It's good for these people to know I have other friends, in case Caroleen has been talking to them. For now I seem reasonably welcome.

"I'm a bit nervous about coming here," I confided to Stephanie and told her about the nasty Instagram post. She looked appropriately shocked and tisked in that French way she does. Then she leaned in to confide something to me.

"I have to tell you something." she said conspiratorially. Her face took on a look of dread seriousness and she leaned closer. "About four months ago, I received an anonymous letter that said horrible things about you."

I was at a complete loss for words.

"I shared it with Magalie because I didn't know what to do. We decided that it would be best not to tell you about it. We didn't want to hurt your feelings."

"What? What did it say?"

"That you were a very bad person and that I should not rent to you. That before long you would sue me. That you were evil and you should leave France and go back to California to your family."

I suspect there may have been more to it but that's the gist of what she told me.

"Was it in English or French?"

"English. It had to be her. But at the time I had no idea about any of this."

I just stared at Stephanie, a little baffled. Four months ago. I was still in the other apartment. I hadn't poked the hornets' nest. I hadn't accosted her. I completely avoided Cépage for at least a month after "*le divorce*". The only thing even slightly confrontational I had done to her was ignoring her. My mind quickly raced through all of the people who could possibly want to write such a letter. Who could have been even slightly annoyed with me and want to do such a thing. It was a quick race because there was nobody! It would be simple enough for Caroleen to figure out who to write the letter to. I probably had told her myself. For that matter, I might have even introduced her to Stephanie. But why? There is no conceivable why. I looked behind me into the restaurant at the banquet she normally lays claim to. Nobody is there.

I spent the rest of the day not able to stop thinking about it. She's crazy! I certainly am off the hook for my going low and posting that she was crazy on Facebook. Her disparagement proceeded mine by months! How can I go back to Cépage? How can I walk down the street? What if I see her?

And then I slept on it. And again. And then I realized. What would Ninon do? Ninon wouldn't post the really disgusting picture I have of her slurping oysters. I won't post the photo either. But I won't delete it. And I'm not going to give her Cépage. I'm not going to give her another thought from this moment on. I win.

Une Petite Soirée

Well, maybe not so fast! I read the letter. And I cannot get it out of my head. Try as I might to be like Ninon, the old 13 year old me keeps creeping back in. This is all so junior high school.

Magalie and Stephanie came for *apéro*. As it was my first time entertaining the two *chez moi*, I wanted to put my best foot forward. Fortunately the chee-semonger returned from *les vacances* the day before and I filled in with wine and champagne from Le Franprix. I arranged what was later declared to be an impressive cheese board with some sliced meats, vegetables and olives and put out champagne glasses, wine glasses and glasses for the stuff that makes their teeth green to finish off the night.

The girls arrived right on time with Bob the dog. Bob, being a not particularly well trained puppy went right for the cheese board.

"Woah!" everyone cried out in unison and I moved the cheese board up to the kitchen counter until the dog calmed down. We opened the first bottle of champagne, poured glasses all around and toasted our friendship.

It was only minutes before Magalie launched into the hot topic of the letter. She wanted to dig deeper. Why would anyone say these things about me? I am such a lovely person. She needed to hear the entire story. She refused to let me spare any detail. At this point I had frankly gotten a bit bored with it all and particularly bored and disappointed in myself for being so obsessed by it all.

"I think I have the letter on my phone," she said. Scroll, scroll, scroll… there it was.

Essentially it was just a bunch of inane nonsense. Lots about my size and how much I eat and my belonging to some sort of dining club. I'm so unhealthy I can barely walk ten steps without sitting down. (By that I must have to take at least five breaks walking to Cépage). The sum of that was it would be dangerous to rent to me because I cannot possibly be healthy and something will happen which, me being American, I will surely sue Stephanie. There was more about me making friends in five minutes and then the friendships turning into drama.

So there, when I write it all down, it seems like really much ado about nothing. Clearly what bothers me most is her nasty remarks about my size, not nearly as obnoxiously stated as me being a grotesque fat fuck, but also just hitting bang on my preteen insecurities. Good God! I spent the last dozen years as a highly successful executive of a billion dollar high tech company. I traveled the world visiting embassies, consulates, government officials and empowering women in developing nations. I influenced and advised very respected business leaders. I was the keynote speaker at a China Engineering Conference! And I successfully retired in Paris. How can one stinking anonymous letter from a clear crackpot upset me so much? Why is she so vile and fixated on my being in Paris? Is it because I do have friends? Because I am invited to dine with a lovely group of expats on a regular basis? Or is it because, like my daughter said, I called her on her bigotry and prejudice? I don't know if you can call someone on something they don't know they are.

Jesus Christ, what am I doing, rattling off my accomplishments like some insecure idiot? Caroleen has turned me into my thirteen year old self; Bucky Beaver, taunted by the likes of Kevin Kelly on Mellus Street. I haven't thought about this old stuff for decades.

"Well, I think I am grateful to her!" I say, bolstered by alcohol. "She has helped me get closer to my character."

They both looked at me completely baffled.

"I've been struggling to know Ninon. And this has helped me a lot. After many frustrated and cranky nights and days thinking about this, I realized that I need to think more like Ninon." I continued, "You can't be famous without your detractors. Of course, I don't think I'm famous. But you can't have any level of notoriety without having some people not like you. For example, for all my success at work, there were definitely people who didn't like me. The number wasn't large, thankfully, but people who were on the losing end of my policies and my decisions were not big fans.

"For whatever reason, Caroleen hates me. Think of all the people who must have been intensely jealous of Ninon. Who hated her. The Queen, Anne of Austria, hated her so much she banned her to a convent. She was rescued by her Oiseaux." I refilled my glasses and the girls. "Caroleen tried to ban me from Paris! And I was rescued by Stephanie!"

OK it was a stretch but it was time to talk about something else. So we did. Vacations in Italy, Vacations in the US. Sex clubs in Paris. Our boozy *apéro* goes on late into the night, consuming multiple bottles of champagne, a bottle of wine and a good part of the Get 77 and cognac. The girls go off into the night with Bob and I go into my room where I find a chewed up slipper and a puddle of dog pee on my bedroom floor. I think that was Bob's last *apéro chez moi*.

I drag myself out of bed, wicked tired because I slept very poorly and spent the night pondering the letter. It's still August and after what has been declared the hottest summer on record Montmartre feels like Autumn. The one tree in front of my apartment window, the one I am calling the canary in the coal mine, has lost two thirds of its golden leaves. The rest of the trees are still green but I know they'll be following soon. It's not cold enough for the coats many Parisians are sporting but it's also too cold for the sleeveless outfits I've been wearing since I returned from California in June. I opted for a light sweater over my regular slacks and threw an umbrella in my computer bag and headed out for lunch and a writing session.

Cépage is clearly the easiest and cheapest option. Barely 100 steps from home and with its daily l'*ardoise* that promises an under twelve euro lunch, it's terribly convenient and comfortable. The staff is lovely to me and while it lacks the *beau* Philippe, I somehow feel that my future with Philippe will be a little enhanced by a bit of absence on my part. (Does absence really make the heart grow fonder? Or is out of sight, out of mind?)

I entered Cépage quietly, looked around the busy restaurant and saw she wasn't here. So I took a seat on the banquet that she doesn't usually sit on. A man was sitting in her normal place. The pretty young Asian girl greeted me and asked if I wanted lunch, the one that Caroleen insisted the manager fire months ago when she refused to let her off the hook for her *café crème* when she realized she was a few euros short. Figuring that the girl couldn't possibly like Caroleen I confided that I was checking to see if *"mon ennemi"* was here. *"Elle me deteste"* I told her, she hates me.

"Pourquoi?" she asked, interested in this bit of gossip.

"Je ne sais pas?" I told her that she had written a letter to my landlord saying that I was evil and that she should not rent to me.

"I don't like her either." she said, conspiratorially.

I pulled out my book and started reading while I waited for my lunch to arrive. I was eating my lovely *tagliatelles au bleu* when Caroleen and her husband walked in. Being absorbed in my book, I didn't notice it was her that walked in front of me until I looked up to see who grunted and caught sight of her husband behind her. Ha! Her entire banquet was full. They had to resort to sitting outside.

I kept my nose in my book and the waitress came over and whispered "She's here!"

"I know" I said.

"Maybe do you think she is jealous?" she asked.

"Of what?!"

Garron went to take their order. First he shook her hand, and then she pulled him in for *la bise*. Strange. I've never seen her *la bise* any of the Cépage's servers. Garron has just returned from a few months absence. He may be the only one of the staff that doesn't dislike her. Other than the owner, who she insists wants to sleep with her.

Caroleen is dressed in a wool coat with a scarf wrapped around her neck. Her finger combed hair is pulled back into a messy ponytail and there's a comb stuck in randomly. She and F read their individual newspapers, talk on their individual cell phones and drink their coffees. After a short time F leaves and she sits alone. I assume she's waiting for her regular table to become available but eventually she asks for a menu and orders something to eat and a glass of wine. It must be driving her crazy that she has to sit outside in the freezing cold 68 degree weather while I'm inside working on my computer.

And I'm still doing way too much thinking about her. This is NOT what Ninon would do. It's time for me to get past all this distracting and negative thinking. I've got things to accomplish. Tomorrow I will break my Philippe fast before I leave for ten days in the US.

Les Vacances moins un jour

I am paralyzed by indecision. Why? Tomorrow I leave for my vacation in the US and I haven't done any of the things I was going to do; buy the little cocktail napkins for Christine, buy dresses for Izzy and Ellie, write 5,000 words. OK, I made an effort to buy the dresses on the way to the bus from L'Ami Jean but the shop has disappeared. And the napkins... they just seem like too much trouble and not really necessary. I haven't been to GCA in a week so I plan to go today to write and to let Philippe know about my vacation.

Oddly, I think part of my frustration is that while my upgrade for the trip to San Francisco is confirmed, the upgrade for the return looks terribly unlikely. Business class is full. Coach is nearly full. I am already thinking about a flight a week and a half away, stuck in coach for 11 hours and it's impacting my view of the world. How utterly stupid. Maybe I need to fly coach to remember where I came from!

I piddle away the morning then shower and dress and head for GCA. No Philippe! The same guy who doesn't like me is ruling the roost. Philippe seems to be on vacation himself! And he didn't even tell me he was going!

Everything is upside down: the bar man is waiting tables, the unfriendly manager (at least he did greet me when I arrived although no handshake OR *la bise*) is behind the bar, a new waitress is acting like she knows what she's doing already! The music track is calm and almost can't be heard. No lively dance music keeping the place rocking and rolling. No Philippe. No inspiration!

I order my lunch; a delectable fish stew with vegetables and a carafe of rosé. No bottle for me today. I have plans tonight with Magalie and Jeff to see

Larry Browne in the 14eme. I met Larry on a Wednesday jazz night at GCA a couple of years ago. He's from San Francisco so we built on that commonality to develop a petit amitie. I love Magalie and I really like Jeff. I have to leave at 6:30 in the morning. I haven't seen 6:30 in the morning since I last flew to SF. I can always sleep on the plane.

The Friday boys arrive for lunch at GCA and take Philippe's round table. I strain to hear if there's any talk about why Philippe is not there. They talk about returning from their vacations, but there is no mention about Philippe. The new waitress gives them all la bise. Interesting.

I wanted to write about Ninon today. The words are not coming.

Maybe I should finish up my wine, Uber to Maille and buy the little napkins and some truffle mustard for Christine (and myself) and then taxi to Jacadi and buy dresses for the sweet little girls. Take back my control.

Tomorrow I will fly to the other place, where I am another person. And all that matters is petite Izzy. When we FaceTimed yesterday she showed me her latest dance moves and asked me to take her to a Super Hero movie. I will go from life in Paris to life at the 3 foot level. And not think about Caroleen or Philippe or speaking French.

But first I'll navigate the long stairway to the toilettes.

A love letter to my stalker

I admit you got to me. You occupied my head for way too long. Even after I was determined to get over it, asking "What would Ninon do?" you still held court in what was in danger of becoming your own personal apartment in my brain. You reached back into some yet unresolved childhood insecure place and the result was not pretty.

The timing worked against me; a trip to California to visit family, where I was no longer a successful career woman, life moves on, people look to someone else for all the things you used to provide. And my happy Paris life was 6,000 miles and nine time zones away. Life in Paris moved on without me as well, as evidenced by postings from a rejuvenated post *La Rentrée Parisienne* on social media. I was in limbo, between two happy places and taken back to my least happy place. So I must say you almost won!

The key is "almost". Long talks with trusted friends helped a little. Scoffs and dismissive remarks from daughters helped a little more. What really made the difference was allowing myself to take a Leap of Faith.

Nobody achieves a degree of success without incurring a bit of animosity and jealousy. Caroleen, you clearly hate me. How does a person go from friendship and admiration to such intense hatred in a moment? While we were friends you occasionally took petite stabs at me; little jabs about my French language *un*skills or my appearance. "Why are those women looking at you like that?" you would point out. A real friend would not do that. This was the behavior of someone trying to plant seeds of insecurity. Why would you do that?

Everytime we would end our meeting in a disagreement about politics, you would later text me apologizing for keeping on and saying that it was so important for people living in Paris. But our true disagreement was never really about whatever she apologized for.

I detest it when people blame bad behavior on jealousy. It's too easy. And having nurtured those old dormant seeds of insecurity in me, the idea of you being jealous of me is particularly distasteful. But it's clearly the case here. Your letter to Stephanie had two main themes, my size and my friendships. You chose the first because you knew you could get to me. By choosing the latter you unwittingly showed your cards. "She makes friends in five minutes." As if that is a bad thing. I admit, it baffled me. Were you saying that quickly made friendships were not worth anything? Were you saying that I was an untrustworthy friend?

And then I realized, you don't have friends! Every person in your life is treated with scorn. Sure, you get la bise from some of the cranky old men your husband sits and drinks with. And you say hello to some of the regulars at Cépage. But I've never seen you share une verre with anyone on your own. I've never seen you having lunch or dinner with anyone other than F. You mentioned my "dining club" as if it was something I should feel ashamed of. Yet, you pled with me to introduce you to some of my network. You asked me to be my "plus one" at a dinner party. You never get invited to dinner parties or aperos or jazz nights. You don't have friends. And because I do and because I chose to walk away from you, you despise me. Caroleen, that is your problem. You cannot fathom how I can have a happy life. Like Queen Anne could not tolerate Ninon having a happy life and friends and admirers so she banished her to a convent! You tried to banish me; to make it impossible for me to live in our little village. Ninon cleverly outwitted the Queen by manipulating her into allowing her to choose the Les Grands Cordeliers for her banishment. Her Oiseaux ultimately got her released.

The good will of my friends and loved ones has helped resurrect me from the purgatory your nastiness sent me into. But more importantly, you brought me into the mind and soul of Ninon. Nobody achieves a degree of success and notoriety without incurring a degree of jealousy. The grace is in how one handles that jealousy. I don't know how to lift you from the mean spirited place you live. And frankly, it's not my job. I do, however, thank you. I was struggling to find Ninon, to get into her soul and you alone allowed me to do this. So for this I am grateful. Merci.

Friends and Enemies and the Blurry Lines Between

You don't get to live a life as extraordinary as Ninon's without making a few enemies along the way. Especially when you sleep with their husbands AND their sons. As mentioned before, Ninon's relationship with Marie, Madame de Sévigné was a complicated one. Her affair with Marie's husband was not a business relationship. Henri was a serial philanderer. He had been married two times before and this one to Marie was only six years old when Ninon and he "hooked up".

Henri was from Brittany in the north, Marie was a City girl, born and raised in Paris. A young girl of not yet twenty, she brought the money to the union. Henri brought a title and flair and although they intended to live in Paris Henri was granted an important position in Provence and the couple was required to leave the city. Marie was certainly no fool. Henri had a history of foolish spending and with the help of an uncle she cleverly kept her finances separate from her promiscuous husband. However, in due time, she found herself trapped, a bird in a gilded cage, in her lovely estate in Vitre, some 300 kilometers away from Paris, while Henri spent more and more time away from her and their two small children, Francoise-Marguerite and Charles. Marie provided the very best tutors for both of the children and they grew to be erudite and prolific letter writers.

Ninon was only a couple of years older than Marie but light years beyond her in terms of worldliness and experience. While Marie was a virgin when she married Henri, Ninon had had at least a dozen lovers and a reputation for being the one to pass on the most coveted lessons of love. They were both beautiful but Marie's beauty was locked up in a chateau in the countryside and of course NInon moved about the streets of Paris, admired by many, a free woman.

It's difficult to say what about Henri appealed to Ninon. By the time they became lovers Ninon was financially independent and Henri wasn't paying for her time. He wasn't contributing to her household. That's not to say he didn't shower her with beautiful things. In fact, their affair didn't last long and Henri, with his wandering eye and his overactive libido was on to his next conquest, a Mademoiselle de Gondran. It was over Mademoiselle that Henri engaged in a duel with Chevalier de Albret, losing and dying from the terrible wounds that were inflicted only two days later.

Marie mourned briefly and then moved house and home back to Paris where she lived near the Palais Royal, raised her children in peace and developed a small but satisfying salon of her own. Marie never remarried and expended her energies developing her daughter into an educated and lovely young woman.

Marie clearly preferred her daughter Marguerite allowing Charles to run wild. It was not long before Charles showed a predilection to follow in the philandering spendthrift footsteps of his father. Charles was not stupid and the tutors and ministrations provided to him by his mother rendered him clever with words if not a bit short on scruples. For nearly two decades Marie's bitter feelings about Ninon's dalliance with her husband incubated quietly only to bloom wildly when young Charles followed his father's footsteps briefly into the arms of Marie's rival.

We know that the relationship was short lived and we have heard Ninon refer to Charles to his mother as having a soul of pulp, a body of wet paper and a heart of pumpkin fricasseed in snow. It had to be very difficult for Marie to swallow her pride and ask Ninon to tutor young Charles and turn him into a man. Ninon, the very woman who had been lover to both her husband and her son, who's Salon was far more esteemed, who enjoyed all of the freedom and liberties of a person who had accepted having a reputation, and earned a wonderfully positive life bountiful with friendships, the respect of those who knew her as well as those who wanted to know her, and the regard of those in the highest positions of State.

La Rentree

How in the world would he know how I feel about him when I don't even interact with him. I got a lovely greeting when I arrived at GCA. He pointed at his watch and looked admonishingly at me. Perhaps he should have pointed at his calendar. He gave me a more intimate *bise* than usual, I think he actually kissed my cheeks instead of the air. Was I on vacances? "*Oui, des Etats Unis. Je me suis réveillée à midi!*" "Ohhhh, jet lag?!" he said.

I ordered from the waitress. He clarified with her how I like my wine. Then he told me that I speak excellent french. I said "J'ai oublie tout!"

Then I opened my laptop and started writing. How is he ever going to know how I feel when I spend all my time writing? How do I take that "leap of faith" and tell him that I love him? And if he says he doesn't love me? At least I know and I move on. But then everything changes. The big dilemma. Can I jump that hurdle? I never have before and I've always ended up the worse for it. Will I grow up finally?

What is it about the man that gets to me? He's not particularly handsome, although his looks are pleasing enough. I actually like that he has a bit of a belly. It makes him less intimidating. Is he smart? He's certainly not smart like the Silicon Valley people I'm used to. But he's smart enough to run a successful business. His staff seems to like and respect him. They all shake his hand when they arrive and leave for work. (Then most of them shake my hand as well.) I can't imagine shaking my boss's hand each morning. "Good morning, Jerry" at the coffee machine was pretty much the extent of my daily greeting. His nearly daily blurb on social media is the full extent of my insight into his literary skills.

Today he taught me a new word; "*maussade*", sullen. He called the day a little sullen. It's grey. It rained a bit this morning. Sweater weather. It's a good word. He's clearly not stupid.

He's always got a song on his lips. When he's not singing he's talking, often just talking to himself.

He's eating lunch with Daniel, the guy who fills in for him when he's on vacation. The one who doesn't like me. They are clearly good friends. But what a contrast. Daniel is a ladies man. Philippe is a people person. Daniel seems cynical and snide. Philippe seems sincere and kind.

He loves his champagne and often drinks it at work. He also likes a glass of red wine, Côte du Rhône generally, but seems to sip champagne in the afternoons. I never knew a man who drank champagne. Well maybe Daniele Chandelier. And always thought it was a bit of a feminine drink.

He doesn't bother me when I am writing. He takes my writing seriously. Sometimes I catch him watching me. I wonder what he is thinking.

He seems happy but a bit wounded perhaps. I want to know that story. Who wounded you, my darling? What is your story?

I do have to wonder about drinking and driving. Soon Philippe will hop on his moto and go wherever it is he goes around 5 pm. He is sipping his champagne and had two glasses of red wine with his lunch. The delivery guy came with boxes of moules (will they be on the menu tomorrow?) Before he leaves he has a tall glass of beer and chats with Philippe and Daniel. When he finishes he will hop in his truck and be off to his next delivery. Drinking and driving and smoking. All seem to be a way of life in Paris.

I drank half a bottle of wine but I'll be taking Uber home. Then I'll be heading out for dinner with my expat friends. At least I'm skipping the *apéro*.

Ninon Tutors le Marquis

Theirs was a complicated relationship. Madame de Sévigné was a bright woman and occasionally spent time in Ninon's Salon, but most often she frequented that of Nicholas Fouquet, the Minister of Finances to Louis XIV, and as such preferred the atmosphere of the Court, which Ninon eschewed. However, being neighbors in the Place Royale, both ladies of letters, it was only natural that their paths would cross.

Madame de Sévigné was closest to her firstborn, her daughter Françoise, and it was to Françoise that she dedicated most of her own attention. She was at a loss for what to do with Charles.

"My dear Ninon," she implored, "It would be such a favor to me if you would help him. He is unfortunately a heart fool. I fear for his future!"

"A heart fool?" Ninon exclaimed! "Charles is a man beyond definition. He has a soul of pulp, a body of wet paper and a heart of pumpkin fricasseed in snow!"

Ninon turned to look out the window at the square below. Autumn was coming to the Place Royale and it was once again possible to open the windows and let in some air. Just the week before Ninon was housebound as a horrendous heat wave plagued the city and the air was fetid. Two days of rain washed away the top level of the merde and mire that accumulated in the streets and on the sidewalks and wedged between the city's cobbles. Only the top level, but the rest was on its way to becoming part of the pavements of Paris, petrified into a kind of permanent grout. Best not to let your hem touch the ground!

Now the leaves were turning gold and some already littered the gravel square below. A few children were running about under the watchful eye of their respective nannies, delighted to finally be allowed outside for a bit of fun and frolic. Servants scurried by, their baskets filled with purchases from the nearby marche, dodging horses pulling carriages. This was Ninon's favorite time of year. Spring was too wet, summer too hot, and winter so very cold. Autumn was perfect. Wise with the knowledge of all that had passed in the year but with just a little promise of what might be yet to come. Ninon thought, "a bit like my life!"

She refocused her attention on Madame de Sévigné. "*Oui*", she acquiesced. "I will speak with him. Tell him to call on me next week and I will see what can be done with the boy." And so it was that Ninon's rather long period of communication with the young Charles, Maquis de Sévigné, began. Ninon took the young Chevalier in charge, intent on making a man of him.

Charles arrived early on the appointed afternoon, very eager to spend time with the beautiful and very alluring friend of his mother, fully expecting to rejuvenate and expand on their their very brief past affair. Of course her reputation was already unsurpassed in the Place Royale and Charles had visions of becoming one of the very lucky men to sample her legendary sexual prowess. He was dressed in his dashing best and was doused in perfumed waters, cocky and ready to roll, twenty minutes before his expected time.

Ninon sat at her desk in her private office, writing to her oldest and dearest friend M. de Saint-Evremond when her maid entered to tell her that Charles was in the salon.

"Already?" asked Ninon. "Well please make him comfortable; but not too comfortable. It is important to educate our young friend that it is not acceptable to arrive so terribly early." She returned to her writing and the maid scurried off with a small smile, ready to school the young man.

An hour later Ninon entered the salon. By this time Charles was fairly stewing in his own juices; alternating between fury at being kept waiting and eager anticipation of the ardour of which he expected to be on the receiving end.

"Monsieur." Ninon said, extending her hand to Charles.

Charles impertinently seized her hand and turned it upward, kissing her wrist, a clever little ploy he had adopted to initiate intimacy. To be fair, it had worked incredibly well with the young women Charles had engaged with thus far. Ninon snapped her hand away and turned her back on him. Oh dear, she thought, this is going to be an even bigger endeavor than I had expected!

"*Monsieur le Marquis!*" she scolded, "I am not one of your young friends! If you behave in such a manner again, our communications will cease immediately!" She gazed pointedly at the Maquis for a full minute as he wilted noticeably before she turned and took a seat on a nearby settee. After another full minute she invited him to take a seat as well, in an adjoining chair.

Afraid to say the wrong thing, the Maquis just stared silently at Ninon, waiting for her next direction. For her part Ninon just watched the young man, taking some satisfaction in his discomfort. Finally she began.

"Monsieur le Marquis, as a friend to your mother, I have agreed to make a man of you. You seem to perhaps have misinterpreted what this means. I fear our lessons will not be at all comfortable for you. I will in fact be sharing with you many secrets of the female heart."

At this the Maquis noticeably perked up and leaned forward a bit.

"But I will also be exposing your own frailties!" Ninon continued. Charles settled back into his seat, looking dejected.

"I am dining tonight with Marquis de la Rochefoucauld, Madame de la Salière and La Fontaine. Perhaps you would like to join us. La Fontaine will tell two new stories."

The invitation made Charles feel that perhaps his transgressions were not fatal. While his tutoring was not to take a path that he had hoped, he was not being tossed out the window like the morning honey pot.

Charles pulled himself up to his full height and composure; "Madame de l'Enclos, thank you from the bottom of my heart for not only including me this evening, but for considering my education in the ways of the heart. I very much look forward to the dinner this evening." Looking anxiously toward the door he was eager to get away.

"*Mais, Monsieur!*" Ninon said, "Make no mistake about this undertaking of ours! We are going to take a course of morals together. Yes, sir, MORALS! But do not be alarmed at the mere word, for there will be between us only the question of gallantry to discuss, and that, you know, sways morals to so high a degree that it deserves to be the subject of a special study. The very idea of such a project is to me infinitely laughable. However, if I speak only of reason to you, will you not tire of our discourse? This is my only concern, for as you know, I am a pitiless reasoner when I wish to be. With any other heart than that which you misunderstand, I could be a philosopher such that the world never knew."

And with that she turned and walked out of the room, leaving poor Charles gazing at her back.

Playfulness and Weakness

Ninon sat at her desk, pen poised thoughtfully above a sheet of paper. Contrary to his fantasies of long afternoons in Ninon's private rooms, her letters to the Marquis de Sévigné were the delivery of her promise to him to educate him in matters of love.

"At your age, being unable to think of entering into a serious engagement, it is not necessary to find a friend in a woman; one should seek to find only an amiable mistress.

The intercourse with women of lofty principles, or those whom the ravages of time force into putting themselves forward only by virtue of great qualities, is excellent for a man who, like themselves, is on life's decline. For you, these women would be too good company, if I dare so express myself."

Ninon paused and thought for a moment about what she was saying to the young Marquis. The handsome young man had indicated that he would like to be next in line for Ninon's affections. While the notion was intriguing for about half a second, she knew the folie of such a temptation.

She continued, "Riches are necessary to us only in proportion to our wants; and what you would better do, I think, is to frequent the society of those who combine with agreeable figure, gentleness in conversation, cheerfulness in disposition, a taste for the pleasures of society, and strong enough not to be frightened by one affair of the heart.

"In the eyes of a man of reason they appear too frivolous, you will say: but do you think they should be judged with so much severity? Be persuaded, Marquis, that if, unfortunately they should acquire more firmness of character, they and you would lose much by it. You require in women stability of character! Well, do you not find it in a friend? It is not our virtues you need; but our playfulness and our weakness. The love which you could feel for a woman who would be estimable in every respect, would become too dangerous for you. Until you can contemplate a contract of marriage, you should seek only to amuse yourself with those who are beautiful; a passing taste alone should attach you to one of them: be careful not to plunge in too deep with her; there can nothing result but a bad ending. If you did not reflect more profoundly than the greater part of young people; I should talk to you in an entirely different tone; but I perceive that you are ready to give to excess, a contrary meaning to their ridiculous frivolity. It is only necessary, then to attach yourself to a woman who, like an agreeable child, might amuse you with pleasant follies, light caprices, and all those pretty faults which make the charm of a gallant intercourse."

Fast forward some three hundred and fifty years. My dear friend Siobhan has been in love with her best friend for three years. He doesn't know. They share a work space and compare notes on their jobs every day. They eat lunch together and go for drinks after hours. During that time he's been in two serious relationships and she has, at emotional cost to herself, counselled him through the ups and downs of each relationship.

The women were each ten years younger than her best friend and pretty much emotional wrecks. The first wanted desperately to get pregnant, finally resorting to the costly expense of in vitro fertilization. When a much celebrated pregnancy ended in miscarriage, the stress and grief tore the couple apart. Siobhan was there to pick up the crumbled pieces of her friend and hoped that after an appropriate period he would recognize that what he was really looking for was right in front of him.

Unfortunately, the friend's appropriate period of time was much shorter than Siobhan could have anticipated and before you could blink there was a new pretty young thing sharing his apartment. This one was a lost soul of twenty five, trying to find herself. Her latest enterprise was an expensive wine training program that required her to travel around Europe learning all the important things about wine. She needed the man, not so much to support her financially (her generous daddy was taking care of that) but to support her emotionally. Often. And a lot. Siobhan took a deep breath and settled back for another long wait. "It won't last," she told me. "I don't see him with her in the long term. Soon he will tire of the drama."

In the meantime, Siobhan rearranged the furniture in his apartment to be more user friendly, stocked his liquor cabinet with things that he would like and helped him negotiate a new employment contract earning him one hundred thousand euros a year more money. He celebrated the exciting windfall by buying himself an expensive watch. He texted a picture of the watch to Siobhan.

Out of the blue I got an urgent message from Siobhan who was on a business trip in Ireland. "He just broke up with her! I am returning to Paris tonight and we are going to have dinner tomorrow. Let's have drinks tonight."

It would seem that Best Friend has been following Ninon's advice for his entire adult life. Do men ever outgrow the appetite for playfulness and weakness? Is it possible for Siobhan to move from the friend zone to a romance with Best Friend?

Elliot told me one time that he contributed to the success of his twenty year marriage to the fact that he "married his best friend". He has confided to me stories of a wild past with multiple girlfriends at the same time; models, ballerinas, artists, all with traumatic problems and neediness. Joan certainly seems to be none of these things, the epitome of self confidence, quiet and stability. Somewhere along the line Elliot figured out how to make the leap from an agreeable child to a woman estimable in every respect.

Best Friend is crushed. Siobhan confides that she needs to give him some time before she tells him how she feels. "But how much time?" I ask? "Look what happened last time!" It's tricky we agree. Or is it just too scary? What if she tells him how she feels and he says he doesn't feel the same? Which would be the greater loss? The loss of her Best Friend? Or the loss of hope? Hope that someday, this man will be hers.

What is required here is a leap of faith. A heroic leap of faith.

What about my own leap of faith? Can I learn from Ninon here? Is the potential reality of something real with Philippe worth risking the loss of the dream of something real with Philippe? After all, if it's never to be, wouldn't it be better just to accept that and move on? Am I brave enough to risk a heroic leap of faith?

The Funk

I'm in a funk. It's ironic actually. I just told a friend that one of the best things about living in Paris was that I had absolutely no worries. I should have known better than to tempt fate. I came home to an email that changed everything. The owner of my apartment, the PERFECT apartment in Paris, was planning to live in it beginning March, the day my current lease expires.

My heart stopped. I had asked Stephanie to get an agreement from the owner that I could rent from her next year. It was taking an awfully long time for her to answer. I should have suspected. Stephanie said that she wants to be here at least until the beginning of September. Did I want her to talk to the owner of a place in the ninth and see if they would like a tenant?

I was still stuck at the idea of giving up my perfect apartment. I couldn't even think about the ninth.

After about twenty minutes the survivor side of me kicked in. On the other side of this roller coaster was a better thing. I just had to buckle my seat belt and enjoy (???) the ride. "It's an opportunity for growth," I told myself. Show what you're made of. "In March you will be remarking how absolutely fortuitous this change was for you."

For the next two days my apartment felt like a traitor. Looking out the window at the produce vendor, the rug man, the Japanese restaurant, they all felt like co-conspirators to the treason. *Je suis la fille américaine!* I belong here. I'm part of the fabric of the neighborhood.

But maybe not. Options ran through my head. I could start looking for an apartment to buy again. Maybe fate was preparing to put the ideal place in my path. After all, I missed the apartment upstairs when it sold for a price I could easily handle. Maybe there was a more perfect place in store for me. Maybe the owner would find, after six months she didn't really want to live in Paris, in Montmartre, on the most perfect street, in the only apartment with the perfect view on the perfect curve of the perfect street. Maybe the summer months will be so horribly hot and miserable that she will hate it and will want to get out fast! Maybe she will find that she doesn't like living in Paris at all. Or maybe not. After all, it is perfect.

Besides, I can't plant myself in a temporary place based on a bunch of maybes.

Then I considered actual survival. How could I ensure that I would have a roof over my head, regardless of whether or not it was the perfect roof? Right before I got the email I was having dinner with visitors from the US who were staying in a little apartment on rue Lamarck, right across from the metro station. My friend Silvie manages it and I always thought it looked quite charming from her website. I wondered about it being on the stairs to the *métro*. Would it be noisy? Dona and Alan assured me it was very quiet. After dinner I went to take a tour of the apartment. It had potential but the furnishings, decor and accoutrements were not at all to my liking. I thought about what I would do if I were to live there long term. The little cafe next door was nice. The bartender took great pains to make me the perfect sidecar. He even invited me back the next night to have another.

But no. Besides, it was right next door to Caroleen! Wouldn't that just frost her balls? The idea actually became appealing for half a second. Maybe for six months while my owner decided that Paris didn't suit her at all? Too many ifs. What if she decided not only did Paris not suit her but she wanted to sell the apartment and she wouldn't sell it to me? What if she decided Paris suited her perfectly and she stayed? What if she decided that she would prefer to go back to short term rentals and make a bit more money? There were far too many uncertainties to just wait around.

And then I stupidly looked at Caroleen's photo blog; her fabulous website that is a placeholder until she launches her actual website that she's been working on for three years. Every day she posts a picture or two with a short caption. Not this day. She posted a picture of a poster with a cartoon of a French woman, terribly thin, terribly stylish.

"Yesterday I happened to walk into my local butcher shop just as everyone was still reeling from the size of an American woman who had bought a chicken.

Knowing I am originally from the U.S. they asked me if it's true that obesity in America has become epidemic, repeating something I'd heard from a group of French doctors I'd been training at The American Hospital of Paris: In Paris, as most hospitals don't have scales to accommodate people of such proportions, they get sent to a veterinary clinic outside the city, in Asnières, where livestock gets weighed.

 Obesity (not to be confused with being *surpoids* or overweight) in Paris, while it exists, is still a visual rarity, as noted with surprise over and over by Anglo visitors. French girls and women are depicted in illustrations as stick thin, which of course is not true nor is it the norm or even desired norm.

But fashion and beauty, synonymous with Paris, is a big part of French culture; most café terrace chairs face outwards so passersby can be seen - and appreciated. If one is to look up at the sky just about anywhere in Paris no electrical or telephone lines will be visible because, as a French architect friend explained, "It ruins the eye!"

I used to wonder if Mireille Guiliano's best-selling "French Women Don't Get Fat" shouldn't have been titled, "French Women *Won't* Get Fat." When I was growing up, my father, who never lost his French accent or sense of élégance, used to admonish all of us, "Take a little pride in your appearance!" This was in the U.S. where, later, because of small "French touches" to my wardrobe - a scarf here, a one-of-a-kind necklace there (I designed my own) - I unwittingly became a sort of "fashion trendsetter" on campus, particularly in grad school.

Concerning obesity, health is one consideration yes, but for now, at least, the French still like to quote Russian novelist and philosopher Fyodor Dostoevsky at dinner parties: "Beauty will save the world."

La beauté has been an integral part of French culture for centuries - besides fashion we see it in French art, architecture, gastronomy, design, not to mention French *savoir-faire* drives the world's luxury market - and is highly valued."

Clearly this was aimed at me. And it's complete bullshit! The people in my neighborhood are so very lovely to me. The butcher is so friendly since I asked him how his vacation was. The cheesemonger the same. The wine seller, the servers at Cépage, the girls at the grocery store. The only person who is reeling over my size is Caroleen. She didn't seem to mind for the two years I was picking up her tabs and buying her seafood platters and lobsters at L'Ecailler. What changed? Clearly not her image of her own wonderfulness, "unwittingly becoming a sort of fashion trendsetter on campus"?

And seriously? Doctors sending their patients out into the suburbs where the livestock gets weighed? Well played, my dear! You managed to come up with the ultimate insult. But like your other fabrications and fairy stories, this is not true.

What changed was that I dared to walk away from her. I dared to challenge her bigotry and her racism. I dared to decide she wasn't worth my time.

And now, six months later it is killing her that I'm still here, still thriving, still making friends, still becoming part of the neighborhood.

Fasten my seatbelt indeed. It might be a bumpy ride. But I've dealt with far more challenging foes than the vain, and evil Caroleen. She will not send me packing. I will come out of this little set back in a better place.

A Tale of Two Meals

I t's fortuitous that my daughter just gifted me an eBook; *On Looking; A Walkers Guide to the Art of Observation*. It was my intended reading material for today's lunch. After reading the prologue I was reminded to stop reading and pay attention to my meal. And while I was enjoying today's delicious selections, I thought a lot about this meal in contrast with last night's.

Last night I had lunch with some new friends. I have to admit I was a bit intimidated to meet Dan and Vicky. I know Dan only from the internet, having connected with him on another social media page. They live in West Hollywood and seem to enjoy a very chic life. When I invited them to join me for Wednesday jazz night in my favorite café in the 9ème, I worried that it would be a bit low brow for them. They are staying in an apartment featured in Architectural Digest and had an amazing lunch at L'Avenue followed by dessert at Le Crillon. Upon meeting them, I warned them, "This is MY Paris!"

I needn't have worried, Dan and Vicky are two of the loveliest people you would ever want to meet! And I mean that sincerely! As soon as they walked in Dan gave me a big hug and introduced me to his best friend Vicky who pulled me into another hug. They are so warm and interesting. We sat for hours drinking wine, listening to jazz, eating good food and talking talking talking. It was one of the best nights I've had ever! And it included all of my favorite things; my favorite French drummer, my very favorite French restaurant owner, and Paris.

But you know, I hardly noticed all my favorite things because I was so enthralled with Dan and Vicky, new friends who had such interesting stories to tell. We have so much in common when it comes to what we love and care about; especially Paris. It was one of those nights when you share stories from your past, and even probably past lives. I know that there is a thread that connects the three of us. And every now and then I heard Daniele doing one of his amazing drum solos, and Philippe came by to be sure that we had everything we needed, and the restaurant was filled with happy Parisians, and outside Sacré-Coeur loomed above us in the Paris night. But for the most part, my focus was on Dan and Vicky. I honestly couldn't tell you anything about my meal! I know I put away a good bit of Côte du Rhône and lingered over THREE cognacs (can that be?!) and I had a bit of a headache this morning (or rather this noon, when I finally got out of bed!) .

Fast forward to today's late-ish lunch. I wandered down to Les Loups where the wonderful Raphael was behind the bar. He is one of the loveliest Parisians you will ever meet. He went over today's ardoise (blackboard) and I got way ahead of myself, ordering an entree and a plat. I turned on my kindle and as I said, read the prologue of the new book. I was reminded of what I have been told by some of my restaurant friends: *Quand tu manges; manges! Quand tu travailles; travailles*! So I turned off my Kindle and paid attention to what I was eating.

My starter was a wonderful *terrine de chevre*; shavings of celeriac with olive oil and parsley, tart marinated peppers and earthy creamy goat cheese. I was mindful to really taste every delicious bite. Then came the osso bucco. The savory, melt in your mouth veal with the bone full of sinfully rich bone marrow (*moelle en français*... if you see it on a menu GET IT!) and a lovely tomato sauce full of carrots and other vegetables. It was amazing. I concentrated on being aware of the cool breeze that wafted in from the wall of windows looking out on an expanse of leafy trees and Parisian rooftops across the way. I listened to the soft music, the perfect accompaniment, not too loud but not muzac. I noticed the only other diner, a good looking mec with a man bun eating steak frites and talking on his phone. I tasted my water, cool and fresh. Wine has become such a habit for me in Paris. Maybe I need to appreciate water more!

And after I nursed a *café américian* while I read the first two of the author's 12 walks.

What I took away from this were several things. First, while I know many people are loathe to eat alone and bring a book or a journal or any number of other distractions to keep them company, it's pretty darn amazing to eat alone and really really enjoy a meal. It is truly the only way that I actually pay close attention to what I'm eating. Second, nights like last night are true highlights of life. Remember to savor every aspect of them; the music (merci, Daniele), the food (merci, Philippe) and the companionship (merci Dan and Vicky). Appreciate the big moments and the small moments. These are the best days of our lives!

On the way home I tried to really notice the things on my street; the things in the window of the pharmacy, the chasses roues next to the doors of an apartment entrance, the waning days of someone's small vegetable garden under a tree, the changing seasonal produce on offer at the produce stand... then I had to go to the bathroom, so I hurried.

Busting Myths

Paris is a big and very diverse city. It's also world famous for many things, some of which are just not true. The French are rude. Parisians never go out without being dressed to the nines and well coiffed and made up. French women don't get fat.

Well I'm here to tell you that those are myths. Paris is made up of so many different cultures and nationalities and neighborhoods that it's simply impossible to stereotype Parisians. Other than maybe, they speak French! And English. And Spanish. And German. And Farsi. And you name it.

Roughly fifteen percent of the population of Paris is Muslim (5 million in France). Just a couple of blocks from my home, the streets are full of colorfully dressed women in African print dresses with their heads elaborately wrapped in colorful fabric tied in creative knots. They walk side by side with women in hijabs, men looking like they may have slept on the sidewalk, men touting watches and cell phones and trinkets and others trying to get passers-by to play their moveable games of which cup is the pea under.

I watched out the window this morning as the street came alive. An old woman with hair color not found in nature wore a strange cotton top, with a big fanny pack hanging from the front, cropped pants and sneakers, pulling her shopping cart. Most people heading downhill to work or school or wherever they go every morning wear jeans and tennis shoes. Moms and/or Dads with kids in tow lug backpacks, some on scooters. Occasionally a pretty girl goes by in a dress with sandals. This morning it was lightly raining so no sandals. Everyone had umbrellas. Everyone in a rush. Nobody really paying attention to what anyone wears. As I type this a young multi-ethnic guy walked by with a six inch spiky mohawk and at least a dozen facial piercings. And headphones. So many people walk down the street with either full on headphones or iPhone earpieces. Everyone is tuned into their own world.

People come in all shapes and sizes. Caroleen wrote her terribly offensive blog post about the obese American in the butcher shop who set the neighborhood reeling. Ironically, the butcher himself is quite rotund; certainly bigger than me. There are a great number of very thin French women. If you watch them on the terrasses of cafés, they are the ones who eat six cigarettes and a glass of wine for lunch, carefully holding the cigarette so the smoke goes towards you and not their dining companion. They are also the women who twenty years later are overly wrinkled and overly tanned. There seems to be little education about the dangers of smoking and tanning. It boggles my mind how many Parisians do both.

I do not find the French to be particularly rude. In fact, I would have to say my experience is quite the opposite. I have noticed when you are hanging out in heavily touristed areas waiters are a bit less friendly. I invited friends to join me on rue des Abbesses and made reservations for four for dinner. I showed up early and wanted to sit on the terrace for a glass of wine. The waiter tried to redirect me from the table I had chosen to one right next to one where a guy was talking into his phone earpiece and smoking. I argued for a different table, saying (in French) that I was waiting for friends and that we had a reservation. He instantly turned into rude Parisian. For the rest of the evening we got pretty lousy service. Maybe he was rude before I asked for the different table and would have been rude the whole time. He worked in tourist central. Can I blame him for being rude?

I've noticed that when the client is rude, a waiter can be really good at being even more difficult. My nineteen year old granddaughter particularly experienced some rude service. But she would relentlessly drill the server about the items on the menu: Was this vegetarian? Describe this! The lesson being, you get what you give. In Paris as anywhere. Ninety nine percent of Parisians I come into contact with in business situations are absolutely lovely and helpful. Just like anywhere in the world, there are crazy people on the street, pushy people who will cut you off in line at the grocery store. A bus driver may zoom off even though he sees you running to get on. My friend who is white insists it's because he was black and we are white. I don't agree.

Some things remain true. I've never seen a French person with a beret. But I have seen plenty of men in blue striped shirts.

The Threat of Homelessness Hangs Over Me

While I filled my days with writing and lunches and daydreaming over Philippe, by night I was met by worries and the fear that I would not find a satisfactory solution to my homelessness dilemma. I lay in bed thinking about all the possible scenarios. If I move out for six months, can I come back and stay for a year? Where can I go for six months? What are the chances the owner will come for six months and decide to stay forever? Is the other apartment near Cépage available? The apartment on rue Lamark My new friends had just showed me their apartment on the stairs by rue Lamarck (just next door to Caroleen): would it be somewhere I could see myself living. Probably not. But in a pinch? Next door to Caroleen? But also next door to the lovely bartender who made me the handcrafted Sidecar. Then Silvie told me the owners were putting it on the market! Would I be interested in buying it? Only 650,000 euros!

"Well, to start with," I replied, "I think it's about one hundred thousand euro overvalued!"

"Noooo, I don't think so." answered Silvie.

That apartment for 650,000 euro! Clearly I am not in a buying mode.

Where do I even begin to look for a new apartment? Am I ready to leave rue Caulaincourt? Am I ready maybe to leave Montmartre? Could I find an unfurnished, unrepresented apartment and maybe pay less and spend the difference on furnishings of my own choosing? And how on earth do I do all of this in French?

I finally drifted off to sleep thinking that this could be my opportunity to really take that leap of faith; to assume that this is all going to be for the better. Six months from now I will look back on this and realize that it was all good. I'll be in a wonderful apartment with perfect furnishings and everything I want. I'll be even happier than I am today!

I spent the next couple of weeks adjusting to the idea, letting it roll around in my head as options presented themselves to me. My long honed instincts to "cross that bridge when we get to it" kicked in and I mulled. The bridge loomed five months and two weeks away. That was a good thing. On the other hand, if I started looking now and found something I was stuck in a lease for that same five months and two weeks. Would I have to pay the lease in full?

The option list grew. Maybe, just maybe, there are apartments that are nice on a street other than mine. Maybe even another arrondissement might not be the end of the world. I spend a lot of time in the ninth. Maybe I should look there as well. Maybe the owner will decide she doesn't like living in Paris so very much and will leave and let me rent forever after. Maybe she will find she doesn't ever want to live in her apartment again and then will decide to sell it! Maybe I can buy it. Maybe I won't be able to afford it! Maybe I should move for six months to somewhere outside of Paris; explore another town or even a little quiet place in the country somewhere. March is cold and rainy most places. But June and July and August are hot in Paris and it wouldn't be so bad to live somewhere different. Maybe St. Malo!

I started sharing my plight with different friends. Each offered their advice, mostly with a personal bias attached. Evelyn said "I will introduce you to Jean-Claude. He was my apartment finder. He is excellent and very very discreet! You can trust that he will not share any of your personal details with anyone." (Evelyn is very private.)

"You want a two bedroom apartment!" she continued. "How many square meters is your current apartment?"

"53" I mumbled

"Oh, too small! You need much more than that."

I tried to explain all of the little details about my apartment that made it perfect, none of which had anything to do with square meters. Yes, it's small, but I'm one person. I don't need big. I need a wall of windows. I need to be on the curve of my street; the very best street in Paris. I need to see the produce vendor set up his shop in the morning and put it to bed at night. I need to keep track of the hours the rug seller keeps and watch him stand in front of his shop. I need to see the Lebanese deli man visiting with the florist every morning. I need to be able to walk out the door and go to the butcher shop, where I have finally cracked the growling butcher into friendly smiles and small talk, to *la boulangerie*, to *la cave* for a word of advice from Monsieur Vincent about what wine will go good with what I'm planning to serve at my *apéro*, to visit my friendly cheese monger and get advice about what cheeses will make my perfect cheese board. I need to be able to pop into Les Loups and Cépage and Café de la Butte. And when I come home, from wherever I've wandered, I need to hear the boys in the minimarket downstairs say "How is the American girl?"

Oh Whaaaa. I won't be the American girl in the building anymore. Somebody else will be that person.

An email comes from Evelyn, I was copied on her email to Jean-Claude:

"Hello Jean-Claude,

I am trusting you and your family are doing well.

My friend, also an American, would like to rent an apartment beginning 15 January 2019.

She has been advised by her current landlord that he wishes to beginning living in her apartment, at the end of her lease. She seeks a large one bedroom or small two bedroom unfurnished apartment.

Would you be able to assist her in this search? I have recommended her to you, based upon the excellent knowledge and attention to detail in this market.

I have copied her on this email so that you can contact her directly.

As always I send my best regards."

Well, sort of. Let's say the end of February. And the two bedroom is Evelyn's idea. For the one percent of time anyone would be staying in the second bedroom, I am not eager to pay the extra euros every month. Besides, what I need when guests come is another bathroom! But more importantly, what Evelyn doesn't get is that the most important thing to me is location. Not only location, but what I see when I look out the window; where I am when I walk out the door.

Following the email a text from Evelyn:

I hope Jean-Claude has made your acquaintance and you will be able to find a new home. I was thinking - you could possibly begin to start thinking about art now. I suggest looking at the prints by Willy Ronis. Also Peter Turnley. I may be able to obtain a Peter Turnley print(s) for only $500 each. Also perhaps just looking at galleries…"

Oh my goodness. First I need a bed. And a sofa and a dining table and chairs. And then book shelves. Art? Galleries? No, first I need an apartment!

An email from Stephanie tells me that the apartment at Cépage is available from March 1 to April 22. That gives me another six weeks in my own neighborhood.

So many moving parts. So many options. Sorry Caroleen, I don't think I'll be rushing back home soon.

L'Appartement de Architectural Digest

My friends Dan and Vicky were invited to stay at the apartment of one of Dan's clients in Hollywood. The client is a designer. Not just your everyday ordinary designer. He buys and renovates *châteaux*, specifically *châteaux* of the Loire Valley. The apartment is in the 8ème, very close to the British Embassy. Dan and Vicki asked me to come for *apéro* last night and then go to dinner at a restaurant nearby.

Fall has officially found its way to Paris. The evening was clear and fresh. Vicky had tex ted me the address but not the building passcode or floor so I texted them from the Uber. I arrived a bit early and noticed a fancy liquor store across the street so popped in thinking to buy a nice bottle of wine. Nope. The store had only very expensive whiskies, all behind glass and subtly lit to show off the bottles' best effects. No prices anywhere. No doubt one of those "if you have to ask" situations.

Still no response from Dan or Vicky so I went to the small cafe on the opposite corner and got a glass of wine. My mind was doing all of its usual paranoid tricks. Is it the right day? Is it the right place? I looked repeatedly at the initial text invitation. Yes and yes. I texted with daughter number two at home. "Are you wearing slippers?" she asked. "Are you walking to school in your slippers on Saturday?" "Maybe they are looking out the window at you laughing!"

I've got enough of my own paranoid delusions. I don't need to add hers to the mix!

Finally, at least half an hour after the appointed time a text came from Dan. "365B"

I enter the lobby of course to find the second door, this one with a buzzer to push for the owner. I push and nothing happens. Suddenly Dan appears to bring me the rest of the way.

The apartment, which I had already perused on the Architectural Digest link I googled, was indeed extraordinary. Facing the street were a large lovely salon, a beautiful home office, a massive formal dining room and one of the two guest bedrooms. There was a smallish kitchen, complete with everything one would need to prepare a meal, but I suspect actual meals have not often been prepared here, and an actual laundry room. The master bedroom was locked, bringing to mind BlueBeard.

It was all a bit too Louis XIV for me (more accurately Napoleon III) and it would take a year to notice all of the details, from the sculpted molded ceilings to the marble fireplaces and crystal chandeliers (in each room) to the vintage antique furniture. As I settled in to an antique white armchair, Vicki thoughtfully offered me a glass of red wine. Dan and Vicky are very Californian and drink Chardonnay but they noticed that I prefer red. Dare I accept a glass of red wine in this room? On this chair? *Mais oui!* On the massive glass topped coffee table, along with piles of design books and other bits of porcelain odds and ends was a beautiful cheese board, a basket of bread and crackers, and a bowl of nuts.

For the next hour we talked about the owner, relationships and our mutual love for Paris while I carefully balanced the glass of red wine and took in all of the rooms decorations. The man must spend all of his time in antique shops! On a table between the two huge French windows was a three foot marble bust, a torso only. I was on my second glass of red when I suddenly noticed two taxidermied foxes (looking a little worse for wear) on the floor in the corner. In my surprise I jostled my glass and spilled a quick slop of wine! Fortunately only on my black slacks, not the white fabric of the chair or the antique carpet beneath my feet!

I could have stayed all evening in that room, drinking wine, feasting on the cheese platter and noticing new things. However, Dan and Vicky had a dinner planned. So we had to leave. We wandered down rue d'Anjou toward Palais Borghese the home of the British Ambassador, where there was an elaborate formal event in full swing. The open doors to the massive courtyard tempted us to slip in and take a closer look, but we continued on rue du Faubourg Saint-Honoré, looking into all the closed but brightly lit windows of the fashion houses, showing off their best for fashion week, happening now. We walked along a few more blocks, Vicki the fashion fiend taking photos of the size zero dresses and the impossible to walk-in shoes in the various windows.

Finally after a couple of turns we found Zo, a charming French restaurant with Asian influences. It was absolutely bustling for a Monday night. We seemed to be the only English speakers. A long table of some two dozen people lined one end of the room; someone's birthday. Other diners were in twos and threes. It was more sophisticated than the jazz dinner that I shared with the couple a few nights earlier but these were people who were comfortable in any environment and with any caliber of people. We carried on our comfortable conversation for hours over bottles of Chardonnay, tapas and teriyaki salmon.

Reluctantly we made our way out into the fall night and walked arm in arm in arm along the cobbles towards a street busy enough for me to find a taxi back home. Although we were only friends for five short days, we felt like lifelong buddies. True aficionados of all things Parisian, I will be as sad as they are when the wheels go up on the plane taking them back to California on Friday.

Coffee and a Cigarette

He came in the restaurant briefly to pick up a newspaper. Then he sat at one of the small café tables outside, just beyond the window from where I was sitting. Handsome face, salt and pepper grey hair - a lot of it. That two day stubble that French men all seem to have (except Philippe who is always very cleanly shaven). He orders a coffee and while he waits for it he lights a Gitane. He's wearing a sharp looking fleece pullover with a violet scarf wrapped around his neck and carefully tucked into the neckline of the pullover.

For quite a while he just sipped his coffee and smoked his cigarette and gazed at the street. What was he thinking about, this very French specimen of a man? He has taken far more sips of that tiny cup of coffee than I would ever manage to find in an espresso. Is he just touching his lips to the hot liquid? He tilts his head back toward the sun and blows out five bursts of smoke. His cigarette has burned down nearly to his finger tips. Another sip.

He stubs out the cigarette and finishes the coffee. He closes his eyes and lets the sun settle on his face. Perfectly still for a few moments until he puts his elbow on the table and rests his face in his palm. A brief nap? A moment of meditation? He nods as if answering someone. The conversation in his head?

I remember sitting in this same seat at GCA, watching a silent snowfall just a few short months ago. Now Fall is here and the weather is crisp and every good Frenchman is wearing a scarf. The days of *La Canicule* and short shorts and bare skin are past. Soon it will be cold and wet and the days will be very short. Everyone will be in puffy coats and boots with big wool scarves wrapped around their necks and faces.

But for now he sits on the terrace with the sun on his face and the internal dialog, whatever it is, running through his head.

Understanding Ninon

I'm sitting in GCA on a Friday afternoon, eating an amazing serving of *moules frites* in the best *marinière* sauce ever (it's all I can do not to pick up the bowl and slurp the remaining sauce right from the bowl when every last moule has been devoured), drinking a good Côtes du Rhône and watching Philippe sing and dance around the restaurant. And between slurps, sips and sighs, I am reading Ninon's letters to the Maquis.

"Do you know, Maquis, that you will end by putting me into a temper?" Ninon writes. "Heavens, how very stupid you are sometimes!"

I wish that I could read the Maquis' letter. What could cause such an outburst?

Is the Maquis truly obtuse or is he egging Ninon on?

"What is the destiny of women?" Ninon asks. "What is their role on earth? Is it to please? Now a charming figure, personal graces, in a word, all the amiable and brilliant qualities are the only means of succeeding in that role."

No wonder Ninon has declared herself to be a man.

Later I sit in my Paris apartment watching the Senate Committee hearing preceding the vote to confirm Brett Kavanaugh as the latest Supreme Court justice. Accused of attempted rape and drunken behavior he simply refuses to answer direct questions. He whimpers. He blusters. He shouts. He pouts. The comparisons and contrasts cannot elude me.

What is the role of women on earth? Is it different in France than in the US? Is it so very different from the role of men on earth? If, in fact, it is as Ninon contends to please, charm and be amiable, I agree. Would I rather be a man. I enjoy being a woman. But at times it may seem less than desirable. Today there is an emerging philosophy regarding gender. One can freely decide to be gender fluid, gender queer or non-binary. How would Ninon have responded to these options? For my part, I'm definitely a woman who loves men. But I've always thought there was a great advantage to be able to think a bit like a man. It's a bit like eavesdropping on a conversation that's spoken in a language that nobody thinks you speak.

Relishing the sensation of enjoying happiness

or

Voulez vous coucher avec moi

Ce sois….. I'm sitting in GCA with the intention of writing. Actually, nothing seems to be happening. Same place, same time, but I'm not feeling very inspired. Maybe I'm tired. Maybe I'm burned out from all of the recent visitors to Paris. I'm re-reading Ninon's letters to the Maquis; still struggling to get a deeper sense of who she is. These are her very words (albeit translated into English by a middle voice). Yet she still eludes me.

I sink back into my seat and take a long breath, not only of oxygen but of everything around me. At first I closed my book and ate my salad with intention. Endive, blue cheese and walnuts. I focused on the flavors and textures of my meal; distinctly salty and slightly bitter the creamy blue cheese took the front stage, dominating as it coated the chopped bases and also bitter solid chunks of endive. The sweet, buttery walnuts perfectly balanced this combination. I focused on noticing the flavor of every bite until I got a little bored and found myself looking at my phone.

Stop. What else is going on around me? Philippe is humming and singing snippets of the songs on the sound system. Today he seems to have chosen a black soul genre. "Stand by me", Philippe sings. I slipped in awhile earlier when he was busy and helped myself to a seat in the back of the restaurant, facing rue Gérando. Soon he noticed me and came over to plant bises on my cheeks.

It's cold outside, Fall has definitely arrived in Paris. Nobody is sitting on the terrace and the restaurant is fuller than normal. In twos, threes and fours, customers are convivially eating, drinking and chatting. It feels good. The familiarity of the scene outside, rue Gérando as the seasons continue to march on. Last week, the young mec sat outside with a cigarette in the sunshine. Today, everyone, myself included, wears a scarf and I see my first puffy coats. People walk more briskly. Where not so long ago the window of the consignment shop across the street displayed mannequins in sportswear and shorts, today they are wearing coats, scarves and hats. Berets actually. I've never seen an actual French person wearing a beret; only tourists. Philippe is wearing his navy pull over, which he hasn't worn in months, since a false Spring presented itself and he seemed to think he could hasten his beloved summer if he dressed accordingly.

"Mrs. Jones... every day in the same café..." Philippe whistles along. Does he understand the words to the songs he whistles?

None of this is getting me any closer to Ninon... or Philippe!

Ninon says, "Love is a passion which is neither good nor bad of itself; it is only those who are affected by it that determines whether it is good or bad…. it drags us out of the rut. It stirs us up."

There! That is precisely what Paris has done to me with all of these crazy infatuations! Stéphane, Daniele, Thierry, Philippe… I have been dragged out of my rut, a long rut of more than a decade, and it has completely stirred me up. It's as if my nerves are always on their ends. Everything tastes better. Music sounds like it's talking to me. Even the changing leaves on the trees have an urgency in them; reminding me always of the passage of time.

"*Voulez vous coucher avec moi…..*" Philippe is whistling and doing his little dance. It's just a bit too much for me. Time to pay my bill and grab a taxi to Le Terrass to meet visiting family for *apéro*.

Tired

I'm just tired. I can't seem to sleep enough, which I think is not a good thing. What is causing this constant fatigue? I have to go to 204 rue Marcadet to pick up the Amazon package I was not home to receive; two grill pans for the stove top, one for me and one for Charlotte. It's a walk of about 400 meters. Two blocks and one hellishly long set of stairs. Going down to get there. Going up to come home. Or I can catch the 95 bus right across the street from where I pick-up my package, a relatively heavy package, and take it two stops to Damremont Caulaincourt, walk a block and a bit up hill to hop on the 80 bus the rest of the way. That seems like the best bet to me. I'm so very tired.

Tomas, the manager of Cépage that Caroleen called an evil little faggot, took my plate and quickly rattled off some French to me. Caroleen said he would never wait on me because I was associated with her. He's actually been very kind to me. I thought he was asking me how my meal was. It turns out he was asking me how I was.

"*Non!*" he said "*Ça va VOUS!*"

"*Ahhh, Ça va! J'ai la pêche!*" I responded, which always garners huge laughs. Maybe I'm not one hundred percent sure that it's an appropriate comment.

On his next pass I said "*Mon français est très mauvais, mais j'essaie!*"

"Noooo" he assured me. "Your French is very good."

Ha! But Tomas is starting to look quite cute to me. He's very compact. It's a shame that he weighs about half as much as I do. Should that matter?

Why am I so darn tired?

Ninon

"**I** have had lovers, but none of them deceived me by any illusions. I could penetrate their motives astonishingly well. I was always persuaded that if whatever was value from the standpoint of intellect and character, was considered as anything among the reasons that led them to love me, it was only because those qualities stimulated their vanity. They were amorous of me, because I had a beautiful figure, and they possessed the desire. So it came about that they never obtained more than a second place in my heart. I have always conserved for friendship the deference, the constancy, and the respect even, when a sentiment so noble, so worth deserves as in an elevated soul. It has never been possible for me to overcome my distrust for hearts in which love was the principal actor. This weakness degraded them in my eyes; I considered them incompetent to raise their mind up to sentiments of true esteem for a woman for whom they have felt a desire."

"What is the world's idea of a virtuous woman? Are not men so unjust as to believe that the wisest woman is she who best conceals her weakness; or who, by a forced retreat puts herself beyond the possibility of having any? Rather than accord us a single perfection, they carry wickedness to the point of attributing to us a perpetual state of violence, every time we undertake to resist their advances. One of our friends said: 'There is not an honest woman who is not tired of being so. And what recompense do they offer for the cruel torments to which they have condemned us? Do they raise up an altar to our heroism? No! The most honest woman, they say, is she who is not talked about, that is to say, a perfect indifference on the part of a woman, a general oblivion is the price of our virtue. Must women not have much of it to preserve it at such a price? Who would be tempted to abandon it?"

"Tell me this: Is a society woman obliged to have an attachment? Is she not exempt from tenderness? It is sufficient for her to be amiable and courteous, everything on the surface. As soon as she becomes expert in the role she has undertaken, then, the only mistrust the world has of her is that she has no heart. A fine figure, haughty airs, caprices, fashionable jargon, fantasies, and fads, that is all that is required of her. She can be essentially virtuous with impunity. Does any one presume to make advances? "If he met with resistance and quickly give over to worrying her, he thinks her heart is already captured, and he patiently awaits his turn."

– "Life, Letters, and Epicurean Philosophy of Ninon de l'Enclos"

True merit is that which is esteemed by those we aim to please.

The Ongoing Saga of My Search for a Home

For about a month now I have known the bad news. I cannot stay in my wonderful little apartment on my wonderful *petite rue* next year. Or at least for six months next year. After that is uncertain. Which makes my options uncertain. Which makes me crazy. It's difficult to speak to anyone about it because everyone else's opinions are truly getting on my nerves.

Stephanie, of course, wants me to rent something from her. She is getting some unknown percentage of the rent I pay each month. Her income is at stake. But the other apartment is only available for six weeks. Will the owner decide that she wants to live in Paris forever? Will she come and decide that it will never be a place that she wants to live and after six months sell it? By that time will the property market it Montmartre be so out of control that she will want to sell it for double the price that the apartment upstairs sold for? Will I even know it is for sale? And if I do, will I want to buy it?

Magalie thinks I need to rent a furnished apartment. She has a friend, not Silvie, not Stephanie, who can help me out. She will introduce me soon. We can look at apartments together.

Evelyn's finder told me it doesn't make sense for us to start looking until January. In Paris it is only required to give thirty days notice so we won't know what will be on the market until January at the soonest.

"You need at least two bedrooms! A much bigger apartment! Jean-Claude will help you!" Evelyn continues to insist that I need a big apartment with my own furnishings and my own art!

"Are you looking at art?!" she urged. "Of course," she said, "to move in you will only need a bed and a dining table and chairs. A sofa and TV would be next." But evidently first is art. *Ooh la la la la la la…* I would think first would be an apartment! I envisioned myself living on the sidewalk in my art fort, draped in blankets and furnished with my wine rack.

Siobhan started an apartment search around the same time. In her case, her employer had granted her a substantial allocation to pay for housing, enough to rent Evelyn's apartment! The timing was auspicious for me because Siobhan is nothing if she's not proactive. She began looking at some amazing properties in Montmartre. The problem is Siobhan's budget had her looking at apartments substantially bigger than I want. She does have good taste and is very interested in the precise area I want to live in so her search left me hopeful. She thinks I need at least two bedrooms and sent me to look at a couple of lovely web postings, within the range of her own budget. She also doesn't mind hills and stairs as much as I do.

One especially beautiful option was very close to me; a beautiful three bedroom apartment, one that would rival Evelyn's. But it was completely empty. Of furniture. Of light fixtures. Of a kitchen! OK, factor in a 20,000 euro budget to outfit the apartment with everything I need and I would have my dream Paris apartment. And a four thousand euro a month rent payment. It's about 35% more than I was hoping for. But it's available NOW. I don't want to move until March, maybe even mid April.

"That's nonsense!" exclaimed Siobhan. "You should not be held liable for that lease given the circumstances."

She showed me a couple of other postings. One on rue Caulaincourt, quite a pretty apartment but in a modern building outside of my 41 to 71 range, a newer building on a noisy part of the street with little charm, but a more charming price tag. Another in the 9ème. I do spend a lot of time in the 9ème.

This would save me upwards of 100 euro a month in Uber fare. Add that to the rent budget. It was a block from Le Clou, two blocks from Le Grand Comptoir, and almost on rue des Martyrs. It could be a possibility. Siobhan ruled it out because of its proximity to the back door of Monoprix She happened to be passing early one morning when the homeless were waiting for expired groceries to be dumped. I passed by in an Uber one noon when the kids were out of school for their lunch break. No thank you.

Maybe I should leave Paris altogether and spend a few months somewhere else, returning to my sweet little apartment on rue Caulaincourt in September, when the owner has gone back to the US. If the owner goes back to the US. And if she's willing to rent to me for another year. Too many ifs!

So the options require all of the talent I acquired in my Quantitative Business Analysis class I had a hundred years ago in grad school. Shall I make a decision tree? Which branches shall I prune? The options seem endless and always moving. I can buy an apartment in Paris. I can rent an unfurnished apartment in Paris and furnish it to my own specifications. I can rent a furnished apartment in Paris. I can leave Paris for some period of time and hope to return in September.

If I leave Paris for a period of time, where will I go? Provence seems tempting but likely to be very hot in summer. Bretagne sounds good and a quick look at potential rentals seems like an attractive option. No doubt I could come back to Paris in the Fall and I would have plenty of time to look while I'm away.

Would I miss Paris? I could visit. Siobhan chose a big three bedroom apartment very near me. Maybe I could rent a room from her. Would I miss Philippe? Would he miss me? I am sitting in my normal seat writing and Philippe is talking to his regular pals at the bar, sipping a glass of champagne, overdue for lunch. What's with these mecs? They stand at the bar and drink and gossip and Philippe goes back and forth between them and his customers. By late afternoon, there are nearly no lunch customers, just a few people drinking on the terrace and these mecs. One drinks chablis, one rose, one beer and Philippe champagne. Other than the beer, it seems a bit odd. Philippe and I just seem to get farther and farther apart. I get my bise. He asks how I am. And then I write. And he leaves me alone. It's time.

J'ai besoin de passer par-dessus lui ou de passer sous lui. I need to get over him or get under him. Or I could find someone new to get under.

So many decisions to be made. So many moving parts.

So Many Fish in the Sea

My friends from Cape Cod were in town and wanted to see some Gypsy Jazz. What luck! Opus 4 was playing at La Chope on a rare Thursday night. So I shot the friendly manager a quick message, can we reserve for three? She responded with a thumbs up emoticon. The world has certainly become a lot less formal!

I invited Miki and Dick for an *apéro chez moi* and then we would Uber over to La Chope, so fortified by a bottle of bubbles and another bountiful cheese board, we headed to Saint Ouen, home of the famous brocantes. Our driver took an odd route and before long we were caught up in a massive jam on the streets of the city of fleas. Our driver nudged into the parade of traffic on rue des Rosiers, Saint Ouen's main street, right behind the two mounted police officers. People crowded the sidewalks and at eight pm cafés were bursting and the shop doors were all wide open. What was going on?

When we arrived at La Chope Opus 4 was in full swing. Watching them kind of makes me think of watching Romanian French Beach Boys. Or what the Beach Boys would look like today, elderly and wrinkled from too much sun, too much partying, too much booze and drugs. Perhaps the first one you notice is Serge, very blonde (must be bleached), very tan, a leather choker around his neck hints that he's modern despite his advanced years, very smiley. He plays a mean guitar and is the lead singer. Pierre is very tall and thin as if it burns a lot of calories to play a steel acoustic guitar as fast and furious as he does. Piotr is from Gdansk. He's small and compact and looks very serious and Eastern European. He seldom smiles and his violin skills are second to none. He sits. He stands. He sits. He stands. I suspect he is standing when his violin is the lead instrument but it seems like he's always on. Once I shook his hand and said "incredible!" and he barely managed a smirk, as if to say, of course! What else is new?

And then there is Frank. He's the youngest of the four and plays the contrabass, an instrument taller than him. He has the appearance of a big solid man but in fact is quite short. He has an amazing beautiful rich voice and a gorgeously handsome face. Everything about him looks strong; strong hands, strong voice, strong expressions. And for some reason he seemed to never take his eyes off of me.

I took a seat at the raised table for four with my back facing the group but able to watch every move in the massive mirror taking up the entire wall in front of me. Normally I find it disconcerting to watch myself in the mirror throughout a meal, but that night I watched the band. And the glimpses I saw of myself, well, I looked rather pretty! I watched Frank and smiled at him. I looked away and looked back to see his gaze still fixed on me. Between songs he said something to Serge and the group launched into a new song, a love song. Frank sang with great determination, watching me. I smiled and listened attentively. At the end of the song, he said, "that was for you."

Across the street a Chinese parade formed with a dragon dancer contorting at the lead. Beautiful women in traditional Chinese festive dress and makeup followed, musicians followed but could not be heard over the sounds of Opus 4. Crowds surged into the street and pushed against La Chope's windows. Only then did I notice the paper lanterns and dragon strewn around the restaurant and across the mirror I had been looking into all night. Of course! Autumn Festival, a week long holiday for China and Chinese across the world.

The group took a break and Frank passed by our table. "Where are you from?" he asked Dick. He didn't speak to me. Nor I to him. I'm fairly certain he knows I live here because he's watched me watch him before. Dick insisted on paying our tab and we left to wait for the 85 bus right outside La Chope. The group resumed playing.

We must have been at ground zero for the nights festivities. The mounted horses passed by and the crowd waiting for the bus grew, many more people than seats on the bus. An empty bus arrived. I've been in Paris long enough to know not to wait politely in line and pushed my way on, taking a seat in the front. Miki and Dick had moved further into the bus and were stuck standing near the middle door. By the time we left the stop not another person could cram onto the bus. Slowly we crawled down rue des Rosiers. At each subsequent stop people tried to press in. I worried I'd not be able to push my way out when the bus got to the Marie in the 18ème.

Most everyone got off somewhere around Clignancourt and it was an easy exit at our stop. There I hugged Miki and Dick goodnight and they headed off to the metro while I boarded an all but empty 80 bus for home. Once again on tranquil rue Caulaincourt I got off the bus and bid bon soir to the guy standing outside the mini market downstairs.

Elliot once told me that I had to be careful, that I was exactly what the north African and Muslim men liked; zaftig and blonde. I've bemoaned that that doesn't seem to be what Philippe likes. But maybe I'm what Romanian French contrabass players like!

"And for always getting what she wants in the long run, commend me to a nasty woman." Edith Wharton, House of Mirth

Joia Is Where You Find It

L ast night we went to Joia par Helene Darroze, the hottest new restaurant to open in Paris. I'd been watching their Instagram page since before the launch and was terribly excited to try it out. Everything posted looked wonderful; food, desserts, cocktails, environment. Elliot had secured reservations, a month out, for six and asked if I would like to go. Absolutely! I told him that Charlotte and I had been talking about going, thus Charlotte and T became numbers four and five. I wondered who would be number six.

As time grew near I began to speculate that going to Joia with Elliot might not be the best thing. Since he trashed Le Clou I had seen him criticize a handful of other places I liked quite a lot. Elliot is the self avowed, and to be fair, undisputed expert in that group of all things wine, spirits and food. I have to admit, his favorites leave me scratching my head. Judging by the number of times we have been, Maison Dong must be at the top of his list. It's pretty much Chinese food. Chinese with spices otherwise unknown in Paris, he will argue. Perhaps my dozens of trips to actual China, paired with a lifetime of not bad Chinese food in San Francisco, left me a bit jaundiced when it comes to Chinese food.

I think after hanging with Elliot for more than six months now, I would call him the anti snob food snob. Or something like that. If everyone else likes it, he will pick it apart. If it's tiny and unknown he's likely to rave about it. Once we went to a Sicilian restaurant. Elliot raved about everything from the *charcuterie* starters to the shared pizzetta rounds to what I thought were horrendously thick pasta spirals, completely inedible. We sat on a sidewalk while hordes of tourists walked by looking at our plates, the table next to us shoved up next to ours and a bush poking me in my side throughout the entire meal. The next day Elliot posted a glowing review on his social media page.

So much to Elliot's chagrin I passed on the *apéro* at 6:15 "just 100 meters away" and met Elliot, his wife, Charlotte and T and happily Magella the number six, at Joia at precisely 7:30. They were already seated in a small room just off the main dining room, I think. I think because there is a rather majestic stairway that heads upwards there must be another level. Our little room turned out to be actually a tiny courtyard covered by a massive patio umbrella, complete with heater. Trellises lined the walls and a round table filled the space. Elliot was already absorbed with the carte du vins. Les bises were distributed and a white wine was ordered. Evidently Elliot would be making all of our drinking decisions for the evening. A nice light white was poured for all of us and Elliot asked for a second bottle right away. The youngish waiter placed it in a wine cooler. Elliot snatched it out. When the waiter returned he tried to put it back. Elliot nearly slapped his hand.

Time to place our orders. The menu had five categories; small bites, as in a bowl of olives, *les amuse-bouches*, as in amusing your mouths, *entrées*, as in starters, and *plats* as in main dishes. Of course all followed by desserts meaning desserts. Based on prices it was clear that the small bites were things that regular restaurants may put on the table while you decide what to eat and drink. I was not clear the difference between the *amuse-bouches* and the *entrées* and some of us ordered from one list while others ordered the other. I had no problem deciding on the *moules*, from the *entrée* list. Charlotte ordered fried chicken from the amuses list. In the end they seemed pretty equal. Joan also had moules, Elliott and T had garlic soup and Magella had *boudin noir*, a blood pudding seemingly favored by Brits and Irish. *Beuck* (Yuck). My *moules* were extraordinary.

The problem came with the plats. The menu had six items, four of which had to be ordered for two or four people and the remaining two which could be ordered for one. The roasted chicken spoke to me; foie gras tucked between the chicken and the skin and a whole roasted garlic presented on the plate. But the *poitrine de porc* - pork belly - evidently spoke louder. Maybe that was a mistake. I expected legumes to be vegetables, not a big bowl of white beans. My pork belly was just ok, the white beans… *beurk*!. Someone had the fish which had to be ordered for two but could easily have been prepared for one. Joan had the pumpkin ravioli, which ultimately looked like the big winner of the night. Elliot and Magella shared the chicken, which was good, but after all, it was chicken. Fifty euros for half a chicken? And the sides had to be ordered separately. Those who ordered roasted potatoes complained they were dry. Elliot ordered polenta and whined loudly that somebody put something sweet in his polenta. He argued with the waiter about the bottle of red that was brought out, complaining it was not what was advertised on the menu; something about coming from the cellar of the daughter and not the mother. Clearly the daughter's grapes were not grown far enough up the hillside.

Nobody ordered desserts and I was disappointed not to see the macha crepes piled high into a *gâteau*, although I really only wanted to see it and maybe take a bite. When the check came, Elliot divided it equally and announced that we allowed exactly sixty seven euro fifty. He was not willing to give the young waiter one penny of tip. He produced his American Express Card only to be told, "Je suis *désolé*." I have watched Elliot pull out his trusty platinum card time after time only to be told no. The 5% charge that American Express requires is just not to be tolerated by French restaurants.

"Strike three!"

Are we really only up to three? "Really Elliot," I say, "This happens every time."

"I guarantee Helene Darroze's Michelin starred restaurants take American Express!" he harrumphed.

I handed the waiter seventy euro, no change required.

"Do you want to share my Uber?" I asked Magella.

"Let me order it!" she protested.

"No problem," I said, "It's on its way."

Quick *bises* to everyone and we were out the door, the Uber already waiting in front.

When will I learn my lesson? I lay in bed later thinking about the evening. I loved my *moules*. The wine was excellent, although I'm sure I could have ordered something equally good on my own. I made the mistake of ordering the pork belly. Live and learn. Would I go back? Yes, for lunch. With Elliot? No! My phone binged indicating a text.

Elliott: "How about Friday night, Maison Dang?"

Me: "Sorry no. I have a lunch date at an Argentine French place in the 18th and I'm trying to limit myself to one meal out each day."

Elliott: "I understand. But we'll miss you."

It could be said that I am learning.

La Fête des Vendanges

Every year on the second weekend of October Montmartre celebrates wine. Specifically the tiny vineyard that grows on the hillside about three blocks from chez moi. It's said that Montmartre used to be home to many vineyards as well as other agricultural enterprises. But this tiny block of grape vines is all that remains. The wine it produces is not very good but it fetches a good price because its 15,000 bottles a year are the only bottles of wine grown and made in the City of Paris.

Saturday found my neighborhood a complete zoo. Rue Caulaincourt was one big traffic jam from ten am until … well, I don't know when because it was still a traffic jam when I went to bed! I spent the early afternoon working at GCA. Philippe and his team were on the run as virtually every table on the terrace and the tables that remained after moving many of the indoor tables outdoors to accommodate the sun seekers were full as well. I almost felt guilty taking my table for so long while I wrote. But not that guilty. I ate moules for the third day in a row, then I drank wine while I worked, occasionally peeking at the oblivious Philippe to see if he was peeking at me. He was not. In fact, he was outside sitting with a group of people chatting. One of the things Magalie asked me was does he ever sit with you. No, He sits with his pals. He's sitting with this family. He doesn't sit with me.

Just as I ordered my unusually expensive Uber to head back to crazy Montmartre a pretty girl walked by and looked at me oddly. Aimee! We exchanged *la bise* and she told me that she was outside with her sister, her niece and her niece's boyfriend. The group that Philippe was sitting with! I looked out and Veronique waved back. I went outside to wait for my Uber and chatted briefly with

Veronique. Her daughter is the bartender at GCA! This world just gets smaller and smaller. She says "Yes, I've seen my picture on your Instagram!" My Uber arrived and I quickly said goodbye to everyone, agreeing with Aimee that we would meet for an *apéro* soon. I hopped into my Uber while Philippe called out "*Au revoir, Katrine!*" Just a tiny bit of recognition to keep me hanging on. Darn.

The evenings plans for La Fête were moving all over the place. First we were to meet at Chez Stephanie for champagne and to meet her latest foster pup before heading up to SacréCoeur for the party. All of this meant lots of stairs and lots of hills. I fretted about keeping up with everyone. Plus, I hate dogs. Then I got a text from Stephanie that Magalie wanted to meet at Place du Tertre, precisely at the corner of Rue de Mont Cenis and Rue Norvins. After we would meet at Le Bistrot Du Maquis, just six or seven blessed doors from chez moi!

I thought briefly about begging off of the party and telling them I'd meet them at the Bistrot. That's what I always do. That's what I did for the last *apéro chez* Stephanie. Don't be so lazy, I told myself. Go outside! Outside is where things happen.

So I showered and groomed and primped and got myself ready to head outside. It was unbelievably hot at 5:30 and all the world was working their way up the hill. I wore a form fitting tank top with cut out shoulders and back, meant only to be worn with my little black jacket with gold zippers and snaps. After about two blocks and the first uphill portion of the trip the jacket came off and I didn't care that my bra straps were showing. So were everyone else's.

It's a good thing all the small streets of Montmartre were blocked off for pedestrians only because the cobbled pavements were jammed with people working their way up towards the party. Fortunately, when I reached the vineyard a crowd had gathered around a performer playing his guitar, singing and telling ribald stories about the Lapin Agile, the famous cabaret on the corner. I sat on a retaining wall and caught my breath. People crowded around the cyclone fencing of the celebrated vineyard, taking pictures. The always present Bride and Groom were on the sidewalk with their professional photographer, adding to the mayhem.

Two more uphill blocks to go. Seriously uphill. By the time I got to rue Norvins I had worked up a good sweat. I turned left and fought the crushing crowds, watching my footing on the cobbles. A couple of portrait artists made brief attempts at proposing a sitting. I glared at them. You've got to be kidding. Do I look like a tourist? Ha! The crowd at the appointed meeting spot was insane. I found an empty table in a café and planted myself there, just fifteen minutes before the designated time. A pretty handsome and not unfriendly waiter dropped by and I asked for a glass of red wine. Small price for a seat where no seats were to be found.

Six o'clock came and went with no Magalie and no Stephanie. By 6:20 I turned on the roaming on my phone and texted Stephanie. "I should be there by seven she said. I'm coming with friends." Evidently she went through with the champagne after all. I texted Magalie. "We are already inside the party. At a table near where the Republique de Montmartre sign is.

What is with these French people? Is it that difficult to make a plan and follow it?

I looked over at the entrance to the venue. The guards who were checking bags before letting people in had temporarily closed the entrance. Too many people inside. People were squeezing up around the sides to get to the front of the line. The French are very bad at standing in line. Evidently the only place they stand in line is at the *boulangerie* and that is due to some extremely rigorous policing on the part of the *boulangerie* ladies. I watched two large women with skin tight clothing and copious tattoos squeeze in at the front. The were followed by an Asian family. This was not going to happen.

I texted Magalie: "I'm sorry, big crowds kind of give me the heebie jeebies. How about if I meet you at the restaurant?" Magalie responded, "Where we are is not crowdy but if you prefer to meet at the restaurant it is 8:00. Up to you." Perfect. I finished my wine, paid the hefty 15 euro bill and headed back down the hill, carefully watching the cobbles and dodging drunks or dodging the cobbles and watching drunks.

The terrace at Cépage was full. I grabbed a seat inside and ordered a four euro glass of red. It came with a bowl of pretzels. What a difference four blocks makes. I watched the traffic jam work its way up rue Caulaincourt, sipped my wine and chatted with the lovely staff of Cépage. At a few minutes after eight o'clock Magalie texted me, "we are in the restaurant!" *Parfait*!

Around the table were a big group of French people, most of whom I didn't know. Magalie, Stephanie and Jeff sat at one end of the table. An empty seat was next to Stephanie. I introduced myself with the others who turned out to be Sebastian, Isabel, Renard, Gils and Eva. They each offered some little tidbit about themselves along with their introduction. Isabel and Gils are married and lived for five years in San Francisco where he was a Software Engineer. Eva is actually Danish but has a French boyfriend (who seems not to be present) and has two French children (who are also not present). Renard tells me that I will not be able to pronounce his name, which of course starts with the guttural "R" and laughs. Sebastian begins his long evening of annoying seduction. He is sitting next to me and can't seem to get close enough, rubbing against me throughout the entire meal.

Suddenly there was quite a ruckus in the small restaurant when a group of Fête dignitaries made their way inside. There were half a dozen men dressed in cere-monial garb; elaborate hats, capes, sashes draped across their chests, adorned with medals, badges and epaulettes. It seems le Président de la République de Montmartre, Monsieur le Maire and their assorted henchman had chosen to eat at the same restaurant. Well done Magalie! Along with them, their wives (or mistresses) and soon their table was overflowing. Three of them chose to be seated in the three empty chairs at the end of our table. Renard and Eva bore the brunt of entertaining them. Oddly, their fare was added into ours and we included them when we split the tab!

Dinner was a lively affair, mostly in French, with some token English thrown my way. The wine flowed freely. Afterall, we were celebrating the noble grape. Because I was a relative novelty, much ado was made of my presence with lots of questions, tidbits and unexpected attention. I was well lubricated between wine with lunch, wine while waiting for dinner and wine for dinner.

Sebastian was becoming a bit annoying. He got closer when it seemed there was no room to get closer. He told me he was forty-five and not quite divorced and embroiled in a complicated relationship. (a "complicated relationship" is a huge red flag for me). It was essential, he claimed, that he gets the best out of life now because he was 45. In 20 years he will be as good as dead! Know your audience, dear Sebastian! He kept making vague references to a "French helicopter" which after about the third reference was clearly some sort of puerile reference to oral sex. It got old very fast.

I gave the last half of my plat to Sebastian, which may have been a mistake because I think he might have thought that made us a couple. Just before the dessert arrived Stephanie went to the bathroom and I took the opportunity to play musical chairs and move onto the couchee next to Magalie. Stephanie returned and somehow managed to get Sebastian's chair next to Renard, her "best friend" (last week Stéphane was her best friend but he just moved to St. Martin so I guess best friends are a fluid thing) That left Sebastian next to me again but far enough not to effect the rubbing.

Finally it was decided that we would head to my apartment, seven doors down the street, where Stephanie and Magalie knew there was at least half a bottle of Jet 27 and a wine rack with at least a few bottles of wine! We paid the bill, a not uncomplicated process with 9 of us and 3 of the forces of la République de Montmartre, and headed out into the night, or at least navigated our way down seven doors. I was walking with Jeff when we passed Cépage and Tomas was outside. "*Bon soir, Katrine!*" he called out. "Do you know everyone?!" asked Jeff.

Six French people traipsed up the stairs, Sebastian got into the small elevator with me. Ugh. By the time we got to my second story apartment the windows were open and every chair was taken. I brought two more out of my bedroom and opened some more wine. Somebody brought out glasses, ice, and poured out the remaining Get 27. There was talk about going downstairs to the mini market for more but I think everyone was pretty well saturated by then.

Sebastian kept talking about French helicopters. Magalie and Sebastian hung out the window and smoked. Somewhere along the way Sebastian asked if I wouldn't prefer to be told I love you even if it were a lie to get me into bed. I would prefer that you just go home Sebastian. The wine kept flowing. The talk kept going. How do you get people to go home once they are in your apartment? I just wanted to go to bed. Alone.

Amazingly something happened at about 3 am. Everyone jumped up to leave in unison. Of course that meant at least 10 or fifteen minutes of *bises* while everyone said their goodbyes. Renard hugged me, proving that French people do hug, and gave me a gift; a small magnet that commemorated La Fête 1969. "The Summer of Love!" I said, before I could catch myself. I stopped short of saying that I graduated from High School that year. He probably was born that year… or later. Sebastian pulled me into a hug and told me that he was going to be getting in touch with me so we could have some one on one time.

They all headed into the night and I turned off the lights and went to bed, breaking my rule about leaving dishes undone. Screw it. I would do them in the morning.

Les Chiens sont Rois

I don't like dogs. You might even say I hate dogs. I suspect that I may have been mauled to death by a dog in a past life. At my throat.

I don't want to touch dogs. I don't like them to touch me. I hate when they jump on me with those nasty little claws of theirs, tearing snags in my stockings or my pants. I hate their drooly mouths and their stinky breaths. And those tongues. Don't even get me started on those tongues.

So I was not happy when Stephanie et al showed up at Les Loups for our dinner with new friends with Bob in tow.

"Bob has really grown out of his bad puppy behavior!" she proudly exclaimed a couple of days before. Thank goodness. Last time he came to chez moi leaving a chewed up a slipper and a puddle on my bedroom floor I vowed it was the end of Bob's visits to chez moi. If I hate dog drool you can imagine how I feel about anything that comes out of the other end.

I'm afraid that Stephanie is fooling herself. Bob was his old badly behaved self. He loped his way through the narrow restaurant on a very long lead. When everyone was seated he wove his way through our legs tangling everyone in his leash. His face was at table level more than it was under the table. He tried to eat from all of our plates and when he was foiled, he tried to eat from the neighboring table's plates.

"*Doucement!*" cautioned Renee as she offered her salmon skin to Bob. He gulped it in one quick greedy grab. "Good dog!" she praised.

Good dog my ass!

He gobbled Magalie's salmon skin, Renee's vegetables, my spinach.

I'm sorry Stephanie. I love you but I hate Bob! Please leave him at home!

Things Still Happen Outside

Wednesday night. Jazz night. It's been a crazy couple of weeks with too many people, too many lunches, too many dinners.

I feel something coming on; strep throat? tonsillitis? Something. Oh God; it's time! I'm going to have to find a doctor. But I reached deep into the depths of me, brushed my teeth and gargled, got dressed and summoned an Uber.

Jazz night with Daniele by myself. It's been a long time!

Philippe met me at the door with la bise, right in front of Daniele, playing his drums. He showed me to my regular "when I'm by myself table" not twelve feet from Daniele. It was very hard not to make eye contact. The restaurant was quite empty for a Wednesday jazz night. Indian summer continued to hang on, making the terrace too good to pass up for most drinkers (and smokers). Before long my second chair was snagged and taken out to the terrace. At the bar was a couple drinking beer; a fifty something man and a young Asian woman. The man was seriously into the music. He danced on his stool and clapped wildly and off beat. At the end of each tune he shouted Bravo. His female friend seemed a bit embarrassed.

I arrived a little late so it wasn't long before the group took its first break, Daniele stood to introduce the guitarist and bass player. The guitar player in turn introduced Daniele. The man at the bar went crazy with applause and shouts. Then Daniele headed right over to me!

He reached out to shake my hand. His hand was very sweaty. Is playing the drums a sweaty job? Or is this something I don't know about him; he has sweaty hands?

"*Votre père?*" I joked.

"*Désolé!*" he smirked. I realized I was still holding on to his hand and quickly let go.

He asked me something in rapid fire French that went beyond "ça va." I just stared at him. Finally I managed "*En anglais s'il vous plaît?*" At least I didn't turn into the giggling fool I was last time he came to talk to me. If anything, he seemed to be the nervous one. He easily switched to English and I noticed how lovely his French accent was when he spoke English. He asked me about Vincent Bourgielle, quoting my Facebook comment to his announcement earlier in the week that Vincent would be playing with him at Pop Up Du Label.

"The most enthusiastic jazz pianist you've ever heard!" he quoted. "Where have you heard him?"

"Oh yes! He is wonderful!" I replied. "I heard him at Sunside. Avec Alan....." and I couldn't for the life of me remember Alan's last name. "An American singer, guitar player, from New York...." Was it seconds? Minutes? Hours? "Harris!"

Daniele knew of the performance, an Eddie Petersen tribute (I personally don't know Eddie Petersen from Bob the dog) but said he didn't know Alan. Yes! I watch someone besides you, Daniele Chandelier! I am not the complete groupie I may seem!

"He will be at the Ducs de Lombard next month," I said. "You should go." He looked doubtful.

"You should come to Pop Up Du Label on Tuesdays," he suggested. "It's mine!" Of course I've known about his Tuesday performances at Pop Up but I've never gone. It's in the 11eme and seems like a young venue. In addition to being too far away it didn't seem like a place I would be comfortable. Of course, look how long it took me to actually go to Le Grand Comptoir for a jazz dinner. Now I practically live there. If I added that venue to the occasional other places I watched him, and my every other week presence at GCA I would really become a groupie!

I looked at him reluctantly. "*C'est trop loin. J'habite dans le dix-huitième.* I don't know," I added. "It doesn't really seem like my kind of place."

"No! It's nice!" he protested. "It's OK, I live outside of Paris! Completely the other way!" (I didn't know that.) "You would like it! It's very nice. There is a restaurant with very good food, *bio*! You should come. It's very nice. You would like it."

Oh my. "*D'accord!*" I said. "I will try it."

As the evening went on I realized that Philippe was giving me space; walking by, doing his little dance, winking but acceding space for Daniele. He thinks I am here for Daniele! And Daniele thinks I'm here for Philippe.

Daniele plays with great enthusiasm. He smiles at me from time to time but we don't talk again. I get my bill from Guillaume and order an Uber. It's one minute away when Philippe brings the cognac bottle to give me a refill. "My Uber is one minute away!" I say, slugging down the cognac. As I walk out the door he comes for *la bise*. I plant a single kiss firmly on his cheek. "*Je t'adore!*" I blurt out. He looks at me with a puzzled look and I get into my Uber.

Who am I here for? Can I be here for both of them?

And the Crazy Goes On

I just had a drive by shooting. As I wrapped up the day's writing at Cépage, answering a couple of texts and emails, Caroleen passed my table. As she walked by she murmured "fucking bitch." Then she actually took two steps back and hissed at me "You are going to pay for trying to smear my name."

I was stunned. I have pretty much gotten over her nastiness and decided that yes her angst really is about jealousy. "She makes friends in five minutes!"

How is that a criticism worthy of warning my landlord? The truth is, she has no friends. It must be very frustrating for her to watch me, the new kid on the block (my block, by the way!) making so many friends. I'm sure she looks at my social media pages and realizes what a rich full life I have. She still can barely get served at Cépage and I get greeted by name and accommodated with helpful gestures to maximize my writing efforts.

It wasn't over. Twenty minutes later she came over and completely laid into me. I am a horrible evil person! Everyone in Montmartre hates me and knows how awful I am. (ok, that should be a clue that she's unhinged). Two men at Cépage were just talking about what a nasty person I was. I suggested she just leave me alone and I'll leave her alone but she insisted that it was too late for that! She said I used her like I use everyone. Then she brought up Elliot and said "you buy him dinners to get him to be your friend!" I said, the only person I bought dinners for was you! And she said "we had an agreement that you would buy me drinks and dinners and I would help you out with Paris info." (we did? And why am I even talking to her?) "You invited me for a drink that night! You had been bad mouthing me for months before that! I liked you. You betrayed me. We were friends."

"Yes" I said, "we were friends and then I couldn't take any more of your bigotry and racism!"

"I'm not a bigot! How dare you! You are just a pansy. You want everything to be the way you want it to be."

Why oh why am I engaging with her? Stop! And I did.

It boggles my mind that she thinks I am the problem here. But why on earth am I giving her any mind space? Her part in this tale is over.

What would Ninon do? Nothing. Although all out warfare is tempting. I will do nothing.

J'ai le Cafard

J'*ai le cafard*. It's pretty much the opposite of *j'ai la pêche*. The latter is a phrase I've taken to using when someone asks me "Ça va." Ca va is what everybody says when they see you. Not the *"comment allez-vous"* that we learn in school. Literally it means. It goes. The result can be a back and forth with both people saying *Ça va* repeatedly. Just put a question mark on it. Just tilt your head a bit. Or perhaps blow a bit of air out the side of your lips and shrug before saying "*ça va*".

One might get clever and respond "Ça va bien!" It goes well. Or if things are not going so well, "*Pas mal*" Not bad. That one has actually resulted in raised eyebrows and a concerned look like, well, what's the matter? Or one might respond *"Comme si comme ça"*. Kind of so-so. But I like to say *j'ai la pêche*. I have the peach. It's something most non French speakers don't know so it says, I know what I'm doing! I've been around the block and I'm as good as French! Well. Maybe not completely. But it also says that things are great. It always elicits a chuckle and a smile and the recipient wants to know why things are so good.

For the last two days *j'ai le cafard*. I have the cockroach. Or what we English speakers would call the blues. I haven't tried using it on anyone. I'm not really sure I will because it's kind of a turn off. Nobody really wants to know why I'm blue. I don't even know why. I just haven't wanted to get out of bed. I certainly don't want to get out of my pajamas, or brush my teeth, or wash my face. My hair is taking on strange shapes.

I got out of bed yesterday intending to perk myself up; to do something fun. I made pancakes. And coffee. I ate them on the couch while I watched a movie on Netflix. When the movie was over I lay on the couch and finished my book. By the time I finished the book the sun was setting and it was too cold outside to really want to do anything fun so I downloaded the next Bruno, Chief of Police, book and started it. I made some dinner but I wasn't really hungry enough to eat. I texted a bit with Elliott. He just returned from a trip to Marseilles and said he really likes it. I should go. I told him I wanted to. I had only been once very briefly many years ago. He said that they say it's getting safer, friendlier, cleaner. That's good. I remember being a bit intimidated when I was there before. But I didn't tell Elliott. I think he prefers it intimidating.

An invitation comes from Magalie, dîner *chez elle avec* Sebastian, the creepy guy from dinner after the Fête des Vendanges and Eva, the nice Danish girl, who turned out to be his girlfriend! I'm not sure which is less appealing; Sebastian, the expensive Uber trip to *chez* Magalie or the five floors up with no elevator. Other than that, dinner with Magalie is always a really nice thing. Something keeps me from responding right away.

I put my dinner into an old ice cream container I use in place of tupperware and put it in the refrigerator. It will most likely be thrown away next week when it grows fuzz. I poured the remains of a bottle of wine into a glass and took it to the couch. I went back to Bruno. When it was reasonable to do so I went back to bed. At one thirty I popped two Tylenol PM and went to sleep, vowing to do something fun tomorrow.

What am I leaving out?

Yesterday was Tuesday. Pop Up du Label day. As soon as I woke up I looked at my phone. "Daniele C has invited you to Mardi Jazz". Now that would certainly be a fun thing, wouldn't it? Good food. Good music. And Daniele. The man practically begged me to go. What more do I need? What is holding me back? All day my (in)activities were punctuated with "shall I go?" And then there was the further dilemma, Daniele would be with the same trio at Chez Papa in the 5eme on Wednesday and somewhere near Jardin du Luxembourg on Thursday. And of course Wednesday was jazz night at GCA, the vocal version. So that forces the answer; am I there for Daniele or am I there for Philippe? And does either really care?

I woke up this morning before ten. That was a breakthrough! Then I dawdled around with my phone. Before I knew it, it was noon and Philippe was announcing today's menu and reminding the world that it's Jazz night. I haven't seen him since Friday. I wonder if he notices I've not been there. Daniele was announcing his gig at Chez Papa. I still have options.

I jumped out of bed, making it up as I went so I wouldn't be tempted to crawl back in. I headed into the bathroom, peeling off my three day old pajama wardrobe and throwing them into the washing machine. I carefully climbed into the tub. This would not be the day I slipped in the tub and cracked my head open, not to be found until Saturday by the cleaners. I scrubbed my hair and soaped every inch of my body, letting the hot water rinse away all my negativity.

I brushed my teeth and let the electric toothbrush run through its cycle twice! I moisturized everywhere. I threw a laundry pod into the washer and turned on the machine, heading into my bedroom to dry my hair and get dressed.

In only a few short days the weather has changed completely and I have to go into the bottom drawer to pull out a turtleneck sweater. Red. To cheer me up. Get me started. Claim my place on this planet! Let the Parisians have their black. I'm the American girl. Well, short of the MAGA cap and dreadful politics.

I pack up my books, my computer, my bag and head to Cépage. Today's feature is *parmentier de canard*, the dish named after the pharmacist who cleverly tricked the French into eating the humble potato. Bruno keeps me company while I eat my duck. I respond enthusiastically to Magalie's invitation and send a friend request to Eva. I send a message to Philippe, "*seulement moi ce soir, s'il te plaît*".

There. Decisions made. Now I'll research a trip to Marseilles with maybe a stop in Lyon on the way. Maybe I need a little break from Paris.

Domestic Bliss (or not)

Ninon kept to her commitment of never marrying but there was a period of time when she was almost as good as wed. Louis de Mornay, the Marquis de Villarceaux was the perfect match for her. He was brilliant. He was confident. He was exceedingly rich. He was handsome. He was very highly placed in Court, but Ninon was willing to overlook that one tiny fault. And he was already married, which took the problem off the table. For over five years she spent most of her time at Louis' chateau in Meulan, only 50 kilometers from Paris but as good as light years away.

In Meulan Ninon had everything she could wish for. She could read, write, play her lute. She had a house full of servants. She could bring anyone to her side with just a wink and a nod. The countryside was quiet. The air was fresh. Birds sang, cattle lowed, cicadas buzzed. All of the hustle and bustle of Paris seemed a million miles away. Ninon was in love. And her Marquis loved her.

It was during this time that Ninon gave birth to a son! Louis de Mornay was a delight to both his mother and father but also the cause of conflict. The Marquis being married refused to officially recognize the child. It did not take long for Ninon to retaliate by taking refuge in Paris where the delights of her salon, her good friends, the stimulation of intellectual discourse and if truth be told, freedom from the infant, reminded the beautiful epicurean what she most valued in life.

Sometimes the heart wants what the heart wants. Ninon's heart was not finished wanting the Marquis. As such, she found herself pregnant yet again. She took her bloated self back to Meulan to await the birth of a second child. Sadly, after nine months of gestating, both the child and Ninon as she pondered her best future, the pregnancy ended in a stillbirth.

The devastation brought an end to the five year love affair with de Mornay. Ninon left the Marquis, the château and the toddler, providing a financial future for him and swearing on her soul that she would never ever tell young Louis that she was his mother. This would have tragic consequences in the years to come.

Seasons

Only a mere month shy of the one year anniversary of my first arrival on rue Caulaincourt as an official resident. Today is the first honestly cold day. Cépage has put up the plastic walls on the terrace and turned on the heaters. Parisians are bundled in coats and scarves. The bright colors and exposed skin of Indian summer, could it have been just two short weeks ago, are gone. Everything is somber colors, the famous Parisian black. It's really only 48 degrees Fahrenheit, not exactly what I could call coat weather and I'm wearing a sweater and silk scarf, the same wardrobe for inside and outside, but it's only a very short walk.

When Laurent greeted me, he asked me to feel his hands. They were cold.

It's Saturday lunch and the restaurant is full. The entire staff is working today and everyone except Garron is friendly to me. He hasn't got a smile or a friendly word for me. I noticed that he got la bise from Caroleen a couple of weeks ago so I suspect that she has been turning his ear. Everyone else seems to be going out of their way to show me that I am indeed welcome and if they had to choose sides, which they clearly don't want to do, they would choose mine. After all, she's tried to get two of them fired and a third she's called a terribly nasty name.

The sidewalk in front of the florist shop is covered what I suppose are cold weather perennials. Still very colorful. In four short weeks there will be Christmas trees. And the quartier's lights will welcome all to Montmartre with Holiday greetings! By then I dare say I will break out my puffy coat.

The produce vendor displays persimmons, pomegranates, and pumpkins along with an assortment of late season fruits; figs, apples, oranges, pears and a couple of pineapples, front and center. I wonder where they have been shipped in from.

Cépage is doing a brisk business from its shellfish counter displayed on the sidewalk, oysters, shrimp, lobsters and limpets. Some of the families inside order big seafood platters. Some shoppers with bags already laden with the goodies from the butcher, the baker and the candlestick maker come into pay for the crustaceans that they are taking home with them. One of these guys has a pineapple poking out of the top of his bags. I wonder what his table will look like!

It all makes me wish I like oysters. The bountiful platters that are brought to the long table next to me, a table full of celebrating young Italians, are so attractive and tempting! They taste like the sea, exclaims a friend who is a fan of the slimy little globs of … there's no other word for it… snot! Dress it up with seaweed, add bright lemons, serve it with wonderful bread. I would rather take a slurp of the ocean. They drink bottles of Pomerol. That part looks good. Garron opens more bottles and fills their glasses. They are having fun. I stick to my French onion soup.

Book Clubs

Elliot and I have been tossing around the idea of a book group for months now; something small, limited to four people at most, and with a longer term duration. Years ago, he, Joan and Charlotte spent every Thursday reading the complete works of Shakespeare and discussing each over an appropriate dinner and wine.

I suspect a weekly effort might be too much. After all, Elliott has his tribe to take care of. Maybe every other week? I've made a couple of recommendations but they were not to Elliot's liking. Yesterday I suggested Proust's seven volumes of "In Search of Lost Time". What could be a better way for me to augment my drinking from the firehose education I'm getting about my adopted country?

"Ha ha ha," responds Elliott. "I haven't read it since university days. The downside is that I don't like reading in translation and it is pretty important when reading something as textually dense as 'A La Recherche' together for everyone to have the same edition to uhm, uh, be on the same page as it were. (insert winky eye emoticon). What about Madame de Stael? I've always meant to give her a thorough read through."

So off to Wikipedia I go. I have never heard of Madame de Stael.

"Her intellectual collaboration with Benjamin Constant between 1795 and 1811 made them one of the most celebrated intellectual couples of their time. They discovered sooner than others the tyrannical character and designs of Napoleon. In 1814 one of her contemporaries observed that "there are three great powers struggling against Napoleon for the soul of Europe: England, Russia, and Madame de Staël". Her works, both novels and travel literature, with emphasis on passion, individuality and oppositional politics made their mark on European Romanticism."

Oh good grief, yet another important contributor to Literature who I know nothing about! And yet, yes, she does sound important. Especially if Elliot is willing to consider reading her in English!

In the meantime, my efforts to understand Ninon better have me buried in Molière, Richelieu, and Cardinal Mazarin, and my online book club with the Earful Tower has me deep in reading about the German occupation during World War II. Throw in a bit of Bruno, Chief of Police in the Périgord and it's a wonder I ever take my nose out of a book. Much less finish writing mine.

Maybe I'll tackle Proust on my own. In English.

The Actor

Jean Baptiste paced back and forth while Ninon read the latest reviews of his play. He grew increasingly impatient which irritated Ninon to the point that she tossed the pages onto the table in front of her and exhaling pointedly stared at her dear friend.

"What did you expect, *mon ami*?" Ninon admonished Jean Baptiste, known to the greater Paris population only as Molière. "You are making fun of their very lives!"

The night before the author had introduced to the public, at Le Palais Royal, his new play, *L'Écoles des femmes* (School for the Wives). For most of his career the author had much preferred tragedies, but his audience and his patrons made it very clear to him that they preferred his comedies. Last night's performance was attended by the brother of the King.

The play, with its twists and turns finds Arnolphe, the lead, played last night by the author, a man terribly awkward with women and scheming for years to see his charge, Agnès, to be raised by the nuns to grow up naive and ignorant enough to believe when she comes of age that marriage to Arnolphe is a good outcome. Of course, nothing goes that easily and nature and hormones take their own course, resulting in Agnès falling in love with Horace, a family friend and much much more appropriate husband for the young Agnès.

Arnolphe schemes, Arnolphe lies, Arnolphe deceives only to be foiled in the end, when Agnès of course marries Horace. Who could not predict the outcome? Yet, the audience had been scandalized. Reviewers complained that Moliere had gone too far. Ninon lifted the pages again and continued to read. "Wanting in good taste, sound morality, and rules of grammar!" cried one critic. "All else aside," wrote another, "the play is horrendously dangerous of undermining the principles of religion."

"And these disturb you why?" Ninon asked. "What did you expect? And more importantly, why are you concerned?"

Molière continued his pacing. He admired Ninon above all others but like every actor and playwright, he lived for praise and positive affirmation. Maybe Madame de l'Enclos was accustomed to being roundly criticized and but the morning's reviews were just too much for the poor aging author to take. He sunk down onto a padded stool near Ninon's chair. Elbows on his knees, he lowered his head into his hands, burying his fingers into his thick curly hair and moaned.

"*Regardez*! Look at all these raves about the work." Ninon flipped through the pages, pointing at the positive, even glowing reviews of last night's debut. The fact that all of Paris seemed to be talking about Molière's most recent work, whether they were at the performance or not, was significant. That alone should have made the playwright ecstatic. After all, silence would have been a far more devastating result today.

Moliere slowly raised his face and dropped his arms to his side. He gradually raised himself back to his feet, regaining his composure as if all of the air that had left his body had found its way back. It was still not easy for him to meet Ninon's eye. He walked to the window and looked out onto the Square below.

Ninon could barely hide her impatience. "Listen," she said, "You will answer these silly claims with a follow up play."

The writer turned away from the window and finally met Ninon's eye. He tilted his head, wordlessly considering the idea. His mind sped. There was nothing more for Ninon to say. Moliere was already writing his great answer to his critics in his head.

Ninon slipped out of the room without him even noticing. An hour later, one of the maids entered the room, finding Molière continuing to pace as he formulated La Critique de L'École des femmes in his head. The maid gently steered

Monsieur towards the exit, him mumbling out loud to himself as he was guided towards the door. As he walked down the cobbles below the window Ninon watched out the window.

The Elephant and
the Six Blind Men

A group of blind men heard that a strange animal, called an elephant, had been brought to the town, but none of them were aware of its shape and form. Out of curiosity, they said: "We must inspect and know it by touch, of which we are capable." So, they sought it out, and when they found it they groped about it. In the case of the first person, whose hand landed on the trunk, said "This being is like a thick snake". For another one whose hand reached its ear, it seemed like a kind of fan. As for another person, whose hand was upon its leg, said, "the elephant is a pillar like a tree-trunk." The blind man who placed his hand upon its side said, "elephant is a wall". Another who felt its tail, described it as a rope. The last felt its tusk, stating the elephant is that which is hard, smooth and like a spear.

"Oh my goodness, David Lebovitz is my favorite author! You know him?" exclaimed my new friend Neel. She's a lovely woman visiting Paris with her husband John and introduced to me by John's childhood friend Elliott. They were at *chez moi* for one of Elliot's "I most miss tacos" Mexican feasts.

Elliot sneers and lets out a disgusted puff of air. "I know him." Clearly he doesn't like him.

"Why not?" I ask.

"I find him incredibly pretentious. He writes about things he doesn't understand and he passes himself off as an expert. And don't even get me started on Peter Mayle. I'd like to assassinate him."

"Well, he's already dead…." I mumble.

Previously I had watched the man come unhinged about the movie Amélie! "It makes me furious! People think that this is Paris! It is NOT Paris." Spittle practically flying from his mouth.

"It is Paris." I countered. "It's one version of Paris. It may not be yours but it certainly is Paris on rue Lepic!"

"Bah!" Elliott grumbled.

Fast forward a few days and I met my fellow expat, Evelyn, for drinks after her first French class. She chose Le Bar at the Intercontinental Hotel near Palais Garnier.

"We live in a five star bubble." conjectured Evelyn. "We drink in luxury hotel bars. We eat at nice restaurants. We live in very nice apartments. Our bubble follows us around." She took a sip of her 30 euro martini, Absolut vodka, three olives, not dirty.

Well, maybe her bubble follows her around. Personally I was noticing that everyone around us was either a business traveler or a tourist. I was wishing we had opted for the cafe across the street from the Opera House where a glass of wine would have cost no more than 5 euro and the people around us more likely to be French. Even chi chi Café de la Paix would have been more authentic. Ironically Evelyn commented that a gentleman at the end of the bar was watching her. She was clearly watching him too. When we started to leave she stopped mid-step and walked back to him. "*Enchantée*" she said and turned and walked away. "Made his day." she giggled. I was thinking that had she gone to the business traveler's room and given him a magnificent blow job, THAT would have made his day. Her *enchantée*?

"I'll see you here Wednesday?" Evelyn asked as I got into my taxi to head back to rue Caulaincourt and my Paris.

"I'm afraid I can't make it Wednesday." I said, my five star bubble deflating, thinking about my plans with my lovely Columbian friend and how I convinced her to give my Paris, after dark, 9eme, jazz, casual dining and Philippe, a shot.

Rive Droit vs Rive Gauche, the Marais vs the Latin Quarter, the Champs Elysee or Boulevard Saint-Germain, La Bastille vs Odeon, Jardin du Luxembourg vs the Tuileries.... Or neither! How about Square d'Anvers where you can see Sacré Coeur up the hill, just three short very touristed blocks away, but where you will only see locals, or their nannies watching the children running, jumping and climbing in the playground? Or venture down the stairway below the bust of Dalida, breasts rubbed to a shiny brass glow (why, I'm not sure) to the tiny Square Joël Le Tac, where you can watch the feisty Montremoise playing *boules*.

Skip stones on Canal St. Martin (like Amélie) or sail a toy boat on the fountain in the Tuileries. Follow your toddler on a pony around Jardin du Luxembourg or take the always enjoyable Bateaux Mouches on the Seine. Find one of the iconic green chairs in the Tuileries, Parc Monceau, next to the Medici Fountain, or in Place de Vosges and read or nap or daydream.

Take your place behind the Chinese tourists in line at Louis Vuitton where they will give you a glass of champagne while you decide which bag to buy instead of paying your mortgage this month, or see if you can get the door man at Dior on Ave Montaigne or at Chanel at Place Vendôme to unlock and let you in. Join the throngs at Galleries Lafayette or their humbler fellow shoppers across the way at H & M. Or shop for pennies on the euro at Tati in the Goutte d'Or.

They are all Paris. Pick yours. Or pick a few.

It's Raining Men

OK, what is the deal with married men in Paris? We've talked about the speculated statistics to death; 99% of married men cheat. I still don't know if I agree with that number. After all, I would suggest that 99% (of married men) are not cheatable. In other words, I don't know where they would find someone to cheat with.

So now I know married men and I know single men. Oddly the married ones seem to be the most flirtatious. Take Philippe. Not married. Not gay (as far as I know). But frankly not very flirtatious. I woke up in the middle of the night last week, sat bolt upright and said "He has a rule about sleeping with clients!" By the light of day, I think that my revelation was probably just wishful thinking… I could always stop coming to GCA. Daniele; married and suddenly very flirtatious.

Renard, from the dinner after the Fete des Vendanges, is single and is going to come to *chez moi* and we will cook together. I have no idea what he expects that will involve other than pasta, a truffle and wine. The only part of this that makes me nervous is that he is Stephanie's "best friend". Stephanie seems to have a lot of best friends and after all, she went straight for Daniele. Not that it got her anywhere. With her green teeth. I will be sure never to have green teeth. A wine mustache, maybe. But never green teeth.

I'm writing at my table at GCA. Philippe is doing some kind of business, whistling, walking back and forth in front of me. I can't say I would call it flirting. I would just call it looking for attention. He's taking my writing seriously. At the bar is a guy I've seen the last few times I've been here. He's not bad looking. Probably mid to late forties, dark hair and beard, I think he works in the neighborhood somewhere. He actually looks a bit like Thierry. Definitely the type that catches my eye. He is turned away from the bar and facing me, maybe looking out of the window, or maybe watching me work. Wedding ring on his finger clear as day. If I smile at him, he smiles back. But he still keeps watching me work. And drinking his Chablis.

Tonight Daniele has a rather special gig at Pop up du Label; a music club and restaurant in the 10ème. He's all but begged me to go for the past month or two. "You'll like it," he assured me. "It's very good. It's mine!" So last week I told him I would go tonight. And now I feel like such a baby but…. I am afraid!

Just like I cancelled my reservation at GCA three times before I ever came, I no doubt will cancel this one. I google street-viewed the location of GCA, the entrance, and where Daniele would be sitting when I came in. There was no way around it, I would have to walk right past him. It was impossible. And today I practically own the place. What about my mantra, "Life happens outside. Go outside!"?

Siobhan said that next week she will go with me. This week she has a business trip. Will absence make the heart grow fonder? Or will I seem like the big loser that I am? *Je ne sais pas.*

Maybe if I turn around and look out the window behind me I will see something really interesting going on. Now both Philippe and the handsome guy are both sitting at the bar looking directly at me. It's terribly disconcerting. Maybe I should speak to him. Maybe I should say *"enchantée"*.

Tragedy

The years passed and Ninon kept her word never to breathe a word of her son. In truth, it was not so difficult because his father swept him off to the Netherlands when he followed the Prince after the Fronde. Ninon thought about the boy from time to time and the anniversary of his birth was always a painful time, with her taking to her salon for days on end, not willing to talk to anyone.

So it was a great shock followed by dismay when young Louis appeared at Ninon's salon in the company of a contingent of Dutch royalty. The young men had heard about the pleasures to be found at the now famous salon, both intellectual and otherwise.

Naturally, Ninon did not recognize her son at first. Always happy to entertain new and very handsome young visitors she showed them her very best. The first evening of their attendance Jean de la Fontaine was reading his new fable, "La Cigale et la Fourmi".

Madame de Sevigne was also in attendance that night. "Ah, she exclaimed, "Le Fontaine is such a delight! Reading his fables is like eating from a basket of strawberries. You begin by selecting the largest and the best and before you know it, you've eaten them all."

Fontaine had read the fable outloud and a hearty discussion was in progress about whether the Cigale represented the improvidence of France when the young gentlemen entered the salon and were announced by the manservant. Ninon was gazing at the young men, impressed by their good looks and obvious breeding, not really noticing their names until the shock jarred her out of her reverie. "Louis de Mornay…"

Never a swooner, Ninon was stunned and could not catch her breath. It could be no coincidence that this young man had the same name as the Louis de Mornay who Ninon had lived with for five years in the countryside some, what was it? Fifteen? Twenty? The dates ran through her head. Seventeen years since Ninon gave birth to her son. Nearly fifteen since she left desolate at the stillbirth of her second child. And when her lover had extracted from her a promise never to tell her child that she was his mother.

While Ninon was busy reeling at the recognition, young Louis was busy experiencing his own *coupe de foudre*. For him, as it was for most young healthy men of his age, it was love at first sight. The years and done little to diminish Ninon's beauty and appeal and Louis was desperate to get closer to his hostess, to this compelling woman. He must know her. He must have her.

But it would not happen that day. Ninon had fled to her private rooms.

Week after week Louis returned to the salon each Wednesday evening. Each week he tried to get close to Ninon. He wrote her notes, he imposed on Ninon's friends to intervene on his behalf. Each week she managed to elude the young man. Finally, after a month of avoiding him, Ninon realized that she had to face the problem head on.

But not yet, she decided to take a break in the countryside.

Without much notice to anyone, Ninon accepted the long standing invitation of Monsieur M to stay at his very small chateau in the shadow of Château de Fontainebleau, on the edge of the forest. She packed few clothes, her writing paraphernalia and one servant.

Just a half day by carriage from Paris, Fontainebleau was nothing like Paris. The air was clean and outside of the grounds of the big chateau one could imagine that there was no one around for miles and miles. Summer was warm but the trees and greenery of the nearby forest made things seem cooler and fresher.

And in spite of the serenity and solitude try as she might, Ninon could not clear the nightmare that occupied her head.

It was on a lovely Thursday afternoon that Ninon was sitting with a book and her journal in the garden nearly dozing in the sun when she heard the clopping of a solitary horse and rider. Minutes later footsteps on the gravel approached where she was sitting. A sense of dread kept her from looking up. Finally she felt a shadow blocking the sun and she had no choice but to look upon the intruder; her visitor, her son.

She didn't speak. After a few moments, that seemed like an eternity to Louis, he finally did.

"My beloved Ninon", he began "I am so sorry to intrude on your holiday like this."

Ninon didn't help him at all.

"But you leave me no alternative," he continued.

Ninon was mute.

"I know that I have yet to prove myself to be worthy of your love. But I am well born, well educated and my opportunities are limitless."

With that Ninon looked at the young man.

"This will never be." she replied quite simply.

"I cannot accept this!" Louis exhorted. For the next half hour he argued with her, if one can argue with someone who doesn't offer any rebuttal. He fumed. He paced. He shouted. He even wept. But of course nothing could change Ninon's response.

"This will never be." she responded once more, with resolution.

"If I can't have you, then I must end my life!" exclaimed the young man in despair.

"Cannot have me?" Ninon looked at Louis with a mixture of compassion and heartbreak. "You say you are well born." She took a deep breath as she prepared to break the vow she made to Louis's father so many years ago. As she expelled the breath it was as if her very soul leaked from her body. "I am your mother."

Young Louis, was stunned. All of the color drained from his face and his bearing drooped. He stood silently in front of Ninon. He had no words. Finally he turned and walked away, his footsteps sounding on the same gravel that warned of his approach.

Ninon slumped in her chair. She had no tears. She had no emotion. She felt dead.

Moments later a single shot rang out. A hunter in the nearby forest? Ninon dropped her book on the ground.

An hour later the body of young Louis was found in the woods; next to him his pistol.

Renard

Maybe this is where my part of the story should end. If it is, it's only fair to warn the reader that things could not be any more unreal than they are. The cliché just gets to be more and more cliché. American woman "of an age" moves to Paris to write and find her new life. She makes many friends and a few enemies. And in the end, the perfect French man lands on her doorstep and they fall in love. Happily ever after. *La Fin*

But life doesn't really happen that way, does it? So maybe it's in the telling that makes it less than a cliché? Maybe Ninon taught me something. Maybe Paris taught me something. I was certainly an eager learner.

I wake up at a leisurely 10 am to a text from Renard. "What do you think, if I come to your flat tonight? I'm a little bit tired with my big working week… but with you (insert smiley emoticon with hearts for eyes) and a good bottle of wine and truffles that is all I need to my body. Or tomorrow if you can?"

We have been texting each other in a playful way since the night of the Fete de Vendanges; talking about his cat, cooking, restaurants, truffles and random other things. Now this.

D'accord! The rubber has met the road. Put up or shut up, lady!

Then he adds, "And with this bad weather we need to cocooning." So his English is good but not perfect. It's cute.

"Tonight is fine. Tomorrow I have plans. Tell me what we need for making the pasta and I can get it today. What time is good for you?"

"OK. Perfect for tonight! I don't working so I can come at 19:00 if it is ok for you? I bring everything for the pasta and a salad for after, and a peace [sic] of meat. You can buy one or two cheese, one cheese goat will be good with truffles and olive oil… and a bottle of wine. I bring a bottle also."

"I just need this," he adds, and up pops a picture of a cheese grater.

"And you have an oven?'

"Of course I have an oven! But my cheese grater is terrible. Can you bring yours?"

"You modern girl! And ok, I bring mine. I need your address again and door code. And I bring bread."

"I bring a bottle of champagne to celebrate our dinner. You know food is very important to me."

Oh the pressure!

In the hours to follow I clean my apartment. I text Siobhan and she gives me the pep talk only a really good girlfriend can deliver. It's interesting that both of my very good girlfriends here are younger than my daughters. But they don't feel like daughters. They feel like friends. My daughters would shriek if I talked to them about this. She offers to make me an appointment where she gets her bikini waxes. Agggghhhh! That is not happening!

But I do scrub myself to within an inch of scouring off all of my skin. And then some.

At 6:30 I resort to drinking from the leftover bottle of white wine in the fridge. My wine rack has grown a bit empty in the last weeks but I have earmarked a really good red that was given to me when I "retired". Is that what I did? How can that be? This feels a lot more like my college days than my retirement days. At 6:45 the wifi goes out!

I spent five minutes trying to get it to reconnect before I finally just switched my phone to roaming and accepted that I'd pay the ten dollars to have access for the next twenty four hours!

Just as I was wondering if he would follow the French rules of being fashionably late, bing, a text. "Can I come at 10 minutes before 7." and then the door buzzer rings.

I push the button to open the second door. Let the games begin.

In moments he's at my door. He has a huge bouquet of flowers. And a bottle of champagne. His expectations become a little more clear.

I honestly don't remember the next half hour or so. I know we started with *la bise*. And then we ended with …

Let's draw the curtain here to allow some privacy. Discretion is the better part of valour and all of that. How we got from champagne on the sofa to waking up together at 10 am the next morning is something best left to the imagination. Suffice it to say that after some dozen years of abstinence and truly never expecting this kind of intimacy again, somehow a charming forty seven year old man made it incredibly comfortable and easy to take me there.

Well, it certainly didn't hurt to have sweet French nothings whispered in my ear. And that he told me he wanted to kiss me since that very first night he was in my apartment after the Fête de Vendanges. And that I had crazy sparkling eyes full of mischief and fun. And did I mention the French? Even when he spoke English it was so incredibly charming and sexy. He opened me like a book that he couldn't put down and I eagerly shared my story. Ugh, that is way too campy. He peeled back my inhibitions. He… let's stick with the book analogy.

Shower, coffee and he was on his way. I cleaned up the dishes from the night before and then reluctantly cleaned up the remnants from the night on my own self. I had a busy week scheduled. Siobhan texted me right after the cleaning was done, her wifi was not working, could she come use mine? She did and we were off to lunch, with wine and confidences shared.

I was still worried about Stephanie. She had insisted that they were "best friends", that he was "like a brother to her." He said they were friends but he was not at all interested in her that way. I guess I can't help wonder why not. For her at least. Back at my apartment Siobhan asked if she could take a nap on my sofa. Sure. Why not.

Throughout the day I got texts from him. "Kiss kiss" "You are on my mind"…. "Answer him!" said Siobhan. I answered in kind feeling like a thirteen year old girl. Then I had a dinner commitment with Silvie, Elliott and Joan. All the while my mind buzzing with Renard.

What would normally have been a fun dinner dragged on and on. Elliott expounding on wine and food and cheese and… blah blah blah blah blah. I was exhausted. I just wanted to go to bed. And sleep. A text from Renard, "I don't want to disturb your friends time but I'm about to go to sleep and I want to tell you…"

Aftermath

Wednesday. Drinks with Evelyn. Why am I continuing this friendship? And even worse, why oh WHY did I tell her about Renard.

"Be very careful!" "I am almost certain he has done some background investigating on you. He knows you have money!"

The very idea that haunted me the week between "we will have dinner together" and our actual night together. Every single thing Evelyn said suggested that my sweet man was a fortune hunter, an opportunist looking for a sugar mama. Why else would he be interested in someone my age? Certainly he had done his research with Stephanie and knew I money and precisely how old I was.

Now let me be clear. I don't have Evelyn's kind of money. I don't live in a five star bubble. While spending thirty euro on a martini is not a terribly big deal, I'm practical enough to know that it's generally a waste of money, and since I seldom stop at one, it's an even bigger waste of money.

"What is the one thing about yourself you would like to change?" Evelyn probed. I knew exactly where she was going. She had just hired a personal trainer. Two weeks into her regime she was past the initial pain all over your body place and had become a disciple. "It's only 1500 euros for a month."

Seriously? If you paid me 1500 euros a month I wouldn't hire a personal trainer. No use trying to explain to Evelyn how I feel about all of this. She's on a mission. She wants to fix me. That's what she does. She wants to put me into a two bedroom apartment with Peter Turnley prints lining the walls at a modest 500 euro per print. She wants me fit and trim and wearing great clothing and with skin that glows from the ministrations of her very expensive day spa.

My eyes glass over, both from the two martinis and her well intentioned advice and I tell her I have to go… I have a reservation at Le Grand Comptoir for jazz dinner. She insists on picking up the check (120 euros for four martinis) and I ran out to grab a taxi.

Le Grand Comptoir is buzzing! My little reserved table, number thirty is sitting ready for me. It is very close to table number 31 where a couple is sitting enjoying their drinks and avidly listening to the music. As I walked in, Daniele looks up and gives me a broad grin. He never smiles that big. Philippe is waiting on some people and the bartender shouts a big bon soir. I nod to my table and he nods back.

Philippe comes over with *la bise*. The people at the next table introduce themselves. They are close enough to me, that they might as well! Bob and Cindy are from Maine. They are musicians. They discovered Daniele on a previous trip and texted him to find out where he would be. They had even gone to the Pop Up du Label the night before.

Guilloume came to take my drink order. "Une bouteille ce soir" I respond. It's always a question… *une bouteille or a carafe*. Never a question of what, Côte du Rhône. Bob and Cindy were impressed.

I got there so late it was time for the group's first break and Daniele made a beeline to my table. He reaches out to shake my hand and I do the two hand intimate version, much more intimate than *la bise*, in my opinion. "Can I sit?"

Are you kidding me? Three years of lusting after the man and now he wants to sit?

"*Bien sûr! Voulez-vous un verre?*" He looks at my bottle. "I can't drink all of this." I say.

"She just had two martinis!" says Bob. Why did I tell him that?

"*Oui, merci!*"

"Philippe!" I shout as he walks by. "*Un autre verre s'il te plaît*". Philippe dances over with an empty glass and I pour Daniele a glass.

"Merci." his dark eyes are sparkling.

Bob and Cindy are so close that they join in the conversation, telling Daniele that they are big fans. Because he sits with me they assume that Daniele and I are friends. I guess we are now. They went to Pop Up Du Label last night and tell him so. He didn't see them there and was surprised. He looks at me admonishingly. I blush and tell him "It's so far." He just shakes his head.

Then he tells Bob and Cindy about a drive he made across the US. LA to San Francisco to Yellowstone to... what's that place with the faces of the Presidents carved on the front of the mountain? Mount Rushmore. Yes!

I don't remember what it was I said when Bob said "You have to watch this one!"

"Yes, I'm learning that." says Daniele. He gives me *le regarde*.

"Oh darn! I have to go back and play."

In the meantime I am getting texts from Renard. He's "remembering our night."

The musical portion of the night ends and Daniele sits in the seat next to me, where Bob and Cindy have just left to make a dinner reservation nearby. Texts are pinging in from Renard. It's time for me to go. I call an Uber. When it arrives Philippe comes to say goodnight. I planted a big kiss on both of his cheeks and then shock him with one smack on his lips. I turn and go out to my Uber.

Hallelujah, it's truly raining men!

Aftermath of the aftermath

Stephanie has returned from ten days in Bali. She arrives with the new cleaner, Sol, to go over the basics of what needs to be done and to see where things may be hidden; the Holiday decorations, extra towels and blankets and pillows. I spent a good hour to make sure nothing would popup, evidence of Renard's presence. Except the flowers. But she either didn't notice or didn't choose to ask.

I had spent a terribly restless night, sending Renard a text in the early evening to try to tempt him to come over. He responded that he was in Boulogne "far away from me". I googled it and saw it was a concert/sports center. OK, I went to bed with my book and pouted. What was it I had warned myself? - not to sabotage this. At 6 am I woke, having only fallen asleep at 3:30 and looked at my phone. Late at night, when I was on a social media strike, he posted pictures of a Cool and the Gang concert. Well he told me that he liked 70s music. And evidently he went with the same guy who he had gone to a Beaujolais Nouveau tasting the night before. Why does he get two nights in a row? There I went, down the sabotage myself spiral. This is not good.

I got up, fixed breakfast and watched a Netflix movie. Then I cleaned my apartment before the cleaners came. I still had some time before they arrived and was looking at myself critically in the mirror. My hair definitely could use some care. It had been over two months since my last appointment at the salon in California and it did the thing it does; suddenly needing a color job in the worst way.

Before I could talk myself out of it I put on my coat and headed out to see the salon down the street. On the way I saw Raphael, the owner of Les Loups. He greeted me warmly with *la bise* and I told him *"J'ai besoin de trouver une coiffeuse!* He pointed to the shop next to his restaurant. *"Elles sont gentilles."* He suggested. So I walked into the shop.

"Bonjour!" I said to the two women working. There were no customers in the shop. *"J'habite ici maintenant et j'ai besoin de trouver une nouvelle coiffeuse!"* I said quickly followed by *"Parlez vous anglais?"*

"Non."

But that didn't stop them from trying to help me help them understand what I wanted. Fortunately my SF stylist had given me the formula for my color which was easy to tell them. And I didn't think they would have that much trouble figuring out the cut. I was just deathly afraid that I would turn out orange. There are plenty of women around here with hair color not found in nature. I want to look a little French. But mostly I want to still look like me, Renard's California girl.

So I ended up with an appointment for 2:00 pm that afternoon.

Back in my apartment I waited for Stephanie and Sol and after they arrived I asked Stephanie if she wanted to meet me at Cépage. I was going to go there to write. I'd love to hear about her trip to Bali.

I wasn't there long before she arrived just at the same time as the carafe of wine.

Bali was great, very relaxing. She booked another three weeks in February, following her two weeks in St Martin and two weeks in Thailand in January. This woman never seems to work. And she sure isn't around when I need something. She had Bob in tow. He was his misbehaving self. I reminded her that I still don't have heat. It snowed last week and I still don't have heat.

"Yes, I will call Magalie on Monday and ask her to have the handyman come look."

The handyman who is Gareth? It seems Gareth never found the fashion job he was looking for but has been making do as a handyman for Magalie's company. He showed up unexpectedly when I asked to have my smoke alarm moved from the kitchen to the hall where it wouldn't go off every time I turned on my oven, or made toast, or boiled water! But certainly Gareth won't be able to fix my heat. And Monday is two days away. And it snowed last week!

"I'm pretty sure that the building has central heating and they don't turn it on until the end of November. That's what happened last year." I lamented.

"But you don't know that for sure."

Well, no, I don't. But I still don't have heat.

Stephanie left for another appointment and I tackled the task of eating another hundred *moules* and writing another thousand words. At two o'clock I braced myself and headed to the salon.

If you want to get a feel for a neighborhood, a couple of hours in the local hair salon is the perfect place. Madame Claudia greeted me and sat me in a seat in front of the mirror. She fastened the gown around my shoulders and started to pluck at my hair. She was whippet thin wearing tight leather pants and a white knit sweater. Her own hair (red!) was pulled back into a severe small ponytail. But she had a kind and reassuring way about her. I decided I was in good hands.

"*Oui, entre neuf et dix.*" she confirmed, repeating the formula I gave her earlier.

"*Et coupez juste une petit peu.*" I instructed. And cut just a little.

Her assistant mixed the hair coloring agent and started to apply it while Madame Claudia went outside for a cigarette.

I have always found the hair salon experience distasteful. Hair plastered to my head with a smelly paste, bare face looking directly into a wall size mirror is not my best look. As the years have gone by it has just gotten worse; more saggy, more jowly, more droopy. I focused on the comings and goings around me.

An elderly man came in for a cut. He took the seat next to me while his daughter sat on a seat across the room and read a fashion magazine. Our eyes met in the mirror and he smiled at me. A well dressed redheaded woman in a wheelchair was brought in by a slightly younger woman. After many bisous and much ado about removing and folding coats and scarves, Madame Claudia and her assistant joined with the helper to manoeuver the woman into the chair at the sink.

Presently it was my turn at the sink. While I may not enjoy the salon experience in general, the hair washing part is at least something I find a little bit enjoyable. Evidently, it's extra nice in Paris. Or at least in the salon of Madame Claudia! Whatever stress I had, admittedly not much since moving to Paris, immediately evaporated with the long and luxurious scalp massage. The water that circled the drain took with it all of my negative feelings, my self doubts, my wrinkles, sags, droops.

I moved back to the chair by the mirror and snuck a peak at the hair color. Not terrible. Of course wet it's not possible to know what it will look like when it's finished. But how was it that I looked better? Somehow less of those things that offended me just fifteen minutes earlier. Madame Claudia started to comb and cut. I was more optimistic by the minute.

Suddenly into the shop burst a very good looking man with a pup. "I speak perfect English!" he declared. Evidently someone had called him and asked him to come translate for me.

"A little late!" I giggled. Did I actually giggle?

He laughed and all the ladies in the shop nuzzled the pup. Madame continued to cut and with every snip I became more confident that she knew exactly what she was doing.

By the time I was blown out I was delighted with the results. Enough to take a selfie on the way home and post it on my Facebook page. Perfect color. Perfect cut. Perfect style. I think it was the first time I didn't go home and wash my hair and restyle it myself.

The first comment on the Facebook picture was from Renard.

"My California girl!"

Girl indeed.

That night I went to bed at 8:30. It was the only place I could be warm. My glass of wine sat on my dresser, just out of arm's reach if I dared to take my arm out from under the duvet.

A kissing emoticon pops up from Renard. I quickly pull my phone under the duvet.

"I'm freezing!" I whine. I sneak a picture of my wine glass, out of reach on the dresser and send it. "I can't reach my wine."

"My poor California girl."

At least he's sympathetic. But he doesn't come to keep me warm.

The Spin Plate

G rowing up my family always ate dinner together at the kitchen table at precisely six o'clock. The five girls had the rotating responsibility to set the table. Our dishes were mostly green with a colonial motif, dishes that we had gotten a week at a time at Safeway, with minimum purchase. One of the plates didn't sit quite right on the table. When you tried to cut your food, the plate would spin. It was very important that whomever's job it was to set the table that week never ever gave the spin plate to our dad.

When it was my turn, I always made sure that I gave myself the spin plate. And the fork that didn't match. And the heel from the loaf of bread.

After a lifetime of choosing the spin plate for myself, I chose Paris. And I after a lifetime of not thinking I deserve the best, I choose to let this lovely French man, twenty years my junior, love me.

Rev 2

Another Monday night and Renard has suggested he come for dinner. He will bring take away. I will get wine and cheese.

I wonder if Monday nights will be our thing. I kind of hope not because nothing is open on Mondays! I considered surprising him with oysters. He loves oysters. But the oyster bar at Cépage is not open on Mondays. Neither is the cheese shop, the wine shop, the *boucherie*. Fortunately the *boulangerie* is open and tarte *au citron* becomes his surprise. As well as grocery store wine and cheese. My wine rack is distressingly empty!

He arrived with another big bouquet of flowers. Last week's bouquet was still quite nice. My apartment was beginning to look like a florist shop! Or a funeral parlor. I opened a bottle of wine and we sat side by side on the sofa. He looked deeply into my eyes and stroked my cheek.

"I love your soul" he almost breathed the words rather than spoke them. I don't know which I like better; when he speaks French or his mangled English with that accent. I am hypnotically regressed to my twenty something year old self…

Again, I will leave the intimate details to the reader's imagination. Suffice it to say it was *tres tres bon*! But we also talked. About anything and everything. There is nothing like the special feeling of a new relationship; two people peeling back the layers of their minds, their hearts, their souls. Feeling as if nobody has ever gotten you quite like this person. Talking between kisses. Talking between touches. Talking between exploring. Not only exploring each others bodies but each other's psyches.

I discovered two Renards; the one who spoke a pretty mangled English. And the one who spoke French. In English he giggled and joked and shared his dreams. In French he became far more serious. He smiled less. And he never giggled. Here I sit, only a year into my living in French and I find myself different in French; not clever, not funny, not interesting. I blame it all on the struggle to communicate in a language I'm not comfortable with. Maybe it's not just that. Maybe the French are not ever funny!

I like both Renards. But I'm glad there are two.

He left and went back to his normal life; the one he had before he met me. Granted he sends texts throughout the day. He posts pictures to his Facebook page that I know are messages to me; him in a park standing in front of the statue of naked couple wrapped in each other's arms, a wolf staring at a lighted window, looking up into the leafy bower of a tree. He told me one night that he wanted to make love to me outside, under a tree.

He left and I stayed. I stayed in my Renard cloud. I didn't write. I didn't read. I didn't eat. When I had to go out because I had to shop and cook a Thanksgiving dinner for the friends I had invited, because I had to meet a friend for lunch because I had committed to bring a cheese board to Siobhan's new house-warming party, I carried my phone with me at all times, looking for a text, wondering what he was doing, wondering when he would be coming back. He went back to living the life that I found so attractive. I forgot how to be the person he found attractive.

It didn't help that I had deliveries arriving, four of them. Everyone I know in Paris agrees that this is something that the French still don't do well; deliveries. Each delivery was to come on a different day. The email notification said *La livraison est pour le moment prévu pour XX nov. 20XX, entre 09h et 18h.* It will come on Friday between 9 am and 6 pm. The delivery person will buzz me when he arrives. If I am not home he will take the package back to the warehouse and I will be left to figure out how to get it. So I'm trapped at home waiting for my delivery. And thinking about Renard. I realize that I am at risk of losing myself. I've done it before. Every time I was in a new relationship before. My own personal sort of sabotage.

Monday came. A wine delivery due. And some hints from Renard that he may come on Monday night. I cleaned the apartment. I cleaned myself. I checked my texts. I listened to the most not helpful music. I leafed through my French cookbooks wondering what I could cook for Renard when it was my turn. I took a stab at writing from home. I pondered all of the reasons it didn't make any sense for Renard to love me. The most not helpful music was not helpful but it didn't drown out the tape playing in my head. "When will he get tired of me?" "What could he possibly see in me?" "I'm too old." "I'm too fat." "He only wants my money." (Be quiet, Dad!)

Stop!

After all, he told me, "I love you exactly the way you are." Why can't I just believe him?

What would Ninon do?

Spring Again

Spring could not come soon enough to rue des Tournelles. It had been a brutal winter and Ninon felt it in her bones. This particular winter saw more snow than usual, cruelly alternating with some short but taunting sunny days, just sunny enough to melt the snow by early afternoon and see the slush freeze by sundown into a treacherous icy obstacle course for man and beast. Even the horses, usually accustomed to Paris winters were slipping and sliding, their carriages and human cargo skidding on the streets. All of this kept Ninon captive in her rooms where even the most robust fires in every room couldn't seem to warm the stone walls and wooden floors.

Ninon's maid kept coal bed warmers and hot water bottles on hand to take the chill off the bedcovers. She stayed wrapped in scarves and knitted gloves. She longed to throw open the windows and rid herself of all these layers of clothing. She craved those first bright green shoots and flowers and birdsong. She wanted to walk in the square, to breath fresh air, to clean the cobwebs from her brain. She wanted to dance. Outside. In the sunshine.

So when the tiny green buds started to burst out Ninon felt warmed to her very soul. And it was this same day that two young men, Abbe Gedoyn and Abbe Franguire, came to Ninon's salon. Both were escapees of the Jesuits and both were greener than the buds on the trees in the square, in their early thirties, well versed in their letters but novices in the way of the world, particularly in affairs of the heart.

Ninon had quietly celebrated her seventy-eighth birthday that winter. It was not lost on her how many friends and lovers had passed and while she still enjoyed undeniable beauty, perhaps at the behest of *Le Noctambule* some six decades before, and the same youthful heart and spirit she had when she was a twelve year old girl, on occasion her joints sang to her. Even the careful and diligent ministrations to which Ninon had prescribed all of her life did not stop the random aches and pains that the bitter cold brought on.

The young ex-Abbés entered the Grand Salon with an odd combination of cockiness and shyness, as if they thought themselves the smartest men in the room, but in their heart of hearts were aware of their inexperience in a world outside of the Church. When they spied Ninon talking with her friend, Marguerite, formally known as Madame de la Salière, all the cockiness melted away and they were profoundly impacted by this strange new world.

"Messieurs," Ninon greeted the two warmly. "Bienvenue en notre petit salon." Madame de la Salière stood at her elbow, taking measure of the newcomers.

If life outside of the Abbey had interfered with the gentlemen's equilibrium, coming face to face with Ninon and Marguerite quite knocked them off their feet. They stood gaping at the two totally at a loss for words.

"Vous avez donné vos langues au chat?" coaxed Madame de la Salière, not unkindly. "Has the cat got your tongues?"

"May I offer you a small beverage?" inserted Ninon, giving the gentlemen a chance to regain their composure. "Perhaps some sherry? Or if you would prefer a cognac?"

Abbé Gedoyn could not take his eyes off of Ninon. "I'll have whatever you are having." he replied grasping for straws.

"I am afraid I don't drink alcohol." replied Ninon. "Perhaps you would prefer a cognac?" She suggested, beckoning over her houseman.

"Merci," stammered the Abbe.

Abbé Franguire, on the other hand, had been immediately smitten with Marguerite and was more composed about it. Putting his hand lightly on her elbow he cleverly steered her away from Ninon and Abbé Gedoyn to a separate corner of the room, leaving his awkward friend alone with the object of his immediate amour.

The houseman came back bearing a crystal snifter on a silver tray. Abbâé snatched it and took a fortifying gulp. The vapors of the heady spirit filled his nostrils and made eyes water. He coughed and drained the glass. Ninon smiled and nodded to the houseman signaling him that it was ok to bring another.

As the cognac took effect Gedoyn's tongue loosened a bit and he became increasingly bold, trying to impress Ninon with how much he knew.

"Yes, La Fontaine! Very famous!" he remarked. "His Fables are drole, but in truth, don't you agree that they are just a retelling of Aesop?"

"Well, Monsieur La Fontaine has been a regular at my Salon for many years." replied Ninon. "He frequently shared his drafts with me, looking for feedback."

Oops.

Example after example Gedoyn proved himself outwitted. Ninon was not only a great beauty but obviously very, very smart. Rather than be embarrassed and turned off by this, Gedoyn's infatuation grew by the minute. When the time came that it was impossible for him to stay a moment longer without seriously overstaying his welcome, everyone else attending the afternoon's salon had long gone, including his friend, Franguire, he was totally and forever être éperdument amoureux, head over heels in love.

Gedoyn lived for the Wednesday Salons. He was loathe to miss a moment that was an opportunity to spend any possible second with Ninon. By the time the leaves had properly burst from their buds and the Square was green and filled with blossoms and children running and shouting and birds singing and dogs barking and horses clopping and fountains flowing, before the days got hot and the streets steamed with muck and horse leavings and air got more fetid, eventually unbearably so, our young Gedoyn was beseeching Ninon to become his lover.

Gedoyn had just celebrated his thirty-fifth birthday, Ninon was half way through her seventy-eight year. She did not presently have a lover. She really didn't want a lover. She was happy with her life, her friends, her books, her lovely home on rue des Tournelles. Sorry, cher Gedoyn, this was not going to happen.

But as the seasons passed; Summer turns to Fall, and the days again becoming bitterly cold and the horses were sliding around the cobbles and the square was icy and empty and the fires were roaring at 28 rue des Tournelles, Gedoyn was still beseeching Ninon to become his lover. Finally she agreed. If he still was of a mind she would become Gedoyn's lover on her eightieth birthday.

On an unseasonably warm day in November in the year of 1700, Ninon made the 36 year old Abbé Gedoyn's dreams come true.

The birds were singing in the square.

Popping the Five Star Bubble

Evelyn asked for another Wednesday, post-tutoring drinks session at Le Bar at the Intercontinental. Part of me wants to put an end to this friendship, but part of me is intrigued and still wants to know what exactly it is that makes her tick. Along the way, she asked if I would mind inviting Judith, the woman we were also introduced to when we met each other, courtesy of mutual friends who were visiting Paris. I thought it odd because she didn't seem to have a high regard for Judith when we met before. I didn't click with her enough to follow up but I didn't mind including Judith, even though it was my turn to pay and the martinis are thirty euro a pop.

Somehow Wednesday turned into Friday. Renard is sick with a cold and in his own words, "When a man is sick the world must stop." Maybe your world dear, not mine. The night before, in our before going to sleep texts he said "so much to say…. just I am sick, and when a man is sick, the world have to stop." "Second…. Is a long story (kissy emoticon)" "And not for tonight…" (another kissy emoticon).

Me: "Good story or bad story." Careful girl, you're getting a bit close to that self sabotage thing.

"No no no… sorry but, not everything can be explain by sentence. Tonight for me is a (insert photo of foil pack of pills) "for my gorge." What an ugly word for throat.

This feels like really dangerous territory to me. My mind is racing through all the possible scenarios that "second" are going to be. He's dumping me. He's giving me bad news. Oh la la la la la la…

I decide it's better to deflect. "OK, you can tell me when you see me. I need to sleep now. Bonne nuit (kissing emoticon).

"Bonne nuit aussi ma douce. (kissy emoticon)

Well, he can't be dumping me if he's calling me his sweet.

The next day he wasn't feeling any better and was whining up a storm. I told him I was going out with friends. Get some sleep. I'll text him when I get home but I hope he's sleeping.

Evelyn and I agree to meet at 5:15, an hour and a half before Judith will arrive. We can catch up. Google maps says it will take 18 minutes. I order my Uber at 4:45.

The Uber takes an inordinately long time to arrive. I was about to give up on him and flag down a taxi when he arrived. For some crazy reason Uber drivers are locked into what their GPS tells them to do and sometimes GPS doesn't seem to know what it's talking about. We headed into the warren of what I call Amelie's Paris, the little one way narrow cobbled streets of Montmartre. Up rue Lepic, turning on very narrow rue d'Orchampt which winds around to where we want to work our way down the hill to Blvd Clichy. Uber's GPS really wants to avoid the main thoroughfare of Place de Clichy but more often that not, it would be the quickest route. Suddenly there was *un bouchon*, a bottleneck. Nobody is moving. I credit my driver in that he didn't honk. Every Uber driver loves to honk. Eventually we backed our way through the little cobbled rues of Montmartre, a funny little parade of cars all going backwards. After about fifteen minutes of navigating the narrow passageways, we ended up out of the maze and onto Rue Blanche, at least in the right arrondissement, the ninth.

I arrived at Le Bar a good twenty minutes late apologizing profusely. It's no small coincidence on my part that it is my deceased father's birthday. Just that day, my sisters and I were discussing the one main lesson Dad taught us. For me it was "Always leave in time to change a flat tire." In truth I could not change a flat tire if my life depended on it, but I had developed a lifelong habit of always being early. Showing up late was indeed disconcerting.

I found Evelyn in the crowded bar half way through her first martini and worrying about how we would find a table that would accommodate three. "Let's just tell the server to watch for one and let us know." I suggested. The server indeed accommodated us by moving two tables together and moving Evelyn's martini and the little trio of snacks to another table. Problem solved.

After what seemed like forever, I managed to get my martini we toasted to the holidays, to life in Paris, to our health. Evelyn asked me briefly how things were going with Renard.

"Wonderful." I said.

"Have you seen him again?"

"Oh yes. We are in that stage where you talk about everything for hours."

"I've never talked about everything for hours. I don't like it when people ask me questions about my life. I don't need to know about their childhood. And I certainly have no intention of telling them about mine."

I don't know what to say. So I say nothing.

"it's really busy here on Fridays. I was here last Friday with a gentleman and it was equally busy."

OK, evidently she wants to tell me about that. I've learned not to probe with Evelyn. Let the story unfold on her timeline. But I need some help here. What gentleman? Did she meet him here in the bar?

"No of course not. I met him through some business meetings I've attended here in Paris." Evidently after retiring from her Marketing Director job in January, she has been consulting with some organizations in Paris. "Antoine" is a Parisian that she met in one of these organizations. He asked her for a drink and she suggested Le Bar. Since he had made what she considered a clever comeback to her remark in the meetings that hope is not a strategy, she decided he was worth a date.

She described Antoine as pedantic, entitled and boring. Gentle probing, one has to be very careful with Evelyn or one would be perceived as pushy and nosy (both attributes which I freely acknowledge), revealed that Antoine is an "aristocrat", a man of high breeding, divorced after 25 years of marriage to a beautiful woman. He lives in the sixteenth arrondissement and has multiple châteaux. But he was a bore, completely unable to carry on an interesting conversation.

Now carrying on an interesting conversation with Evelyn is a bit of a challenge. It generally means getting her to talk about herself, without actually asking her any direct question which will render one borish and nosy. Don't ask about her dead husband. Don't ask about her kids. It is ok to ask after the health and happiness of her young grandson, but not about the discipline problems she alluded to last time we met. It's ok to ask about her language tutoring, but not the status of Michael, the Financial consultant in New York who she plans to have dinner with in a couple weeks.

As the martinis go down, a little more comes out about Antoine. "It's funny," she said, "he thought the date was a success and is looking forward to our next one."

I tilt my head and look quizzically, a trick I learned from an old colleague who always had me spilling my guts. Best not probe about these things.

"Well of course I sent him an email, thanking him for the drinks."

One does not send a thank you email to someone one hopes never to see again.

"He responded that he was hopeful but did not have a strategy." I tilted my head to the other side. "I will probably go to dinner with him."

Give a handsome aristocrat with an apartment in the 16th and multiple chateaux in the country a second chance? Really? My how our standards are diminished….

Finally Judith arrives, about forty five minutes late. She looks quite beautiful. She orders a martini "comme James Bond" she tells the server. He has no idea what she's talking about. She points to Evelyn's drink with olives (mine has a twist) and says "comme ça".

"So, how are you?" Evelyn asks. And Judith launches into a long story about the trials and tribulations of her new job. She is just ten days away from becoming a regular employee at an English language school. The ten days are crucial because once she passes that probationary period, she becomes, what is in France, impossible to fire. She tells us about how her French company has been acquired by a bigger US company. The acquiring CEO came to visit her location and she took the liberty of asking questions in a meeting that essentially embarrassed both her manager and her local CEO. She thought she was demonstrating how savvy she was and didn't understand how dangerous her actions where in getting her over the ten day hurdle.

"I'm working twelve hour days, doing my job and my assistant's job. My boss seems invisible and clueless. The local CEO doesn't care and replies to emails with 'that's a stupid question'. Nobody respects either of them. My assistant thinks she should have gotten this job and seems to be out to get me fired."

Evelyn is on fire. Business issues, particularly management issues fall right in her sweet spot. Evidently it's ok for her to ask probing questions.

"How old is your Manager? Tell me about her. What does she look like? How many kids does she have? How old are they? How tall is she?....." Judith tries to answer but she can't keep up with the questions.

"How do you think you made your boss and your CEO feel when you asked their boss those questions?" An obvious question that I wasn't going to ask because I'd rather just enjoy my martini.

Two hours and more martinis passed with Evelyn grilling Judith about the actions she did and didn't take; with her boss, with her bosses boss, with the big boss, and with the recalcitrant employee. This is what Evelyn does best. Try to fix things. When the focus turned to me; Madame HR, what would you do? I deflected. Honestly, what I picked up early in the conversation was that Judith wanted this job because it was a paycheck but truthfully, her heart isn't in it at all, she doesn't respect or like any of the players and frankly I would probably try to talk her into cutting her losses and finding another sort of job. But that isn't where either Evelyn or Judith wanted the conversation to go.

I finished my second martini and was looking for the waiter to order a third.

Finally Evelyn decided it was time for her to go and Judith said she'd really like to go out for a cigarette and then come back and have another drink. I was rather eager to hear about the other aspects of her life so I ordered two more martinis and sat back enjoying the ornate room with it's incredible chandeliers, it's gargantuan mahogany doors and the soft background music of the gentleman playing the grand piano tucked into the back of the room.

An Ending

What happened to my great love for Philippe? One night with Renard and it has vanished. Here I sit at GCA on Wednesday night jazz night by myself. Somehow it feels important to do the normal things I do.

Getting ready Renard was texting me, mushy romantic texts. Then suddenly about his plans to organize my kitchen.

"Maybe I need to organize your kitchen in a different way... don't be surprised. I am just crazy about food and the way of a kitchen supposed to be..."

"This is going in the book."

"Good!" (smiley face emoticon and thumbs up)

Monday, after a week with the horrible cold mon homme sauvage decided he was well enough to come to me.

"I'll cook for you." I said. Damn, why did I say that?

"I'll bring wine," he said.

"It's OK," I assured him. "I have wine. You don't need to bring anything this time. Just yourself."

Mondays are a difficult day for our dinners. Everything is closed except the *boulangerie*. Man cannot live on bread... and wine... alone. Of course the grocery store is open. That means really cooking something.

I decided to keep it simple; gnocchi with a brown butter sauce and parmesan, a salad, some cheese and Magalie's Christmas cookies and clementines for dessert. But a surprise to start, oysters. At the last minute I popped out and Thierry at Cépage prepared a platter of oysters on a bed of crushed ice with a lemon.

Renard was delighted. I had a nice sauvignon in the fridge. He definitely approved, especially when I poured myself a glass of red and he realized I had gotten the white just for him and his oysters.

It went downhill from there. Renard is a chef. Or rather he was a chef. So I'm going to say on his behalf that he just can't help himself. I went into the kitchen to prepare the gnocchi. I had the directions for the brown butter sauce written out onto a small square of paper, on the fridge under the magnet he gave me the night we met.

He popped up and followed me into the kitchen.

"You, on the couch!"

He went to stand on the other side of the kitchen island.

"On the couch!" I repeated. He acquiesced.

"You can help with the salad." I conceded. I hadn't really thought through the dressing anyway.

"After the gnocchi." he said. "Hot food and then cold." How very French. My dinner was turning into a five course meal!

I served the gnocchi which wasn't beautiful and the store bought dumplings were a little dense. But he had seconds so it couldn't have been too bad. I poured him a glass of red wine, the one he loved before. And a new glass because I know he likes a new glass when he changes wines.

When it was his turn, he fairly sprang into action. I got the leavings of the oysters and headed out to the garbage. That's when he took a good look at my fridge. I hadn't planned on that scrutiny. Admittedly there were some things that had started to take on a life of their own. Thank goodness I had already dumped most of the Thanksgiving leftovers. And I snuck the rest of the meat stuffing the butcher had prepared for me, I wasn't sure exactly what it was but I didn't like it, into the oyster trash that I had taken out.

We ate the salad. We nibbled the cheese. Renard ate two cookies. We opened another bottle of wine. And we talked. For hours. Then we went to bed.

Without going all *50 Shades of Grey*, it was a long night that seemed like a short night. In the morning I made coffee while he took a shower. Evidently I can make coffee well enough, even amid the mess of last night's dinner. I haven't quite figured out why leaving the night's mess until tomorrow is ok. He snuck into the kitchen and took another look around.

"I will come later this week to organize your fridge."

"Your fridge," I said. "Going forward the kitchen is yours."

"Yes!" he responded, obviously beyond pleased.

"But the bedroom is mine" I added with a small smile.

He grinned. "Yes, the bedroom is yours. And now it's important that I go to the *marché*, before it's too late."

With a kiss he was out the door. A few minutes later a text: "I think the clock on your stove is wrong."

"You mean the clock on your stove. You forgot to change it after daylight savings time ended."

Wednesday night jazz night. I went alone and sat with my notebook, writing. I treated myself to a piece of tarte citron. Philippe came over to ask about my book. Is it almost done?

"Yes, I think so. Only a few more chapters." He grinned. Pleased to be part of the process. "Merci, Philippe." then I switched to English. "I am so appreciative for all you have done to accommodate me over the past year." He glowed.

"*Un cognac*?!" he suggested.

"*Non, merci.*"

"*Non? Pourquoi?*" I always had a cognac and sometimes a second. Something he seemed to like giving me on him.

"*Je bois trop.*" I frowned. "*Ma foie!*"

He laughed and said "*Moi aussi!*"

I flagged Guillaume down and paid my bill, slipping outside in the rain to wait for my Uber. Philippe came running out after me to say goodbye. I kissed him soundly on both cheeks and said "*Au revoir.*" I doubt he knew the meaning of my *au revoir*. I even cried a little in the Uber.

L'Ecoles de Filles

A thousand years ago, when I was pretending to study at University, I had a boyfriend who brought the audio version of a book that was making the best seller lists at the time. Actually there were two; one for men and another for women. I can't for the life of me remember the names of the books but the authors were just a single initial. So "J" wrote the version for women, "How to please a man" and "P" wrote the version for men. My clever boyfriend brought "J's" version and we sat in his car in front of the house and listened on an 8 track or cassette or whatever archaic device we listened to music in the days before Bluetooth and digital and even CDs. Pretty smooth move on his part, now that I think about it oh so many years later.

Suzanne and Fanchon. Ninon had pulled it off. Her book was certainly causing quite the scandal. But Ninon cared naught for scandals. Everyone in Paris and beyond was searching for the true identity of Ange but ironically nobody suspected Madame de l'Enclos.

How was a young woman to learn about love; more specifically about the art of making love?

"Belles et curieuses damoiselles, voici l'École de votre sagesse, et le recueil des principales choses que vous devez savoir pour contenter vos maris quand vous en aurez ; c'est le secret infaillible pour vous faire aimer des hommes quand vous ne seriez pas belles, et le moyen aisé de couler en douceurs et en plaisirs tout le temps de votre jeunesse."

Beautiful and curious young women, here is the school of your wisdom… all of the things you must know to please your husbands…

Or perhaps not your husbands.

It is impossible to find a copy of the actual book translated into English. It's also evidently not possible to find a copy in French. But I did find an excerpt on a pdf file, in French that included the "Mystical and allegorical table according to the moral and literal sense of School girls." After a year in France, my language skills had progressed sufficiently to get the gist of this, but I popped the lengthy Table of Contents into Google Translate and came up with a general idea of what Suzanne had to share with Fauchon, her young protégé.

Hardly the Kama Sutra. In fact, hardly titillating by today's standards.

1. Note of age cleaner to marry girls.
2. First testimonials of love of boys towards girls
3. The rigors of mothers and the foolishness of girls who refuse them boys and their caresses.
4. Girls ignorant not to listen to words of men.
5. Excellence of the pleasure of love.
6. Simplicity of a girl who does not know what love is, nor what is it clean. (???)
7. Preparations for girls pleasure instruction of love
8. Age to start loving boys and girls
9. Short description by parenthesis and necessary in this place, of a man who pisses and lives when he does not band.
10. Generality of the pleasure of love and the large number of people who are involved, with a division on it.

OK, I'm going to need help understanding all of this. Google translate must be mistranslating some things…. A quick text to Renard.

"I think I may need your help with something for my book." I suspect he will like this. He quickly responds, "Yes, you will explain to me."

The list goes on, some things intriguing "Speech of fools", others sound more technical; "the proper names of things". Some don't seem to make any sense at all; "How does the boy to push him live in the corner and the pleasure the girl receives".

18. Third resumption, and more specific description of the lives only before; inner anatomy of the con, which he nothing is so difficult to peel; with the beginning, the end and duration of the pleasure of love.

And this way before Viagra but maybe after the African wood that Renard talked about looking into.

19. Of the liquor of love (I'm going to have to try using this phrase next time!), which comes about in this law. (law?)

20. Fourth recovery, as the living goes out after the function of the pleasure of love, and as the girl can make it return stiff with hand.

21. Great and different virtues of the girls' hand to give pleasure to boys; where it is inserted something of the kiss of the tongue."

OK, now we're going somewhere....

24. Possible and new remedy for girls who are con itchy for lack of life to put in, rubbing it with the finger.

It? Which it are we talking about?

25. Advice to girls to take a friend...

NO! Don't do it!

26. Reasons that prevent girls from being entertained, and refutations of these.

- First reason.
- Second reason.
- Third reason.
- Fourth reason.

OK, I'd like to see these....

32. How many times he withdraws, or how many rides in one night.

Good question....

37. Nice comparison of the noise that makes a live con when he comes in and goes out... Learning necessary for girls to move well the buttocks. More about the ejaculation of love liqueur (liquid d'amore)...

My Google translate is sighing and moaning. I'm a little confused. I put it aside until Renard can lend a hand (so to speak).

Evidently Ninon's book is in fact titillating. Or so it would seem on a rainy Saturday afternoon, after a long lunch and an excellent bottle of Margaux. I explained a bit about Ninon and her life to Renard. Then Ninon's book. He was interested. I opened the PDF file, 19 pages introducing the tome and listing the Table of Contents.

Renard struggled as much with the translation as Google translate. "This is not common French." he kept saying, as he scooched towards the edge of the couch, closer to the computer.

"No" I responded, "remember, it was written in 1655."

"Yes, it's very old... not typical."

Well, typical enough to get him interested.

"Oh, this is very good!" was his most common remark. As he got lost into the book he mumbled and smirked and smiled and nodded. The most common theme seemed to be "riding" which he punctuated with a funny gesture, like two hands around a girl's waist and plopping her down on his "lap".

45. How to get sex quickly (in fifteen minutes or less) on the *coffre.* He spent several minutes trying to describe to me what a coffre is, finally googling it and showing me pictures of chests or trunks. Exactly what I thought it was. That seemed to baffle him. Why would anyone want to get sex on a coffre? At this point though, he seemed willing to go with it.

In the end, Ninon's book seemed too distracting and he proclaimed we needed a break. "A nap, perhaps?"

364 years later Ninon's L'Ecoles des Filles is doing its job.

October 17, 1706

Termini

Qu'un vain espoir ne vienne point s'offrir,

Qui puisse ébranler mon courage;

Je suis en âge *de mourir;*

Que ferais-je ici davantage

Let no vain hopes come now and try

My courage strong to overthrow;

My age demands that I shall die.

What more can I do here below?

November 26th

A year ago today, I boarded (again) a plane to Paris. I know, I've flown a lot of planes to Paris in the last 10 years, but this time it was different. This time, I was going to start a new life. (And yes, I returned for the month of January to finish up some loose ends, but this time, I knew that returning to SF would be different, a "visit" short).

The past year has been extraordinary. I had the chance to make wonderful friends. Charlotte, my "Fairy Godmother and Elliot, my Fairy Godfather" of friends generously opened up their networks and the result was so rewarding. It's hard to believe that the people who populate my days I've known for less than a year. I cannot imagine my life without them!

People say that Parisians are hostile and rude. I must say that nothing is further from the truth. Owners and servers of the cafés and restaurants, my butcher, my cheese maker, the charming man who manages the produce store, the boys downstairs in the mini market, the cashiers at the G20, the ladies at the bakery ... everyone in my little section of rue Caulaincourt, everyone made me feel so welcome and part of the fabric of my little neighborhood.

My French is appalling, but less dreadful by half than a year ago! I have eaten thousands of mussels, a mountain of cheese and other things that I will not even try to quantify. And I drank gallons of wine! Every bus or taxi ride through the city takes my breath away. Every day I am stunned by the reality that I live in this amazing place. The ghosts of Montmartre have become my friends. I love to walk on the cobblestones at night, the same pavements on which Lautrec,

Degas and Picasso tread. And I am so grateful to add my own echoes to these nocturnal footsteps.

After all the stress of impending homelessness and trying to figure out where I belonged, Stephanie came for our American Thanksgiving dinner, chez moi, with news to be truly thankful for. The owner of my apartment agreed to let me stay as long as I liked, beginning in June of next year. The apartment in the Cepage building was available for seven weeks of the gap, the time the owner will be in Paris. I have a world of options for how to spend the other seven weeks. It seems my perfect apartment would still be mine. It probably helped that I offered her more money.

A year ago, I opened a Google document and wrote the first sentence. I was not sure if I could write. But I wrote! Tens of thousands of words! I even suspect that with a serious editing, these words are worth reading!

So now that Paris is lit up again by the lights of the holidays and the champagne corks burst and the oysters are slurped and the foie gras is tasted and we wrap ourselves in layers of scarves, hats and gloves, I start my second year here. Paris changed me. I like the person that I've become. And I love the fact that Paris and the Parisians have embraced this Californian.

Il y a un an aujourd'hui, je suis monté (encore) dans un avion pour Paris. Je sais, j'ai embarqué de nombreux avions à Paris au cours des 10 dernières années, mais cette fois-ci, c'était différent. Cette fois, j'allais commencer une nouvelle vie. (et oui, j'y suis retourné pour le mois de janvier pour en finir, mais cette fois, je savais que retourner à SF serait différent, une "visite" courte).

L'année écoulée a été extraordinaire. J'ai eu la chance de faire de merveilleux amis. Ma "fée marraine et fée parrain" d'amis m'a généreusement ouvert ses réseaux et le résultat a été si enrichissant. Il est difficile de croire que les gens qui peuplent mes jours que je connais depuis moins d'un an. Je ne peux pas imaginer ma vie sans eux!

Les gens disent que les parisiens sont hostiles et impolis. Je dois dire que rien n'est plus éloigné de la vérité. Propriétaires et serveurs de café et de restaurant, mon boucher, mon fromager, le charmant homme qui gère le magasin de produits, les garçons en bas au mini-marché, les caissières au G20, les dames à la boulangerie ... tout le monde dans ma petite section de la rue Caulaincourt, tout m'a fait que je me sente si bien accueillie et qu'elle fasse partie du tissu de mon petit quartier.

Mon français est épouvantable, mais moins épouvantable qu'il y a un an de moitié! J'ai mangé des milliers de moules, une montagne de fromage et d'autres choses que je ne tenterai même pas de quantifier. Et j'ai bu des litres de vin! Chaque trajet en bus ou en taxi à travers la ville me coupe le souffle. Tous les jours je suis abasourdi par la réalité que je vis dans cet endroit étonnant. Les fantômes de Montmartre sont devenus mes amis. J'aime marcher sur les pavés la nuit, les mêmes pavés sur lesquels foulent Lautrec, Degas, Picasso. Et je suis si reconnaissant d'ajouter mes propres échos à ces pas nocturnes.

Il y a un an, j'ai ouvert un document Google et rédigé la première phrase. Je n'étais pas sûr de pouvoir écrire. Mais j'ai écrit! Des dizaines de milliers de mots! Je soupçonne même qu'avec une édition sérieuse, ces mots méritent d'être lus!

Alors maintenant que Paris est de nouveau illuminée par les lumières des fêtes et que les bouchons de champagne éclatent et que les huîtres sont gorgées et que le foie gras est dégusté et que nous nous enveloppons de couches de foulards, de chapeaux et de gants, je commence ma deuxième année ici. Paris m'a changé. J'aime la personne à qui il m'a confié. Et j'adore le fait que Paris et les parisiens aient embrassé cette californienne.

FIN

Acknowledgments

Merci Beaucoup

It's dangerous to begin thanking people for any major undertaking because there are so many that will be left out. That said...

Building a new life would not have been nearly as much fun or as easy without two people who opened their networks to me and became my go-to guardians for all things Paris, Forest and Fred. Along with them, to all the lovely friends who have shared their adventures with me; a big merci.

Stephanie and Magalie, the *soeurs de ma coeur*: I love you both and look forward to many more bottles of champagne on rooftops, wine in our living rooms, gossipy lunches, and explorations of other parts of France!

Beverly, my editor, cheerleader, creative consultant and smart reader, you have been invaluable and I am so excited to work on Book #2 with you!

Lily, my French editor, merci cherie! You are both brilliant and fun.

Lina, who's cover illustration absolutely captures my relationship with Ninon and the Grand Comptoir, you are so gifted.

To all my *voisins* and the denizens of my little neighborhood on rue Caulaincourt, a big merci for allowing me to become part of the fabric of life in this very special place. You have made me proud to be the American girl, but maybe just a little bit Parisienne.

And to R. You taught me that tomorrow can bring the most amazing surprises.

Coming in 2021

My Paris Kitchen - The Good, the Bad and Everything In Between

(Once taste is learned, there is no return…)

Oscar Wilde wrote that when they die, all good Americans go to Paris. Not trusting the Almighty's decision as to whether or not I have been a good American, I decided to go a bit early. Visa renewal application completed, long term lease signed. Year number two of my life in Paris has officially started. So let's recap.

I moved to Paris after a long and fruitful Silicon Valley career. I arrived a bit worn out from long years of business travel, twelve hour work days, horrible commutes, high pressure decisions to a life where my only decisions were where to spend my day writing my 1,000 words five days a week, which restaurant to eat in and what kind of wine to order. I made enemies (one) and friends (dozens).

As the seasons passed on my little street in Montmartre, as well as the rest of Paris, I got to know the commercants; the helpful handsome butchers, the lovely cheesemonger, the man with the Lebanese deli (who took a liking to my little granddaughter when she came to visit), the ladies in the boulangerie, the men at the produce stand, the girls at the G-20 all greeted me with familiarity. When I walked down rue Caulaincourt, Rafaele came out of Les Loups to give me la bise. Claudine, my hairdresser waved out the window. Tomas called out a hearty bonjour from Les Capages. The florist nodded and showed me what was new today. I had indeed become part of the fabric of my little quartiere.

Siobhan texted me regularly to ask me to meet her for a quick coffee. Stephanie came by often to share a bottle of champagne at the end of the day just because we liked to celebrate our happy lives. Magalie joined us often after work and our after work bottle would turn into several that lasted late into the night.

When I ventured further out of my neighborhood, and even out of the 18eme, I would find myself writing or enjoying jazz dinners at GCA where the bartender welcomed me by name, Philippe ran over to give me la bise and finally Guilloume stopped calling me Madam W. Daniele started to join me during his break. The same at Le Clou where Maulo rewarded me with la bise and the rest of the staff warmly shook my hand, more out of respect than anything else. I had dinners with Elliott and his tribe of expats, met Silvie to try out new restaurants, had regular drinks with Charlotte, and met Lina and Oliver to consult on ideas and guests for their podcasts.

I navigated the challenges of living in a different country, in a different language, in a different culture. I dealt with repairmen, delivery men, changing bus routes, stranger followers on the street. I cooked a turkey dinner for my French friends on Thanksgiving, figuring out how to get all but the most elusive products not regularly found in France. I bought a Christmas tree. I endeavored to live in French. "*Si j'habite à Paris je doit parler seulement francais!*" I declared to anyone who tried to speak English to me, or who complained about my French. My French got better by half.

I learned to eat differently. I actually begin to taste my food. One lunchtime at home I marveled of the exquisiteness of an artichoke eaten by itself, with a glass of wine. I ate thousands of moules, mountains of cheese and kilos of foie gras. I drank gallons of wine; wine with lunch, wine with dinner. I made coffee every morning in my French press. And I lost weight.

I dabbled in love. First with Daniele, the drummer. Then with Philippe. I flip flopped between the two, never really making progress with either. And then at the tail end of Fall, on an uncharacteristically hot day in October, Renard fell into my life. He said it was un coup de foudre for him. For me it took a couple of weeks of texting to fall in love with him. What a cliche. An American moves to Paris. Deals with the challenges of a new country, a new language. Meets a French man. Falls in love. And they live happily ever after. Well maybe. Maybe not. Does anyone ever really live happily ever after?

I wrote. An entire draft of a book. And I gave it to someone to read. And now, as that someone applies their first round of edits, I'm not ready to stop writing. Especially since my next book found me.

I've always thought of myself as a reasonable cook. Certainly cooking in a Paris kitchen (small) with Paris ingredients (different) and French methods presented a learning curve. I'd had some successes (Thanksgiving). I'd had some failures. Renard was trained as a chef a thousand years ago. While he hasn't worked as a chef for the last two dozen years, the habits and techniques have stayed with him. I would call the first dinner I cooked for him a failure. It wasn't bad but my methods proved unsatisfactory to him.

He confessed to a certain obsessive compulsive behavior the first time he cooked for me. I was probably too caught up in the passion of that night to really notice, but I certainly noticed the night I cooked for him. While I prepared the gnocchi I told him to go sit on the couch. He went to stand on the salon side of the kitchen island. "The couch!" I said, waving him to the other side of the living room. He grudgingly went. I conceded by letting him make the salad. That's when he started to complain about the condition of my fridge.

Finally, as we sipped our wine and he munched the cookies I presented him for dessert, I told him, "Going forward, this is your kitchen!" He was delighted. While we were lying in bed a couple of hours later he said "I will come later this week to organize my kitchen."

"That's fine," I said. "But before you get carried away, this is MY bedroom!"

"Parfait!" was his happy response.

Renard ran out of my apartment in a rush on a Tuesday morning. "I have to get to the marche! It's very important to get there early before the good things are gone." Ten minutes later I get a text. "I think the clock in your kitchen may be wrong."

"You mean the clock in your kitchen! You didn't change it after daylight savings time ended."

Renard spends only a couple of nights a week *chez moi*. That leaves me a lot of meals I must prepare for myself in his kitchen. Some have been pretty good. Some have tasted fine but looked less than picture perfect. And some have been inedible. None have been prepared in the fashion that would make my sweet French boyfriend happy. Fortunately he doesn't get to see those.

On my bookshelf are a few of my favorite Paris cookbooks. David Lebovitz's My Paris Kitchen may be my most favorite. As I was leafing through it one afternoon, trying to figure out what I should tackle next my new book found me. My Paris Kitchen - The Good, the Bad and Everything In Between

So begins my second year in Paris. Happily ever after? Or the rest of the story? This is about what happens next. And the other five days of the week.